I0739492

Books by Lauren Lynne

All Ages:

The Secret Watchers Series
Visions
Whispers
Insights
Perceptions
Destiny

Young Adult / Teen Dystopia:

The Recalcitrant Project

More from Wyvern's Peak Publishing

The **Charlie Sullivan and the Monster Hunters** Series
by D.C. McGannon & C. Michael McGannon

The Butterfly Stone
The Stones of Power, Book I
by Laurie Bell

The RECALCITRANT PROJECT

The RECALCITRANT PROJECT

LAUREN LYNNE

WYVERN'S PEAK PUBLISHING
An imprint of The McGannon Group, Ltd. Co.

The Recalcitrant Project

Written by Lauren Lynne Walker – www.LaurenLynneAuthor.com

Published by Wyvern's Peak Publishing. 2018
An imprint of The McGannon Group, Ltd. Co.

Cover design by www.FlirtationDesigns.com

The Recalcitrant Project / by Lauren Lynne Walker – 2nd Ed.

Summary: Elise is a student programmer who is unknowingly being used to develop a game that the government is using to eradicate an entire graduating class nationwide. She and the resistance—the Recalcitrants—seek to stop the game from going online, and establish a new way of living.

2   4   6   8   10   12   14   16   18

ISBN-13: 978-0-9990212-0-0

www.WyvernsPeak.com

Acknowledgements:

Many people build a book; it isn't just one person. Everything I see and experience has the potential to inspire me. Each interaction helps to mold my ideas and give them shape. This is for those who aren't afraid to get dirty; to dig in their gardens and to splash in the puddles of life.

With special thanks to the following people who helped make this book a reality: Nathan and Bryan Beals, Marge and Stan Walker, Cipriana and Sharon Mabaet, Cindi Etten, Amanda Wall, Judi McLaughlin, Susan Chipman, Rachael Fetrow, Julie Postlewait and Laurie Bell. You guys are the best and a simple "thanks" will never be enough!

With a special thank you to the following Oregon retailers: Mail House Plus in Milwaukie and The Latest Trend in Clackamas!

re·cal·ci·trant

\ri-ˈkal-sə-trənt\

adjective
1. having an obstinately uncooperative attitude toward
authority or discipline.

noun
1. a person with an obstinately uncooperative attitude.

History books tell us that after the Third World War everything changed. Our government, in an effort to protect those of us who remained, took away nearly all of our personal rights and freedoms. A universal way of living was established for the populace, supposedly for our safety. At the time the citizens agreed it was for the best, but as always, there were a few who were unafraid to speak out. Dissenters were identified and made to be an example. Many simply disappeared. During that time a legend was born and even though the government tried to kill the idea, it lives on. It says that one will come who will break the system and save us from our crushing government. Personally, I don't care about all that. My life is fine, but then I've never known any differently. I know it is best to just go on, do your job and not cause any trouble. Last night's news release confirms this.

"Citizen Informational Update JEA042B — As a result of the civil unrest that has broken out among our citizenry, new laws will be strictly enforced. Those who do not conform to the lot they are given and choose to defy our great nation shall be reconditioned. On this day, April 26, 2034, we the government will begin a new system of eradication of those citizens we find to be obstinately uncooperative in their attitude toward authority and discipline — end update."

. . . And so begins the Recalcitrant Project.

11100010 10000000 10011100 00101110 00101110

00101110 01110111 01100101 00100000 01110100

01101000 01100101

Black-clad public safety officers swarm the dimly lit tunnel shoving my people out of the way. I can smell the fear and hear panic in voices as the thud of fists land. I am shoved into a wall, my face scraping along its rough surface. Tears spring to my eyes from anger and pain. My heart is beating so hard and fast it hurts. The officer releases me just enough to put a hand on someone else; I have to run. I lunge, hoping for escape and fall out of bed.

"Are you okay?" Malorie asks in a whisper. Her big gray eyes look huge in the darkness.

"I'm fine," I half snarl more from embarrassment than anything else, but then I'm no morning person and Malorie knows it. I shake the nightmare off — working on the game must be getting to me more than I want to admit.

"You're not! It was another nightmare, wasn't it, Elise?" Her tone is accusing but also concerned.

"I guess."

"Why don't you tell someone? They can take those away you know."

"Sh!" the girl in the next bed exclaims, then mashes her pillow over her head.

What does it say about me that I've slept next to her for two of my seventeen years and I've never bothered to learn her name? I stare at her pillow for a moment, then quickly make my bed and hurry through the dorm's murky dim toward my assigned closet. The wood floor is cool on my bare feet but not as much as the tiles just outside the bathroom. I sigh and go back for socks. Malorie gives me her classic mother hen look and moves past me in slippered feet. We'll be early for exercise but so what? No one has gotten into trouble for being punctual — yet.

And then I wonder why I thought that. '*Yet.*' I have to assume that my increasingly frequent nightmares still have a hold on me. I can't possibly be one of the troublemakers, right? I hate confrontations. I would never be one of those Recalcitrant people we heard about from the Citizen Information Updates, or CIUs as we call them.

We dress in our matching school uniforms; the only difference being the color of our shirts to match our area of study. I guess it's easier to keep track of us if they can tell what division we're from at a glance. My communications wristband tells me that mandatory exercise is in fifteen minutes.

Malorie and I wait for her friend Jill, who has nearly made

us late daily for morning stretches since she was transferred here six months ago. The chill in the air encourages me to keep moving. The little hopping motion is waking me up, but not improving my mood. I take a deep breath of the fresh air and remind myself that being outside is supposed to improve my mood. It almost works, until I see Jill. Her hair is pulled up into a smooth ponytail and her makeup is flawless. I know what takes up her time in the morning. She puts my messy bun to shame. The smirk she gives me turns into a real smile for Malorie.

I stuff my cold fingers into my armpits and follow the girls to the workout yard, yawning all the way. I may not be a morning person, though I can program all night long. Malorie and Jill are happy morning companions. Gross. They have learned to just ignore me early in the day until I am fully awake and functional — usually after lunch.

Jill and Malorie continue to whisper and giggle. They aren't loud enough to get into trouble but I still feel torn between being jealous of their easy comradery and disgust that anyone can be so happy in the morning, and a rainy one at that. Ugh. What I'd give for a cup of coffee and a cozy chair to read in or better yet — bed. No caffeine required.

"Reach up," the instructor says into her headset with a bored voice, from her raised platform. The sound is amplified over the public address system so we can all hear clearly. "Bend to the left . . . and hold, 2, 3, 4." She drones on and on, every morning, the same routine. I could lead it myself by now. Even the littlest of kids up in front move in perfect unison with us near graduates in the back. Why she even has to instruct us I don't know, seeing as how the government approved routine never changes.

We head for the dining hall where the clatter of the dense plastic trays hurts my ears. This morning the smells in the air make me nauseous and the LED lights are too bright. Most kids are sitting with their aptitude group, but I can see a few exceptions. I pick a relatively empty spot and slump onto a bench near a boy dressed in the red of medical branch. He looks down his nose at me, which has to be pretty difficult since I'm a little taller than he is. He breaks eye contact first and returns to his breakfast. I pick up the one small mug of coffee that students are allowed in the morning, ignoring my food and scooch away a little to escape his pungent aroma after morning exercise.

"You know, you should eat your oatmeal. It's good for you. It has fiber and breakfast is the most important meal of the day," he says in a snooty tone.

I scowl at him. *Really? And I should take advice from a boy with questionable hygiene? What's the good of studying medicine?* I feel relieved when Mal and Jill sit down and distract me from the unwanted advice before I lose what little control I have and punch him in his stubby nose. *Please let the caffeine help my pounding head.*

Conversation swirls around me, but I only half listen as I peel my hard boiled egg and eat the white. I slowly spoon up a couple of bites of oatmeal as I wait for Malorie and Jill to finish. The tone of a coming CIU silences the cafeteria.

"Citizen Informational Update JEA042C. There has been an 8.65 percent rise in overall crime and 13.28 percent rise in disappearances. Citizens are asked to exhibit due care. Patrols will be increased. Evidence is being gathered. Our government is here to help us. That is all."

Conversation slowly resumes.

Malorie's coffee sits untouched so I trade my empty cup for her full one. She sends me a quick smile but Jill's eyes look hard as pebbles. I'm bending a rule today by exceeding my caffeine limit and she doesn't like it, I guess.

I give the boy one last spiteful glance as I dump my mostly uneaten tray of food and head for my assigned class, knowing in my heart that breakfast is totally overrated. He gives me a sad shake of his head which only irritates me further. Superior son of a . . .

Mal takes my elbow and jerks me toward the exit before I can open my mouth and get myself into trouble. Jill hovers near her. I hate it when she does that.

"Now what? You are seventeen, not three," Mal says, giving me a look of frustration as if I get into trouble daily.

"He can't even take care of himself and he's telling me what to do!" I snarl in return.

"You need to have more patience with people, Elise. You'd have more friends if you would," Mal answers calmly, knowing that my grouchy attitude isn't about her.

"It's hard to be patient when you have a migraine," I mumble instead.

"Another one? Go to Medical."

"You know they're not helpful."

"You just don't want them inside your head." Malorie lets my elbow drop, giving me a sad look. "They only want to get to the root of your problem, you know."

I catch a look on Jill's face. What was that expression?

Malorie sighs and walks away with her to talk to another girl I recognize, whose face brightens when she sees them. I feel a little jealous again as I enter the flow of student bodies headed for classes and workstations. It's almost a relief to get to our part of the building where it's quieter and peaceful with all the blue, the color of our aptitude, softly reflecting in the walls and carpet. The hum of computers is a welcoming white noise that helps me to drown out most of the unwelcome sounds of humanity around me. Why can't I just be happy and content like everyone else? Why do I have more than my fair share of headaches and nightmares? I should probably listen to Malorie, but I never go to Medical voluntarily. My motto is that if it's not broken, leave it alone. Medical makes me feel . . . uneasy. Maybe it's the stark red and white that makes me think of blood and death or maybe I've suppressed something from when I was younger.

As I enter the doorway, my presence is recorded by the automated voice. "18A294E." I slide into my assigned seat and log in to my student account. We sit in a grid of widely spaced rows facing the front so that we can see the big screen that shows the instructor's computer screen and our daily announcements. The room's high windows are positioned so as not to distract from our learning, with posters and diagrams filling the rest of the wall space. If you look out the window, you can see a strip of sky and a few tree branches.

I jerk my eyes up from my computer screen and quickly look around. I have that feeling again — the one where the hairs on the back of my neck raise and my skin prickles. I've felt watched, especially in here over the last few months and I don't mean the normal observations by the instructors. I wonder again if it's a side effect of *The Curse of the Underworlders*, the game I've been working on for technology lab. They've had me and a few other students at it for months. I'm usually really good at figuring out scenarios but not this time. Usually in games you play over and over, you die and respawn, but this game is morphing. It's almost like it's learning from me. It makes me wonder if I am creating a monster. Is this my Frankenstein? It's dark and makes me feel uneasy. I don't mind fighting dragons and trolls. I know they're not real, but the stuff in this game has made my palms sweat and sometimes my gut clench.

In that virtual world, I've built scenarios where soldiers can be fought and the underworlders suffer The government provided me with MOV3 and MP7 files of these tunnel dwellers, or underworlders, and the brutal way they've been treated, like a rat infestation. It makes me feel sick. My graphics are to look and feel real. They taught us that there aren't many tunnel dwellers left and no underground cities exist anymore — it's just mechanical stuff down there to run the city, but now I'm unsure because what they've given me to work with is recent, some of it with hidden time stamps they don't know I've seen.

I wish I could talk to someone, but there are some things we just don't talk about. I'm beginning to sense that what they teach us isn't the truth. Instead, it's a made-up story of how they wish things were. They certainly want us to believe what they say; however, *Underworlders* portrays the very things they don't want us to know about, so I'm left to wonder . . . Why would anyone create a game that reminds us of the things the government wants us to forget? Are they trying to turn them into urban legends? Maybe it's to give us the sense that if they are in a story or game, they can't possibly be real.

I shake off whatever has made my skin crawl this time and return to my assigned task, artificial intelligence for non-player character behavior. Not only are the images and sounds unlike anything I've experienced before, but *Underworlders* contains some of the most elaborate random algorithms I've ever seen. Every day instead of getting easier, it feels like it's getting harder to beat and more complicated to build.

Last winter I asked to be removed from this program cycle, but I was denied and now I'm afraid to draw any more attention to myself because I know they are watching me more closely. I can feel it. In the game world, I roam the underground tunnels weaponless, searching for a way out. I am continually attacked by all forms of monsters, including public safety officers that I programmed. Traps and optical illusions, that someone else created, surprise me at every turn. Maybe this is part of my final testing and finding an escape is the way to graduate. I have yet to determine if it even has an end or if the quests are virtually limitless.

Are they really going to release it to the public with their limited free time? Few vacation because of lack of time and money. Some visit a virtual world because it's cheaper and easier. Right now, the only breaks I get are for fitness, food, and sleep—a little vacation would be pretty awesome. I haven't had any real free time in weeks. It doesn't feel fair that I keep getting more game work heaped on while others get free time.

I should have never complained.

I scan the room again quickly. There are others working on *The Curse of the Underworlders*, but it looks like I've gotten further than anyone else. We aren't allowed to talk about it. One young man who tried to discuss the game over dinner about two months ago was removed. We have not seen him again. I heard he's wearing orange now which means he's part of construction, transportation, and maintenance. The rumor is that he's not right in the head anymore and that he's headed for sanitation. The job is necessary but not fun. Somehow the "not right in the head" part really scares me, because I remember when he was fine. Other people laugh about it, but I'm afraid it could be true. What if what happened to him was no accident? Am I getting paranoid from the game or am I seeing a reality that I should not see?

Now I'm looking forward to my own trial because once I've passed it, I will go to live in the city with the other programmers of the technology group. We will be housed in small apartments and life will go on much the same as it has at school, except with a little more freedom. We still have to wear our aptitude colors for work, but there are more clothing choices. I will be able to pick what I want to eat. I feel that same excitement building in me like I always do when I think about esca — I mean . . . *graduating* from here.

At long last, the bell rings and I log out of my station to reenter the student world. I glance at my communication device to confirm the time. I head to the cafeteria where I grab an apple and a sandwich. I don't bother to sit down to eat; instead,

I walk right back out with my food hidden in my pockets. I wander over to the library where food is prohibited and go to my favorite corner where I can't be seen. There are still many old paper titles here. Most students check out material on their eReader, but not me. I like the smell of printed books and love the weight of them in my hand. The far wall of the library is a floor to ceiling glass window and I love to sit here and watch nature with my back to the wall of the alcove. I know some kids come to the library to make out. Between the shelves of books is one of the few places not covered by cameras. I've gotten a really good education about boys from watching. No one notices me in my corner. They are too busy with each other and I prefer my books anyway.

I've read all the history I could get my hands on, but the rumor is that history is written by the victors. It is nearly impossible to find books or articles from before the last war, back before we became known as the New North. I remember learning about our beautiful, sparkling city where there is not so much as a leaf out of place. In the CIUs, it always looks so perfect, so pristine, and so peaceful, but I know that something festers just below the shiny surface. I tell myself it has to be the influence of *Underworlders* and my mind processing my day through dreams.

Sadness washes over me when the bell rings. I reshelve my book, toss my trash, and exit my little corner of paradise for another day. I can't help but sigh inside as I'm forced to push through the swell of student bodies. I feel a wave of exhaustion crash over me just thinking about going back to that rotten AI I'm creating for the public safety NPCs. I swear it's sucking the life out of me. I used to love gaming.

I log back into my station and stare at the screen as the game loads. A movement by the door pulls at my attention and I slide my eyes in that direction. Jill is there, hovering in the doorway. I hide behind my screen when I see her eyes start to sweep the room. My instructor rises from his desk to walk toward her, but she is already darting away. What is she up to now?

At dinner, Malorie's face lights up when she sees me. "There you are! We missed you at lunch. Did you skip it again? You know that's not good for you."

Jill is watching me and something about it makes my skin crawl. I choose to ignore her and focus on Mal. "Yeah, I just took a quick break and got right back to work."

"Uh-huh," I swear I hear her mutter as she gives me an odd look, but I keep my face blank and pick up my dinner tray. I head to a quiet table where I can look out a window. Malorie sits down across from me; Jill chooses to sit right next to me. I force myself not to scooch away.

"How goes *Curse of the Underworlders*?" Jill asks.

"Fine," I reply, focusing on my food.

Jill won't let it go. "I was able to sit in on some actors doing voice overs for it today. What are you working on?"

"I program."

"Come on, Elise. Loosen up. We know you program," Jill tries again.

I've had enough. "I'm not supposed to talk about it and you know it. I don't want to get into trouble, so just drop it, okay?"

"Whatever you say, Super Star."

What is that look on Jill's face? Frustration?

"I've got to go. I'm expected back at the lab," I say before they can ask anything else. I pop up, turn in my tray, and leave. I stroll back to the lab to finish my hours there and consider going to bed early.

One day blends into the next. I still feel like Jill is overly interested in my business but when I bring it up to Malorie she thinks I'm being paranoid and unfriendly. I try to be gracious, I swear, but Jill is pissing me off so I do everything I can to avoid her. Somehow wherever I am she's nearby. She eventually finds my spot in the library. I sigh inside. Four days until our trial. I will survive this craziness and the loss of my sanctuary.

Two days before our trial is the final parent visitation day. Mine won't be coming. I haven't seen them since parent visitation when I was fourteen. I touch my earrings, remembering that last visit and that they gave me these as a gift just before . . . the crash — the one that took their lives.

As far as I know, no students live with their parents past age three. That's when we begin school and enter the dorms. The government tells us that we are living in a utopia styled after the ideas of the great Plato who recognized that family was unimportant and the business of procreation and raising children should be the responsibility of the government. I bet those Recalcitrant people would disagree!

Virtual visits over the internet are allowed but that time is limited. Most citizens work sixty-hour workweeks and no one questions it. Or are they made to forget how things were before the war? We are taught that too much free time was the cause of all our previous woes, so now we are too tired and too busy to get into trouble or cause it. Besides, punishment is harsh and swift, so who is dumb enough to try?

From the student lounge, I watch vehicles pull into the lot that is virtually empty most of the time. Parent visitors spill from open car doors. A strange tightness squeezes my throat when I catch sight of Malorie's mom giving her a hug. A stern looking woman who looks nothing like Jill approaches her. They don't hug but fall into step side by side. They glance around and quickly head toward the walking path that loops the grounds. Others are headed into the building for refreshments or toward the benches scattered around between the buildings.

Feeling the urge to spy on Jill for a change, I do a fast walk down the hall, down the stairs, and out the door at the end. I see a flash of Jill just ahead, disappearing around the corner of the gymnasium. I walk nonchalantly in that direction. Here and there, instructors are visiting with parents in impromptu conferences. Jill and her companion have stopped near the grounds keeping shed with their backs to me, and appear to be having a serious discussion. I need to know what they're saying because their body language does not say "family" to me. I move to the far side of the shed and wait for several beats before slipping around the corner.

". . . all set then?" Jill asks.

"Yes. Remember to stay close. It's not all covered."

"I know what I'm doing," Jill snaps.

"If that were true, you would have delivered more intel on—"

"Miss Andrek!" I jerk upright and move quickly away from the corner. My level five programming instructor is striding toward me.

"Yes, ma'am?" I ask like I hang out here every day.

"What are you doing loitering out here?"

"I thought I'd get some fresh air and exercise."

"This is parent visitation day, so where should you be?"

"In one of the designated areas," I sigh.

"Now you will serve detention. Show me your communicator."

I want to grind my teeth, I want to run, but I'm caught. I hold out my wrist.

"It's just, I don't like visitation days. It gets harder every year, wishing my own parents would show up," I say, hoping her attention stays on me, and maybe, just maybe, she lets me off this one time.

She waves her handheld mini computer over my wristband and touches the screen. My band emits a few beeps in response. I glance at the readout. *Detention. Computer lab. Of course.*

"Yes, I'm sure it's difficult, but this is for your own protection. Your safety is my priority. I am simply looking out for you. Now, let's go back inside and make sure this behavior doesn't happen again."

I follow the instructor but look back to see if Jill noticed what happened to me. Maybe I got lucky because she and her "mother" are showing no interest and have moved on up the path.

I enter the computer lab. "18A294E detention." Another student and our monitor are already in the room. The monitor scans my wristband which beeps with the newly added data. I slink over and sit at my usual workstation. At first, I clench my jaw, too angry to work. Then I force myself to breathe. I log on and glance at the electronic work-order added to my instant messenger account. Apparently, I will be debugging a glitch in the student tracking system. In no time I'm sucked into the code. It swirls before me and then . . . *what is this?* I freeze. I give myself a shake so that I won't give anything away. Our lives are orchestrated from who we sleep beside, to who we sit with in class. Our personalities, habits, quirks, and aptitudes are listed. We've been deliberately profiled. I want to tell Malorie, my only true friend, but I can't. As quickly as I can, I fix the assigned issue and then I send the work-order back. I log out and go up to the room monitor to check out.

He checks his tablet. "You are to report to the headmistress."

"Yes, sir," I reply, my belly clenching. I did give something away. I square my shoulders ready for more punishment. The halls are oddly quiet with everyone in the public areas visiting with their families. I take the stairs up to the instructor level. A bored public safety officer meets me at the door at the top of the stairs. He scans my student wristband and then he passes his own in front of the door panel to unlock it for me.

Skylights and white painted walls brighten the hallway. Up here, smooth, glossy wood covers the floors. A touch of artwork adorns the gaps between the doors. Straight ahead, the school secretary scowls at me from behind her glass window. I start to speak. She merely points to the door to the left. I step in, but she doesn't even look at me over the counter.

I barely register the room. More white walls and our headmistress waiting in front of her office. She has a wrinkle between her brows and her purple clad arms are crossed. I sigh inside. I know better than to let it show.

"Sit."

"Yes, ma'am," I say as I slip past her to sit across from her desk in the "naughty" chair.

She moves to the other side, sits, and looks at her computer monitor. "What were you working on?"

"There was a glitch in the student management system."

"I'm aware."

Her weird pale blue eyes are drilling into me so I stutter on, "Some . . . some students were not being logged as they entered classrooms."

"Did you fix it?"

"Yes, ma'am. I believe so."

"Why did you freeze?"

"What?"

Instead of answering she turns her monitor around. A split screen shows the two camera angles in the computer lab where my focus is on my screen. My fingers are moving and then I definitely pause for a moment. Crud. "I, um, was trying to figure out how to correct the issue of having more than one student band pass through the door at once." I let my eyes glaze over and pray she thinks I'm another vacant girl.

She stares at me for a full minute. "You may go."

I have to resist the urge to run. I still have the urge to spy on Jill, but I don't dare, so I go to my corner of the library. I've been in enough trouble for one day. I've seen things I shouldn't. When I was asked to repair the school counselor's computer not long ago, I saw some behavioral notes on some students. Within days of my discovery, Jill arrived. Coincidence?

I feel like computers understand me better than people do. Maybe that's why I find Jill odd. Maybe she's normal and I'm the one lacking in social skills. She sure made quick work out of becoming Malorie's friend. A shiver dances along my spine as I realize that Mal could inadvertently tell Jill all kinds of things about me that she may not even realize she knows.

Thinking of Malorie, a smile touches the corner of my mouth. She's always been good to me, but she isn't the only friend I've had. I remember Bren, our teacher's assistant from two years ago. When I first saw him, I felt like one of the magic spells I read about had fallen over me. His shirt stretched over his shoulders and I could see the muscles in his arms move under his gently browned skin. He had a light dusting of hair on his arms when most boys in my year group didn't and I couldn't stop staring at it. Sometimes I could feel his gaze on me and I'd have to rip my eyes away. His eyes were dark and serious with golden flecks and I could have gotten lost in them easily if I'd let myself. When I caught him looking at me, he was nearly always looking out from under his low, slightly curved brows as if he could hide there. His hair was longish and slightly unruly; always looking like it was time for a haircut. It had just enough curl that it tended to have a mind of its own. He had a wide jaw and his chin was a bit dented. To call it a dimple would be too cute and girly. I haven't been able to decide if his best feature was his eyes or his amazing lips that seemed to curl up slightly giving him the illusion of smiling even when he wasn't. He was beautiful.

I have often dreamed of Bren and still do sometimes. My dreams are the one place the government cannot go. I remember being sad when he left for his trial. I knew that I wouldn't see him for at least two years, probably longer, and perhaps never again. They often choose your partner for you based on a compatible gene pool after you've worked for a while. I still miss him, which is weird because we barely spoke, so maybe it's just the idea of him that I secretly love. Did I mention he was beautiful? Of course I did.

The day of our trial dawns cloudy and cool. The misty fog hanging in the air is unusual for this time of year but fits my mood perfectly. We've run many mock trials over the last year so I'm not too nervous. I know they want to be sure that our aptitudes match our actual abilities. They've told us that it's important to prove that we can do in real life what we showed in school. They took us to an office building on campus set up specifically for these live action drills where we were to interact with the other divisions and solve a technology problem. Check and recheck, test and retest. Those who don't pass spend more time at school preparing, often after a slight change in career path.

Everyone must be nervous because the bus that heads for the city is strangely quiet. Seats have been assigned and I get to sit next to the girl from the dorms who hates me, so I have nothing to say anyway. I wish I was sitting next to Malorie, but I distract myself by staring out the window. We are allowed to bring nothing with us, not even our communication wristband. I admire Mal because it's people like her who design these amazing all-in-one microcomputer tools. You can access the internet and pull up GPS of any building in any town and road maps to get you there. You can contact friends, if you have any, and they have a full arsenal of other apps and widgets. Playing with it now would have been a lot more fun than this vast nothingness. There isn't even music playing; however, I can see that our orange clad driver is wearing a wireless earpiece. Lucky.

I must have zoned out because the last few students are leaving the bus and moving into our preassigned groups. Technology students from all the area schools are lined up in front of one building and engineering at the next. I step onto the square with my student number on it and look around. For quite a ways in both directions, I can see student groups preparing to enter their assigned building. Each is dressed in our identical student work uniforms; we look like a bunch of dolls on an assembly line I saw once as a child. I roll my neck on my shoulders and wait for our group to move forward. It all feels a little strange. I look down the rows again. What is it? A feeling of unease skitters through me as a vision of cattle in a pen headed for the chutes slashes through my mind. Could it be the armed guards that have me spooked? Had I not noticed them before or was this new? The usual speech is being given, but I can't concentrate.

Finally, our row is marched into the building's lobby to await our turn to take the elevator to the practice floor. I thought students were always taken to the same building each year — this doesn't look like the one that was in the video clips they made us watch, but maybe I'm wrong. Things never look quite the same in real life as they do in a video, right? The row in front of us is swept away by the elevators, we move forward and another group enters the building behind us. I notice Jill in that group. Her eyes meet mine, but she doesn't smile. She looks . . . mean, but I don't have time to think about it.

"Move forward, please." I snap my head around to face the elevator. This is the least hospitable hospitality person I've ever seen. He's wearing the right uniform but his look is unfriendly and his voice is harsh. I'm surprised he's not a member of public safety.

The doors slide open and our row moves forward. Eleven techies enter with me and the doors clang shut. With a lurch, the car begins to move, but I'm startled when it feels like it's moving down instead of up as expected. The numbers are moving up but the motion . . . Malorie twitches nervously at my side. The other occupants seem overly nervous too. This is where we are supposed to be, so my senses must be playing tricks on me. It's just nerves, I tell myself angrily Stay calm or you won't perform well.

The doors open and the expected guide is waiting for us. I take a deep breath and shake off my sense of dread.

"Find your way to your station." His voice comes out sounding almost mechanical. There is no smile on his face either. I give my head a shake to clear it. Two inhospitable hospitality personnel in one day? It's a statistical improbability.

I take in the oddness of the carpeted corridor we're standing in. There are no signs or directories. It moves off to the left and then turns the corner to the right. It's the only way to go, so the signs must be around the corner. We start to walk forward en masse.

"Two at a time," the guide barks. He may be dressed like hospitality but he isn't living up to the aptitude expectations. He should smile and be warm and friendly. What is going on? My mind whirls. There is a less than five percent chance that a true member of hospitality would behave in this way. They are empathetic by nature and friendly to a fault.

We obediently line back up and wait for the signal to move forward. Mal and I are in the middle of the pack. I watch as two by two the students ahead of us walk down the hall, turn the corner and disappear. It's eerily silent except for the occasional whispered voice and the swish of a far off door. When it's our turn, I walk forward with my head held high, trying to look confident. We turn the corner and a double door slides shut behind us. We take two steps and the floor begins to move. Malorie gives a startled squeak. I brace my feet and look all around for a way out. The wall ahead of us is painted to look like a hallway but is only a dead-end. I don't have to touch it, to see that it's moving upward. Soon the painting ends and there is nothing but gray concrete wall. Now what? This isn't right. We should be in an office with computer banks everywhere. Is there a sublevel computer problem we are to fix in one of the mega-computers? Why the games and illusions?

The floor stutters to a halt and another door opens to our

right. The overhead lights flicker out so that the only light comes from the corridor ahead. We step forward into the dim light. Mal clutches my hand. I could tell her it is going to be okay, but I don't know that it will be, so I say nothing and try to exude calm.

"Show them confidence," I whisper just loud enough for her to hear. Mal drops my hand and straightens her spine, but I can still feel her shaking.

This hall is not carpeted, nor is there any signage. Paint has been sprayed on the walls and ceiling in a sketchy manner and drips have hardened on the concrete floor. The moment we clear the doors they swish closed, ending with a bang that echoes in the empty space. I look for cameras and can only see a couple. Their coverage will be spotty. There has obviously been a mistake. We need to find stairs going up because we can't go back the way we came. Doors line the hallway. I listen for a moment but I don't hear anything except our breathing. Where is the welcoming hum of machines? By mutual unspoken agreement, we cautiously move forward, but I can't bring myself to try any of the doors.

As if she's read my mind Mal speaks softly, "Should we try the doors?"

I shake my head and wonder why I did at the same time. Trying the doors makes sense but somehow it feels wrong. The next step has us tumbling down a chute as the floor gives way. We must have stepped through a false floor. I fight to keep my feet in front of me so that I won't land head first. I'm too scared to scream as the metal shaft flashes by faster than my eyes can process. Next thing I know I'm flung off the end to crash into a pile of trash. Wait, not trash — nothing is too sharp or rancid smelling. In fact, it seems like there is nothing bio-based in the heap at all. It's mainly cardboard and packing material like you'd find in a pile of sorted recycling. A strange sense of déjà vu whispers past my senses. With a scream, Malorie flies out the chute and crashes into me so hard the breath leaves my lungs and I hear something crack. My shoulder blade erupts with pain. We both groan, but Mal has gotten the worst of it. My shoulder will be bruised, but her nose is bleeding.

I quickly scrounge around to find something to stop the flow, but all I feel is an incessant need to keep moving. As I hold some soft paper up to Mal's bloody nose, I wonder if we've been dropped into the wrong scenario. Is this the trial scenario of the public safety students? We must have been sent to the wrong place. Could we possibly have a task with them? How could that happen? The government never makes mistakes . . . or did they? Or worse, was this intentional?

"I'm okay. I don't think it's broken," Malorie squeaks in a stuffy sounding voice as she pushes my hands away and holds the paper herself. "Where are we, Elise? What is this place? This isn't what we trained for or practiced. We should be in an office, shouldn't we? Did they make a mistake? Except they don't . . . they don't make mistakes so why are we here? What's going on? Should we call for help? Is this an accident or a test?"

"I wish I knew, but I feel strongly that we should keep —" A scream echoes down the chute interrupting me and then there is silence. "Yep, keep moving — definitely," I whisper in a shaky voice I hardly recognized as my own.

"But what if it's one of our friends? What if they need help?"

"Friend or not, this is no place for us. Come on, Mal. Better safe than sorry, right?" I'm not going to wait around and see what will happen next — this move will be mine.

I pull her up by her hand and hurry into the shadows. I'm glad for the first time ever, that our uniforms are mainly gray with a touch of blue and not white like engineering. Light colors would practically glow, especially in the dark. Please let the gray be enough to hide us. I surge from shadow to shadow and move behind any objects in our path hoping they will obscure us to unfriendly eyes — my brain has gone into survival mode. I didn't play all those battle games in beta for nothing. I will use what I learned. Every — single — awful — bit — of — it! In real life, I hate hurting people but in the game world, it doesn't bother me. I'm one of the best. I just have to pretend this is a game. Could that be it? Were they testing me to see what I'd learned from the game? Then that would make Mal an innocent bystander in my final exam and that wasn't fair, but when had the government ever been fair?

I'm so focused on our surroundings and my own crazy thoughts that I block everything else out. I finally notice that Malorie has grown silent. She follows me, eyes huge, and hands shaking, but she hasn't uttered a sound in what would have been about three city blocks at ground level. Her nose has stopped bleeding but she is so utterly quiet that I wonder if she is in shock. Maybe I need to get her some water or something. We will need some soon anyway — first rule of survival — fresh water. My ears have gone into hyperdrive and my eyes are busy searching. My mind constantly evaluates all that has happened, making a single idea snap into sharp focus — I know this place. I go over the pieces again. The elevator didn't go up as indicated. I felt it go down and it had. I know it for sure now. Damp feel, no windows, cold concrete walls . . . we are in the underground and I have the horrific feeling that we are not just below ground but we have entered the live version of *Underworlders* that I helped create and has caused my nightmares.

"Where are we?" she whispers.

"I had to study this when I worked on . . . my game, *The Curse of the Underworlders*. I know I don't usually talk about it, but I've watched videos so that I could build the game world to look like this. We're in the underground, a place the government tries to hide. They send crews of black uniformed public safety officers down here to eradicate the infestations of humanity that try to survive among the rubble. This is where people who are desperate come. This is where you can get drugs and other things frowned upon by the government. This is also where prisoners who escape come and anyone who gets crosswise with the government. We aren't supposed to know about this place, but there have always been rumors. To students, it's almost glorified — a mysteriously dangerous place that holds exciting allure," I mumble as quietly as I can.

"Not for me. I don't want to be here," she says, sounding scared. "I thought this was all closed off for safety reasons."

"It was."

"Then how do you know?"

I lower my voice again. "Remember when some government

people came to our school a few months ago, looking for anyone who could solve their communication issue? I was asked to see what I could do to boost the signal for the public safety crew working down here. I couldn't help but see snatches of video — I had to in order to confirm my adjustments. They claimed it was a training exercise. I pretended that was true, but I had this creepy feeling that it wasn't. I know now for sure that they lied, even though I didn't want to admit it to myself at the time. At least I knew even then to keep silent. I hoped they had bought that I was a dumb sixteen-year-old kid, but now I wonder. Why else would I be here, in the very spot I saw on those video clips and with a tumble down a chute just like at the start of the game? What kind of a test is this?"

"You and your conspiracy theories! Just get us out of here."

Maybe she's right and I'm being too suspicious — I've been fascinated by what the government tries to hide for as long as I can remember. I looked for information in the library and on the internet using the secure server. I know how to research and cover my tracks by bouncing my signal all around and using a revolving IP address. I figured it out in my eighth year of training and I never let on.

The school staff knew I was talented. I knew that they shared all information about us with the government. I learned how to cheat the system. Even on tests, I can almost feel which questions to answer wrong so that they can never get a clear understanding of how I think. I figured out what to show them and what to hide by the way questions were being asked and by how they presented training exercises to me. Now I am thankful that they don't know as much about me as they might have.

"Which way?" Mal's voice still sounds stuffy from her banged-up nose. It brings me back to the present.

"Try not to talk. I'm sure they're watching if not listening," I mumble, tilting my head down to cover my mouth so they can't read my lips. "Follow me. I've seen this before."

"What? How?" She says it aloud, still not believing what I've told her.

"Please, Mal. I'll explain more soon. Just trust me, okay?" I mumble again. A skeptical look crosses her face, but she closes her mouth and swings her arm up and flicks her hand out, letting me know she is ready for me to lead the way again.

I walk slowly and carefully with my senses on high alert. I can't help but feel grateful that she is following quietly. It just might help me save her life. I've only seen bits of the labyrinth of passageways down here, but I have a feeling about what I need to look for. Scanning our surroundings for any sign of human life, I know our best bet is to look for the people who hide down here. I know they're not all criminals and dangerous. A small movement — a sound . . . I freeze and stare ahead. What have I seen? There it is again; something that doesn't belong. I hear the sound of air moving and see a bit of fabric flutter where there should have been none. I creep forward cautiously. Is it a clue or a trap? Up close, I can see the opening, but from a distance, it had been completely hidden with an optical illusion.

I sense Malorie watching me. The muscles in her neck look tight and her eyes are overly bright. I can tell she's unhappy, scared and confused. Her eyebrows draw together and her eyes go from wide to squinched up. A streak of dirt on her cheek has a clean line running through it. I know it's marred by a tear. I take her hand and give it a gentle squeeze because I can't bring myself to smile. Not here, not now.

We step into the opening and ease down the narrow passageway that is more like the area one would find between commercially constructed walls than a real hallway meant for foot traffic. Soon it widens out and branches off, so I pause to listen. I peer right and left from the end of the alley we are in. I look for footprints and how used each direction looks. This area is strange. It looks like an actual hallway, and perhaps it is. Public Safety would need passageways to move troops around, right? Unfortunately, I can't tell a darned thing, so I pull Mal to the left hoping to get even further away from the building we started in. I figure we have to be across the street from the building that engineering started at by now.

I close my eyes to visualize. Who had lined up across from them? I wrack my brain. Who had been standing there? Color flashes and I remember; it was the aqua of science. If we are entering their scenario I can deal with it. I'm good at both science and engineering. They tie for second on my final aptitude test scores and both ratings were high enough for me to go into the field. It was no surprise that I had the lowest known score on record for hospitality. In what little free time I had, I read every book I could get my hands on about science, engineering, and history. I never went for the fluffy pretend stuff. Another movement catches my attention, so I pick up the pace to get a better look.

"What are you doing?" Malorie complains, sounding completely frustrated.

"I saw something move and my gut tells me to follow it."

"I'm not sure that's a good idea. I think we're moving away from our building."

Should I tell her the truth? Should I lie? I look into Mal's eyes. She's scared and isn't sure she should trust me. Crap.

"I'm certain this is the way back," I lie smoothly, feeling sick inside.

"Okay," she answers softly in an unconvinced voice. "I just wish they'd left us our wristbands so we could use the GPS."

The GPS would have been nice, but I say nothing as we face two more choices. We can continue in this passageway or we can go down a flight of stairs. I start for the stairs.

"No! We need to go back. What's wrong with you?" Mal hisses angrily. "I may have North, South, East, and West confused, but I sure as heck know up from down!"

"Mal, remember the scream? We need to find another way. We can't go back."

"Then we should stick to the lit hallway and not a dark stairway."

"We need to go in a way that is not expected. They are herding us with the lit hallway. It's what most people would do." I know it's also where we are likely to run into someone from public safety.

"That's why it's a good idea."

"That's why it's a bad idea. Think! Remember the scream."

"Public safety and medical have helped her by now."

"What if they didn't? What if it was the test administrators who made her scream?"

Malorie grows angry. "I don't believe it. You've been watching too many CIU broadcasts." She's referring to the Citizen Information Updates broadcasts. "The government isn't against us. CIUs are meant to inform. You read things into them that aren't there. That's your crazy conspiracy theory again."

"Mal, if I'm wrong, I'll take the blame and you will be retested. But what if I'm right?"

Malorie's face pales as her pulse quickens at her neck. "Fine. We'll do it your way, but if we get into trouble, so help me, I — I, well — I'll never speak to you again."

I have a sudden urge to giggle but instead smile a sad, hurt kind of smile. "Fine. No hard feelings."

The light behind us fades as we descend the stairs, making it hard to see. It almost feels like the dimness is becoming denser and the shadows more menacing. The stairs become slick and the walls cold, wet, and tacky to the touch. I can smell moisture in the air. Malorie is slowing down and lagging behind. She frequently looks over her shoulder like she wants desperately to go the other way, but she is more afraid to be alone than she is to follow me into the inky dampness. We stay close to the wall but soon my leading hand is touching a foul, slick dampness that I don't want seeping into my clothes.

I pull away just as Malorie speaks, "What *is* that smell?"

I take another whiff. "It smells like . . . vegetation. And not the fresh kind."

"Is that normal?"

"How should I know? I've only seen this in JPEGs and vids. A section of the game looks like this."

"You and that game." Malorie goes quiet again. The way her nose is wrinkled, she must be thinking. Whatever her thoughts are, I don't want to hear it, so I shrug and move forward.

Near the bottom of the stairs, I can see a grayer kind of black. My feet touch what must be the floor because there isn't another step. I pause for a moment. I can see most of the room except for the corners that are still the deepest black. The room has a strange greenish cast that has to be caused by the algae and slime. The floor is slicker than melting ice with water oozing over it in a fine sheet. The smell of rotting vegetation presses in on me in a smothering cloud, making me gag. Malorie retches behind me. I move faster because if she really loses it, we will definitely leave evidence that we've been here.

This is not a part of the game that I recognize, but I can sense the value in it. They would never expect anyone to walk through here and the moving water and thick scent will cover our passage, even from scent dogs. I start to take off my shoes and socks.

"What in the world are you doing?" Mal asks me like I've lost my mind. I can tell that she is mouth-breathing, trying to cut the stench.

"I don't want anyone to know we were here. If we put our shoes back on, on the other side, then we won't leave footprints when we exit."

"Gross! How about we wear our shoes over and then take them off on the other side until they dry?"

"Okay." At least she is willing to follow me. I could do some things her way.

I quickly wipe my foot off on the bottom of my pants and replace my sock and shoe, then I target the doorway that is diagonally opposite to our current position. I keep my knees slightly bent and my stance wide as I move slowly and carefully across the slick floor, watching where I place each foot. As Mal asked, when I reach the edge where three steps lead to the next level, I carefully remove my shoes and socks before placing my feet on the clean step. Today, I'm thankful for morning stretches each day. I imagine myself falling over into the awful stench and then I'd never get it out of my nose. We shake and scrape as much gunk from our shoes as we can and then slink up the steps and down the gritty hallway to the left. *Hallway* really isn't the right word because on this side of the swamp room it is more of a cavern with partially rough-hewn walls. I wonder if the slimy room we just left has a side that backs up to nothing except earth or maybe even the river. We would have to be closer to it by now and one side of this passageway offers no doorways.

The lighting is changing. Up ahead the roof of the cavern-like passageway almost seems to glow. I look for a light source and discover strange bulbs I've only seen in history books, held above the surface of the rock with exposed wires running from light to light. I am reminded of pictures I've seen of old mine shafts. Here and there is a burnt out bulb that has not been replaced. How could there be light here at all? Surely public safety would have ripped it out. I'm thankful they didn't.

I check my shoes repeatedly until finally, they seem dry

enough to put back on. I can't tell if the odor of that nasty room is still clinging to my shoes and the hem of my pants or if it's soaked into my skin and will linger in my nose forever.

Mal and I walk on. I have the creeping sensation that we're being observed even though I haven't seen an obvious camera since we've come down the stairs. I peer into each crevice, ready for a public safety recruit to jump out at me. It takes a little while for me to realize that it's growing lighter up ahead and the sounds of humanity are faint in the distance. Mal must sense it too because she starts to hurry past me, but I grab her arm and hold her back. I shake my head and quietly push her into the shadows. She gives me the angriest look I've ever seen on her face and I can feel my heart breaking. I try to convince myself that it's better for her to hate me and be alive than it is the other way around.

I approach the sounds cautiously, using outcroppings and random stalagmites as cover until I reach the edge of an enormous man-made cavern. I slide behind a large crate and watch for a bit, soaking in the scene before me. Mal gapes, eyes wide at the traders and their market.

Traders. I run my hands over my body. What can I give up that isn't necessary for survival? Earrings! They're gold wires with real pearls at the ends. The last gift from my parents. I would mourn their loss, but I want to live more than I need them.

All that I learned and suspected about the black market seems to be true. The smell is just as I imagined; rich, warm, and inviting with a whiff of wood fires burning, blending with roasting meats and a hint of unwashed bodies. People are dressed in simple, mismatched clothes so that I can't tell which job class anyone is. They are relatively clean but worn looking and the strangest part is they look . . . happy. The wrinkles and callouses on their hands tell the story of a life that's hard yet free. Their voices are low and their eyes are constantly moving. Their shoulders are hunched and the fabric of their clothes is rough and patched. Here and there small generators are running strings of lights and other strange little machines I've never seen before. Most of the crowded space is set up with vendor stalls but some only have tables, crates, or wagons. It's hard to tell where one ends and another begins. Those without generators have gas or battery operated lamps that I've only seen in pictures until now. It's like all the stories I've read were coming to life. "It's real," I breathe in awe.

Mal waits with her back to the crate, thinking I don't know what. I could sit here observing for hours, but I watch the traders until I have one selected. She's more raggedy than the rest, off to the side, and quieter. I whisper to Malorie to wait and then I use my surroundings as disguise. I pick up a bit of fabric from the back of a stall as I pass by. The vendor is focused on a patron at the front and misses my theft. As I put the fabric over my hair like a scarf, I swear to myself I'll repay him one day. I quickly move behind a display of rugs and turn my jacket inside out. I weave my way over to the vendor I've selected, careful not to make eye contact with anyone else.

"What will you give me for these?" I ask in a harsh whisper. "I need something to carry water and a knife." She doesn't jump. She must have sensed me coming. She turns slowly to face me, one hand still on her small wagon of kitchen supplies.

"I'm a poor old woman. I don't have much." Her eyes are watchful. She's not just looking at me, she's looking into me — assessing me.

I take a breath and try not to give anything away by my expression. "But you have what I need and you'll want these," I say as I hold the earrings within her sight but out of her reach. "You'll get a good price for them and all I want is a small knife and a flask of water."

"We will be punished if we aid the children of the school," she murmurs, looking everywhere but at me.

"I see," I whisper, feeling devastated. I start to turn but she lays a weathered hand on my arm. How had she gotten so close without my noticing? Her eyes are black as the night sky, wreathed in deep wrinkles but somehow kind and gentle looking. A bit of ivory colored hair has escaped from her bun and I can't seem to tear my eyes away from her face. She is beautiful in her own way and I feel as if she's looking deeper into me, to examine all the dark and ugly places that I like to hide even from myself.

"I can't believe you made it this far. You must be special. Besides, what more can they take away from one such as me?"

I feel my eyes widen and words lock in my throat. From her voluminous skirts, she pulls a small blade with a metal handle and finger holes. She wraps my numb fingers around the handle and plucks the earrings from my other hand before I even realize what's happening and then she turns and is gone, leaving the wagon behind to disappear into the market. I feel my body thaw and start to call out but manage to hold my tongue. I take a step and kick an old fashioned canteen lying on the ground where she'd been standing just moments before. Next to it is a small parcel. I snatch them up and return to the shadows, making my way back to Malorie.

After the woman's reaction, I know we have to get away from the market as fast as we can because soon they will be looking for us here and I'm sure there are many who would turn us in for a reward. I touch Mal's shoulder and point to a crumbled section of wall just to our right. We step through, leaving the odors of the market and its people behind. Malorie keeps close to me like she did when we first entered the elevator.

"How did you know what to do?" Mal whispers in amazement as we walk shoulder to shoulder.

I see no reason not to tell her now. If I'm wrong about all this, I'm in plenty of trouble already. "The government had me do all kinds of research so that I could build believable non-player characters, or NPCs, for the game. I have bartered in the virtual world. I just tried what works in the game. Besides, some of us read in our down time instead of sneaking out to meet up with boys." I finish with a half-smile to let her know I'm not mad.

"Whatever. I read. I just enjoy other things too." She smiles back and it relieves some of the pressure in my chest. "Now what do we do?"

"I hope this was all a mistake, but if it isn't we still need to find a way out of here. This is not where we belong."

"Is that water?" she asks pointing at the canteen. "And what's in the package? Food?"

"I hope so. I haven't really checked yet." We pause by another half wall in a darkened area where it looks like part of a building has crumbled away, leaving a large void the size of a city block. I examine the canteen in the weak light. It's heavy enough to hold water, but as much as I've read about science, it doesn't make me part of the school of science. I'd have to rely on my senses and hope for the best. I carefully unscrew the top and give it a little sniff.

"Why are you so paranoid?" she asks. "It's water, right?"

"Really? After what's happened to us so far, you ask me that?"

"Okay, you win. What do you smell?"

"Nothing."

"Well then let me have a little taste."

I hand it over and Malorie gives it a sniff. Then she puts a little on her tongue and waits. "I think it's fine."

She takes a bigger drink and hands it to me. We wait for a few moments and when nothing happens I take a sip. She's right. It seems to be plain old water.

"I didn't realize how thirsty I was," Malorie says with a relieved sigh.

"Me either, but we better make this last until I figure out how to get us more," I say, shifting back into game mode.

Malorie really smiles at me for the first time today. "I don't know how you learned to do all the stuff you just did, but I'm glad."

"Somehow I think all that game building and beta testing I did trained me for this. I just don't know why." I say it with a weak smile because deep down, I really am terrified. I push the feeling away and then I check the package. It looks like some kind of jerky and crackers. Malorie and I shrug at each other. We had our regular morning meal and it was a little early for lunch so I put it in my pocket and clip the canteen to my belt loop. "Come on. Let's get out of here and go home."

"That's the best thing you've said yet, Elise. I'm sure this was all a mistake and we just ended up in the wrong place. I hope we don't get into too much trouble." I bite my lip so I won't speak and turn my head away to roll my eyes. *Yeah, Mal, it's all a big mistake*, I think sadly.

We edge around the basement, keeping to the shadows until we find another opening. We shrug at each other, thinking this way should be as good as the next and walk side by side down the strangely dark corridor. Spider webs hang down from above but the ground is relatively clear, leading me to believe other people have walked this way often. Yet it seems strange. It's oddly quiet with no sounds of humanity and no street noise above us. There is not so much as a vibration.

Soon I lose track of what part of the city we're under and then I begin to question myself. When we had started this way, it felt like the logical way to go. I wasn't sure how I knew it, but the sense of familiarity was strong. I know the thought is crazy because students are never allowed down here. We prepare for our trial our whole lives, except this wasn't what we had trained for. We had always been taught the trial was to see how we would function in real life situations. This was not real life, at least it wasn't our real life — this was the underground.

I again wonder why we're here. There is a chill in the air we aren't dressed for. Malorie and I are meant for office work and computer programming and not . . . I swear this is where the warrior divisions are tested and not our aptitude, but maybe the government is trying to see if we have something to offer that all the other testing has missed.

Our surroundings change again. The walls are looking more finished and now its antique fluorescent lights that flicker overhead among the pipes. This area is definitely old school and is as wide as a city street. The walls are damp; their paint chipped and clearly run down. Graffiti and garbage, along with a heavy helping of dirt decorate the area, yet I can't shake the sense of familiarity. This is definitely not from my real life so I know it's from the virtual world.

"What is it?" Malorie grumbles. I guess she has a case of the creepies too or maybe she's starting to believe me.

"I don't know but something just doesn't feel right." Something has told me to stop and look closely at the intersection just ahead. I feel like I am indeed standing on an underground city street where no one is about. It feels like a ghost town.

"Geez, Elise, you're creeping me out worse. You're supposed to make me feel better. That's your job as best friend. You aren't supposed to tell me the truth about that." She wrings her hands together, clearly not at ease. "How do you really know how to do this stuff? It's not our aptitude. At the market, I thought it was kind of cool, but now you're scaring me. You've gone all quiet and watchful. I want to know what you're think —"

Mal is cut off by a crash. Just in front of us two men burst through the first glass window we've seen down here. They roll around on the ground fighting and I'm seized by the strongest sense of déjà vu I've ever felt. Malorie turns to run back the way we came but my arm snaps out and I take hold of her sleeve without even thinking. My eyes shoot to the window the two men have been disgorged from. Two more men are fighting with strange crescent shaped weapons that glow as if lit from within. And then I know . . . I have seen this before. I can feel Mal shaking and trying to pull away, but going back is the wrong answer. More dangers await us there than if we move ahead, but it's crucial that we do it at the right moment. Right — about — *now*.

The men with weapons roll out the door and would have cut us to shreds had we moved too soon. While all the attention is on the men brawling in this underground street, I yank Mal behind me and move forward past the bar. The moment we clear the doorway, the image shatters and the blades whirl to a stop; with a grinding of gears, they slowly begin to reverse direction. I pull a stunned Malorie out of the way.

We make it about twenty steps when I hear choking. I turn to glance at Mal. A sob has seized her and fat tears streak through the dirt on her face. "We aren't supposed to be here. This is not our scenario. What was that and why are they letting it go on?"

I have no answers so I take her hand and pull her on. I will give them credit for one thing: that was the best hologram I've ever seen.

We stumble through the underground street marked by closed shops with barred windows and boarded-up dwellings.

By instinct, I keep us to the shadows. Every time Malorie tries to talk I urge her desperately to be quiet. Her eyes are now white all around the edges and she is shaking visibly, although her tears have stopped. We come to another intersection and have to choose. I know nothing good will come from going to the left, so I pull her to the right.

"We should go left," she hiccups.

"No, trust me; this is the way to go."

"But the other way is better lit. It must be the way back to our scenario and people."

"They want you to think that, Mal. Looks can be deceiving. Now come on."

"How do you know? What if you're wrong? I've been following you and we're not out yet!" She waves her hand in the direction they just came from. "We almost got sliced to ribbons. I don't want to do this anymore. Our trial should be over now."

"Trust me, I'm not wrong and I swear I'll tell you more later. Now please, just keep your eyes open and your mouth shut for a few more minutes. It's dangerous here."

She swallows hard and gives me a single nod. Here and there, signs of humanity become visible. I can't decide if we're safer among the underworlders where there are less likely to be hidden traps or away from them. We keep walking but I become afraid that our school uniforms will be frighteningly out of place if anyone really pays attention to us. I wonder if there is a bounty on us. There is no doubt in my mind that someone will turn us in for profit. It's fortunate that there aren't many people around, and the few who are keep their heads down or are too busy to notice us skulking in the shadows.

Soon the area widens and slopes down. The wall to our left ends and becomes a railing. I chance a glance over the edge. We are entering a large open area of about thirty by sixty units. Many tables with benches have been arranged in rows and students from our year group are starting to gather. A very young guide is struggling to give instructions as the trial participants arrive from a variety of directions. Again something feels terribly wrong on my personal radar.

Everyone appears to be waiting, watching, and anticipating. I have the sense they feel like they are finished and are waiting to be picked up but are confused about what they've just been through. I can feel fear slithering through the air, and I speculate about where our other teammates are. Malorie must feel relieved like many other students obviously do because she starts to surge forward, but I hold her back.

"What is wrong with you?" she snaps. "Can't you see we made it?"

"Did we?" I ask softly as I release her arm, but I'm not sure she hears me as she rushes forward to hug another friend. I lag behind and watch. Malorie smiles and laughs, ready to put it all behind her. I can't.

Where are our other friends? Where are the other students from our section? As I watch the gathering crowd waiting with anticipation, I know. They aren't coming. There will be no graduation ceremony for them — no tomorrow — ever. I can see that our numbers have dwindled, a fact no one else seems to see. I hang in the shadows, watching for familiar faces, but I see no one else from our division. Fear grips me and I fight for breath. We need to leave. It's not safe here.

We are down to two. The other divisions have varying numbers. I count the students of each group by the color of their uniforms. I notice that one group is especially subdued and all are sobbing quietly. Their uniforms are in tatters. They had jackets like the rest of us but instead of pants, the girls have skirts in soft lime green that reminds me of sherbet from our infrequent desserts at school. Now the green of nearly every skirt is at least spattered if not smeared with blood and things I don't wish to identify. There are only three of them, all girls. The skirts are incredibly impractical in this environment, but they are from hospitality. I'd always thought of them as silly and fluffy but now . . . with dawning horror, I realize what has likely happened to them — rape. They will never survive and if they do physically, can their minds take it? It all makes sense — the ripped clothing they try to spread over their bare skin, the shaking, the cuts, scrapes and bruising, and worst of all, the hollow look in their eyes. They've been through a different kind of trial.

What is wrong with everyone? How can they wait here so calmly? But I know in my heart, it's because each of them is wrapped up in their own little world, celebrating that they made it and still believing that the government wants to help us.

In a panic, I search frantically for Malorie. We have to get out of here before it becomes chaos. My eyes land on the group wearing black uniforms. What a joke the word "safety" is; they are the warrior class, the enforcers. By my count, nearly all of them have made it. I move closer and eavesdrop. They are bragging and laughing at the rest of us. Most of the crowd still hasn't caught on. They are still expecting their friends to show, but an edge of fear is developing as students begin to notice what's left of hospitality. It looks like the guide is starting to get a bunch of questions that she has no answers for. It's time to move.

My eyes land on Malorie and while everyone is diverted, I grab her by the arm and hiss in her ear, "Come on, the next phase is about to begin. We need to be ready."

"What are you talking about? There is no next phase. This is it. We made it and any minute they are going to come and pick us up and feed us lunch."

"No, they won't. This is something . . . different."

"How do you know?"

"I'm not really sure, but it's like I've seen it all before. You know, like in *Underworlders*. It's like I've played the scenario, a lot. You play, you die, you respawn and you learn from it and I'm telling you, I know what happens next."

"I've worked the Beta Game division too," Malorie interrupts. "But I've never seen anything like this. I say we wait for Jill and then decide."

"Don't you get it? She's not coming. We've got to get out of here. Something bad is about to happen and it's going to be soon."

"But the guide hasn't dismissed us."

"Have you looked at the girls from hospitality? They're traumatized, Mal, and not because they're just afraid. Have you seen how young our guide is? She doesn't know what she's doing and she's not showing any loyalty to her own division. Watch her. It's weird. She's got to be a plant."

"Why are you so paranoid?"

"Please, let's just go. I told you; if I'm wrong, I'll take the blame, but what if I'm right? Haven't I been right so far?"

Mal sighs and lets her shoulders drop, a sure sign she's caving in.

We slink over to the far wall without drawing attention to ourselves. The volume is going up as students struggle to get the guide's attention. I quickly scan the room and just as I suspected, kids are catching on and moving like a mob toward the guide. Malorie's eyes meet mine and then they fill with tears.

"Hold it together. Please. You have to hold it together." At my words, she nods and bites her lip.

They will notice that we are gone, but it will take some time and I want as much of an edge as I can get. I pull her further into the murky shadows. The noise level is rising again. Hospitality is still huddled and crying, and the guide looks like she has lost control. Mainly it's the public safety people who are catching on. A number of them are still laughing like this is the best trial ever and why not? It's totally rigged in their favor — at least for now.

I must have mumbled aloud because Malorie sucks in a breath. "We're not trained for this," she cries softly. "Technology yes, but nothing else."

"Somehow, I think we're getting our training right now. Call it on-the-job training."

"You're not funny," Malorie says sounding as distressed as she looks. "They can't do this. People will complain."

"My money is on the fact that they are doing this *because* people complained. They're the government. They can do whatever they want. I just know we need to keep moving."

"But look, other groups are sitting down to wait."

"We need to move now," I hiss, experiencing a new wave of urgency as I feel a small tremor in the floor. "Down this tunnel."

We only go a few feet when we are faced with a ragged opening. It looks as if someone had broken through with old fashioned chiseling tools. We are at an underground highway, and it appears to be deserted, yet it's spotlessly clean. How long until some sort of vehicle zooms through here? It stretches further in both directions than we can see. I look both ways one more time and start to pull Malorie to the left.

"Wait, this is a road. We shouldn't walk here! We'll get run over."

"We have to, Mal or we'll be trapped."

"Look! Some students are moving off. It looks like mainly public safety and engineering. There's got to be a safer way. We could follow them."

"Wait," the hostess bellows at them. "We're supposed to wait for the instruction video."

"We need to keep moving," I yelp in a frantic whisper to Malorie. No one seems to have noticed us yet . . . yet. "Quick while all the attention is on public safety, science, and engineering."

"We're leaving," a tough-looking boy from public safety yells boldly above the din.

Malorie digs in her heels like the stubborn mules I've seen clips of. "We don't know what's going on. We need to find out.

We'll be in so much trouble if we don't follow orders. We'll be punished. I won't let you get me in any more trouble!" She yanks her arm out of my grasp and moves cautiously back toward the group where most of the students are waiting. I hang in the shadows and watch.

Some are quiet and some are argumentative but all are swathed in fear. The sense of wrongness is spreading — the agitation clear. Malorie looks desperately from one face to another. I can't stand it anymore and lunge from the shadows to grab her arm and yank her away.

Student voices echoed in my head.

"No, this is wrong."

"It's not right."

"Someone, help us!"

"What's happening?" Malorie's voice penetrates my brain above the others, "What do we do?"

"We —" I begin.

An intercom crackles. *"Phase two!"*

Malorie looks at me, her eyes huge as a whimper escapes her lips.

"Quiet, Mal. Let me listen." I tune out everything else.

"Citizen Informational Update JEA042E-1. Congratulations to the assembled students on the completion of the first phase. The next session is about to begin. In an orderly fashion, please prepare. As a result of the civil unrest that has continued among our citizens, a punishment has been determined. Per the accords reached on April 26, 2034, we the government, have decided on a course of punishment for those citizens we find to be obstinately uncooperative in their attitude toward authority and discipline. As

is our right, and the law under the Recalcitrant Project, you shall be hunted down like the children of the animals you are. You will pay for the sins of your parents."

Screams erupt as an ear-piercing alarm sounds.

There is that vibration again. What is it? Then I know — feet, marching. "Come with me now!" I yank Malorie through the opening we'd found. This time, she steps onto the road without complaint. She clutches her hand to her chest and mumbles a prayer but follows me docilely.

Now a new vibration claws at my attention. This is not marching feet, this is . . . "Run!" I take hold of Malorie's hand and race as fast as I can up the road. My breath comes in gasps and sweat begins to run down my back. When I glance at Malorie I can see that her face is red, sweat is beading up on her forehead and running down the sides of her face. She is slowing but we will die here if we don't move faster. The sound grows to a roar, completely crushing the screams and the sound of the alarm.

The vibration increases, making my teeth rattle.

Up ahead I can see a break in the concrete wall. I dive behind the nearest pillar, pulling Malorie in after me. A tram whizzes past, stirring up grit in its noisy wake. The thought that it would have smashed us flat sets me to shaking. I can hear nothing else except our wheezing and my pounding heart for several minutes and then other noises begin to trickle in. I sense movement and turn; a cat peers at us from around another pillar.

I scan the area trying to figure out where we are. Mostly it feels like we are ants among blades of grass or that these pillars are a legion of soldiers and we cower at their feet. Off in one corner, a faded and dusty, vintage vending kiosk stands alone. It looks like it had been jimmied open years ago, its contents long gone. At the far end, a set of stairs leads up to another level. This area must have been a station at one time. Movement in the far corner attracts my attention. It's more of the raggedy people, the tunnel dwellers, but these don't look as healthy as the ones from the market. Obviously, there is a whole subculture eking out a living down here. I have seen them in the gaming scenarios and black market history books. Everything useful here will have been picked clean years ago.

These people are not afraid of us. They are cautious yet curious. It's doubtful they have seen any news, so they wouldn't know about us. That is my guess since they watch us like the cat did. I'd bet my last credit they've never seen students before but can sense that we're no danger to them. Malorie clutches my arm, her fingers digging in painfully. There's a small sound and the people vanish like smoke in the breeze.

I glance toward the stairs and see a young woman walking down them sideways, her back to the wall. She wears the black of public safety and the insignia of a new recruit. I'm seeing a whole new side to this group now. Mal draws in a breath to speak, but I slap a hand over her mouth. Unfortunately, I'm not quick enough; we've been spotted. "What are you doing here? You should be with the rest of the trial participants."

I rise slowly to my feet. Her wristband beeps and she reaches a finger toward it, most likely to send in a report about us. My hand snaps out knocking her hand away. I know she's a danger. She's stunned for a split second and then reaches for her weapon. I've never been taught to fight, but I've won plenty of battles in the game world — *Underworlders* and otherwise. Suddenly fighting moves are playing out before me like I'm viewing them on the screen all over again. I knock her weapon from her hand and smash my elbow into her throat. She makes a strange gurgling sound and drops to one knee. I kick her in the head and watch in horror as she falls to her side, lying still.

"Oh my God, Elise. What did you do?"

I grab the downed girl's wristband but leave the weapon. Then I snatch Malorie from where she sits staring at the girl. "We have to help her," she stammers.

"We stay here, we die. Move."

We rush toward the stairs. I can hear a feeble beep so I dart back into the shadows, dragging Malorie behind me. I look at the wrist communication device. It's still, nothing lit, so this is something else. A small wheeled machine lumbers past. We freeze by one of the many pillars and watch. I should have hidden her body, I think wretchedly. She will likely be unconscious for a while but that darned machine will find her any second. We have to move.

As quietly as I can, I move to the pillar closest to the stairs, always keeping at least one pillar between us and the little robotic machine. In moments it will realize what it's about to bump into.

I jerk an uncooperative Mal up the stairs just as the little robot sets off a piercing alarm. I scan the area at the top and, seeing no clear choice, I yank her to the left. She digs in her heels — her body rigid and angry. "Stop it," she snarls. "Let me go!"

"Mal, no. It's not safe. Yell at me later. Just not now. Come on. Please. It's not safe."

I have never seen her look so angry, so defeated and confused. Tears well in her eyes but she gives her head one brief, jerky shake. "You're not safe," she whispers in a broken voice. Faint screams echo up the stairs, galvanizing me into action.

Again, I pull her arm, going left. It's lit fairly well here and I feel exposed, but up ahead I can see a darker area. There are no shadows and nothing to hide behind in this section. Bits of barely legible signage cling to the wall like starfish to rock. I move quickly, almost jogging, wanting to hurry past the well-lit part but afraid of another trap. I recognize this piece from the game too, but it isn't so familiar that I know which way to go. We move down the corridor as fast as we can and still keep our feet quiet. Old cameras are mounted to the walls, but they are still and no indicator lights glow. I estimate the angle of their lenses and stay out of their range as best I can. I don't trust that they are off.

When we reach the darkened area, I see that it would be brightly lit if nearly half the lights weren't gone or broken. Here our dark uniforms could be mistaken for black as long as no one gets too close. I change my approach. "Mal, pretend you're from public safety. Stand tall and walk with purpose. It will fool anyone who sees us from a distance."

She smooths back her hair and squares her shoulders, giving off the illusion of confidence. I wonder desperately where we are and if we can pull this off. Empty, broken kiosks march in a nearly endless row. As we walk, I search frantically looking for a lesser used, more secure area. Most of the kiosks are gated closed, but some look like they are broken. One with a partially raised gate catches my eye. It looks like it has an opening to the back.

I urge Malorie over to the counter, and apply pressure to the gate and get it open far enough for her to slide between it and the counter but then it jams. I pray that I'll fit. I rescan the area quickly and then struggle through the opening. My head, shoulders, and chest make it through fine, but my pants catch by the back pocket and the sound of ripping fabric screams loudly into the quiet. The quiet? The faint sound of the alarm must have cut off with the shredding of my pants. "They're coming," I breathe as I force myself through.

I look around and seize a rag that has been left near a sink. I smudge up the spot we wiped virtually clean by sliding through and then try to push the gate back down. It sticks, then moves unexpectedly, breaking free, rattling, to bang against the counter. I grind my teeth and search for a place to hide.

"Now we talk!" Mal scolds in a violent whisper. "What is going on?"

I just shake my head.

"Don't do that!" she all but snarls. "You know something, but every part of me is screaming to turn ourselves in."

I open my mouth but stop when the wristband I'd lifted off the unconscious girl beeps and a text appears. *Spread them out. You may now shoot any strays you find. Mark the bodies for later retrieval.*

Malorie stares at the wristband and then looks at me. "I don't care," she says in denial. "We don't know what that means. It could be a private joke, meant for her. I don't know what's happened to you or why you're acting like this, but I'm turning myself in. I'm done with this, I'm hungry and I'm done with you!"

"Mal, please —" The sound of pounding feet silences me. We freeze. A boy marked with the purple of government sprints toward us. His eyes are so wide that the white shows all the way around. Sweat and dirt fight for space on his face, hands, ruined jacket and pants. He glances to the side, catching my eye. A bang splits the air, his feet stop churning but his momentum carries his torso forward even as his shoulders and head jerk back. He falls with a splat, blood spattering, while his eyes are still locked with mine yet looking different — glazed — unseeing. I know this boy. I sit by him at meals sometimes. His name was . . . Griffin. He was nice and had a voice you could listen to without growing bored. I always thought he should record books or do voiceovers for video. I glance at Malorie whose fists are jammed against her mouth as tightly she can get them.

I have to do something. I have to save us because it's too late to save him. This is too real, and Malorie is beyond rational thought. I quickly search the space we have jumped into as I listen hard. They must have sold hot dogs here once but now everything looks dejected and lonely. I focus on the exit at the back, and silently creep over and open the door slowly with my jacket sleeve covering my hand. Looking both ways, I can hear the soft fall of unhurried feet. The band beeps softly again. "Body on level sub one, section 12." Shit. This thing has GPS. I find the app and turn it off, grab Mal and pull her through the door. Junk litters the back hall. I quickly pick up a piece of metal and brace it between the door knob and the floor and put my ear to the crack of the door. Seconds tick by, but all I can hear is my heartbeat and Mal's heavy breathing.

"Did you hear that?" A voice speaks way too closely to us and I almost jump.

"Nah, don't be dumb. We gotta get your kill outta here before another stupid student finds it. That would ruin all our fun. Though, the look on their face would play great on the training video." They chuckle at each other, as if trading simple knock-knock jokes.

I didn't wait to hear more. Taking Malorie's elbow, I propel her on and on until my throat is dry and my feet are aching. I've lost all sense of time but the band tells me it's after eight at night. It will be dark soon and then maybe we can sneak up to the streets and somehow hide among the workers.

We find our way to a quiet corner and slide down the wall to sit and rest. We split the water and share some jerky. Malorie doesn't want to talk and neither do I. I'm sure that just like me, she's watching Griffin die over and over again.

I think that we are so dirty now that we can blend in well with the underworld masses. This almost has me laughing but fear keeps me silent. Our government wants us dead, there is no doubt in my mind, but why?

My thoughts chase around my head like a thousand cats on a tear. Malorie puts her head on my shoulder and is asleep in an instant. I wonder how she can sleep — how she can trust that she is safe. It takes me quite a bit longer to finally lose myself to slumber.

A hand touches my shoulder and my eyes fly open. I smack the hand away and spring to my feet ready to fight. Malorie falls to the side with a surprised sound.

"You!" bursts from my lips, the heel of my hand hovering a breath away from a very familiar jaw, caught short just before the strike.

"Come on, you've got to get out of here. They're looking for you." His voice is whispery, low, and rough.

"Why are *you* here, Bren?" I ask in confusion.

"Can I explain somewhere safer?" he begs with slightly more volume.

"Why should we trust you?" I ask as I narrow my eyes to glare at him. I'm not entirely successful because a stupid part of me is so happy to see a friendly face that I'm half afraid I'll throw myself into his arms. His eyes dart over both of us and the place we've been dozing.

Malorie starts to speak, but he strikes fast as a snake and

has the band out of my hand and crushed under the heel of his boot before I can stop it.

"What are you doing?"

"They can track you with that." He scowls angrily at me like he expected more of me.

"I was tracking *them* with it. I already shut off the GPS and I could still read their texts. Now you've ruined it."

"You think you turned it off. They can listen to you with that too. They know where you are and surely know you have it. What else do you have on you?"

"Nothing!"

"I'll be the judge of that." He lunges and twists my arm behind me to pat me down quickly and efficiently. Malorie's eyes grow huge, but she doesn't move. He releases me and does the same to her. "Put this band on your hips," he whispers, pulling a stretchy band with metallic threads running through it from a backpack I hadn't noticed until now.

"Why should we?" Malorie asks, her voice sounding abrupt and rude.

"Please. It will interrupt your tracker signal."

I start to put mine on, but Malorie just stares at him. "What tracker signal?" she asks in a voice that is both calm and frightening yet sounds accusatory.

"All students have them. They put it in your hip when you're young. Now come on."

"Wait. I know who you are. You're the teacher's assistant from our tenth year programming class. B . . . Brad . . . Brendon . . . ? Why would you be here now?" Malorie accuses.

"It's Bren and yes. That's who I was, but not anymore. I'm here to help you. I'm not part of the school or the government. Come on. Please hurry."

It's the way he says it, I suppose, that has me believing him. *Please let my instincts be right on this one.* I sigh inside, adjust the band around my hips and pick up what little gear I have. I'm tired and hungry and I desperately need the help. I can tell that Malorie isn't happy, but she doesn't have a better idea, I guess, or she would say something. She looks from me to our new ally and sighs aloud. She finally steps into her band and settles it around her hips like a low slung belt.

Bren leads us no more than a couple of hundred meters when the sound of marching feet grows behind us. "Hurry," he breathes as he takes my arm to rush us on. He slips between another section of wall where you can only see the opening if you look right at it. The underground people are amazing with optical illusions.

We don't go far before he starts speaking with no sound, using hand motions in the near darkness. *"Over there and down behind the wall . . ."* he says with sign language that even I can understand, so we hunker down behind a broken bit of wall. *"Hold still,"* he adds with his hands. I'm a terrible lip reader so the hand motions help.

Malorie gives him a disgusted scowl, but that is the last attention I pay to her. I listen to the marching feet, but with nothing else to look at except a crumbling wall I watch Bren. I realize that I'm free to look at him now because no one will know or record it in a file. I study his hands and notice that they are no longer soft and smooth like I remember. These are not the hands of someone who manipulates a touchscreen, mouse, and keyboard. Though his nails are still short, clean, and neat they don't look the same. Now his skin is darker and I can see scars and calluses. He has more hair on the part of his arms not covered by the pushed up sleeves of his shirt. I notice that the arm I've been staring at is resting on olive green cargo pants that are similar to the ones public safety wears, except that theirs are regulation black. He's wearing combat boots like they do too. Interesting.

My gaze wanders up his chest to his face. His jaw is stubbled now. I wonder if he's had his twentieth birthday yet. He looks older and even more drool-worthy than he had in school. He looks dangerous, but I'm not afraid of him. I guess it's his calm and alert, yet watchful manner that puts me at ease. He looks confident and I feel lost.

I'm tired. I want sleep. I want food. I want . . . I glance back at his hands and began to wonder what they would feel like on my skin. What would the stubble on his jaw feel like? What would . . .

"What?" he asks softly, jerking me back to the present to find him watching me in return.

"Uh," I clear my throat quietly and realize the sound of marching feet is gone. "I was, ah, thinking."

"Oh really?"

"Absolutely," I reply, trying to sound calm and sure. He gives me a spectacularly executed look of disbelief. "I was deep in thought," I add for good measure.

"Deep in thought about what?" he asks with a half-smile on his face.

I just stare. I'm caught. His eyes gleam and crinkle at the corners. His smile stretches so that it reaches those amazing eyes. I realize he's smiling with his whole body, white teeth shining in the darkness. Before I'm completely lost in distraction again, I snatch at the only other thought rattling around in my head. "I was thinking about how I knew things." *Oh hell, shut up you idiot. You don't know if you can trust him.*

"You'll have to tell me later. Right now we need to move before they come back. They've lost your signal so they'll soon begin to scour the last place you were known to be, though they may not have been focusing on you. They have a lot of students to eradicate before dawn."

That word again. Why did the government want to get rid of a bunch of students? Bren stands and begins searching the far wall. Malorie sends me a disgusted look but then turns it into a soft giggle. "You like him," she whispers softly.

"No. Absolutely not."

"Liar." She smiles bigger and walks toward the man in question who is now waving us over to follow him.

Bren leads us through another optical illusion and then down a narrow passageway. In short bursts, he begins to tell us his plan, which is to get us out of the city and join the resistance in the wilds beyond the city's borders. I have never been outside the city to where farming, mining, and the collection of other raw materials happens. Even those workers who live at the edge of the city are transported to their jobs and are watched over by public safety. I don't see how we can possibly get past all that. The schools may be away from the city hubs but even they are inside the boundary.

Bren and Malorie keep giving each other frustrated, irritated, and disgusted looks. It's getting on my nerves, but there's no way I'm letting either of them out of my sight. I brought her into this and I will bring her out safely. I did well enough on my own, but I now realize that I had no idea the underground area was so vast. It seems that the whole city has layers and there is so much I don't know. I hate to admit it, but we need Bren, who seems to know his way around. If he wanted to kill us he would have already done so, and if he wanted a reward he missed his chance earlier.

We come to rungs set into the concrete and brick of a wall. Bren signals for quiet and crawls up without a sound. He waits for a bit and then eases open the grate. He waves his hand for us to come up. All I can see besides his shadowy face is the night sky beyond the buildings. I crawl on up and take my first breath of fresh air in what feels like days instead of hours.

Bren touches my arm and I feel electricity travel straight to my heart. "At the corner turn right and enter the first door; it's a service entrance that is unguarded tonight. Remove your jacket and tie it around your waist. Take your hair out of the ponytail and try to blend in with the people inside. Make your way toward the front of the building and act like you belong and know what you're doing. When you get to the front, watch for the guards — they will pass at 1:00 a.m. Once they're out of sight, you walk out that door and keep going at a 130-degree angle until you hit the park at the foot of the bridge. You got it?" He looks at me worriedly.

"Yes but —"

"I'm going to create a diversion so we can cross the bridge. We've got to get out of the city."

"How will we find you?"

"Keep walking until you hit the park. Find a place to hide and I'll find you." He reaches out and clasps my shoulder. "You can do this."

"How do you know?" I whisper, but he's already on the move again. I swallow my fear. A siren goes off and I'm afraid they're onto us again. I take a deep breath and lead Malorie the way he indicated, looking back before turning the corner. The grate is back in place with a box over it and Bren is just turning the corner the other way. The street is nearly as dark as the alley on this side.

We quickly follow his instructions and head up the street. I try to look everywhere without giving us away. Mal and I slip into the doorway he indicated only to find it locked. *Now what?* I'm just formulating an alternate plan when the door handle is yanked from my hand. The largest man I've ever seen takes hold of my shirt front and hauls me inside. Malorie barely has time to utter a squeak before she too is drawn in. He shoves us out of the way and bolts the door.

"Two? I was expecting one." He looks us up and down and then shrugs as if he's answered his own question. He again takes hold of my shirt, this time at the shoulder, and drags me forward leaving Malorie to follow behind. Big and demanding as he is, he strikes me as more of a gentle giant. I take in his clothing and it finally dawns on me that he's public safety. I begin to panic and fight. "No, no," he says softly as he holds me aloft in front of him so he can look into my eyes. "I'm helping you."

I just stare into his big brown eyes in his big brown face and I'm again struck with his gentleness despite the fact that I'm hanging in space. He enters a door to his right and dumps me unceremoniously into a chair. A small Asian woman with bright, intelligent eyes is waiting. She smiles at us and then quickly turns and begins pulling things out of a box on the floor next to her. The big man leaves the room and she hands us new clothes. "You change. Put bands under you clothes. This room shielded. No spy here." She smiles and waits.

It takes a moment for her thick accent to penetrate my tired brain. The room is about the size of a large walk-in closet with a barber's chair and a large mirror taking up much of the space. The woman briskly cleans us up and cuts and restyles our hair. Now we look like part of the workforce. The whole thing has taken less than twenty minutes with her quick efficient hands.

She looks at her wristband and makes a sound of disgust. "You running late. I expect one, not redress two. No help for it. My friend watch for night patrol. You go wait for his signal then head to you next destination." Her twisting of our language makes me smile despite my fears.

"We weren't expecting you or your friend either. Why are you helping us?" I ask cautiously in a soft voice.

"You have allies. Many people hate government and want change. You the catalyst."

"But we're just students, and we were only trying to surv—"

She stops me. "No. Not students. You. You are the catalyst."

As she finishes her work, I try to dislodge my stunned mind and manage to ask, "Why would you pick someone like me?"

"No time talk. You must go. Hurry. Good luck."

"But—"

"Meet Mr. Bishop. He help."

"But—" I sputter again.

She shoves us back into the hall and starts cleaning. I watch as she dumps all of our old gear and hair clippings into a huge metal bin and pours chemicals strong enough to make my eyes burn over the top. She replaces the lid and begins to open a trap door. Every trace of us will soon be gone. She glances up at us and then flaps her hands in a shooing motion. I look to Malorie who shrugs and we walk to the front just as Bren instructed.

The big man is standing with his back to the wall containing the windows, but his head is turned so that he can see out. He waves us forward and has us stand by his side. I suck in a sharp breath—not a moment later the first patrol walks by. I start to move, but he pushes me back without even looking at me. A second unit is sweeping the other side of the street. Our enormous angel holds up a hand and begins to count down on his fingers. At the count of one he shoves us out the door and locks it quickly behind us.

I hear glass shatter a block to our right and around the corner, but I force myself not to look and don't allow myself to slow. I have hold of Malorie's elbow again and I'm not going to let go until we have walked into the park—twelve long blocks away by the diagonal route we are supposed to take.

The streets are strangely quiet and nearly deserted. Most windows are dark and many of the street lights are off. In a mostly empty bar to our right, I see an entertainment screen on and pause to watch. Faces flash across the surface. I can hear nothing, but by watching the images and reading the occasional messages at the bottom of the screen, I can tell who they are talking about. I can't seem to catch my breath. The government put the city in lockdown for the people's safety. They're claiming there was a huge accident and many students have died. Tomorrow flags are to be flown at half-mast. The reporter is interviewing our principal. She appears distraught but as I watch closely I can see that she . . . knew. Her body language is speaking to me in ways I've never noticed before. I look into her eyes on the monitor and I know . . . no one needs to blot at eyes that aren't really crying and her speech looks rehearsed. She is not choked up and never pauses.

"El," Malorie hisses.

"You two." I spin to find a youngish man from public safety addressing us. "What are you doing out?"

"I'm so sorry. We were on our way home from work. We had a deadline so we had to work late. I saw the newscast was on and paused to watch. We're just leaving," I say smoothly waving my hand toward the bar.

"I.D.?" he asks as he steps closer. I attack, taking him by surprise like I had the girl in the abandoned underground station. The elbow, used correctly, can be a powerful weapon. He grabs his throat and I kick him in the stomach. He bends over the kick and I use my elbow again to drive him to the ground. Malorie snatches the Taser from his belt and gives him a burst. He twitches once and is still.

By unspoken agreement, we each grasp him under an arm and drag him toward the alley. It takes ten long minutes we don't have to stuff him in a dumpster. Mal tosses the Taser in after giving it a long, hard, covetous look and then we let the lid fall shut as quietly as we can. We run back up the alley and peek out the other side before speed-walking our way toward the park again.

Sweat dampens my back despite the chill in the air. The park looks brooding, dark and empty. We approach carefully and even though nothing looks out of place, we stick to the shadows. Guards walk the upper levels of the bridge above the park and patrol cars move back and forth through the entrance and over the bridge. There seems to be a road block and officers are checking each vehicle leaving the city. Nice. Now how will we get past that, I wonder. I find us a dark corner and help Malorie climb up the bridge support so we have a better vantage point. Then we settle in to wait.

Malorie watches one side of the park and I take the other. I'm so relieved when I see Bren that I want to shout and run to him but I know better. I clamp a hand over my own mouth just to be sure I don't let out a sound. He doesn't look quite right somehow. Then I see it; he's limping. I lurch to my feet but keep to the shadows. "Bren," I breathe. Malorie elbows me in the calf. I clamp my lips together and breathe heavily through my nose. He must have heard me or sensed me, I don't know which, but he walks almost right to us.

"What happened to you?" I gasp when he's close.

"Nothing. Keep moving." His voice is rough and sharp. He's frustrated and angry, but he's alive. "Were you spotted?" he nearly snarls at us.

"Yes."

"No."

Malorie and I answer at once. We look at each other.

"Yes," I say again, "but it's taken care of."

Bren wipes a hand over his face, smearing blood and sweat. I reach up to touch the cut over his eye but he slaps my hand away. "Now we really have to hurry." This time, his voice sounds weary and resigned. "Come on."

He leads us over to another support and begins to climb. This one is different from the one we'd hidden under. A ladder of sorts is embedded into the smooth metal, if you know where to look. We have to feel for the hand and footholds in the darkness and it takes a lot of time, but strangely the further into the air we scale the safer I feel. What is wrong with my thinking? Is falling to my death better than being captured? At the top, hidden within the infrastructure of the bridge is a catwalk. It will be slow going, but we can make it. Inch by tedious inch we'll have to go, but . . . doable.

The cold steel bites into my hands and the wind tears at my

hair. It's cold up here. I pause to look at the sparkling water. How can it be so lovely and yet so deadly? Hitting the water from this height would be like diving onto concrete.

What has happened to my simple life?

I feel my eyes tear up and try to pretend it's the wind making them water. I pause to swipe at the moisture before anyone notices, but my foot slips. I grab at everything and touch nothing. One foot slides further out into space and for the longest moment of my life, I hang in empty nothingness too scared to scream. My other knee hits the catwalk with a bang. My hands slap down hard on the rough surface. Now tears are not my only problem.

One warm hand grabs my elbow and the other my armpit. I look up into Bren's face, half hidden in shadow. How could he look so calm, so in control and so . . . appealing?

"I can't do this." My voice comes out like a squeak. I feel ashamed and like I will throw up all at once.

"Yes, you can. Don't look down. Just put one foot in front of the other. We're almost there."

Malorie has kept quiet, maybe too quiet. What's wrong with me? Everything, right? Bren is waiting for an answer so I give him a nod as I bite my lip. I glance at Mal. She looks . . . determined. Her lips are smashed into a straight line and I can see the muscles at her jaw flex.

Bren was right. In eight hundred ninety-seven more steps he calls a halt. I'm not ashamed to admit that I counted each one. My whole body is shaking. Malorie and I silently hug the support on the far side of the bridge. We watch Bren slowly climb up for a quick look. I'm scared to death of what he'll find or that he'll fall as he hangs suspended out over nothing but the water far below. Now my life is counted not in steps but in breaths as he struggles to hold himself awkwardly out of their sight.

The minutes tick by. I feel Malorie's eyes on me, but I can't tear mine away from Bren's barely visible, shadowy form, high above my head. I finally glance at her. Her eyes hold fear, anger, and accusations. Her lips are tightly compressed together, her knuckles white on the support.

"I'll never forgive you if this doesn't end well," she murmurs.

"I'm sorry," I whisper back. "I had to . . . do this. I had to follow my gut. The system is wrong, and I don't want to die. I couldn't . . . just let things happen. I had to try. I couldn't risk being captured and I didn't want us to end up like Griffin."

"So I was in the wrong place at the wrong time? Am I lucky or not, Elise? Why do I have this weird vibe that you feel guilty? Did you . . . I don't know . . . do something to start all this?"

"Malorie, you're my best friend. I would never"

"Don't say it," she interrupts. "I know you wouldn't hurt me on purpose, but don't you see . . . you did. This isn't the first time you've gotten carried away with something crazy and dragged me into it. You have got to stop."

"I'm—"

"I know you're sorry. You always are. I just wish you'd . . . think first."

I open my mouth to reply, but a noise silences us and draws our attention back upward. Bren is almost upon us. The moment his feet are on the deck he speaks rapidly in a hushed tone. "There's only one patrol on this side of the bridge. We can make it past, no problem. Stay close to me and for heaven's sake, don't talk — try to blend in."

He takes off, only looking back once to spy on the guards before he deems it safe enough to move back to the ground. He leads us on a circuitous route away from there and deeper into the Northeast part of town. Buildings are still closed and dark but there is more vehicular traffic and an occasional citizen is on foot. Public safety is patrolling mainly by car or motorcycle over here. They are not walking the streets. I'm grateful but so tired that I seriously begin to contemplate how bad it would be to get caught.

The sky has changed from true black to an unidentifiable shade of dark blue-gray when Bren finally stops. I'm about dead on my feet and I'll bet my last coin Malorie is too. I've never been up all night and the adrenaline has long ago burned away. Mal doesn't trust Bren and I probably shouldn't, but by now I feel . . . lost. I have rarely been on this side of the river and never on foot. He pauses in front of an abandoned building. I watch him reach above the door, knock a key from the frame, use it in the lock and walk through. He beckons us in, relocks the door, and encourages us up the stairs. Plastic sheeting hangs in raggedy strips from several places. It's joined by cobwebs and dust. Long dead leaves, cigarette butts, and wadded-up papers litter the tiled floor.

Upstairs is only marginally better, but at least the floors are wood and mostly clean. Old fashioned windows with several cracked panes look out in three directions. From here, in the early gray of predawn, the river looks sullen. Lights are winking out and the city is waking up. We settle into a corner and try to rest. It doesn't take Malorie long to fall into an uneasy sleep, but tired as I am I can't seem to close my eyes.

"Rest, Elise. I'll keep watch."

"Tell me what happened to you and then maybe I can relax enough to rest."

He sighs heavily but unbends enough to talk. I can see a little better in here than I could under the bridge or out on the streets as day gains leverage over night. Light from the windows cuts a swath across half his face allowing me a glimpse of the man he's becoming. His nose is straight but turned up a bit at the end like I remember. For the first time since he found us, the light hits his eyes just right and I see it — a flash of green. Then I notice the freckles that lightly dust his nose and cheeks. I hadn't really noticed them before. How had I missed them? I guess I've never been this close before. He turns his head a little and I again catch sight of the blood. This time, he doesn't slap my hand away as I try to blot up the worst of the damage with the edge of my sleeve.

He gently takes my wrist and holds it against his leg so he can look me in the eye when he speaks. "I wanted to create a diversion. One was to be set up for me four blocks from where I left you, but when I got there, a patrol had found it. Lucky for me they set it off while trying to figure out what it was. Unfortunately, I wasn't ready and they saw me. Two of them chased after me and I couldn't get away without a fight. I left them unconscious, but by now they'll be all healed up and giving reports and I'm . . . It's going to be a long two-day walk to the pick-up point with this —" he trails off indicating his leg with a flip of his hand.

"I'm sorry." It wasn't enough but it was all I had.

"I'll survive. Don't worry about it. What happened to you or should I even ask?"

I told him about the bar, the entertainment screen and the officer who caught me off guard. "I need to be more vigilant," I end, shifting my gaze to my feet.

"You're tired and untrained, but your instincts are good. I think you're a fighter and you'll learn."

I smile at him and realize how very tired I am. I had felt lost moments ago, but now when I look at Bren I feel something else . . . hope. I dare to hope and to dream that this will come to an end and that I can make a difference. I drift off with the strange predawn noises scratching at me like a bit of rough clothing abrading my skin. The sounds weave themselves into my dreams. I can see a lake and hear the lap of the water on the shore. I'm surrounded by lush green plants blooming with bursts of bright color. The water is smooth as glass; the trees beyond the far edge are tall, dark and bristly. Beyond them a mountain looms, its tip frosted in snow and its perfect reflection mirrored in the glassy surface of the lake. There's a strange sound and the animal noises cease. Then it sounds again and the birds take flight. Run!

My eyes pop open and it takes me a moment to realize where I am. My eyes flit around the nearly silent room until they land on Malorie who is curled in a ball, shivering. "Mal," I whisper. "What is it?" She doesn't respond. I can feel myself tensing with fear as frightening thoughts race through my mind. She starts to shake uncontrollably. It must have been the chattering of her teeth that has awakened me. "Malorie!" I hiss louder in a frantic voice.

I touch her shoulder to turn her over. She's way too warm. She's cast her jacket off to one side and with her shivering and writhing her pants and band have worked low on her hips exposing a swath of skin . . . where a blue glow shines right through. "What is this?"

"It started about an hour ago," she croaks softly, finally awake enough to answer.

"Why didn't you wake me?"

"I was scared and I thought we were waiting out the day here anyway. Besides what could you do?"

"Mal." My voice sounds sad and broken. Bren mumbles and rolls over, but doesn't wake.

"Y-you . . . sh-should leave me. I think they're onto us."

"No, Mal. You're sick. Let me help."

"The . . . weird . . . blue . . . glow. Did they? I . . . I don't . . . know . . . I feel . . . sick. It's . . . it's like . . . the worst flu . . . ever but . . . I wonder," she stutters between chattering teeth.

I put a hand on her forehead. "You're burning up. You were fine. How could you get sick so fast? Is it because you're scared?"

"No, Elise. I . . . I mean yes. I'm scared but that's not it. Look." She weakly paws at her pants to give me a better look at the blue glow. Her eyes roll up in her head and her body convulses. I rip off my jacket and jam the sleeve in her mouth so she won't bite her tongue or scream and give us away. She thrashes violently. I move back and feel more helpless and afraid than I could believe possible.

Bren springs to his feet. "What?" He doesn't have to finish. He sees the blue glow and drops to his knees. "No! I was afraid . . . but I hoped —"

"Afraid of what?" I bark at him as I scramble back out of the way to wait out the seizure.

"Her capsule's been activated. It must have taken too long to kill you off, so they flipped a switch. I thought we could get out of range and that the band would help. I thought they wouldn't be able to track us past the river. I didn't want to cut it out. I only have my knife and it's not sterilized. I was afraid I'd hurt her. Someone who knows what they're doing —"

My own thoughts are interrupted by Malorie, her back arches violently and I hear a crack. She collapses back limply and lays still.

"Oh my God. Malorie! Mal?" She doesn't move . . . and barely seems to breathe. I feel for a pulse. It's weak and irregular. Bren's talking, but I'm not listening. I can see his mouth forming words but I can only hear a ringing in my ears. I take my jacket from her mouth and tilt her head back, checking her airway. "Get . . . me . . . help," I grate in a harsh voice.

Bren scrambles away and I work on, wiping sweat from her brow and trying to make her comfortable. I try to get her back into her jacket, but my attempt is clumsy and she is no help. My adrenaline begins to wear off and my body aches as I wait for Bren's return. I listen to every sound, watch Malorie's shallow breaths, and move my eyes around continuously. Suddenly fear takes hold of me again. What about me? What about my chip? I start to look, but Malorie moans weakly. Focus. I need to focus on her. "Come on Mal, please," I beg as tears run down my face and drip from my nose. Maybe my nose is running. I shouldn't drip on Mal.

She wheezes and her eyes flutter. "El?" she rasps.

"Yes?" I push past the lump in my throat.

"I can't feel my legs, El." Her eyes roll up in her head and she is still once more.

Poor Mal, I did this to her. Her hip's blue glow is receding but she isn't waking up. Bren comes around the corner with an elderly woman dressed in rags.

"You can't stop it, youngling," she wheezes at me.

"No . . . I have to —"

The old woman kneels by Malorie. She feels her pulse and touches her forehead. With a flash, she has out a knife and has sliced into my friend. I swear I feel it in my own hip. She pops out a capsule from the three-centimeter long cut and tosses it onto a piece of shredded plastic. Bren crushes it under his heel. I watch as they began to remove all traces of our presence here. Malorie remains unmoving and unchanging except for the thin stream of blood that runs from her damaged hip. They don't even bind her wound.

The old woman looks over Mal one last time and shakes her head. "I can't help her." She picks up the crushed capsule and flicks it out the window.

Bren pulls me up and I collapse into him and sob. "No," I croak, my voice echoing back at me. Somewhere nearby water drips slowly into a puddle. It has begun to rain. A ship's horn blows and the sounds of traffic increase. Was I the only one who cared? A few breaths pass as tears slide down my cheeks.

Bren clears his throat. "We need to . . ."

Oh my God, what about me? I push away and begin stripping frantically so that I can search my body. My jacket hits the floor and I reach for the snap on my pants.

"What are you doing?" Bren yelps, as I begin unzipping them.

The old woman speaks but I barely register her words. "That really isn't necessary."

"Where's mine? Is it blinking? Am I glowing anywhere? I don't want to die . . . like that." I push them down far enough to see my hips and thighs and then I'm ripping at my shirt. A button flies off and clatters to the floor.

"Stop! Your chip was wiped from the central computer," Bren ends on a sigh, grasping my bare shoulder and forcing me to look into his eyes.

"How do you know?" My voice cracks.

"Because one of my tasks during my final year of school was to match all the numbers on the chips to the recipients and set up the coding sequences. I . . . I recognized your name . . . and I . . . I liked you. I knew things were not what they seemed. Even then I was leery of authority, but I didn't let on. I inverted a couple of numbers on your information. I just wish I had miscoded her chip too." I must look silly standing there in my underwear with my pants pooled around my ankles, but he doesn't laugh. I shiver and I'm not sure if it's from the cold.

Without another word, Bren lets go of me and picks Malorie up. I yank my pants up and stuff buttons back into the holes in my shirt. He follows the old woman who has already started down the stairs. I stand there for a moment, staring at his back. He turns to look at me before he walks away. His eyes beg me to follow him, his mouth in a grim straight line. I pull myself together, snatch up my jacket, and walk behind him. I don't even care where we are going.

The old woman leads us out one door and in another, weaving through the nearby buildings until we reach stairs leading down and into a maze. The last thing I hear just as the door swings shut is sirens in the distance.

In moments I completely lose all sense of direction. We walk past some people who seem to know her and they look at her with respect. She leads us silently on through a series of rooms where she finally stops and indicates that Bren should put Malorie down. She looks her over one more time, shakes her head and leaves.

"No! We have to save her. What can we do? Help me. I promised her. I . . . promised."

"We'll try but it looks like we're too late; the virus is in her system and her seizure may have damaged her spine beyond what we can repair. We don't know what strain this virus is so we may not have the antidote ready. Even if we could wake her, she'll likely die soon anyway. It's best if she remains unconscious."

Malorie convulses again and then stops breathing. I try to lurch toward her but Bren stops me. "You don't understand how elaborate their plan is. Let her go. Let her suffering end. It's for the best."

Tears run in streams down my face as I shove him away. I tilt her head and blow in one breath and begin compressions. I work and work. Bren looks on and whispers, "Let her go." I can't listen. He is heartless. I work until I'm shaking and my back and arms burn.

"Come back to me Mal, I'm sorry. Please don't leave me. Please. Come back Mal. Come back."

A man walks into the room with a bag. A woman comes in right behind him and they squeeze in beside me and begin to work on Malorie. Bren wraps his arms around me forcing me out of their way.

"Let them try," he says softly.

Minutes pass and I become numb. I can't even hear their voices through the buzzing in my ears. I feel my heart beating through my whole body as frustration, fear, and rage tear at me. They look to me, sadness written all over their faces and start to collect their gear.

"No!" Was that me who screamed?

"She's gone, Elise. It's over. They are the best doctors we have and even they can't undo the damage the government has done."

"No." This time, it's a whisper. I look at Malorie. She is so still, staring at the ceiling, her jaw relaxed so that her mouth hangs slightly open. She almost looks like she is singing but her eyes are empty. They no longer look like they had just moments ago . . . when she'd been alive.

I feel myself crumpling, falling toward the floor. I hope it will open up and swallow me whole, but Bren won't let me go. I shut my eyes to close it out.

There is fabric beneath my cheek. Bren's steady heartbeat and the rise and fall of his chest where my head rests take the edge off my pain. There's a pebble poking me in the knee. Some-one else is in the room. I open my eyes to find the old woman looking down at me with pity. I don't know what my face holds nor do I care.

I watch her walk over to Malorie and gently close her eyes, nod at Bren, and leave the room. I pull myself to my feet and then move over to Mal slowly. I bend and kiss her cooling forehead. "I'm so sorry, Mal; so very sorry. I wish . . ." the rest of the words stick in my throat.

I find myself shaking as silent sobs wrack my body. Bren puts his arms around me again, holding me until he feels me collapsing. He eases me gently back to the floor and lets me sit. I stare into the distance with unfocused eyes. Minutes pass and then Bren gives my shoulders a little squeeze and leaves. It's just as well.

The room is cool and damp, and I can hear water drip in the silence. *Drip, drip.* I close my eyes, clear my mind and just listen for a moment, pushing all the ugliness down deep where it will never see the light of day. The dripping is from my right. I roll my head and search for it with my eyes, the rest of me too drained to move. A rivulet of water makes its way down the bumpy uneven surface of the gray wall. That drop is going somewhere. I, on the other hand, am not. Part of me acknowledges that I should do something, but despair holds me rooted to the floor.

A dog's bark echoes in the distance. I should move. I roll my head back so that I can look at Malorie, then crawl over to her and straighten her clothes. I feel her pockets and find nothing so I zip up her jacket and fold her hands over her waist to hide the damage. I finger-comb her hair and think how nice her new haircut looks. "I'm so very sorry, Mal. I wish I'd been a better friend. I wish I'd gotten you out of this. I'm scared I'm going to end up like you. Come back, Mal. Please. Don't leave me here alone."

The only answer is the bark of the dog and a soft footfall. I turn toward the sound ready to fight, only to see Bren. He holds a chipped mug in his hand.

"You're going to be okay, Elise. Here. Drink this. It will help."

I look at him but make no move to comply so he encourages me to take it by putting the mug in my hands. I take a small sip. It's hot, but not scalding, sweet, cinnamony and smooth with the slow burn of alcohol.

Bren wraps me up in his arms one more time and leads me from the room. I suck in some air and try to pull myself together, but at the moment it feels like a hopeless cause. He leads me down a corridor and into another room. This one is dry and holds a lived-in feel. He gently pushes me into a wooden chair that rests near a rough-hewn table. I hold the mug in both hands as I stare into the opaque contents.

"Drink it, Elise. You'll feel better." His voice is soft and warm like the brew, whatever it is. I take a few more sips. I feel a little better, not good, but not so utterly exhausted and defeated. Dropping my meager gear onto the floor, I round my shoulders and hang my head.

The old woman returns and leaves a pot of tea, some bread, cheese and fruit. She ignores me and speaks to Bren, "Sleep here today. Tonight you must move on. It's too dangerous to keep her here."

I look more closely at her. There is something . . .

"Yes, Melodia." Bren answers.

She smiles a soft smile and shuts the door behind her.

My brain starts waking up. "Wait, you *know* her?"

"She works with us. We've been watching and helping where we can."

"But *I* know her . . . she's the lady from the market. She traded me a knife and canteen for my earrings."

"I bet she did," he answers with a soft smile. "She notified me right after she left the market. Down here, she is like the queen and she has an impressive network of spies."

"If she's the queen, does that make me the court jester?" I ask, fearing the answer. I can feel tears coming back again when a more frightening thought seizes me. "All this time, they've been tracking us through GPS hidden inside of us. Nothing they sent, no scenario they tried, killed us and now . . . now they just killed Malorie by activating a . . . a chip that was injected years ago. I vaguely remember when they did it. How do we stop this? Is it magnetized? The bands obviously don't work. Can we cut it out?" I slam my mug onto the table sloshing the contents. "They can't kill me, but what about the GPS?"

"I miscoded it. Your chip is worthless to them. It was never activated. I swear."

"Even if you're right, maybe I'm better off dead. Look at all the trouble I cause." My voice catches and cracks.

"You have to live, Elise. You have to tell the world your story and stop this."

"I'm just a kid. No one will listen to me. No one has ever listened to me, so I just quit talking." I know my eyes are welling up again and mostly I don't care. They have chosen the wrong girl. I fight to keep them in but the tears begin to spill. Bren slowly puts his arm around my shoulders and then he hugs me gently. Like he's afraid I'll break or maybe that I'll bite.

"Breathe. I'm here for you. I was only supposed to bring you in, but now . . ." He holds me away from him and looks me right in the eye, "Don't feel defeated. Get angry. Fury will sustain you! They haven't won yet, but they will if *you* let them."

"How did I know what to do? How did I know how to fight and how to hide?"

"You've been building and testing the game. The game has been learning from you, but you obviously have been learning from it. You recognized the game elements in your reality and you acted accordingly."

"I'm not special. Why didn't anyone else see what was happening or learn from *Underworlders*? The game, I mean."

"You are special. Only people in programming touched the game, but you aren't like everyone else. You see things and remember them. You have a spark. I saw it right away."

"You never talked to me at school. How would you know?"

"I couldn't give anything away. I was afraid they would see in you what I saw, but now I think they only saw what they wanted to see. They thought you were smart. You are more than just smart. Way more. You remember things that the others don't because your brain is wired differently. Their tricks don't work on you. They train students to forget or reassign them if they have to but none of it really works on your brain." I realize that I'm staring at his lips. I blink. He pushes me slightly away like he noticed it too.

Yeah, I think. I'm sure I look and smell fantastic; besides, what he says is crazy. Bren walks toward the table that holds the food. "Come on. Eat something. Knowing you, you skipped breakfast before the trial and you've only had a bit of jerky since."

"How did you know that I didn't eat breakfast?"

"I'll let you in on a little secret," he says with a sad smile. "It wasn't just in class that I watched you."

One corner of my mouth turns up in response. I plop down at the table and shovel in a little food and then just sit. Bren leads me over to the cot and sits me down. He perches next to me and then tilts me over. He pulls his legs up and holds my back to his chest. In no time his breathing is slow and steady. I can faintly feel his heartbeat again and try to close my eyes and focus on just that. Instead, I keep looking at his hand that lays relaxed on the cot just centimeters from mine. Maybe he doesn't hate me after all. I wiggle into his warmth, lace my fingers through his and finally close my eyes.

In no time Melodia is shaking my shoulder. Bren is already at the table eating like he won't see a meal again for a long time. It's a good bet we won't.

"Malorie?" I ask.

"I'm sorry child. We had her taken back to the warehouse for public safety to find. It was the last place they might have gotten a signal from her and we can't have them finding you. We hated to lose that hideout, but you're worth it. Have some breakfast; it's going to be a long day for you."

"What about my capsule?"

"We do not have the medical facilities here to remove it safely. You could get an infection or worse, we could hurt you. We won't do it."

"Won't they wonder about her capsule?"

"They might but then they may know you got a knife from an old woman at the market. I'm not the only one with spies."

"They don't know who you are," I guess.

"You're right and with luck, they'll keep thinking that all I'm good for is selling kitchen equipment from a broken down wagon. I find that I can trade way more than a pot in that place. It's where I get my best information. Now eat."

"But, what if my capsule . . . ?"

"Hush child," she interrupts. "Bren made sure it was never activated and he will take care of you. He will get you where you belong — where you can do some good. Hurry now, we must erase you from this place in case they come looking here."

I watch her walk away and wonder if I will ever see her again. How had she wormed her way into my heart in such a short time? She is like how I imagine a favorite grandma might be. I walk over to the table and sit across from Bren. It only takes two bites before I see it . . . the resemblance.

"You don't just know her. You're related to Melodia. I may

be the court jester, but you're a prince. Holy crap, Bren. What are you doing helping someone like me?"

His fork dangles halfway to his mouth. The eggs fall off with a plop. It looks like he's forgotten they'd ever been there.

"It's not what you think."

"It's exactly what I think. I can't let you risk your life for me. You have a real family and I have . . . I have . . . no one. I am . . . no one."

"You don't know who you are, but you will." With that cryptic message, he returns to eating his eggs. I stare at him for several minutes but he won't meet my eyes so I give up and shovel in a few more bites of chow. After I stop eating, Bren silently gets up from the table and picks up a tote bag from near the door that I had not noticed. He hands it to me, puts on a ball cap and a different jacket. I realize that he has a bandage over his eye and his clothes are different. He is dressed like maintenance and construction personnel.

He pulls me toward him by the strap of the tote. For a moment I think he's going to kiss me. I almost hope he will, but decide it's a silly thought at the same time. I feel disappointed when he merely ruffles my hair to rearrange it. "Grab your gear, change and meet me outside," is all he says.

"What about food and water?"

"It's taken care of."

Bren steps out of the room and closes the door behind him. I quickly change into my new clothes. Now we will run. *Awesome,* I think sarcastically.

01100110 01101111 01110010 00100000 01110100

01101000 01101111 01110011 01100101 00100000

We wind our way along numerous passageways. I have no idea where he's taking me. I just silently follow.

Bren stops at what looks like a dead end. He slowly slides a panel back to reveal a rainbow of polyester jacket sleeves. He waits a moment and then pushes aside the jackets for us to step through. We have to be in the basement of a retailer. Clothes hang on racks next to skis and other sporting goods. I raise my eyebrows in question but he just gives his head a slight shake and moves the panel back into place. Next, he redistributes the jackets so that the opening is completely hidden.

He eases over to the foot of the stairs and tilts his head to look and listen. I follow him up the stairs to the main level of the mostly deserted shop. A sales clerk dressed in the green of hospitality approaches and I suck in a frightened breath. "Weather's not looking good, sir. May I interest you in some raingear?"

Bren cuts his eyes to the door through which mist is gently falling from a darkened sky. "I suppose that would be in order."

The clerk walks us over to the rack of waterproof coats. I start to reach for a pretty teal blue one that catches my eye, but Bren shakes his head and hands me one in chocolate brown instead. I give him a look, but he nods firmly so I sigh and put it on. Brown is not my favorite color. Next, he hands me a day pack in a gray as dark as the angry looking clouds outside.

We walk up to the counter where the clerk goes through the motions of ringing us up for the few real customers in the store who don't seem to notice us. We step out the door and under the awning before arranging our new gear. Most people have their heads down in the rain and aren't paying any attention to anything but their own business. While I load the backpack, Bren leans in and whispers, "Keep me in sight but don't follow too closely until I tell you otherwise."

He sets a brisk pace and I follow, watching everywhere yet trying to hold him in my peripheral vision. Sometimes I walk close and sometimes I let other pedestrians come between us. Bren leads me in and out of buildings when he can. We walk on and on, always heading generally east. When he senses public safety personnel he moves out of sight quickly. I can tell that he's trying to avoid them all together. Usually, he ducks into a building, but sometimes he simply crosses the street or turns a corner abruptly to change up our route.

Just as my stomach is beginning to growl he enters a diner, and goes straight to a booth at the back. He picks up a menu but I don't think he's reading it. I sit across from him and wait. The waitress brings water and pulls wrapped sandwiches out of her pocket which she sets discretely on the table. Fast as a blink, they're off the table and Bren has them hidden. The waitress sets down a ticket which Bren slides to me.

My eyes go wide for a moment. I have no spending credits on me. We had entered our trial with nothing but the clothes on our backs and this wasn't a place to trade.

I look up to meet Bren's eyes. He's giving me a disgusted look. Then he flips it over to show a note on the back. *Go out the back toward the restrooms. Change into the clothes from the bag by your feet — then wait in the hall. He'll be with you shortly. Take your backpack.*

Feeling silly, I take one last sip of water, stand, pick up the backpack and bag and walk to the back. The hall is dim, deserted, and musty smelling. I enter the women's restroom, quickly make use of the facilities, wash my hands and face and look in the bag. I peel off my rain jacket which I now see is reversible. I give it a good shake, dry it a bit under the air dryer and turned it inside out. Being damp inside will suck, but what choice do I have. My hair that had been artfully arranged by Bren is now a damp straggly mess. I quickly braid it and tie it off. I pull off my shirt since there's a white one inside that will mark me as an engineer. I have one arm in the sleeve when the door bangs open, a panicked looking Bren stands framed in the doorway.

I freeze. We stare at each other for a beat. "You weren't in the hall. I thought . . . I was worried. I apologize."

"Oh-kay." I draw the word out slowly. He stands there for another moment and then steps in and slides a bolt on the door I hadn't noticed, which takes me by surprise. I finish putting on my new blouse, feeling embarrassed and nervous. Bren drops his backpack and begins fishing inside. He too pulls out different clothes. Right in front of me he quickly changes into engineering clothes as well, like it doesn't bother him a bit if I see him in his underwear. I am struck by his beauty. So much so that I think he should be one of the entertainment personalities. Muscles move under his skin and I can't seem to pull my eyes away. Then he turns and studies me before he approaches. He has something in his hand.

"You might need this." It's an ID badge showing that I work for a local company as a civil engineer. He clips it to my collar and starts to unbutton the blouse.

"What are you doing?" I'm irritated when my voice comes out breathy.

"You're crooked. They'll notice. Unless you want them to think you were having something on your lunch hour other than lunch." It takes a minute to sink in. I look down as he releases the next to the last button. He's right; I hadn't lined up the holes with their matching buttons.

"I can dress myself," I snap, angry at one of us and I'm not sure who.

"Sure you can," he replies with a smile. It isn't mean, just a little sarcastic. Somewhere under there he maybe even likes me a little. He slips the last button from its hole but doesn't let go of my shirt. He just looks at me for a moment, moves in closer but then pushes me gently away. "Hurry up. We need to go."

I'm not sure how to feel, but humiliated is top of the list of contenders right now. I quickly rebutton with shaking fingers and then tuck the shirt in. I put my reversed jacket back on and pick up the bag.

"No, leave it. Take this now."

He hands me a messenger bag and stashes my old backpack and the bag full of our old clothes under the sink. He has me check the hall to be sure it's clear. At the end of the hall sits a crate. In it is another messenger bag which Bren slings over his shoulder. He takes my elbow and we step through the back door and into the rain.

It starts with a few drops, but as the rain increases, the visibility diminishes. It is beating down in ever increasing sheets and the streets quickly clear of pedestrians. Cars still splash by, but the walkers and cyclists are smart, they have disappeared into all the surrounding buildings. Bren keeps his hand on my elbow and keeps urging me on.

"Why can't we take a car?" I whine. Even with my hood up, water is leaking down my neck.

"Because they are searching all the cars."

"You're kidding!"

"Not even a little bit. They're looking for you. The waitress is one of ours. She tipped me off that they are now aware that they've lost a student due to a miscoded chip. They can't have the true story getting out so they feel the need to find and neutralize you. Your picture has gone out and you're wanted for questioning as a terrorist. They found Malorie by the way. They claim you are suspected of kidnapping and murdering her. Now I wish we'd handled it differently. I never thought they'd . . ." Bren stops talking when he realizes I've dug in my heels.

I stare at him, my mouth open like a fish. How could they?

"Don't fall apart on me now. We have to keep moving and we're drawing attention."

I try to suck in a breath but nothing happens.

"Elise, it's going to be okay. Just keep walking." He takes my elbow again and practically drags me down the street.

In my mind, I imagined the rain would make it difficult for them to track anything smaller than a truck, but Bren becomes even more careful about avoiding intersections with cameras. He moves away from businesses with digital video surveillance as well. Perhaps he had been all along and I hadn't noticed.

Finally, he pauses and looks at me. "Don't look up. Keep your head down and your hood on. Don't turn your head toward any cameras, and don't make eye contact with anyone."

"There has got to be a better way," I whimper. I'm miserable. I hate being cold and wet. Perhaps I was a cat in a past life. I wish I was one now, then they'd never find me.

"This is best. They won't expect it."

I sigh inside. I've never seen so much rain in my life. It hits the ground so hard that it splashes back up. The puddles grow noticeably and soon many stretch to touch their neighbors form-ing small lakes. The moisture in the air presses in on us like a dense fog. Finally, Bren gives up and pulls me under the awning of the nearest building. The rain comes off it like a waterfall as we huddle against the brickwork. I figure we should move, but this is ridiculous. We'd be wet to the skin in no time. I feel like I'm standing in a cold shower with my clothes on. Gross.

Bren looks at something in his hand.

"What is that?" I ask.

"A device that helps me know where the cameras are. They emit a signal this can read."

"Oh." I'm not surprised really, just kind of amazed and freaked out — make that very freaked out. I watch the nearest puddle move towards us purposefully like it has a vengeful agenda and its mission is to drown us. As the puddle touches our boots the wind picks up, screaming between the buildings, rattling everything that's loose and bending the few trees that are visible. The leaves on those trees shudder violently as they are pulled by the wind. I would think our government had set an angry mother nature upon us, but not even they hold that much power.

The rain changes direction. It no longer splashes us with puddles — it's coming at us from the side. "Come on." Bren takes my hand and we run. Water wicks, spreading over my pants and seeping into my boots. I can barely see past the rain dripping down my face. Each cold drop stings like tiny needles and my life becomes nothing but misery. I fantasize about hot cocoa, fuzzy socks, a fire, and a warm blanket.

With a crack like thunder, a nearby tree loses a limb. It slams into the ground with a thud we can feel through our boots. Bren screeches to a halt and then alters direction to avoid more debris from its fellows, dragging me behind him.

A few blocks later I begin to tug on his hand. This is crazy. I can't see anything through the pounding rain and the wind's howl has all but deafened me. The black clouds are forcing us into an even earlier nightfall and I'm shivering.

"What?" he barks at me as we come to a stop in the space between two buildings where part of the storm is mercifully cut off.

"They won't chase us in this. We should hunker down and wait it out."

"The fact that they won't want to chase us in this is exactly why we should run now. They'll be looking for us by car in this weather. We'll be hard to spot on foot if we stay away from the main roads. This storm is a gift and we have to take advantage of it."

"But I can't see or hear. I don't know where I'm going. I say it's a curse."

"I know where I am. Trust me. They can't track us in this. Their cameras will be next to useless and the water will wash away our footsteps and scent. It's a great opportunity. Besides, we still have about six hours of walking to make it to our next stop."

My mouth drops open. Bren reaches out a hand and touches my face. His voice is gentle. "Hey, geek girl, trust me. You may have mad computer skills, but now we're in my realm. I have survival skills."

"You were assigned to tech too. You had to be or you couldn't have been our teacher's aide."

"That's true but in my free time, it was all about survival skills. My family insisted. You should be glad. I've been living with the Recalcitrants for over a year. You'll make it. I'll be sure you do." Bren sounds confident yet I am unsure.

"I want to believe everything you tell me, but what little

you say goes against everything I've understood and I've been taught. You say I remember things I shouldn't because my brain is wired differently. You say they trained us to forget, but it didn't work on me. I saw people die, and yet I still want to believe it's all a mistake. I can't believe the government would do this to its people."

Bren sighs, "The government wants control of its children; they don't believe that citizens can make good choices about who should breed and how the offspring should be raised. You know they've tried hiding a contraceptive in the water, but they were found out. Remember the scandal?" I nod mutely and he continues. "The people are standing up to defend the rights they should have and the government is striking back by killing off the students in your year group. It's not an accident. They're telling the general public it is but they have sent a message to the Recalcitrants. They are telling us to stand down and give ourselves up or more children will die. We believe the people need to decide their own future, not the government. While this 'accident' is happening they are pressing for legislation to put contraceptives back in our drinking water and people must apply to the government for the antidote. That is the last piece; then they will control all aspects of our society. Don't you see? They already control education, medicine, and the workforce. Do you want them to control who and even if you'll marry and whether or not you will have kids? They are turning us into mindless drones. They want to control everything. Everything! Who would you be if you had no choices left?" Bren speaks with passion and I can see the truth in his eyes.

I turn my lips in and bite them, to hold myself together and everything in. I close my eyes and hang my head. I feel his hands come to rest on my shoulders.

"Just keep walking. Don't think."

I nod and open my eyes. I can tell that he wants to say something else but he stops and lets his hands fall away. When he turns and walks on, I do nothing but follow. This is not my . . . what had he said? Realm? I belong at a computer. I can find glitches and bugs. I can fix programs that aren't working and can even write my own. This is not where I belong.

We walk on and on. The buildings get further apart and there are now more houses than businesses and that means fewer cameras. The rain has slackened but it's prematurely dark. I am so tired that I can barely feel my legs. Neither of us has said a word since Bren's passionate speech. I try not to think, but when I do, his words weigh heavily on my mind and heart. I want to choose. I want to choose lots of things, especially who I will marry or not and have children with if I do, but am I brave enough to fight for it?

The further we walk, the more my fear and anxiety grow. I can feel tension in my whole body. My gut clenches, my stomach feels nauseous, a cold sweat lingers on my skin and mixes with the rainwater making me feel completely drenched. Soon my shivers grow to tremors. My joints and muscles have begun to ache, especially up my neck where a dull pounding has settled across the front of my head. Suddenly raw fear grips me. Am I dying like Malorie? I try to search my skin again and keep walking, but I'm distracted and stumble.

Please don't let me die! I know the people have to know the truth. The government says they're here to help us, but they have become cancer that feeds upon us. They take everything the people can provide and then sugarcoat what little we get in return. I'm so weary, but someone has to stand up, right? Could it be me? Today I don't think so. I'm nobody, but at least I can share what I've seen. Maybe someone who can do something will listen and believe me.

I look at Bren and just leave my eyes there. How many times had I watched him when I was in my tenth year and he was in his twelfth? How many times? Now he is here and he needs me for an impossible task. It's absurd. I dreamed about him and now he is part of my living nightmare. This was not how I imagined we would meet again.

I begin to fantasize about a different life — I am past my trial and in the workforce. Why couldn't I have met him in normal times, under normal circumstances? *What would that look like?* I wonder. My mind snaps to the present, unable to hold the daydream. Why did they send him, of all people, to bring me to the resistance? We have been walking for hours and are now so far away from the city that we can walk together into the misty fog-filled night. Maybe I should pretend we are on a romantic stroll.

"You're staring," his voice rumbles softly.

"Yes," I answer and he laughs, low and soft at my one-word answer.

"You're not shy like you used to be. Somehow I thought you'd still be shy and perhaps nervous to be alone with a male.

You always stayed away from boys."

"What's the point, Bren?" I sigh wearily.

"What do you mean?" he asks like he actually cares what I think.

I snort softly. "We're going to die anyway, so I figure I can throw social niceties and rules out the window."

"Mmm," he answers. "So that's it. You don't fully trust me, but you don't have any alternatives right now. Well, just so you know, it's my job to see that you live, so you don't have to trust me, but at least trust that."

"I might trust you a little," I hedge. "I don't know if I believe everything you say and I don't think I know you. I thought I did a year and a half ago, but now?"

I close my eyes and drift as we walk on. In my mind I'm back in the classroom and I glance up to see Bren watching me. He can get away with it. His back is to the camera that looks in on our classroom with a malevolent eye. Besides, he would be expected to be watching the class. I feel my heartbeat increase in rhythm and my cheeks grow warm. I look at his hands so that I won't get caught looking at his face. I am mesmerized by his long fingers, light brown skin, and short clean nails. Capable. That's it; his hands look capable, not like other boys in my year group. Bren's fingers are tapping — a code — Morse code. I learned a bit about the ancient means of communication from one of the many books I read in my limited free time. I tilt my head to the side and focus. *You are watching me*, his nimble fingers say. I jerk my eyes back to his face, blush and look away. I glance back for just a moment. He's smiling.

I open my eyes and turn to watch Bren again. I can't seem to help myself. It feels like nothing else is worth looking at — not the houses and businesses that are growing further and further apart — not the fields and not the trees. Finally, I break the silence as all the thoughts and ideas that have been swirling around in my head come together. "Why us?"

"What do you mean?"

"Why was my year group chosen?" I ask.

"I don't have all the intel, but there were rumors about a student in our city who would break the system. If that isn't scary enough, civil unrest is increasing. Numbers are on our side with the increases in population. Getting rid of the year group that student is in makes sense. By taking them all out they get the system breaker in the sweep. You hit people where it hurts; their children. Did you know a boy named Daniel McGarvin?"

"Yes."

"He's the nephew of one of the Recalcitrant leaders. The government wants people under control. They need us to do as we are told. It's so easy for them to say, 'We're so sorry. It was a terrible training accident. It won't happen again. A glitch in the system; nothing more. Don't worry.' Then it will all be brushed under the rug until they can do it full scale across all of the New North. We won't let that happen. They will be accountable."

"You're serious?" Looking in his eyes tells me that he is. I've never seen him look so sad, so desperate, so — lost. "I guess the rise in crime and disappearances makes sense now. It's not the people getting surly, is it? It's the government making people who resist disappear and the ones who remain are made to think it's the populace turning against itself. When there is more crime we need more protection. They are hiding the fact that they are building troops."

Bren's eyebrows leap toward his hairline. "You know about that?"

"I think I know all kinds of things that I'm not supposed to. They found that I was really good at running scenarios, creating algorithms, debugging and fixing glitches. They could present me with a problem and in a short time, I could create a program to run all contingencies. At first, I fixed problems on the school computers that no one else could solve, then I was fixing the district computers and soon after that, I was asked to fix the rural computer problems. At first, I was flattered and then . . . I knew it was something more but I didn't let on. It wasn't long before I was fixing city problems. I was afraid to admit that I knew what they were doing."

"The government needs workers to provide for the elite, but too many workers are a drain on the system. There is a critical mass. Just like there is a critical mass when it comes to how people feel. Do they feel appreciated or abused? Do they dare stand up when they are treated unfairly or are they afraid? Push people far enough and they will fight back! Your year group must have been the one that would tip the scale so the government decided that your group should be eliminated. There are no young people related to any council members among your year, so it was the perfect time to execute a test run of the master plan. Besides, you had created the unbeatable scenario and it's always best to tie up the loose ends."

"Me?" He just looks at me like I'm smarter than that. "*The Curse of the Underworlders*… I helped them figure out what events would . . . what kids like us couldn't get past. They're all gone now, aren't they? They're all gone because of me!" A sob catches in my throat and guilt washes over me in a crushing wave.

Bren grabs me roughly by the arm and gives me a shake. "Not YOU!" he nearly shouts in my face. "Don't you dare blame yourself. It was them. They used you. Now help me fix it."

"They're dead because of me. You can't fix that."

"You're right; I can't bring back the dead. I hear a few, mainly public safety were allowed to live. They have sworn allegiance to the government. The ones that died and Malorie — we don't have to let it be for nothing. We don't have to let it happen again!" He is waiting for something, I can tell, but the guilt still has as firm a grip on me as he does. "Elise, you made the system. You can take it down."

"Why didn't you stop it? Why didn't you stop me? You could have killed me, there could have been an accident and no one would have known. One life, Bren, one and not three thousand and some and now where else will they try it? How many more will die?"

"We had no way of knowing when they would execute their plan. We didn't even know for sure what they were planning until it was too late. Now we know they had been setting up parts of it for years. At first, we thought they were trying to trap the people of the underground. We still believed that even when they cleared all of their people out. But then we saw students entering the condemned areas. We realized that the rumors were true and that we were almost too late. We just couldn't believe that they would harm their own children. Besides, I could never . . . the resistance wouldn't kill you, we need you. There was an eighty-five percent chance it was you designing the war game without realizing it. It would take us months to find someone as qualified as you to undo it."

"How do you know all this? Did you have someone inside watching me?"

"I watched you after I was recruited my senior year. Later we were worried about some chatter we heard about some students working on a new game. Our intel hinted heavily that the game was not what it appeared to be, so we sent in someone else to confirm what was happening and, if necessary, to protect you."

"Jill, Jill watched me. She was always asking questions." My head was pounding with thoughts and . . . and everything. I swiped at my brow. Was I hot?

"Jill? A student?"

I nod.

"No, we have a teacher on the inside now. The scientist who works with technology . . ."

"No, the only one who watched me was Jill. She . . . gave me this feeling . . . I can't stand it. I can't do it. Leave me here and save yourself. Run away. Find someone else." My voice has gone high and hysterical even to my own ears, then my throat closes on a sob and I shiver again. The expression on Bren's face changes from earnestness to worry and then blackness takes my vision to a pinpoint before it vanishes.

01100011 01101001 01110100 01101001 01111010

01100101 01101110 01110011 00100000 01110111

01100101 00100000

wake up. I've had the craziest dream. Everything with our trial had gone wrong. I turn my head to look at Malorie but her bed isn't there. I'm looking at a wall. I snap my head the other way and pain shoots up and down my neck. Most of my body aches and then I know why. I'm looking at Bren now. His neck is gonna hurt too, judging by his position in that chair. I must have made a sound because he stirs. When his eyes land on me a slight smile touches his lips. When he stretches I hear his joints and tendons pop.

"I'm sorry," I whisper, realizing my throat hurts too.

"For what?"

"For everything," I croak, feeling teary.

"You're sick. It's okay."

My eyes open wide and fear takes me again. I throw back

the covers to discover I'm in an oversized t-shirt that isn't mine. Good. That will save time. I yank it up to look again for the tell-tale blue glow that will signal my imminent death.

"I told you it's deactivated. You're just sick," Bren says, pulling the covers back up around me.

I huff out a breath, drop the t-shirt and let my shoulders slump. Bren brings over a thermos and opens it so he can pour out some broth.

"Where are we?" I rasp.

"When you passed out, I had to bring you to the closest safe house. I was trying not to use them, to protect the people of the resistance, but you gave me no choice."

"I'm so sorry. I can't help it." Tears form in my eyes and threaten to run over. I've killed enough people already.

"No. I am. I should have noticed sooner and then I . . . maybe I shouldn't have told you everything at once. I've had over a year to process this stuff—you haven't."

"No. It's better that you did. It's just overwhelming." I move my neck again and wince.

Bren has me drink a few sips of broth and then he sets it aside and moves behind me. He sits down, squeezes some minty smelling goo onto his hand and starts to work on the knots in my shoulders and neck. His hands are warm and gentle, the callouses scratching lightly over my skin. The firm pressure of his fingers soon has the knots easing. He must have had a shower because he smells really good; safe—warm—inviting. I smell like rain, sweat, and the funky, minty goo. I sigh and lean into him. I close my eyes and drift. My last thought is to wonder if he put something in the broth.

When I wake up again, I'm back under the covers and Bren is laying outside them curled around me with one arm thrown over my waist. His slow steady breathing makes me believe that he's asleep. He might not like me but I want to remember this. I want to pretend that this is real. I take a moment to just feel and imprint it into my brain, but I want to see him.

I slowly roll over so I don't disturb him. He was right — crazy, but right. He is here for me. He's probably saved my life. I brush some hair off his forehead and look at the wound by his eye. It has closed up nicely; the scar will barely show. I figure I must have lost my mind. This is what it is to go insane. My life is in danger. I don't really know who I can trust, yet all I can do is watch him. I slide my hand up his arm and then over his shoulder. I move in closer so that I can take a deep breath of his neck and feel his warmth. I slip my hand under his arm and rest it on his ribs. I wish I was even closer, that he really did like me, but there's a blanket between us and a whole lot of other stuff I don't want to think about. I have an alien urge to crawl under his skin and forget everything.

His breathing changes, so I pull back a little and find him watching me. His eyes are light brown in this light with inviting flecks of gold and green. Did that make them hazel? Maybe they change with his clothing or mood. He blinks and I notice how long his lashes are. I'm jealous. All my eye enhancements have long ago been washed off with tears, rain and from rubbing my tired eyes. I'm pretty sure I look and smell awful, but at least he's here and doesn't look offended.

"Hi," I offer shyly. My voice sounds better and I realize my throat doesn't hurt.

"I take it you feel better?" I feel like a thief must when they're caught. I blush and wish I'd died after all. "It's time to move on," he continues like we woke up this way every day. I find there is something really appealing about his voice. I can feel the rumble in his chest as he speaks and I want to stay here.

"Okay," I sigh instead.

Bren quickly rolls over me and rises from the bed. He moves around the room gracefully. My brain clicks. "How's your leg?"

"Almost as good as new. I'm sure you could use more rest, but the longer we take to get to the Recalcitrants, the thicker the patrols will be. I have a feeling they won't stop until they find you."

I bite my lip. That isn't what I want to hear. I want this to go away or maybe I want to stay in this room with him and pretend my life is nothing but this moment.

"Go take a shower and dress in the new clothes. After you eat we are hitting the road again."

Fantastic, I think sarcastically. Bren hands me a robe and then leads me to a small bathroom. I'm pretty sure we're in a single wide trailer. Not that I have any personal experience with such places but I've seen them on the internet. Who would choose to live like this? The government provides housing for its workers. Did the government know about these people? Was this housing authorized? *Stop analyzing*, I yell silently at myself.

It takes me a few moments to figure out how to turn the water on. Then it takes what feels like forever for it to warm up. When it does, it's hot enough even if the pressure is a bit lacking. The shampoo is simple yet clean smelling. When I'm done the towels are rough yet absorbent. The whole experience makes me feel like I've gone back in time — way back — decades maybe. Malorie would have hated it. Roughing it would have given her a pain. I smile at the thought and then my throat tightens with tears.

I miss you, Mal.

A hot meal of biscuits with real pork sausage gravy must be waiting for me judging by the smells that are invading the entire trailer. Today zip-off cargo pants, hiking boots, a t-shirt, fresh underwear and a different jacket have been provided for my use. I rebraid my damp hair and try to pinch a little color into my cheeks. I don't know why I bother. Bren doesn't pay any attention to me. He's too engrossed in the news displayed on a funny little entertainment screen that's shaped like a cube and on our host who reminds me of old time photos of a mountain man.

Maybe he is a mountain man. Deer antlers are mounted on one dark colored wall and a rifle hangs over the door. There's a strange fibrous carpet on the floor that speaks to the age of the place. It certainly is clean and neat. All the blinds are closed and I realize that I don't even know if it's day or night.

"What time is it?" I ask them.

"Four thirty," the mountain man answers in a deep rumbly voice without looking up from the . . . I know what it is — they used to call them a TV.

Bren smirks. "Maybe you should ask what day it is."

"Okay, I'll bite. What day is it?" I ask with an eye roll as I belly up to the plate of steaming biscuits swimming in thick, meaty gravy.

"Your trial was five days ago."

My fork clatters to my plate. "What?"

"You're lucky that Josiah is a naturopathic healer. He knows all the local herbs and remedies," Bren answers with an approving smile toward my healer.

"How could I sleep for so long?" I ask perplexed.

"It's a trick I know for speed healing. You should be able to make it into the forest now," Josiah answers with a kind smile before his eyes zip back to the TV.

"Into the forest?"

"The city belongs to the government, but the forest is ours," Josiah answers again.

"I thought the government had control of everything."

"They want you to think that, but they don't." It's Bren who answers this time.

"What's been happening?" I query, waving my fork at the screen.

Bren reaches forward and turns up the volume.

"In a recap of our news this morning: food prices are anticipated to rise and brownouts should be expected due to the energy shortage. Remember to back up your data to Cyber Comet, the government approved virtual storage answer for all your storage needs. It's important to prevent data loss during brownouts."

Josiah laughs a deep throaty laugh. "More like upload your data so we can go through all of it and see if you are any kind of a threat."

Bren smiles, but I keep most of my attention on the broadcaster.

"In other news, most of the storm damage has been repaired, but some areas are still flooded. Our hearts go out to the families of the students lost in the training exercise five days ago. Our government wants you to know that every precaution will be taken before the next district goes for testing. All trials have been indefinitely postponed while evidence is gathered. A faulty gas line is believed to be the culprit at this time. Rumors of a terrorist attack are being put to rest. The girl assumed to be a terrorist is now known to be a mentally unstable student. Please don't approach her, but call public safety immediately if you spot her. It is believed she was overcome with fumes from the explosion and doesn't know what happened to her and is both dangerous and delusional. She escaped with another student who was found dead hours later some blocks away. Our government assures us that she will be apprehended."

The tone signaling a citizen's announcement sounds.

"Citizen Informational Update JPA987T — All citizens are to remain vigilant. All citizens are to put their trust in the officers of the public safety department. We are all the government and we protect our own."

My picture flashes across the small screen and I think I might throw up. "I've gone from terrorist to psycho, awesome," I quip sarcastically. "Now what?"

"We get you out of here. We need to travel through several miles of forest to reach the Recalcitrant compound. We believe that phase one was to get rid of the students from your year group and then they will broaden the scope by expanding to more cities. Controls will be put on food, water, and energy consumption for the masses. Birth control will be placed in the water again and people will have to apply for the antidote for which the government will charge exorbitant prices. Authorization will be given based on genetic superiority. The government is moving to control everything. The underground network is ablaze with conspiracies."

How could Bren speak so calmly? How could he act like this wasn't a big deal? "I want this to end. I want my life back. It wasn't great, but it was mine."

"Don't let them win, Elise. Fight. Fight with me."

I snort. "You don't want me. You want someone brave and strong and smart."

"You are exactly what I . . . what we need." I look into Bren's eyes so long that our host clears his throat. I look away as a flush creeps up my cheeks. I like Bren and I want him to like me back. Was his slip-up a sign that he does like me some or just misspoken words? I shake my head. I'm doing nothing but causing problems and slowing him down. I push my half-eaten food away. I don't want it and he can't want me.

"If you're ready, then let's go," Bren says calmly like nothing is wrong.

I nod mutely and then quietly thank Josiah. Now I have another debt to repay that I probably won't live long enough to even touch. His eyes are kind with crinkles in the corners. I want to say more to him, but I don't know where to start. I hope he isn't caught.

Bren hands me a waterproof shell, fleece jacket, and a different backpack. I bite my lip and follow him out the door. He keeps looking at me but I just bite my lip and look away. Soon we leave all civilization behind. Bren quickly walks off the road and continues on a path. I take deep breaths of rain washed Douglas fir, musty, mulchy leaves, and cool crisp air.

It feels wonderful to be walking through the trees I've often dreamed of, but as beautiful as they are, I find my eyes drawn to Bren. No matter how hard I try, I can't seem to keep my eyes off him for long. I watch the way he moves, smooth and confident. I admire his fit form and the way his hair changes from dark brown to gold depending on the light. My gaze lingers on his shoulders and the way his muscles bunch as he moves. He stops so abruptly that I almost walk into him.

He turns to give me an almost angry look. "Stop it," he growls.

"What?" I ask blankly, not understanding.

"Looking at me like that."

"What?" I ask, still confused.

His gaze shifts to my mouth and I involuntarily lick my lip. "Oh hell," he breathes in a soft, low whisper.

"Wha—" I start to ask again, but he pushes me back into the maple that is just to my left. One hand cups my neck, his thumb stroking along my jaw. His other hand comes to rest on my waist and his eyes never leave mine. They're impossibly dark, the golden flecks almost glowing. He moves closer and I stand transfixed. The ability to speak has left and I'm afraid to move. I'm both scared and hopeful . . . and then he slowly tilts his head as he closes the distance between us and touches his lips to mine. I don't want him to stop. Each place his body touches mine is filled with warmth and energy.

Magic, I think. I actually believe in magic. His lips on mine have made me believe. Nothing has ever felt like this. This is so much better than I've ever imagined. Then I become aware of my lungs screaming for air. I've stopped breathing. I must have made a sound because Bren lifts his head. I draw in a ragged breath and he smiles the best smile I've ever seen. He laughs softly, the smile never leaving his lips. For a split second I'm angry, but then I realize he's not laughing at me. He couldn't be, not with that beautiful smile lighting his eyes and making them crinkle at the corners. I begin to laugh a little too.

"You have to remember to breathe, Lise." It's the first time he's called me that. I like the way it sounds when he says it. At school, he'd always called me Andrek, student 18A294E, or merely, Girl. It's clear to me now. He's been holding back. He's been disguising his feelings. He's trying to protect me and now, for once, no one is watching. I forget what I was going to say. I can feel his warm breath puff across my cheek. One hand still holds my neck, the other he moves slowly up my ribs and then down my back. I try to remember to breathe. He kisses along my jaw and down the side of my neck. "I've always wanted to do this," he whispers softly against my skin.

"You barely knew I existed," I accuse, but I smile anyway.

"I couldn't let on that I was interested in you. They were watching me."

"Why would they watch you more closely than anyone else? I always felt like it was me being zeroed in on, but maybe everyone feels that way."

"I guess you could say I come from a family of troublemakers.

Within our family, we call ourselves spies, or even terrorists if we're feeling extra rebellious. We do not believe in our current government. My family began by speaking out and protesting but things only got worse, so we got quiet and the subterfuge began. We started networking — using our connections to make subtle changes. We've been mostly underground for two generations. Now we are actively pulling threads to unravel 'that which is corrupt' as my great uncle says." He ends making air quotes and I smile again.

"You sound like you had that memorized."

"I kind of do, I guess," he says, turning serious.

"How did you get into school if you're part of the resistance?"

"Everyone has the right to an education. Even the children of field workers get to go to school. Not all of my family is literally underground; some of us hide in plain sight."

"It's all so surreal. The world I lived in and the one I suspected — it's all so —"

A sound — a rustle of leaves. We grow still for a split second and then Bren flips me around the tree. We melt into the underbrush. For the first time, I realize that his clothing is made to blend in with our surroundings. I find myself holding my breath again — this time for a whole other reason. Bren snaps his head left and right and then pushes me into a depression under some salal and covers me with his body. My clothing is not as camouflaged for this environment. I'm dressed partly for hiding in the city and partly in the woods. I wouldn't look quite right in either place but Bren and his rebels have done their best for me. I hold as still as I can.

If I'm completely honest with myself I would be ashamed that my mind is not fully on the public safety officers creeping through the woods. On the other hand, I'm too busy thinking about Bren to be freaked out by their proximity because he is a whole lot more interesting.

A group of three soldiers moves past us. They have their hands on their weapons but aren't actively looking for something to shoot. One pauses near the tree where we'd just shared a kiss and examines the ground. He picks up a handful of Douglas fir needles and then throws them back down to the ground in anger.

"Come on. We'll find her. She's alone and scared and knows nothing about living on her own. We'll get her, someone will turn her in, or the weather eventually will do the trick."

We stay where we are, barely breathing. As the soldiers move away, I became less aware of them and more aware of Bren. I can tell he's listening to their retreat with his whole body. His eyes stay trained on the last spot they were visible. The minutes tick by and I finally tentatively reach up and touch his face. His eyes jerk to mine, a slight wrinkle in his forehead mars his beautiful face.

"Let me try again," I whisper just centimeters from his lips as I grab a handful of his shirt to pull myself closer. His hands still rest on either side of my head. He neither pulls me in nor pushes me away. His eyes hold the look of indecision for a brief moment as he watches me and then he moves. His fingers spasm in the fallen leaves and then his head descends to meet me part way. I smile slightly and start to speak, but his mouth covers mine and my words are lost. I know in a moment I will be lost too. This is more than just his lips on mine. When I inhale all I can smell is him. Heat rushes through my body and I begin to shake. I'm aware of every place his body touches mine — I want more.

I must have done something wrong because one moment he's pulling me in and then like a switch being flipped he's pushing me away. "Come on. We're burning daylight." His voice sounds rough. He's right, something has been burning and it isn't just daylight. How will I ever find the strength to walk away from him now? I decide I've loved more than just the idea of him for a long time and just hadn't admitted it to myself.

He pulls me to my feet and we head out without a word. Bren takes off at a right angle from the way the soldiers have gone. He moves cautiously without a sound. I have to watch each place I set my untrained city feet. I'm meant for an office, a touch screen, a keyboard, and a mouse, not this stuff. I'm so busy watching my dumb feet I can't even admire his fine physique. I know I'm missing a great opportunity.

01100110 01101001 01101110 01100100 00100000
01110100 01101111 00100000 01100010 01100101
00100000

My feet are starting to hurt and my stomach is getting pretty loud with its complaints since we've missed both lunch and dinner. Bren finally stops near the ridgeline by an old fallen tree. He clears out an area that will provide a little protection and then he covers it with fir needles, moss, and leaves. I start looking for kindling, trying to be helpful. When I bring the first pile back he lays out a thin silver blanket and holds it down with his pack.

"Sorry Lise, no fire tonight. They're too close."

"Then why did you let me collect —"

"I'm sorry," he interrupts. "I needed time to think and we can still use it to cover this side over here," he says indicating the left side near the remaining roots.

He takes the branches from me and quickly camouflages

part of the open side. Now I feel awkward and unsure. I stand there looking at him and I feel like he's going to break up with me, which is dumb. We aren't dating — we'd shared some kisses, that was all. He doesn't owe me anything, but I can still feel the cracks fissure across my heart.

"Elise," he says snagging my attention, "we need to focus. I can't protect you if . . . what I'm saying is . . ." I can feel my eyes tear up and it makes me mad. I don't want to hear whatever he's trying to say. I want to have a temper tantrum. Instead, I sit on the edge of the blanket with my back to him. I pull out two apples and a peanut butter sandwich for our meager dinner and thunk down my water bottle.

"Elise," he tries again.

I push an apple and the sandwich toward him and take a drink of water. I can feel his eyes drilling into me, but I won't turn around.

"We'll be there tomorrow." He says it softly and then he sits down next to me and eats.

I close my eyes and try to pretend he isn't there, but it's impossible. I swear I can feel the heat of his body and that unique fragrance that's his. I'm dumb — it has to be in my head, but I can still feel his touch.

"I don't understand you," I whisper after a whole apple's worth of silence. I hadn't meant to say anything. I want to keep it all in — the hurt, the humiliation.

He's silent for a long time, so I watch the sun finish setting through the trees. When he finally speaks, his voice is low and sad. It even holds a note of pleading. "I remember the first time

I saw you. You were in ninth year. I didn't know it then, but you and probably Malorie had twisted your hair up the night before so that it was all waves and curls. You were laughing with your friends and I saw your amazing smile and your dimples. Dimples. Who has those? Well, other than you? I thought you were the most beautiful girl in school and you walked right by me. Later I figured out that your hair was straight and that you were usually serious. I learned that you don't have patience for people who do stupid things. Wearing a uniform gets on your nerves, but you tolerate it because you have to. You're basically a rule follower, but if you don't like a rule you don't mind bending it a little or even a lot when it suits you and you are smart enough to get away with it. You are loyal to the friends you have but you keep most people at a distance. I also found out that you are practical and have a sense of humor. You like to pretend that you don't care what other people think, but I've seen them cut you deeply. I also know that you figured out a long time ago that the government did not have your best interests at heart."

I don't know what to say. I don't know how to feel. I turn slightly to look at him even though I've promised myself I wouldn't. I'm pretty sure I look both broken-hearted and hopeful and I'm not sure I care anymore whether or not he knows how I feel.

He smiles a half-smile, seeing he has my attention. "I saw your spark, but I didn't see your fire until I cheated the system to become your teacher's assistant. I was so glad I'd miscoded your tracker. At the time I wasn't completely sure what made me do it. They didn't chip my class. Yours was the first. Perhaps it started out innocently enough. We were to be tagged like people's pets had long been tagged. Then if you get lost, strayed, or stolen it's easy to see where you belong. The kill feature was snuck in with the rest of the programming. The government would say that it was for our protection — should we be captured by terrorists, we could be killed before we gave away any secrets. The Recalcitrants would say it is a way to eliminate anyone who is a problem — anyone who knows too much. At the time, it just felt so wrong to put chips in people and I didn't even know then what I know now. I knew there was something about you." He pauses for a moment to look up at the stars and let out a near silent huff like he's disgusted with himself. "I think I fell in love with you the day you read my Morse code message. I saw the recognition in your eyes and I was doomed, hooked, or maybe both."

I feel my eyes go wide and my heart skip a beat. "What?" I ask stupidly and he's right, I hate stupidity.

"I volunteered to be the one to come get you and bring you in. If I fail . . . I . . . I will never forgive myself. You are too important."

"You volunteered?" I'm stunned.

"We have eyes everywhere. We knew the government was setting something up but we weren't in on the crews. They were very careful. We didn't know what they were up to until it was happening. I knew you were up for your test. I was supposed to approach you shortly after you went to work. I was planning to lure you to our side and then . . . when the reports started rolling in that your scenario went live . . . I . . . I guess I went a little nuts. I pulled in every favor owed to me and we set our counter plan in motion. We weren't ready, but I had to save you. I've seen part of the feed from your trial. You were amazing."

"Feed? What feed?"

"Remember the cameras that you dodged? Well, you missed a few. You were so good at avoiding them that we had trouble tracking you ourselves, but we got a guy to trace Malorie's chip and that's how I finally found you. I had kept a copy of all the chip coding I did. It wasn't allowed, but I snuck it onto a mini travel drive anyway. I wasn't officially working for the resistance then but my family was and I knew I'd stumbled onto gold. We also have some facial recognition software the government doesn't know about. They would have found you eventually. I was motivated and we were quicker."

"If you found us, why not them?"

"The government was watching over three thousand students. I was only watching for you. At first, I think they viewed it as entertainment. They were pleased with their work and were so busy patting themselves on the back that they didn't notice one missing girl in a crowd that big. When you ran into the girl from public safety . . . we started an alternate plan, but you handled it."

"They saw that?"

"We hope not. There is a brief delay between events and replay. Only so much can be live feed at a time so they only saw it if that view was active. They have thousands of hours of digital feed to go over and our hackers erased it so when they go back that clip will be gone, the time stamp altered, and a loop of the empty station will play. The upstairs hall we had to handle differently, so to them, it should look like an equipment failure."

"So you don't know for sure what all they may have seen."

"That's true," he nods as he talks, trying to let me know he thinks it will all be okay.

I know better. They are coming to kill me and they'll kill him too if they find us together. Can I do what has to be done? Can I walk away and . . . what? Hide? Live in the forest alone and untrained? Hide in the city? Or at least die alone and not take him with me?

"So now they know I slipped through the cracks and they're spreading lies," I say to get him thinking.

"Yes, they are. They can't let you talk. They're trying to reduce your credibility. It's called damage control. Now get some rest. I'll take the first watch."

"Bet they wonder why my kill chip failed. I hope they're not looking for you."

"I was just a student. It was someone else's job to check the work."

Someone will pay. I know it. It kind of hurts that he can be so callous about it but I guess he had to learn to be that way for the greater good and all that. I have more questions but he turns his back to me and returns to gazing at the stars. I move as close to the fallen tree as I dare, zip my jacket all the way up, hide my hands in my sleeves and pretend to sleep, but my thoughts have more tangles and knots than computer cables thrown in a bin.

I keep expecting Bren to shake my shoulder and wake me. One minute I'm cold and then . . . I'm not. I start to move and find myself trapped. A brief moment of panic passes and then I realize what or better yet who I'm trapped by. I had pulled my knees to my chest to keep warm and he has curled around me again and covered us both with another thermal blanket. I know I should get up and keep watch, but I don't want to move. I want to have one last spectacular memory before I leave him — and I have to leave him to keep him safe. I've lost Malorie, I will not lose him! I roll over and boldly throw an arm and leg over him. He smiles and pulls me closer. Then he freezes, coming fully alert.

"Elise, this is not a good idea. I just wanted to keep you warm. You were shivering."

"No one can see us. No one knows. I don't want much. Please, Bren, just hold me and let me pretend for a moment that . . . that this isn't my life . . . that I'm not on the run . . . that I didn't kill my best friend."

"Elise, you did not kill Malorie." His voice is so soft and gentle that it makes tears burn at the back of my eyes.

"Maybe not, but I sure didn't save her."

"Sweetheart, she would have died either way. Know in your heart that you made it less horrible for her."

"But not for me. Every time I close my eyes, I see her and that boy from the government branch and those girls from hospitality. None of them deserved their fate. The boy, Griffin was his name, was looking right at me when he died. His eyes were begging me to save him." The tears I've been holding, pool and drip into my hair.

"I'm sorry," Bren whispers, pulling me close. I rest my head over his heart and try to remind myself I'm not alone . . . yet.

He pushes my hood back and kisses my forehead. "It's going

to be okay," he breathes into my ear, his lips brushing over the surface making me shiver. He must have thought I was cold because he unzips our jackets and then pulls me close once more. Now I can feel his heart beat through my chest. I bravely kiss his neck. His skin is warm and the stubble on his jaw tickles my nose. He becomes very still but he doesn't push me away. I pull his t-shirt free of his pants and run my hand over his wonderful skin. I close my eyes and kiss his lips as I hold him close and concentrate on the rapid steady beat of his heart. Warm — safe — the flash of light. Wait, what?

Bren tenses. There it is again — a flash of light. I hold as still as I can, knowing he's listening with his whole being.

He silently disentangles himself from me and rolls to his feet. My heart beats faster and faster, slamming against my ribs so hard it hurts. Adrenaline bursts through my chest leaving me feeling dizzy and hyper as the chemicals activate every muscle.

The light flashes our way again and I can hear the crash of feet in the underbrush. I hold as still as I can once I've freed myself from our blankets. I crouch low to be out of sight but ready to fight or run.

"Stay here. If I don't come back . . . hide and then keep heading east — always east. The Recalcitrants will find you. Understand?" he whispers in my ear.

I nod, too scared to do anything else. I watch him move away from me on nearly silent feet. I want to scream out, "Don't leave me." It takes everything I have to hold my lips clamped together. He knows what he's doing. I guess if I believed that, then I really have come to trust him.

I hear a crash, a thud, a moan, and then the sounds of fists hitting flesh. I can't stand it. I have to help. He's here to protect me, but I can't let them hurt him, capture him, or worse — kill him!

I quickly stuff the silver blankets and backpacks deep into the crevice and cover them with brush and leaves. The moon gives just enough light for me not to kill myself as I move toward the fighting. Tree branches scrape my face and my feet trip over hidden roots. I fall, hitting my knee, and bite my lip to keep from crying out. "Bren, please be okay," I silently beg.

I scramble forward, holding my hands in front of me. The sounds of fighting increase with each faltering step I take. How had they gotten so close? I'm so scared I hurry too fast and crash into a tree. How did Bren navigate through the dark forest at night without hurting himself or making a sound?

I burst through the trees and onto the path where three public safety officers lie on the ground, but one more is swinging at a bleeding Bren. Rage tears through me. I launch myself onto the back of the last man standing. I lock my legs around his body and my arm around his neck using my other arm to pull tight and choke him. He swings around, staggering, trying to dislodge me and finally slams me into a tree. The air flies out of my lungs in a burst and black dots swim before my eyes, but I hang on for all I'm worth until we both fall to the ground with him landing on top of me. My grip slackens and I slide into the welcome black.

"Are you okay?" Bren barks at me. "Lise, answer me! Are you okay?" He touches my face and I blink at him. Suddenly air rushes back into my chest with a wheezing whoosh.

"Fine," I gasp.

He must have pulled the man off me because he's out cold next to me. Bren pulls me to him in a brief hug. "What were you thinking?"

"I wanted to help," I wheeze. He smiles a little and shakes his head.

He releases me and I watch him pat down the nearest officer. I carefully pull myself onto my hands and knees. I cough and try not to throw up the apple I'd eaten. I watch him collect gear from all four men and smash their communications equipment and wrist communicators. He stuffs what he can in his pockets and hands me some to put in mine. Then he grabs my hand and pulls me away.

He sets a blistering pace back to camp where he quickly repacks our gear and brushes out our footprints. "You left a clear trail, so now we really need to hurry."

"Shouldn't we hide the bodies or something?"

"They'll wake up soon anyway. Let's not waste time. Now is the time to move." He starts to walk but looks back at me. "What were you thinking? I had it handled. I asked you to stay."

"I know but I heard the fighting and I had to be sure you were okay."

Bren sighs and looks to the sky. It's showing a hint of the coming dawn. I still can't see worth a darn and I find I'm incredibly tired now that the adrenaline has worn off. I long for a bed, but follow Bren up the hill feeling every sore muscle in my beat-up body. My face stings from my unwelcome close encounter with the branches and my back will have an awesome bruise from the tree. I've had my butt kicked by a forest.

We walk on and on. Bren doesn't say a word, so he's probably listening again. I try to not feel sorry for myself, and quit paying attention to anything except being quiet. Finally, Bren pauses at a log and hands me some water. I slump onto the makeshift seating he offers and close my eyes. I yawn and let my head hang down. I can hear the forest waking up and Bren rustling around in the packs.

"What are you doing?" I mumble without cracking an eye.

"Checking the stolen gear for tracking devices."

"Oh," I yawn again.

Bren pushes a bar of some kind into my hands. "Eat."

"Mmm hmm," I answer.

Bren slips his fingers under my chin and lifts my head. I open my eyes to look at him. "Please, eat, and then we need to keep moving. We have several hours to go before we get to the Recalcitrants. There are public safety officers in the woods and they are on to us. They will catch us if we don't hurry."

I sigh and nod. I open my bar and take a bite. It's their rations and it tastes terrible. Bren finishes his bar and takes another swig of water. He pulls out a first aid pack, opens some disinfectant, and then he starts messing with my face.

"Stop. That stings," I yelp, fully awake.

"It's supposed to sting. It's first aid. You've got a couple of ugly scrapes."

"Have you looked at yourself? You have a pretty spectacular black eye."

"Yeah, I know. Hurts too."

I can't help it. I giggle a little.

"There's my girl. Come on now. Rest time is over."

I throw an eye roll his way and then pull myself to my aching feet. Who am I kidding? Aching back, sore shoulder, bruised all over, and horribly blistered feet is more like it. When had I last peed? I was probably dehydrated too.

"I want a steak — a rare one — with a baked potato. The potato is gonna have cheddar cheese, bacon, sour cream, and green onions. And I want a big salad with plenty of good Italian dressing. And a hot bath or maybe just a nice hot shower with some tangerine-mango body scrub and I want a big comfy bed with extra pillows and a soft blanket. I also want a massage and pie. I forgot the pie — I want marionberry. It's my favorite."

"What are you mumbling about?"

"I'm making a list of all the things you're going to owe me when we get to this camp of yours."

Bren smiles big. "I hate to let you down, but it kinda is a camp. It may not quite live up to your expectations."

"I don't want to know. I've had plenty of disappointment lately. I'm gonna pretend that we're going to one of those fancy luxury spas for the rich like I've seen in video clips."

He shakes his head and smiles some more. I will always remember that smile.

We walk on and on, always east, just like he said and then we hear it . . . the *whomp, whomp, whomp* of a helicopter. Bren changes our route. We sprint from tree to tree, trying to stay in the densest part so that they can't see us. The sound grows louder and softer as it circles and sometimes we can catch a flash of metal between the boughs overhead. About the time I can't run anymore it moves away, and I wonder if it picked up something to the south of us. Just when my breathing eases a new sound grabs my attention. A high pitched hum can be heard over the whispering of the trees. They must have seen us after all and moved the helo away so as not to interfere with the drone.

We slow to a walk looking for the thickest cover. My breathing is loud even to my own ears. I attempt to keep up, but I'm lagging behind. It's a good time to lose Bren, but I'm afraid he'll find me before I've gotten twenty units away from him. I'm relieved when he pulls a map from his pocket and pauses to look at it — then I almost cry. I lean against a tree to catch my breath and put my cheek to its rough bark . . .

Bark! Bark!

Holy crap! Now there are dogs after us! My eyes burst open and I look to Bren. He's already stuffing the map back in his pocket. He tears hell-bent through the trees to the north without even trying to be quiet or stay out of view. He must have a plan. I fly behind him as fast as my exhausted body will move. Adrenaline and fear are my allies as I push myself. He jumps into a creek ahead of me and runs upstream for a ways before exiting on the other side. I slip, fall, pull myself to my feet, and clamber on. I scramble out at the same rocky spot he did and try not to lose sight of his retreating back. Maybe we should split up? Or maybe he is the only thing that can save me . . .

Pain shoots through my hip, like a strong pinch that doesn't end. Tingles radiate over my skin. Have I been stung? I gaze down to see a dart sticking to me. Oh hell. "Bren, run!" I gasp as I fall to my knees. How he hears me, I'll never know, but he turns and our eyes meet.

"Run," I whisper.

He hesitates a moment more and then he's gone. I fall onto my hands and then roll onto my butt as my limbs give up the fight and turn to gelatin.

"Well, well, looky here. We've been trying to capture you for quite a while, you elusive little bitch. You aren't just any rebel; you're *the rebel*, right?" The public safety officer laughs and it isn't the friendly kind. "What do you think, boys? Is she a rebel, terrorist, crazy girl or just plain dumb-lucky?"

Another of the officers holds a device over me. "I'll bet she's had some kind of help. She doesn't emit a signal. What'd you do to your chip, girly?"

"I thought I saw another person," someone behind me says.

"Call it in, Len," the guy with the most symbols on his uniform says. He must be the leader. "If someone was here, we'll get them."

The blond-haired officer answers. "There's no way she could take us. She wasn't public safety trained."

Oh no, not the guys from last night. I cringe on the inside and try to focus. I bite my tongue to keep myself from speaking. One of them walks away and begins speaking into his communications device. I can't make out what he is saying. I'm scared for myself and for Bren. Why am I not dead?

"No matter, there'll be a nice bonus for us. What, nothing to say, nerd girl?" the man with the scanner asks.

I force my head up; it takes all the effort I can muster.

"I can't believe that dart doesn't have you all the way out. Tough little fighter, huh? I'm impressed you can stay sitting up. Don't worry it won't last. They don't care what we do to you as long as we don't kill you or break your fingers. They decided they've got a job for you and you've got to be able to use the tools of your trade, right?" he ends, wiggling his fingers. I have the urge to bite them or even spit in his face, but my mouth has gone dry. There are six in this group. I guess they figured out they weren't sending enough soldiers.

"Do we have support coming, Len?" the leader asks. I get a better look at him. Crap, he is the guy I choked. Couldn't I catch a break — just once? He jerks his head in my direction and two of them yank me to my feet. My legs won't listen to me or hold my weight.

"Yes, sir." I roll my eyes in the speaker's direction. He's been fighting too. No wonder they hate me. They think I've done this to them.

My hands are being zip-tied behind my back, but I can't seem to make my arms function. I work hard at memorizing each of their faces. Leader — tall, dark and buzz cut. My mouth feels like it's full of fabric. Len — smaller, blond with brown eyes, wiry. My ears are ringing. Ginger-haired guy, blue eyes, freckles . . . blurry vision. He's the one who scanned my chip.

"There she goes. It's working now." I can feel myself crumpling between the two men holding me. My head lolls to the side. Guy on right . . . barely taller than me . . maybe Asian? *I'll remember you guys.*

"Thanks, Mike. I can see that. So who wants her first?" I gag and make a feeble attempt to shake them off, but my body won't cooperate. Remember, Mike is the redhead.

"Not if she's gonna puke all over me!" the Asian guy says.

"Now, Jay, don't be a baby."

"No time anyway. They're coming."

Mike, Jay, Len, leader — remember. I fight to stay conscious and lose.

01101111 01100010 01110011 01110100 01101001

01101110 01100001 01110100 01100101 01101100

01111001 00100000

open my eyes or at least think I do. It's completely black, so I blink several times just to check. I hold still and listen really hard, but all I can hear is a gentle hum in my ears, my heartbeat, and breath entering and leaving my body. My cheek is on a hard gritty surface, and I can smell concrete and iron. Wait, not iron, blood. I'm bleeding. The arm I'm lying on is numb and will hurt like hell when my circulation returns. I evaluate the rest of my body. I'm sore everywhere, but nothing seems to be broken or damaged beyond a couple of days recovery. My hands are still tied or retied because they took my backpack, fleece liner, rainproof jacket, boots, and socks. All that is left is my t-shirt and cargo pants. I slowly maneuver onto my other side. My head pounds with the effort and I swear my tongue feels like it's shriveled. I can't even work up enough spit to swallow.

A light pops on, searing my eyeballs. I squinch them up tight, but they water from the brightness. My nose begins to run, to keep my eyes company I guess, and I can't even wipe it. Ugh. I can't be too dehydrated then, right?

"Student number 18A294E, you are no longer missing. Your body has been recovered. You were killed while conspiring with the Recalcitrants who tricked you into helping them or so the news will read. You have no family. No one will save you. You are nameless. Everything here is earned and you will start with nothing." The voice is male and deep, yet somehow almost mechanical sounding.

I blink and turn my head trying to locate it, but it feels like it's coming from all around me and the light is so harsh and bright that everything is thrown into silhouette, shadow, and glare.

"You helped design the perfect game. Congratulations. You are responsible for the deaths of 3,787 students. How do you plead?"

"Not —" A hand comes out of nowhere and slaps me across the face, smacking it against the ground. My head explodes with pain and I shudder.

"No talking! We are generous — you shall be rewarded for your crimes. Free her hands."

What is he saying? Does it make any sense? Boots appear in my field of vision. They are black, heavy-soled and laced. A needle from a Douglas fir is caught in the lace. Black pants are tucked into the boots — public safety from the woods. That is all the further I can scan when one of the boots kicks me so hard in the stomach that my breath explodes out of my body. I cough and gag, bringing my knees to my chest. A knife cuts the bonds at my wrists but also cuts into my skin. My deadened arm can't really feel it yet, but the splash of warm blood against my other wrist gives it away. The pinpricks begin their own assault on my arm.

"She's a mess. Take her to be sanitized."

"Yes, sir!"

My arm is in a full attack of pinpricks as circulation returns. I feel a strong compulsion to move it, but they have it wrenched behind me. My shoulders scream in complaint, yet I can barely discern it over my pounding head. My arms and legs begin to cramp. I want to fight them off but I can barely stand. They lift me higher so that my toes just touch the floor and then haul me out of the room.

The bright light of the hallway reflects off the white walls, ceiling, and floor to stab pain through my eyes. They go through another door and drop me onto equally bright white tiles. I barely catch myself but then my hands slip out from under me. I turn my head to save my nose but my cheek slaps onto the tiled floor. A smear of red now mars the once perfect surface.

"She's still drugged," a new voice accuses.

"You think? On the bright side, she'll be easier to manage this way." Did that voice belong to the guy who kicked me?

Rough hands grab me and flip me onto my back. I want to roll away but knees come down on my arms and hair pinning me in place. The guy is practically sitting on my head. Gross. Black pants, black shirt — he has to be public safety too. Gee, and I don't feel a bit safe right now.

"You might have been kinda pretty before you got all beaten up."

Yeah, thanks. Awesome, you sick waste of human skin. Him, I will remember. His is the first nose I'm gonna break.

"Grab her pants."

Oh hell no! I scream in my mind as I buck my hips and flail my legs. My arms scream in pain and some hair is pulled from my scalp. Someone sits on one leg and my pants are unfastened. I try to kick with my free leg. I smack the guy sitting on my other one pretty good, but all I accomplish is to make them mad.

"Whoa. We got a fighter here." It's the new voice again — another public safety guy with black hair. "Give her another shot, strip her and hose her down."

I strain with my whole body to break away but a needle pricks my arm anyway. I can feel myself slipping away and fight it. My life shrinks to little bursts of consciousness like the previews of a movie. My pants are yanked off. I can't feel my legs. All are dressed like public safety except one, who's dressed like medical. I can't control my limbs. They pull my shirt off. I should stop them. No, not my bra. Leave me alone. Move! I manage to swing an arm in a clumsy arc, smacking someone. A slap to my battered face makes stars burst across my already screwed-up vision. My poor head.

I'm lying on the side of my face again. The cool tile eases some of my pain and dizziness. I want to curl into a ball. Just kill me and get it over with. I feel my underwear go and feel utterly helpless and hopeless. I try harder to roll into a ball.

Water bursts over me. I shiver. They move me around. I pray I'll drown. The blackness is welcome.

I awake with a start. Obviously, I've had a horrible nightmare. I attempt to roll over to tell Malorie, but I can't move. Tears burn at the back my eyes. I've been strapped to a hospital bed, in a room I've never seen before — except I can't really see it now either because it's so incredibly dim. The tears I'd felt building up start to well, and one escapes to run into my hair. It feels warm against the side of my face. I find a bandage on the wrist that was cut and another on my head tells me this is no dream . . . it's my living nightmare. I do a mental inventory of my body. I'm filled with aches and pains but none . . . down there. It's one of the few places I don't hurt, so that's good, right? I can't even check to be sure there is a bandage on my head because I can only manage to touch my hip with my hand, but the funny tightness and pull tells me there is. I close my eyes to wait for whatever is going to happen next.

I try to relax but it's not really working. I try counting the seconds, lose my place and have to start again. I figure I must still be drugged because it's hard to concentrate.

Eventually, I find a rhythm. *Three million, nine hundred, fifty-four thousand . . .*

"Run!" I scream and my body jerks awake. Where am I? I was running in a forest. Bren gives me a desperate look. He wants to help. I can see it in his eyes, but the odds are not in his favor or mine. It's better to run away and fight again another day when the chances are better. He disappears into the foliage. I physically reach out a hand, hoping to recapture his image, but my hand is yanked to a stop by the strap holding it to the hospital bed I'm on. There is something hauntingly familiar about that.

It takes me a moment to come back to myself and realize I'm no longer in the forest. I'm in a room that smells of antiseptic, not dirt and loam. I look around, realizing that the pounding in my head is down to a dull ache. The room is small, square, and made up of concrete and metal. Shelves attached to the wall hold bottles, tools, and wrapped gauze. Harsh lights flush with the ceiling, hurt my still sensitive eyes. I shift my gaze down to the floor and find it covered with rubber mats, a drain in the center. Thinking about why that is necessary makes me shudder. I turn my head the other way and see a shiny metal panel. I can almost make out my reflection, but if that's me . . . what have they done to my hair?

I twist my body and try to touch my head. My arm is covered with fine powder. I move a leg out from under the sheet and it looks the same way except that most of it has brushed off. I'm covered by a hospital gown so I can only see so much, but it's a big improvement over how I was in the shower room. What have they done to me? Is this ash? Did they burn the hair from my body? I look to the reflection again. My face is still pink so they must have covered my head but flash burned my body. Why? Why go to so much trouble? Why didn't they just kill me?

The way the door clangs open tells me that it's made of

metal and also gives me the feeling that I'm underground. No natural light, no windows, hollow sound . . . I need more data. Someone walks in.

"Will you cooperate?" I turn my head in the direction of the voice. He is medium — everything about him screams average, normal, don't notice me. His voice sounds both educated and professional, yet neither tenor nor bass His hair is brown and his eyes are the color of old weathered wood. His uniform marks him as a government employee. Something clicks — purple — government — royal purple. Long ago the royals showed their status by wearing purple. There was something about the dye being expensive and if you could afford it, you had to be, well, royal. Did he think he was royalty? He is neither thin nor fat and neither tall nor short. So what is it about him that freaks me out? Perhaps it's the lack of expression on his face and the completely dead eyes evaluating me that has shivers skittering up and down my spine.

I'm afraid to look away, but I have to see if I really have the goosebumps rising on my skin that I think I do. Yep, the worst case I've ever had. I must have taken too long to answer because he repeats the question. I look back at him deciding my answer.

"You will answer quickly and truthfully."

I say nothing.

"You have had new hardware installed." He holds up a small device. I don't know what it means. Did I now have a chip like Malorie's? Was he going to kill me? Why go to all that trouble when they could have just finished the beating.

I stare at him saying nothing, waiting.

"You are prisoner number 18A294E. Your name was Elise Andrek. True or false?"

Again I just stare. My name was? What is he asking? He shows me the remote again and deliberately pushes a button. Pain shoots through my left arm. I look at it to see if it's really on fire like my brain screams it is.

"Yes," I gasp as tears run down my cheeks.

The pain stops. "Good girl. Will you cooperate?"

I look at him and close my eyes, wishing that I could wake up from this new nightmare. My arm bursts into flame again and I bite down hard on my lip, trying not to scream. I try to roll into a ball, but my restraints stop me. "Yes," I sob through gritted teeth.

"Good girl." The pain stops as quickly as it began.

"Who was with you in the woods?"

I think about what to say. I've taken too long. Pain.

"No one." Pain.

"Try again, my dear."

"A boy," I gasp.

"Who is this boy?" The sound of his voice makes my skin crawl.

"From school."

"All students were accounted for. Who was he?"

"I . . . I don't know."

Pain.

Lie, I tell myself. "There was another boy."

"Yes?"

"In the woods — one of the wild people who live outside of

the cities and outside of the government."

"Who is he?"

"We aren't supposed to talk to outsiders. We aren't supposed to know about them."

"Okay, how do you know about them?" he asks in his oily voice.

"I used to read."

"What is the boy's name?"

"He didn't say."

Pain slices through my body.

"I don't know. I swear. Stop. Please stop!" I beg because this time, he does not stop it.

"How did you meet him?"

"He found me."

"Where?"

"In the woods."

Soon it doesn't matter how I answer so long as I do. When I finally faint, my agony ends.

When I wake up next I'm in what is essentially a box. It looks like I can get anywhere in this room in about three strides. Along one wall a narrow slab hangs by cables and I'm lying on it. The only other things in the room are a toilet and a sink. I sit up and my head spins. I carefully put my bare feet on the floor and try to rise but fall to my knees. I crawl to the sink and turn it on. Cool water trickles out of the faucet. It smells fine so I stick a finger in it. I rub a bit between my fingers and sniff it again. It has to be water. I wait a few seconds to see if it will sting or burn, but nothing happens so I scoop up a little and test it with my tongue. Still, nothing happens, so I splash some on my face and wash my hands. I wait another moment and take a small sip and then another.

I hear a faint noise and twist around. A slit opens near the base of my door and four soda crackers are pushed in on a plastic tray. The slit closes and there is silence. I shake my hands dry and wipe the remaining water on the hem of my hospital gown. I crawl over to the crackers and go through the same slow, agonizing procedure eating them a bit at a time. I crawl back to my bunk to wait. I roll up in a ball. I'm cold and I have no blanket, no soap, and no towel. They didn't even leave me any toilet paper.

Then I remember the cut on my arm. It must not have been too bad. It looks to be held together with some sort of glue. I search my body for the new chip. I find another glued line at the back of my neck, in line with my spine. Dear God, they wired the pain chip right into my nervous system. I'm doomed.

I keep the crackers down and drink more water. Eventually, I'll have to pee, but I'll worry about that later. For now, I pray for more food and a blanket. Questions bounce around in my head but the answers elude me. Did Bren make it to safety? Did he believe that I was dead? Will he come for me or is it better if he doesn't? What is their plan for me and what did I tell that man?

Hours pass. I'm so hungry that I feel dizzy. Surely they haven't done all this to leave me to starve to death? I hear a small noise that turns into the scrape of a bolt moving. Two of the guards from my shower experience are waiting for me. I back as far as I can into the corner of my bunk, up against the far wall next to the sink and think seriously about climbing under it. They approach looking confident. I hold out my arms to push them away, but I'm enough of a physical wreck by now that they just laugh.

They easily haul me to my feet and half march, half drag me down the hall. I count the doors and cameras. Why it matters I don't know, but it gives me something to do instead of panicking. They guide me through two sets of doors and into a room that is a lot like the hospital room I'd been in. They force me into a chair and strap my arms and legs to it.

I begin to shake. More pain is coming. They are going to interrogate me again. My nose, cheeks, jaw joints, and teeth begin to hurt as the pressure builds up in my head. My eyes and nose water. I pull at the restraints. I'm so scared I can barely think. The public safety men are behind me. I can hear them, but I can't see them and then *he* walks in.

I swallow hard, trying to hold myself together.

"Who helped you?"

"Malorie?" I answer in a small voice, seeing the device in his hand.

"Who else?"

"Griffin?" I hedge.

"What did he look like?"

"I don't know." His thumb nears the button and I talk faster. "He's a boy. He was studying for the government branch. He had a nice voice."

"What did he look like?"

"Taller than me and slender. He had dark hair and dark brown eyes."

"What was his student number?"

"I don't know," I whine in fear.

"Think! What was his student number?"

"I don't know — we never talked about that."

"Who else helped you?"

"I don't know." Pain.

"Who else helped you?" His voice is still calm sounding but his eyes flash.

"J . . . Jill?" The pain stops.

"You said previously that there was a wild boy. Tell me about him."

Oh no, what did I say last time? "He found me in the woods. I was sick. He helped me."

"Where in the woods?"

"He hid me under a fallen tree and fed me herbs."

"Did he attack the public safety officers?"

"I don't know."

"Did you attack the public safety officers?"

"Did I?" I want to sound delusional. I have to mix truth and lies.

"We need to know who we're looking for. If you help us, I'll see that you get a blanket."

"He was dirty. He brought me water."

"What did he look like?"

I thought again of Griffin, whose face would haunt me

forever and described him. A wrinkle forms between the brows of the man questioning me. I'm not sure what that means and I don't have time to think about it before he is changing tracks.

"When did the scenario give itself away?"

"What?"

"How did you know?" he asks in that oily voice that makes me cringe.

"Know? Know what?" I ask. I don't want to guess at what he's asking but his questions are confusing and . . . pain shoots up my arm to explode in my chest. "The elevator . . . the elevator went down not up." The pain stops.

"When were you watched at school?"

"Always." This is the truth as far as I know. It sure felt true when I was at school.

"Who were your friends at school?"

"Mostly Malorie. Jill. I don't know."

"You don't know? Who doesn't know who their friends are?" His voice changes to cajoling.

I match his tone. "Who does? I mean really?" Pain.

"I'll ask the questions." He pushes a button and the pain stops. "What programs did you work on?"

"Mostly the game."

"And?"

"They asked me to fix glitches and bugs. Whatever they asked — I did. I don't know. I just looked at the problem and fixed it. What do you want?"

He had warned me not to ask any questions, and I know I'll pay even before he begins to charge at me, I slam my head into the back of the chair, but I'm trapped. He puts his face centimeters from mine. Rage purples his face making it clash with his uniform. "I'll ask the questions," he shouts so loud my ears ring in response and spittle flecks my face. "I want the truth!"

He rears back and jerks his head once to the side as if he'd just had some kind of episode and then he starts his questioning again. On and on it goes and I once again lose track of what he asks and how I answer. It seems like he asks the same questions over and over but in different ways. Finally, he gives me a jolt of pain so strong that my chest seizes up and I pee myself. He throws the controller at me, I jerk my head to the side, but he hits me in the temple. Blood runs down my face, dripping on my shoulder.

"Get her out of here!" He screams. His head jerks with another tick.

The guards grab me, remove my straps, and drag me into the showers where I know I'll get to be humiliated all over again.

"Strip," one says.

"Leave and I will."

"Strip now. You are to be watched."

"Turn around."

He grabs me by what is left of my hair and uses it to force me to look at him. The other officer comes up behind me, grabs the back of the gown and pulls. I hear the Velcro rip away. The officer drops me and I hit the floor hard, landing on my hands and knees.

I cover my chest.

"Underwear."

"No!" I cry.

I hear a sound and look up in time to see a baton whizzing toward me. I don't even move. It hits me in the shoulder with a ferocious crack and I pass out.

wake up briefly in the hospital with my shoulder and arm immobilized in a strange device. I close my eyes and pray for death, or at least oblivion.

When I wake up again I'm back in my box with stitches in my temple, my hip, the back of my neck, and under my collarbone. They have left me a thin blanket and toilet paper. They leave me in the box for days. Food comes through the slot at intervals just as I'm getting shaky, but it is never quite enough. I am reduced to judging the time by the healing of my wounds. I see no one but know they are watching. A black dome in one corner hides a camera — I can feel its evil eye on me.

Someone from medical comes to see me after what must have been two weeks post-surgery. He is accompanied by two guards so that I don't cause any trouble. The irony is that I really don't have the energy to. He examines my incisions and takes out the stitches. I'm back in interrogation the next day and the next. Some days it's the remote in the plain man's hand that brings the pain, other days it's the fist of the guard captain. One day when the purple uniformed man isn't getting the response he wants he tries a knife. As it first slides over my skin, I feel nothing but friction, then the line of red appears followed by the sting.

"What do you want?" I beg for what feels like the millionth time.

"I want you to tell me everything."

I'm breaking on the inside, but outside, the surgical scars are a pale pink. I will have more of them than I can count. The man from medical appears and paints the cuts with glue that smells awful and stings worse than the cuts do. I look at him, begging for his help. A wrinkle appears between his brows but he says nothing and leaves. I feel despair.

I shake every day before interrogation. There is nowhere to hide and nothing to kill myself with — that's when the drugs begin. I pray they will finally take me. I hope he will crank his device one notch too far and burst my heart. They break bones and set them with the weird device in the hospital. They cut me and glue or stitch me back together, but I don't know anything worthwhile and I can't let go of Bren or how I knew what I knew about our trial. I'm not sure how my brain works so how can I hope to explain it to *him*. It doesn't matter what I say, they seem to believe my lies more often than the truth, including my stories of the fictional wild boy. I have lied about him so many times that I almost start to believe he's real. I can see no pattern in anything they do, but I am still learning from it. I learn how much pain I can take and how much damage my body can withstand. I make sense of the answers I have given as they ask questions over and over and I adapt my story. Soon I won't know what the truth is anymore. Soon I will be a beaten, ruined animal.

A deep depression takes hold of me. I care about nothing and do nothing but sleep when they leave me alone. At first, my dreams are filled with nightmares, but then I begin to see Bren. Comfort fills me. The world is fuzzy and unclear, but Bren is in sharp focus. He smiles as a breeze ruffles his hair. He looks healthy, his skin a warm golden brown. I hug him and nestle my face into the soft skin of his neck. He smells of forest and human and home. My lips touch his neck and I awaken.

He has come to save me in the dream world and when I'm fully awake, I know he did, somehow, in my present nightmare as well. Just like he did before I was captured.

For the first time in days, I feel not good but better. Fear has burned its way out of my body. I can take the pain and I will accept death if it comes, but now I hope it doesn't. The pain comes and the pain goes — it is survivable. I know what it is to have stitches and broken bones — they heal. My friends are dead, Bren probably is too. Having no one gives you freedom; it means they can't hurt you anymore — they have no tools left.

I realize that I had not been paying attention. After inter-rogations, if I was cooperative and gave them some information they thought they could use, I would get a gift. First, I got soap and then a day at a time I received a toothbrush, toothpaste, and a towel. That spark of hope helps to sustain me. I begin to take more interest in the nourishment they provide. It's not good, but I force myself to eat it all. Maybe today I will get an item of clothing. I start a new routine. I begin with stretching. I add sit-ups and pushups and then I add lunges. I cannot allow myself to waste away. I have to be ready. Looking back I guess the food had been getting better too. It is plain and tasteless, but I'm not starving anymore. I can't tell what they are feeding me most of the time. I cannot allow myself to grow weak and I figure if they are going to poison me there is nothing I can do about it anyway. One death is as good as another from where I'm standing.

I choose to walk to questioning between my guards and sit in the chair voluntarily. The man I have come to think of as the Inquisitor studies me for a long time before he asks me the questions that I have nearly memorized. He rewards me by not strapping my feet to the chair, but he doesn't let the guards leave the room. I smile inside but leave my face completely blank. When I return to my cell I'm fitted with a wristband. There are no buttons for me to push and the readout is blank. I watch it warily for a long time. Periodically it emits a beep or two, but I don't know what they mean. I know I will eventually work out the pattern — I have nothing else to do.

After several beeps, another nameless public safety officer brings me food. He is followed by another with a small stack of gray fabric. They leave and I explore my new gifts. The gray fabric is clothing. They are nothing special but feel like a luxury after weeks of wearing nothing but the hospital gown. I happily pull on the socks, cinch pants, and a t-shirt. Heaven. I rub my head and measure the length of my hair. It's almost as long as three of my fingers stacked up.

Every day becomes the same and when I say the same . . . I mean exactly right down to the food I am given the same. Every morning a stack of clean clothes scrapes through the slot in my door. They are always clean and always folded exactly the same way. I never see anyone but public safety deliver the food or clothes. I only see the guards who take me to the Inquisitor and the man himself. They have not hurt me so badly that I need to see the medical personnel in what must be weeks. Either they like what I'm telling them or they need to heal me up to put me to work. I don't know which scares me more.

My nourishment — their word — not mine, becomes identifiable but it doesn't ever alter. I always get oatmeal, a hard-boiled egg, and apple slices for breakfast. A chicken breast, green beans, a slice of bread and an orange are my lunch menu and dinner is like lunch except they give me carrots, a banana and some kind of white fish. I fondly remember pasta and I still dream of the steak and potato that I told Bren about. I thought the food at school was bland. It wasn't so bad. I've learned that when you're hungry enough, food is food.

Every day *he* tries to get into my head. The Inquisitor is such a funny little man, colorless except for the purple in his uniform. I seem to really frustrate him. It looks like someone has drawn the line at maiming because as many times as he sprays my face with spittle, looks like he's going to pop a blood vessel, or hits the pain button, he has not damaged anything beyond what the hospital can repair. I'll have a scar from his remote, where he hit me in the temple, and many others to go along with that one, though. My bruises are spectacular, multihued, and many. Some even run into each other and vary in shade from blue, to black, to reddish, and yellow-green.

I wish I knew how I was able to mix truth and lies. I've played dumb and I've shielded Bren. His name still has not crossed my lips and I try very hard to not even think about him. How do I know to mix things up and to tell a twisted-up version of the truth? That never was part of *Underworlders*, was it? When I did repairs had I seen interrogation clips? I barely remember who I am through the haze of medications they pump into me in their attempt to get the truth. The funny thing is, I don't know what that is anymore.

Lately, they have tapered off the drugs and now I suffer a whole new kind of agony. My stomach hurts all the time. My muscles cramp for no reason, my bowels are in revolt and I have the sweats. My skin is pale with a yellow tinge and I'm just thankful I can't see my hair.

The door opens and I sigh. My wristband had pinged so I know it's my least favorite time of day — time to see the Inquisitor. The guards march me down the hall, but I almost fall over one of them when I expect them to turn and they don't. The one on my left roughly grabs my now bony elbow and we walk on for the first time in what has to have been about six weeks, though I have no real way to count the days or even know for sure when it's day and when it's night.

We go past a guard station and enter a new room. I work

really hard at keeping the surprise off my face as my guards bring me before the Inquisitor's desk. Today a secretary is stationed nearby with a tablet. Ah, today we will be more civilized. I look longingly at the tablet out of the corner of my eye but try not to look as if I am. I'm afraid I'll give myself away. My brain had begun to fester on all that is happening here and now I wonder if this place is self-contained or if it is run remotely. My eyes wander around the room taking it all in. I almost forget the man behind the desk . . . almost.

"Did you have help?"

"No."

"No? Let me help you think."

Pain courses through my body with such force that I fall to my hands and knees. "Yes . . . maybe . . . sort of." My voice comes out with a whimper.

"I need names."

"Malorie helped —" More pain cuts off my words. My brain flashes with pieces of the trial. I describe the men from the bar that were no more than an illusion. The pain stops. The Inquisitor gives me a strange look. I wonder if I'm on the right track. I sense his confusion. A part of me wonders why I did it. Why did I have to protect Bren — because he is so much more important than me and every day I get away with it is another opportunity for him and the rebels to extinguish our crushing government. I wonder about the chip they've planted in me. If he comes, can it be removed safely? Is it affecting my brain or my nervous system? Have they activated its GPS and does it have a kill switch?

I also lie because every piece of information I learn, I can use to help the resistance. The government believed I was a silly girl who was decent with computers. I'm not sure what they believe now. I'd love to see my file or better yet, corrupt it and plant a virus in their system.

The Inquisitor stares hard at me. "Who was in the woods with you?"

"The men looking for me."

"Who was in the woods with you?" he repeats, his voice more intense.

"The men looking for me and their dogs."

He sighs. "How did you get there?"

"I walked."

"Where were you going?"

"Away."

"Away to where?" he presses.

"Away from the city."

"To where?" he raises his voice.

"I just wanted to get away from the city. I thought I could hide in the woods."

"You told someone to run."

"I thought I should run." Pain.

"Who did you tell to run?"

"Malorie," I gasp.

"Malorie is dead."

Because you killed her, I yell in my mind, keeping my face blank.

"Who? Give me names!" The vein in his temple pulses and I observe his strange tick again as his head jerks to the side.

"Griffin?" Pain. "Jill?" This time, it goes on and on. I fall onto my side and writhe. There is a clatter and it stops.

I lie panting as the secretary finally speaks. "Enough, Bartholomew. Clearly, she doesn't know anything. If she did, she would have told you long ago."

How careless, now I have a name.

"She does know something; if you'd just give me a little more time."

"This is a waste of time. Reprogram her and stop this nonsense! You have been wasting our time for almost two months. No one could take that without breaking. If she had something worthwhile to say she'd have given it up long ago to stop the pain. No trace of anyone else was found in those woods — none. Whoever this 'wild boy' was, he is long gone and for all we know he may have been a figment of her imagination. Enough resources have been wasted. It's time to move on."

This man is not the Inquisitor's secretary. He must be his boss.

"She had to have help. There's no way she could have gotten away and beat up those men. We need to find that boy."

"The public safety officers heard her say 'En.' Maybe she was confused and it was Griffin, she yelled after all. Maybe the 'wild boy' was all in her head like I said before."

"Griffin died in the old commuter station," the Inquisitor insists.

"She was distressed. She could have made a mistake. She had been through trauma, perhaps she dreamed it. That can happen."

"I don't believe it."

"She's just a girl who got lucky in her escape. She has skills we can use. Reprogram her and put her to work."

"What about the officers?"

"Maybe she tricked them and they beat up each other in the dark and confusion. They were ashamed they were beaten by a girl. Perhaps they stretched the truth. Now, send her up and focus on what's important."

"They know there was a male there."

"I said, stop this!" the Inquisitor's boss bellows.

"Fine!" the Inquisitor all but snarls back.

"I have a few questions for her first," the government man says calm once more.

The guards haul me to my feet. I'm sweating, shaking, and the way my legs are behaving, incapable of standing on my own at the moment.

"Why did you run from your government?" he asks softly.

"They were trying to kill me."

"I want to know, who are you really?" His voice is still smooth and calm. It reminds me of silk.

"I am Elise, a student. I am no one."

"You helped to create *the game*." He sounds almost awed when he says it.

"I didn't know what I was doing. I was just designing the game elements I was assigned."

"Why do you hide a piece of yourself away?" I can almost touch his curiosity, it is so strong.

"I don't."

"You do and I want to know how." Again he sounds more curious than anything else.

"I don't know what you're talking about." He moves right up next to me and looks into my eyes with his ice blue ones that are wreathed with wrinkles and bags. His white hair is slicked back and up close I can see his pink scalp through the strands. His breath is odd. It almost smells like . . . chemicals. He continues to stare into my eyes and then breaks our connection.

"Get her shoes and send her up. Her slot is ready."

Physically, even I could beat up this old relic, but there is something about him that speaks of power. I look at him and I am afraid.

The guards half drag me through another door and down a hallway. We stop before metal doors that require a keycard. We step into a metal, buttonless box. They don't remove their hands from me even after the doors close and we begin to raise one level in the secure elevator. We stop by a counter where another public safety officer is waiting to serve us. He looks at my feet and hands over a pair of simple athletic shoes. A non-sensical part of me wonders if they had any paint that wasn't black, gray or white. I miss blue. Technology blue made me happy. Heck, I'd gaze at any color right now, even brown like the jacket Bren had given me. *Don't think about Bren.*

They still have a hold of my arms. Instead of releasing me they throw me to the floor. "Put on the shoes," the tall one snarls as he throws them at me.

I do as I'm told and wait for further instructions. This time, I don't get any, they just yank me to my feet. They lead me through a hallway, past a cafeteria, and out the doors. I take a deep breath of the first fresh air I've had in two months, according to the white-haired gentleman. It must almost be September. All too soon we are entering another building. A guard stands in the entry. I capture a brief glimpse of a bathroom and then we're in the barracks where long skinny windows rim the room just under the eaves. They are too high to reach even standing on the top bunk and although they are plenty long they aren't tall enough to fit through, but I can look through them and stare at the brilliant blue sky. I can't take my eyes off those windows.

The tall guard shoves me between my shoulder blades, propelling me forward. We walk down the row. I would guess a hundred people can sleep in here, but I don't take time to count. We stop about three-quarters of the way down the row.

"No fighting, no hoarding, no stealing, no loud talking, no sex." He doesn't need to tell me what will happen if I disobey. He points to a bunk with my number painted on it and another number below mine. The bunks are similar to the ones we had at school but not as nice. This time, I get the upper bunk. "Be here when your wristband shows fourteen. At fifteen it's lights out."

They leave me. I don't know where I'm allowed to go, so I stay and enjoy this new freedom. First I study the wristband. It is simple in design and streamlined. It doesn't show the time but has a place where a readout could appear. It has no obvious buttons. I wonder what kind of data is stored on it and what Malorie would have made of it.

Thinking of Malorie makes me sad so I let my eyes travel around the dormitory, but the windows still draw me back to them. I climb up on my bunk to get a better view and just sit there, looking out the window and watching the clouds. I find

I've grown stiff from sitting without moving so I turn and count the bunks. There are twenty-six on each side with a double foot locker at the end of each one. The space in the middle looks like it could hold two more bunks end to end. I notice that not all the bunks have numbers on them. It is warmer here than it was in solitary.

No one brings me food or tells me where to go, so I continue to watch the sky. At fourteen beeps, people of all ages and both sexes walk in. Most look tired and beaten, but the strangest part is that they are nearly silent. Everything is soft — subdued — muted. Apparently, I'm not the only one who's had lessons in pain. I watch them all closely for my cues as to how to behave. One thing stands out, although they wear the same type of shirt as I do, they are wearing canvas pants.

After seeing many go to their footlocker I do the same and find my meager toiletries from solitary. They must have brought them up while I was still with the Inquisitor and the other government official. I follow two women with their toothbrushes in hand into the bathroom that is a lot like the one we'd had at school. Here the toilets are in open stalls and the showers have no curtains, just a half wall that the few who are showering use to hang their towels. I quickly avert my eyes from the ones in use. The sinks are the kind where several people can stand at once and there are no mirrors. At least there aren't any cameras, but we share the bathroom with the men. This will take some getting used to.

People are changing into pajamas right next to their bunks. Someone has been through and delivered a pair for everyone and hampers have been rolled into the center aisle. I follow the example of those around me and drop my dirty clothes into the bin. Prisoners roll them back out when it appears that everyone had made use of them.

I crawl onto my bunk and spread out my thin blanket. I lay back and try to sleep when the lights go out, but after the silence I've been in, there are too many human sounds. Each mattress creaks, people snuffle, snore and their breathing almost startles me. It is too dark after learning to sleep with the light left on in my cell almost continuously. Now I would have to get used to the red light strip that shows the way to the unisex bathroom. I give up on the sleep idea and just work on relaxing my body, but it's difficult with my growling stomach. All I had today was breakfast.

I guess deep down I am just too scared to sleep.

Eventually, the rustling of people trying to find a comfortable position slows and the breathing becomes steady. I listen, trying to soothe myself with the sounds of humanity, but the sounds change. A mattress groans and then another. There is the faint scuff of a shoe on the floor. It grows nearer and then the breathing around me changes too. I am yanked from my bed blanket and all. Had I been asleep I would have taken a lot more damage. I get in a decent punch on the way down and am rewarded with a grunt in return. A fist connects with my shoulder and I take a kick to the gut before I roll under the bunk and the one next to it and pop up on the other side. My two attackers seem momentarily befuddled.

I climb the foot of the nearest bunk, find an attacker as his feet hit the red light strip and launch myself at him. He falls flat onto his back. I hear the air rush from his lungs and his head smack against the floor. I knee him the groin on my way back to standing, but his friend doesn't appreciate my efforts. He helps me up by the back of the t-shirt I've been given to sleep in and flings me into a bunk. I hit the corner and fall to the floor.

The barracks goes silent. Not one person comes to my aid. I attempt to roll away again but he gets me by the neck and squeezes. I pound on his arms with my elbows, but it isn't working. I can feel myself losing the fight and my breath. The lights pop on. My vision is marred by black spots but the squeezing has stopped. Guards march in. The three of us are hauled to our feet, cuffed and pushed out of the barracks before it's returned to darkness. I'm glad that I remember how to defend myself.

We are led up a guarded flight of stairs to a hallway that has benches running the full length on both sides. Each of us is pushed onto one to wait. Concrete, metal and gray are once again the main thematic elements. So far the only real difference between rooms that I have discerned is size, shape, and function. I just about have the above-ground part of the building mapped out in my mind.

I get my first real look at my attackers. They are both bigger and older than I am. Both have hair cut close to their scalps. Perhaps they are new here. They look scared but not as much as I would expect. They say nothing but are not worried about scowling at me. They fidget enough to make me think they aren't comfortable, so I guess that they don't spend a lot of time here. They aren't sure what to expect either. It feels like someone has put them up to this. I also get the sense that they aren't particularly bright. The looks they give me aren't filled with hate or loathing. In fact, they seem to be just as curious about me as I am about them.

Only the rustle of the public safety officers' uniform and the squeak of shifting leather gear holsters disturb the utter silence of the hall. A door opens and one at a time my attackers disappear with a guard and don't return. The minutes are ticking by but I have no real way to count them. I just know it is still very dark out, judging by the high round windows at each end of the hall. All I can do is wait for the pain that I know will be administered for my infraction. I try to relax; it will hurt less if I can manage to relax.

It is down to just me and two guards, the one who has control of me and the one from the upper hall. Can I take them? Should I make a break for it? No, I have to get the pain inducer out of me and I need to know the layout, guard schedules, and camera angles, let alone get out of the handcuffs. The door opens and it's my turn.

This room is completely unexpected. My mind reels with the enormity of the change. The walls are darkly paneled and nearly every one holds shelves of books. The carpet is dark red like drying blood and the furniture is all dark wood, perhaps walnut or mahogany. So much rich color after the nothingness amazes me. But as warm as the colors should feel, the room comes off as oppressive, dark, and heavy. I can almost feel the weight of it pressing in on me. Just as I swear the bookcases are starting to tilt inwards a sound breaks the spell.

It's a small sound — the squeak of a laptop being squared up on a desk. My eyes snap to it and focus in like a camera changing focal distance. The Inquisitor sits behind a desk that is meticulously, compulsively neat. Now, after all our time together, he has given me the biggest clue to his nature. This is his real office, not the one in the basement.

I'm surprised to find him dressed like always. Does the man never sleep? His nails and hair are perfect. It's like he has them professionally trimmed every week, I think suddenly. He stares at me, saying nothing. I become aware of a faint ticking. Ticking? Who has that kind of clock anymore? There is no way it's a bomb. He would never ruin an office as elegant and neat as this one. He works hard to keep it this way I realize.

"Leave us!"

"Sir?" one guard queries.

"I said leave us. Wait outside for further instructions."

"Yes, sir," the guards reply smartly with crisp salutes.

Before the door even clicks shut he begins talking, "You think I give myself away by allowing you to see this room, but it is you who does that. I know how your fingers itch to touch the books and electronics around you. You crave the knowledge. Your curiosity is insatiable. I admire you and yet you frustrate me. I must get into that mind of yours, but like a piece of fine art, I don't wish to ruin it, just examine it . . . for now. You have shown me you can think in a crisis and you have some fighting skills. I wonder how that slipped through all the testing we did when you were in school. Unless . . . No. No, I think it was a mistake or even chance. You shall be reprogrammed as public safety. That is what this latest test result has shown."

The silence stretches until I can no longer stand it. "Why?"

"Why? Why you ask? I find that interesting. I just compared you to art and you still ask why. There is no way I'm ever letting you near a computer again so engineering and science are out. I had to see what you could do. You shall become a weapon. You shall be a tool . . . no, an instrument. My instrument. It is amazing that you have survived. You show that my modified chip can work and can be used for training purposes. You have been part of a pilot project. You are a test subject, a pawn, less than human. And yet a small part of me still admires you. In some ways, you have proven to be tougher than many public safety officers. Yes, you shall become my special toy."

He pauses to look at me, but I find that my mouth has gone dry and I don't know what to say.

"You are tougher than I expected. It is unfortunate that my supervisor chose not to let me finish my earlier work with you. Just when we were starting to get somewhere. Someone thought you were being mistreated. They just didn't understand our relationship."

I fight to suppress a shudder.

"Just know that I've got my eye on you. I would suggest that you do exactly as I say, or one of your school friends would be hurt but then you've already taken care of that for me. Maybe your parents then? Oh wait, they are dead too. What do you care about? Don't worry, I'll figure it out. Nothing to say? Then you may go. Your new training regime starts bright and early." He taps his tablet to activate it and pretends to become engrossed in it. The door opens and the lone guard who had escorted me in comes to walk me out. At the door to the barracks, he uncuffs me and leaves.

I can't believe it — it had all been a test. I'm not really sure if I passed or failed. I walk through the barracks as quietly as I can, counting bunks as I go. Maybe everyone here doesn't hate me after all or maybe they just don't have the energy to dish out any hate and discontent. I carefully check my bunk for unexpected surprises and finding none, climb under my blanket.

I attempt once again to sleep, but tired as I am I just can't make it happen. I listen to the humans around me and make note of who gets up in the night and where they seem to go. I also discover that darkness has many shades.

00110001 11 00110001

00100000 01101001 01101110 00100000 01110100
01101000 01100101 01101001 01110010 00100000

Clothes are delivered for each prisoner just when the sky is a paler shade of black. I'm thankful that I was not assigned that particular task today or if I was, no one told me and I haven't been punished for not showing up. I had watched them leave an hour ago. In all that time my wristband, or prisoner tag as they call it, has signaled nothing. Just before sunrise, when the sky outside the windows is an interesting shade of blue, so pale that it's almost green, the lights come fully on and a guard blows a shrill whistle. Everyone gets up and begins dressing. Bunks are neatly pulled together and night clothes are dumped into the hampers that have once again been placed in the center of the aisle.

We stumble out into the courtyard, rubbing at our tired eyes. A guard leads morning stretches much like we'd done at school. Then another whistle blows and everyone begins to run. There is no air of panic so I start at a slow jog and drift to the back of the pack where the old and infirm reside. Here the stress level is oddly a bit higher.

The feeling fascinates me. Why are they so anxious? It isn't like they are in competition for first place. I'm not a runner, I have never been. I guess I only ran when chased or was required to and lately I've been malnourished, abused, confined, and I'd had no sleep last night. Ugh. At least it's still cool from the night. I know that later the heat will be ugly and they will never give me another day to just sit on a bunk.

When I slow too much, someone whispers a word of encouragement. When I stop to bend at the waist, hands on knees to catch my breath, an older gentleman takes my arm and pulls me on. He immediately lets go when the whine of a motorized cart behind us lets us know a guard is coming. I struggle to jog or at least keep up a decent walking speed. I keep wondering why anyone would bother trying to help me now. Where were they all last night?

I start paying attention to where I am. I will need the lay of the land if I'm going to get out of here. As much time as has gone by I have to assume that a rescue is not coming and therefore it's up to me. Next, I need a plan to deactivate my chip. Perhaps I'm being ridiculous, but I have hope and planning is a better activity than worrying. Thinking of Malorie makes me sad so I push that away. My mind wanders and lands on Bren. I hope he is happy and safe.

Distraction is apparently a good tool — I have survived my first run.

We line up outside the dining hall. One by one we are allowed to enter, wash our hands, pick up a tray and wait to be served our breakfast ration. I watch the other inmates for clues and examine the food choices. To me, it looks like the choice is pretty much take it or leave it, which isn't that different from my time in solitary except here I get to eat with a crowd. I don't trust anyone so I look for a place where I can put my back to a wall. There isn't any so I settle for a spot with as few people behind me as possible. It's not silent, but there is very little talking since most folks are hunkered down over their plates, shoveling in the chow before time is up. I don't want to sit too close to anyone nor invite any conversation. I put part of my attention on my food and tablemates, but most of it I put behind me so that no one can sneak up on me.

With as little talking as there is going on, I can sense when something changes. Silence pushes toward me like the prow of a ship cutting through the water. I suspect it's the guards by the way eyes shift and shoulders hunch. I wonder if I should turn and look or if that's a bad idea. Before I can decide, I'm grabbed from behind and my head and chest hit the table, sending my tray and the rest of the food on it flying. They don't even wait to see if I will cooperate. They hold me while they thrust my wrist into a device.

"18A294E?"

"Yes, sir," I gasp.

"Download her." Download me? What does that mean? My wristband beeps. One guard still holds my shoulder to the table, but I manage to turn my head. He pushes down a little harder on me but doesn't interfere with the head turn. The second guard pushes buttons on the device he holds around my wrist, covering the wristband. Several electronic sounds of various pitches grumble out of the machine.

"Schedule downloaded," the machine responds in its bored, flat voice. They release me and step back as if I'm a feral cat they're afraid will bite.

I turn slowly and look at them. "What does that mean?"

Both stand at the ready with their hands on their tool belts. "You'll figure it out."

I work hard at keeping my face blank.

"Clean up the mess you made, prisoner," the burly one commands.

I watch them go. Most people return to their breakfast, but two move close enough to help a little. One is the elderly man who assisted me this morning.

"I'm fine," I grumble under my breath. I don't want to owe anyone anything I can't repay.

"Most folks just say, 'thank you'." That was not the voice of the elderly gentleman so it must be the other.

"Thank you," I mutter and then look up into the most fantastic blue-green eyes I've ever seen. The rest of her face nearly vanishes, I'm so amazed by her beautiful eyes.

"We're not all bad, evil, or mean. Just so you know. They just gave you your personal schedule. I suggest you follow it closely." She quickly picks up her tray and disappears into the crowd making its way out of the cafeteria.

My wrist device beeps. I glance at it and for the first time, something is on the display. It's a code C-PF-103-112, but I don't know what it means. I turn in my tray and observe where people go. I watch some folks head to the kitchen and some to a building marked laundry. I realize it has a number on it I can see through the window. I smile to myself. I glance at my prisoner tag again. A bunch of people are headed down the wide hall past the kitchen. I quickly step outside and look at the building and then again at my wrist device. 103, the same numbers are on both the building and my wristband. On the readout, they are followed by a dash and three more digits. I think I have my floor and room number. I follow the crowd down the wide hall and see numbers next to doors. It doesn't take long for me to find 12, my assigned room. My wristband emits a different sound when I enter. I have found my classroom.

I get a better look at the woman who helped me with my tray. She is taller than me, slender and fit. I want to be her when I grow up if I live that long. She isn't glamorous but there is something about her. She moves like a dancer with a grace that leaves me feeling both jealous and wanting to be her friend, but I don't know if I can trust her, so I watch instead and think about what she said to me in the dining hall.

The next thing I notice is the smell in the room — distinct and almost bitter. It takes me a little while to identify it — it must be the tang of sweat. The floor of the room is covered in pads, as are the walls. The only furniture in the room is racks of free weights. An armed guard stands in the corner looking bored. The instructor is the biggest, scariest public safety officer I've seen yet, and that's saying something. His head is shaved bald and he sports a black goatee and mustache flecked with gray. He stands with his feet apart and his hands are clasped behind his back. I think he might be able to stop my heart with just a look. Over his shoulder, showing on the wall is a physical fitness plan. Looking at the ceiling I can see a document camera has been released from a movable panel.

I feel my heart squeeze when he finally glances my way with his cold gray eyes. Although he had glanced at me, he begins class as if I'm not even there and he seems to expect me to know what is going on. I follow the lady with the fantastic eyes and try to keep to the back of the room and out of his sight. Some of the students actually want his attention and I plan to use that to my advantage. We begin with stretches. This I can handle. I had begun doing them on my own anyway. It's when we start lifting the free weights that I quickly get into trouble.

This is something that I've never done before. I'm thankful for the little bit of exercise that I started doing on my own, but the weights feel cold and alien in my hands. My arms shake with the effort of holding them steady. My arms also hold an interesting burn that I am not used to. It reminds me of the burn in my legs when I ran up the stairs to the roof at school.

In time, our wristbands beep in unison and students quickly clear the room. Judging by the number on my watch I should be right next door. Most students walk out of class without looking at their bands so I guess there must be a routine to what we do. I follow the main group headed next door. They walk in, in front of me, but I run into an invisible force shield. Someone snickers. I look at my wristband and then at the number next to the door. I am in the wrong place.

I head down the hall in the opposite direction and find my assigned room. This one is much like the first. The smell is the same, the mats are the same and the armed guard in the corner is the same. The exceptions are that the mats are blue instead of red and there are no weights. This instructor is long, lean, dark haired and dark skinned; when he speaks the whiteness of his teeth flash in comparison. His voice is low and well-modulated. He is scary in a whole other way. Looking into his eyes I sense that he is like a black leopard, full from a meal, but you never know when his appetite may change.

"I see we have a new student. Half of you will work defense, half offense. Kate, you get the new girl. Try not to bloody her up too badly. Partner up and ready to go in ten, nine, eight . . ." Everyone moves quickly. Amazing Eyes stands before me.

"Seven, six," the instructor continues.

Amazing Eyes, I mean Kate, pushes my body into position.

"Five, four, three."

She takes a defensive position.

"Two, one."

Kate throws a punch at my shoulder. It isn't hard, but it knocks me to the side. The instructor comes and stands right behind me. "Defend yourself, newbie."

I step forward toward Kate. I don't want to be anywhere near him. With the guards, it is best to just curl into a ball and take it until the beating stops. This is different, I need to think like the game. How did I behave under the city? I bring my arms up in front of my body, bent at the elbows and close to me.

"Go!" the instructor barks from behind me.

Kate moves in again. This time, as her fist moves toward me, I try to deflect it to the side. I am slow and she hits me again. The pain I can take, I've lived through plenty. Hands back up, I am ready again. Our instructor just watches and then finally moves off. He does not offer any advice. Kate begins to mumble tips to me when the instructor is out of earshot. I can feel that she is holding back. I'm afraid he will notice. I work hard at keeping my guard up, but I can feel my arms burning and my body wilting from the exertion.

He finally calls a halt and I fall gratefully to the mat with many others in the class. He picks a volunteer and does a few demonstrations. Then he asks us to practice. He leaves me with Kate and I am incredibly thankful despite the bruising that is going to be covering most of my upper body. With anyone else, it would be much worse.

When my wristband finally beeps, signaling the end of class, I want to weep with relief. I am stiff and sore, hungry and incredibly tired. I stumble to my next class wondering how I will survive any more exercise.

I am greeted by a room done all in gray, their favorite color, and rows of desks. Although the chairs look to be incredibly hard and uncomfortable the thought of sitting down feels like a gift. After running this morning it was difficult to get my body to cooperate with the demands of weightlifting and fighting, so that now that I'm in a lecture on weapons, I doze off despite the armed guard standing in the corner as usual.

I wake up as I'm thrown from my chair. A black boot crashes

down on my chest. "No sleeping in class!" the instructor yells.

It must be my lucky day. My favorite head guard from solitary, I think sarcastically. I'd swear he wasn't the one who was in the room earlier.

"You get a promotion?" I ask before I can stop myself.

Smack. My cheek stings sharply where he's struck me. "No backtalk. I thought we'd trained you better than that, but it doesn't matter. You will be my special reform project from now on. I will dedicate my life to rebuilding you. How long do you think it will take until you are begging me to do whatever I want?"

I know better than to answer. He lifts his boot and I start to move, but he stomps back down knocking my head into the floor and the air from my lungs. I lay stunned for a moment aware enough to see the malicious gleam in his eye and the slow reptilian smile spread over his thin lips.

He moves away and nods to the instructor who blinks twice before he continues his lecture. I roll to my hands and knees, right my chair, and drag myself back onto it. A couple of students send me a sad look and then put their attention back on the instructor and so do I. The hairs on the back of my neck tell me that I am being carefully watched. The way things are slightly out of focus tells me that I probably have a concussion and the way my side hurts tells me I might have a cracked rib. As if I wasn't handicapped enough already.

It's an enormous relief when lunch comes. I try to stay away from everyone hiding myself among the other prisoners. I force the food into my stomach which seems to be in a state of revolt and drink as much water as I can hold. The readout on my wrist-band tells me that it's time to show up at workforce. At least it gives me a location, south of the main structure. I walk to the south side of the building hoping for the best. I don't think I can handle another beating today.

Instead, another kind of cruelty greets me. I walk up to the small group of inmates. A guard grabs my wrist roughly and reads my band. He runs his scanner over it, it beeps and he nods once — my attendance is logged. Judging by where we are standing, it looks like today's job is to weed the gardens and pick the ripe produce. The bite of pungent plant and soil tickles my nose. I look over the workbench and rack of tools with a sigh. No one tells me what to do; I must observe everyone for clues and dig out of my brain everything I've ever learned about vegetables and fruit. I decide to grab a hoe like the person in front of me, but the guard waves me off and shoves an old nasty basket into my hands instead. It's big enough that I can just touch my fingers if I ringed the top with my arms. I doubt I'll be able to carry it when it is full.

Another guard grabs my arm while I'm trying to figure out what to do and where to start. "No eating. Pick only what's ripe and if you damage anything you will pay for it."

Pay for it? With what? I wonder. I'm afraid to ask any questions and I'm given no other tools so I'm not meant to pick some things. I will be working with my hands. That leaves tomatoes, green beans, squash, and berries. Berries would be ruined in the bottom of this basket so I headed for the squash behind another woman whose dark hair is pulled back into a sloppy bun. She has a piece of cotton fabric twisted around her head like a headband. Her tank top and canvas capris look much better for this type of work than my cinch pants and t-shirt.

I watch her pick two squash, with a quick twist and snap away from the vine and settle into the other side of the row from where she squats. Initially, the warmth of the sun feels good on my sore muscles, but in no time, I'm sweating. My t-shirt sticks to me, making me feel even hotter. The sun that was at first welcome begins to feel mean as it beats down on my aching head. I notice some of the prisoners have gloves. They would be hot, but they would protect my hands. I've got to figure out how to get some.

We are given a brief water break and I'm so thankful it's in the shade, I almost cry. When we return to finish our shift the melting heat of the sun pours over my head and shoulders. They'd kept me buried underground and now they are going to burn me out here. As I fill another basket with squash, hot as I am, I do my best to keep my skin covered by my clothing. I have to assume that having us in the garden would have to be nothing less than punishment at this time of day. If I were in charge I would assign this task to early morning or evening crews.

My clothes are wet with sweat, my hair hangs in snarly, damp lumps and I feel a distinct urge to throw up. I wipe the sweat from my forehead to keep it from running into my eyes and look to the trees just across the way. I barely noticed during our early morning run, but they aren't what I'm used to. The needles are longer, stiffer, and sharp. The cones are woodier, the sap more prominent on the strange bark, glowing in drops of amber. It makes me think of drizzled honey. Then there is the smell . . . bitter, dusty and sharp, biting at my nose. Perhaps it's because it's so much drier here. It's as if things are disintegrating in the heat and dryness. I miss the mossy dampness where decay happens by things rotting away, creating a rich loamy smell.

I'm extremely happy when my prisoner tag beeps until I see the readout. Next, I get to clean the bathrooms. I briefly wonder if being in solitary and getting beatings is better than this new form of torture but I want to live and my chances of escape are better out here, so I grit my teeth. I'm not even given a mop which I could use as a weapon and certainly no chemicals. I get to scrub the floors by hand with rags and soapy water. On the bright side, it cleans the dirt from under my nails. On the downside, by the time I'm done my hands are chapped and sore.

Apparently, scrubbing floors was not to be the end of my humiliation today. When I get to the dorms I find my footlocker has been dumped out and the meager contents spread around and walked on. Not one prisoner will make eye contact. I bite the inside of my lip, my eyes burn, and a quiver zigzags through my knees. I'm so upset about the trunk that I don't notice the guard right behind me until it's too late. "Clean it up," he snarls, shoving me between my shoulder blades. I pick up as fast as I can, doing a quick mental inventory. Nothing seems to be missing or damaged beyond being dirty. I just want to be alone, but the guard watches until every bit is neat and tidy. When my day finally ends my uncomfortable bunk feels like heaven and I'm asleep before the lights go out.

12

01100001 01110100 01110100 01101001 01110100
01110101 01100100 01100101 00100000 01110100
01101111 01110111 01100001 01110010 01100100

The days creep by, ever the same; the only change is the weather. Some days are hotter than others, but it's always nastiest in the afternoons when the cloying pungent odor rolls off the pines and the heat makes everything sticky and dusty. Each night there are long lines at the showers. It seems that everyone wants to cool off and get the day's stink and dirt off of them.

I know time is moving past just by watching the fruits and vegetables. Nothing new comes on, but some begin to disappear. All the beets were pulled and the blueberries and blackberries have run out of fruit. It's getting cooler at night. Some of the wealthier inmates are starting to pull out jackets and warmer blankets. No one has offered me any pay yet, but I keep observing. I've seen some prisoners trading with each other and even a guard or two but what do I have that anyone would want?

I am quickly assimilating the rules and bell schedule. The one thing I have trouble accepting is the random dumping of my footlocker. Nothing is ever taken. I have nothing anyone would want but I'm punished if I don't clean it up quickly. I don't seem to be the only victim.

Every night I pray for an escape opportunity or for Bren to come save me. He has probably been captured as well and is imprisoned elsewhere or he may even be dead, but hope feels better than despair, so I keep my head down and press on. Yet each night when I close my eyes, I see him. It is my mental escape if not a real one. I wonder if I am weak because I have come to look forward to it. I relive each touch, each word, each moment. He has helped me in an unexpected way. When I close my eyes at night, I can almost feel his touch and what it was like to run my fingers over his soft warm skin. I remember his scent, the way he looked at me and that one last beautiful smile; a photograph stamped forever in my mind. He will always be my escape even if he isn't really here and even if I never leave. I would much rather think of him than . . . *NO, stop. Just think of Bren.* The nightmares will come soon enough — they always do and not just for me. I'm not the only one who screams at night.

Now that I am not as exhausted each night from my daily exertions, I'm finding it difficult to sleep again. I keep a low profile and stay out of the way of anyone in a black uniform. I remember all the rules of the dorms, but not everyone follows them. The lucky ones don't have my special hardware installed for when they misbehave. Some only lose a privilege, but I get to be part of the pilot program. Lucky me. The soft grunting and rhythmic squeak of the bunk next to mine and below me tell me my neighbor is going to be in big trouble if she gets caught. I'm learning that it depends on who you get caught by — some will warn you, some will beat you and some will trade something for their silence. I have seen both male and female prisoners make trades with their personal belongings or sex. It makes me sick but I've been able to avoid it so far. I'd give up every one of my meager possessions before I let one of the guards touch me. I can't imagine willingly offering myself.

Maybe I'm a fool, but I believe that love is real and that there is someone out there for everyone — no exceptions — and that what you find here isn't love. I also believe that things don't always come to us in the way we expect, but we need to make the most of every opportunity. My dreams are my opportunity to escape what my reality has become. They still cannot control them or my thoughts. I just can't let my sharp tongue get me into trouble. I am so thankful that my mind is safe.

I find it interesting that both the guards and the prisoners appear to be of all ages though the prisoners have a wider age span. I am one of the youngest, but there are a couple of others still in their teens. It's the old ones that fascinate me most. When I can, I get them to whisper stories about what things were like when they grew up. In my mind, I begin compiling some local urban legends and history.

I continue to watch Kate and interact with her some. It is her care and kindness to others that I appreciate the most. Today it looks like she has another new recruit under her wing.

This time, it is a young boy. Judging by the over-large hands, feet, and ears he must be about twelve or maybe thirteen. He is incredibly skinny and I find myself worrying about whether or not he will be able to run with us or even survive here. Where could he have come from and why would someone so young be here? He is by far the youngest prisoner here.

My mind turns to more urgent needs. I am missing something. How are the prisoners getting extra things? Some have locks for their footlockers. If I had one, I bet my locker wouldn't get dumped out as often. I need to be more proactive. Who do I trust enough to ask? Perhaps Kate? She is nice to that boy. I experiment with following a few prisoners when the population is on the move but I don't find anything useful, so I go back to watching Kate and the boy.

The hint of bite in the air this morning makes me worry about the coming winter. Kate has been generous with her knowledge, giving me a bit at a time in the snatches of conversation we can get away with. I finally bite the bullet and pull her aside when it's time to turn in our trays and head for class. "I need to prepare for winter."

"You need to ask for extra work." I'm not sure what she means, but the guard's eyes are on us so we must stop. I still don't completely trust her, but then I don't think she trusts me either. Everyone is wary here and dances around each other like they are taming a dangerous wild animal. I wonder if that is what we are becoming.

In personal fitness, Kate touches my hand when we both reach for a weight. She is not careless so I know she is telling me something. I glance at the instructor and guard who are busy talking to each other and then look at her.

"You'll need a coat. You have to earn it and you're running out of time," Kate whispers quickly. I make eye contact to let her know I am listening. "You have to sign up for an extra work detail. They won't tell you that, but it's what you have to do."

"How?" I whisper back.

"Go to the supply desk and ask the officer there for extra work. They'll give you the worst of it first. Just so you know. You can also trade, but no one will be fair with you in the beginning so watch people and figure out what they are dying for and trade up for that. Someone who's hungry enough will do almost anything for food. Stock up in the offseason for trade in season. Earn a lock for your foot locker first so that you have a place to keep your stash." The guard looks our way and Kate melts into the crowd. I never even got to say thanks. I guess if it all works out I can give her a gift.

Why didn't I think to check the supply desk? I guess I was too scared to look there and risk getting caught. I associated it with solitary. I see no reason for Kate to lie to me about this. She would have nothing to gain by leading me astray and she is right about the lock. Theft is a serious crime here but so is hoarding so no one says much when extra items go missing. The guards are known to break in and appropriate our belongings but mostly they don't bother unless a prisoner gives them cause. I have nothing of value so they have only dumped out my stuff a few times. I never know why they do it. I just figure it is part of my conditioning. I know I'm still watched pretty closely, but enough new people have come in that I can feel the oppressive stares and scrutinization beginning to lessen. I have not caused any more obvious trouble either so I become less interesting by the day.

I let a day go by watching everyone carefully and mulling over Kate's words. On our morning run, I decide that today is the day. Instead of going in for breakfast, I head to the supply desk. I wait my turn and eavesdrop on all the conversations happening in front of me. The guard manning the desk looks mildly surprised to see me when I approach.

"Whadda you want?"

"I would like an extra work detail."

"Let me see your band." I tentatively extend my wrist. He looks at the readout on his tablet and appears confused. "Well, okay, I guess. You know anything about electricity?"

"Yes," I lie. Well okay, I knew a little, but mainly I know about how it pertains to computers.

"We got an emergency. Report to Lieutenant Brenton in five minutes."

"Who?" I ask wondering how I will find someone I've never heard of in that short time. The guard hits some spots on his tablet and turns it around to show me a picture of a young public safety officer with bright blue eyes and sandy blond, buzz cut hair.

"You'll find him at the main stairway."

"What about my class?"

"Do you want to work or not?"

I nod and rush into the cafeteria to see if there is any chow I can grab on the fly. I take a banana, hard-boiled egg, and a piece of bread. I munch as I do a fast walk to the stairs. I see officer Brenton at the bottom of the flight and he really does look more approachable than most. I take a deep breath and go stand in front of him and off to the side as I've been trained to do.

"What?" he asks, but it sounds more bored than snarly.

"I'm here to help the electrician," I say boldly like I do this all the time.

"Band?"

I obediently hold up my wrist. He swipes his handheld device over it and checks the readout.

"Wait here."

In less than a minute a small man in blue coveralls, a massive tool belt and a bucket of tools comes in the front doors. My first impression is that I'm looking at the characterization of a mole. He has thick heavy glasses perched on his narrow nose and they look like they may slide off at any moment. It's odd that he wears glasses. You hardly ever see them anymore. Perhaps he has an eye condition that cannot be corrected by the surgery they usually do.

We head up the stairs and I pray this electrical problem will get me near some computers so that I can find out about my chip. If nothing else I might get to see another part of the building. I've only been up here the night I thought I was in trouble and found out I was being tested again. I think I can count on the fingers of one hand the times I've seen prisoners go up these stairs.

Part of me is full of dread as I imagine that this is another test or trick to get me into trouble. They can't possibly imagine that I will be able to retain every bit of knowledge I gain from this little excursion, but I'm not sure how much the Inquisitor has pulled out of my brain. Lately, he seems to have lost all interest. I hope he has too many others to torture and it's not that he has me all figured out.

I had not appreciated how old the building is until now. We have climbed up into the attic and I can see wires running everywhere like crazy oversized spaghetti thrown from a pan. The dirty pink insulation tickles my nose and makes me itch. The old electrician shows me where to put my feet and gives me heavy bags to carry but says little. Even I can tell that they have overloaded their circuits. What a mess.

A piece of plywood is positioned and a chair has been added for a guard to sit and observe us. Another waits at the foot of the ladder. The electrician has to show me which tool is which but he appears to be pleased that he only has to tell me once. We keep our voices to a low murmur and the guard's body language tells me that he is not happy to be here and that he is bored. He pretends to ignore us and plays with his rifle and knife. He spends his time cleaning the former and sharpening the latter.

"Hand me the wire cutters." I do so without a word. "I used to wear orange you know."

"I guessed," I reply softly.

"Name's Marvin." He looks up and I smile at him. "Thought about engineering but I like to work with my hands," he adds as he preps the wire. "We're gonna split this here junction box and rewire. It has too much load and keeps tripping the circuit breaker. You do as I say now, hear?"

"Yes, Marvin."

"God forbid the officers and government officials should be without AC or computers, aye?"

I smile. I like this old guy. "It would be a tragedy."

It's cramped and miserable up here in the attic and it's quickly heating up. I can't imagine how horrible it would be up here in full on summer. I try to distract my physical discomfort by focusing on Marvin's stories as we work. My stomach growls and I know we've missed lunch. I'm about dizzy from dehydration when we finally finish. I'm half worried about missing class but they gave me the job so it must be okay, right?

I drop through the opening and can immediately feel the temperature difference. We stagger to the dining hall and grab our share of grub. By the look of things, we've about missed dinner too. I need to remind myself to eat and drink slowly so that it doesn't all come back up.

The water hits the back of my parched throat and I can feel its coolness flow to all parts of my body. Even my eyes water a bit in response. I know it's a reaction of my nervous system and my imagination, but it is so weird to feel that zing of cold move through me. I almost feel like my body is coming back alive.

Apparently someone new had been added while we were working. When it is her turn to be served, the cook looks at her and his face changes. Ugliness shows through his otherwise neutral façade and color creeps up his sweaty neck, flooding his cheeks. I am fascinated and can't tear my eyes away.

"Your share," he sneers flipping the serving spoon over so

that only a few grains of rice cling to it and fewer hit her tray.

She looks for a moment at those few lonely grains and then up into the cook's eyes. "Thank you for your generosity and may your kindness be revisited upon you."

Okay, it sounds a little goofy like she is a walking, talking fortune cookie, but it still has an interesting effect that even I feel. The cook swallows visibly as sweat pops out on his brow. Then he laughs and serves the next person in line. The girl never looks back as she walks away, but I can still feel her power. I lose sight of her as she moves down the line, but I see her again sitting alone as if the whole room is afraid to get too close.

I stand up as a group passes our table, walk over and set my tray by her. I'm curious. If she is new, how did the cook know her?

"For your own good, go away," she says so softly no one else can possibly hear.

"I apologize for intruding," I reply smoothly as I pick up her tray instead of mine.

Her hand snakes out and touches mine. "I appreciate what you are trying to do, but don't do it again. They will catch on and punish you."

She lets me go and I move away. I can do without a meal and if I have been kind, she will owe me. It's how it works here. I notice the prisoners' dining hall is extra quiet today. A few people stare at the new girl, a few at me and the rest are hunkered down over their food like usual. I will pay for my defiance, but so what? I've always hated unfairness, and the punishment, if they catch me, is just a lost meal. I can live with that.

I quickly finish what little food is on her tray, turn it in and go back to the supply counter to collect my voucher for the work on the electrical system. My *favorite* guard is leaning against the wall with a mean smile plastered on his thin lips. His dead eyes drill into me, his stance is wide, his beefy arms crossed and his hands fisted. Something is definitely up. I slide my gaze from him to the guard behind the counter who is trying to stare at me with a completely blank look on his face. He fails. Maybe he needs lessons from the captain here, who I am trying to keep in my peripheral vision so I can see him coming.

"May I have my vouch —"

"What voucher?" the guard behind the counter interrupts like he can't wait to get the words out.

"May I please have the voucher for my electrical work today?"

The old electrician walks up as I am speaking. "Evening, boys. Elise."

"Marvin," they return. He is handed his voucher without even asking for it. He smiles and wanders off.

I stand waiting. The guards look like they are holding back a good laugh.

"I was Marvin's apprentice today," I prod.

"Sorry. No voucher for you." Funny, he doesn't sound a bit sorry.

"I did the work. I get a voucher." The man I think of as "the Captain" roughly takes my arm and spins me to face him.

"You don't get a voucher." He speaks harshly, inches from my face, his spittle landing on my nose and cheeks. "You worked longer than the allotted time. Deduct. You missed class. Deduct. You traded trays with the new girl. Deduct. About now, I figure you owe us. How are you going to pay?"

I stare at him with my mouth open in shock. Fear and disappointment go to war within me.

"Look at you, acting all surprised and stuff. How about this, I've been needing a sparring partner. Today's your lucky day. I want to see how you brought my friends down in the woods. Let's go."

He hoists my shoulder into an uncomfortable position and yanks me down the hall to the sparring room. It strikes me as strange every time I walk in here how much it's like the dance studio that the hospitality folks used back at school. There are no bars or mirrors here, just wood floor and plain walls. And the blue mats of course. Today they are stacked off to the side. Sometimes there are racks of weapons but not today, I notice as I'm thrown across the floor's shiny surface.

"Get up!"

I scramble to my feet and face the Captain. He rushes me, but I turn at the last moment and he stumbles past. He turns with a sneer on his face and comes at me again. He has both height and weight on me. I will have to be quick. He tries to tackle me, but I roll out of the way. This time, he smiles. Oh crap, he's moved me into a corner. He charges and I change my strategy. I run toward him, put a foot into his mid-section and my hands on his shoulders to flip myself over his head. It doesn't go as I imagined and I land badly. Pain shoots through my ankle. I hope it isn't serious. I limp a little as he comes around and smiles bigger.

Again he charges me. This time, I don't try to run, I focus on defense. He throws a punch and I block. Over and over he tries to hit me. My arms are killing me from both being exhausted and bruising. I know my form is horrible and that I'm dropping my guard. It feels like he has boundless energy. He is landing more hits than I'm blocking. I get in a good one to his jaw with my elbow, but it barely fazes him and I miss the upper cut coming at mine. I feel my body fly backward . . .

I wake up on my bunk. It's dark and the barracks are quiet. I realize I'm not alone and scoot backward so fast I almost fall off.

"I told you not to help me. I knew you'd pay a price. You're going to be a bigger project than I thought."

"Who are you?"

"Don't worry about that now. Watch who you trust. Some people you think you can trust, are not who they appear to be."

"What?" I ask, but it's too late. She has swung down and is gone. It is too dark to see where she went. At the moment I'm not sure I care. My head hurts. I feel a lump on the back and figure it's where it smacked the floor. Ugh. My jaw is so sore, I can barely stand to touch it.

I am still awake when the first hint of lightness hits the windows. I ease my aching body out of the bunk and limp to the bathroom. If my blood spattered clothes are any indication and with the way I feel, I must have taken a fantastic beating. I'm pretty sure I look as amazing as I feel. I decide on a hot shower before anyone else is up. I attempt to stretch and loosen my knotted muscles. A sound alerts me. I turn off the water and grab my towel.

"Don't get dressed on my account. I was just admiring my handiwork."

"What do you want?" I half snarl, not wanting to be too disrespectful, but I can't shut it all off.

"'What do you want, sir,'" The Captain corrects me. I just look at him. He waits. I wait. Finally, he speaks. "Do I need to beat you again?"

"No, sir," I say with as little emotion as I can manage.

Having made his point, he lifts himself from the doorframe, turns and walks back through it. I had always had a thing about hurting people, but I'm pretty sure that I can hurt him . . . a lot . . . and not feel a bit guilty. I dress quickly, run a comb through my hair and head back to my bunk to do some more quiet stretches. My bed has been made and my work voucher from the electrical job is on the end of it with a single grain of rice. I look around, but no one is moving. The girl with the rice has more than returned my small favor. I don't know her name or what bunk is hers, but she knows me it seems.

Today I will stay low, quiet, and out of sight. I will only take what is given to me and volunteer for nothing. The usual routine begins and I try to stay in the middle of whichever crowd I find myself in. Unfortunately, it gives me time to think. I try to count the days that I have been incarcerated, but I'm not allowed to have anything to write with and if we are caught damaging property we get double chores. I'm not even allowed to have a calendar, but they have made a few mistakes. I can see outside and I know the days are getting shorter. They have me in the garden long enough to watch the tomatoes die in a frost and the other plants wither. This morning they upgraded my wrist device so that I can see my entire daily schedule. All the data in my head swirls and coalesces into patterns telling me it has to be moving well into October. It makes me want to cry to think I have lost so much, but I won't let myself.

Being here has done one thing for me — it has made me appreciate school. I used to feel like I was tossed around and had no choices, but now that I truly have none. I look back on school with a whole new attitude and longing, and wonder again why they keep me alive. If I've caused so much trouble, why not just pull the trigger. I want to live but I hate it here. The stress is making me crazy — that and the lack of frogs. When I was at school, I could hear a chorus of frogs every night. It's peaceful somehow, the sound of frogs, but now the night sounds different. It is empty and mournful without my frogs. Only the pines whisper and I don't think I like what they're saying.

13

A week goes by and I do not volunteer for any extra work. I use every spare moment to watch everything and heal. Most of my attention is on one thing, or person. I still think of her as the girl with the rice. She has skills that I both admire and find a bit scary. I'm fascinated by her. I know deep in my soul that I need to become more like her. She doesn't talk to many people and she appears to carefully select the ones she does deign to speak with. She also spends a lot of time observing and I can't help but think that she is recording each bit of it in her brain. She just seems so precise and purposeful about everything she does. Because of her, I now find myself watching the prison population and guards even more carefully. Something is going on. It's like seeing a hidden code for the first time and not being able to quite make it out, but I will.

More and more patterns begin to appear where I had seen none. Sometimes the prisoners are jostled at unexpected times, like for an early morning run, a shortened or lengthened class, or an unusual job cycle, but there is a pattern in that too, I discover.

The guard shifts finally become clear to me as I learn their faces and demeanors. They are on ten hour staggered shifts. In addition to the two personnel stationed in each of four watch-towers, there is one who patrols the top of the compound, one at the gate and one on ground patrol at the back. There are also twenty guards on duty at all times to handle the inmates. At full capacity that would be about one hundred four prisoners in our wing, but not all the bunks are in use. Right now we are at eighty-eight. The other wing has to be about the same. Then there are the public safety officers who teach our classes, but they don't run a full school here. Eventually, I will puzzle it all out.

I have also discovered that about the time someone new comes in, someone tends to disappear. It pays to be useful and not make a nuisance of yourself. It also isn't wise to get too sick. There was an old man who went to the infirmary with pneumonia and never came back. Dying of something like pneumonia just doesn't happen anymore, so I wonder, was he put down? People with useful skills seem to have better luck sticking around, but why most are here is a mystery. I swear it looks like some people are kept here only because their skills are needed. There is a lady with gray buzz cut hair who appears to be some kind of a handyman; Kate, the nurse who works exclusively in the infirmary, and then there is Marvin, and I know there are others. They are the strange few who barely even seem like prisoners anymore and get lots of special privileges.

I am amazed that the boy is still with us. I haven't gotten to talk to him but I enjoy his ready smile and quick humor. Kate is still watching out for all the underdogs but has taken a special interest in him. I've seen her slip him some of her food when I catch sight of them at meal times. He has charmed me enough that I have slipped him a roll now and then and I'm not the only one. Several people have given him gifts of their extra whatnots. I figure it must be the way he brings a bit of sunshine into whatever room he's in.

My thoughts turn to the Inquisitor, Bartholomew. He seems to make up his own rules and the man I now assume is his boss only comes in once every few months. He is the only person I ever see leave. There is a story between those two I'm certain.

Since I can't figure that one out yet, I think about the girl with the rice and the cook. He knew her from somewhere. Did they work together or was she imprisoned before? My mind then shifts to how things work in the kitchen and beyond to the prison in general. We have two cooks and inmates fill in the rest of the slots. Prisoners cook, clean, do laundry and repairs, and groundskeeping. Some jobs are more popular than others. They make all of us run, but classes seem like they are varied among us and some inmates appear to only work. Thinking about the prison population makes me realize that I have noticed something else, sometimes prisoners disappear but I have never actually seen them leave. There has to be another entrance because when officials come, they enter through the front gate in a big production complete with a shiny black limo with flags mounted to the front corners. New prisoners also come through that gate, though that "show" is completely different. It has to all be calculated, but what are they trying to teach me?

My mind circles back to Kate, having hit a temporary dead-end. I have accounted for most of her movements. She appears to work a ten-hour shift in medical. I usually see her at meal times and she has a bunk near the front of the dorms which I assume is so she can be easily retrieved in the middle of the night if the need arises. I think she takes the physical fitness class to stay in shape and relieve stress. She doesn't talk about it, not that we have much time to talk, but I see the worry lines forming between her eyebrows and they always are less prominent after class.

They say that people graduate to new jobs on the outside, but I haven't seen it. It looks like most are retrained here as public safety or maintenance. A select few, like Kate, get to work in the infirmary. Starting this week, Bartholomew, *he'd stroke if he knew I called him that even in my head*, will have me meet with the prisoner assigned to repair and maintain the computers. I will be allowed to touch nothing, only coach, but it sounds to me like my skills are so far superior it will be laughable.

Wait a minute, I have something else to figure out. I have never seen supplies or equipment come in and no one talks about it. They appear as if by magic, so they either come in while we are asleep or they come in underground.

After breakfast today, I am dismissed from regular classes and sent to meet with the computer guy. I go to the stairs and check in with the public safety officer assigned there. He sends me up. The guard in the upstairs hallway leads me into a room where a small sweaty man is literally and figuratively wringing his hands over a computer with nothing but a repeating blip flashing in one corner of the screen.

"Are you the one who's going to help me?" Even his tone sounds worried.

"Turn it off."

"I already tried that and it didn't work."

"Do it again," I say.

He argues with me every step of the way, but it's no skin off my nose—I don't want to help them anyway. We get that computer running and move on to the next one. I let him argue. I keep my voice calm. He is wasting time and I'm glad. It gives me more time to figure him out and determine if I can trick him into revealing any information. I would send a message out, but I have no one to send it to. Maybe I could send something to the cloud for when I get out, but I'll have to hide and encrypt it really well.

They keep us at it for a week, all day every day. Even now, I hold back. I give the minimum of tech support and sometimes I play dumb to cause them frustration. I don't want them to know what all I can do and I don't believe they realize that just by seeing their setup and knowing bits about their system, I can guess at the rest.

I go to bed, my mind in a swirl, but I don't forget to check my bunk like always. Most inmates lack the initiative to harass anyone else, but there are a few bullies, troublemakers and friends of the guards to be wary of. Some days I also wonder if there are also plants to spy on us, but who would choose that kind of life? What cause is worthy enough to put up with being treated this way? Perhaps someone they love is threatened or perhaps the rewards cannot be turned down. My thoughts spin as I rub my eyes and then run my hands over my bedding. I feel thankful that no one has dumped out my footlocker for quite a while.

Tonight there is an unexpected lump. It's slight, but I can see it when I really look. I cautiously move my blanket, not sure what to expect, finding fingerless gloves . . . with a single grain of rice. I ease myself back off my bunk and look around. I still don't know where she sleeps. I scan side to side as I make my way back to the latrines.

It almost startles me when I see her brushing her teeth. I haven't seen her all week. Hardly anyone is left in here. I slide by her and whisper. "Thanks," as I set the only extra item I have on the far edge of my sink. It's just some dental floss, but I want her to know her gift is appreciated and I'm still saving for a coat, though my work this week really helped. I can certainly earn more floss before I run out. I proceed to wash my face and then leave like the floss was never mine. She doesn't look at me or say a word.

I check my bed once more, crawl in and think again about her and the cook. What is their story? She isn't allowed any-where near the kitchens and I find that interesting. Tomorrow it is my turn to help there and I plan to do a little spying of my own. I try to stay with that train of thought but soon my mind drifts to Bren. I imagine him free and happy. It's how I want to remember him.

Morning comes much too early. Fear is the only thing that gets me off my bunk and out into the crisp, dark morning. My day drags on and I fantasize about coffee and then about the outside world. I've been so busy analyzing how this place works that I've barely thought about anything outside except for Bren. I pretend he has a happy life out there and that one day I will be able to share it. I do not make the mistake of falling asleep in class anymore even if I have to pinch myself to stay awake. At least I can sit here and I usually view it as a kind of rest, but today my mind is already on the kitchen.

I can hardly wait for the buzzer to sound, signaling the end of class and then I'm off to kitchen duty. When it does finally buzz, I have to remind myself to act calm and not run for the kitchen as I would like.

A guard checks me in. As I look around, I can't help but take in the wonderful array of weapons. What I would give for one of those knives, but we pass through a metal detector and the cook has no ceramic blades so we can't steal them.

The assistant cook gives me and another inmate some basic instruction and then turns us loose. I go and wash my hands as instructed and put on an apron. I quickly learn the head cook loves to whine and complain. To him we are nothing; he ignores our existence and only speaks to his assistant and the guard, who, I'm pretty sure could care less by his expression. Unless he's barking a command, he yammers nonstop. I'm forced to listen so I won't miss one of his instructions.

At least I learn a lot just by eavesdropping. It takes all week, but eventually he lets slip that he was stuck here because he was a hospitality dropout. He also talks about a girl he recognized that he worked with in the kitchens in another institution. She had made her escape one night by stabbing him; he has the scar to prove it. His fat, white, hairy belly is now seared onto the back of my eyeballs. He said he was relieved when she had been recaptured, but sending her here? What an atrocity! I laugh in my mind but keep my face blank and let him ramble on as I peel what had to be my one millionth potato of the week.

My luck with flying under the radar holds out for two more weeks and then the moment I've been dreading most arrives. At breakfast, I receive a summons. I almost throw up the food I have just eaten and there is no way I can take another bite. I feel like I have to pee and that my bowels have turned to water. I begin to shake and sweat. My escorts barely give me time to dump my tray. I guess it's a good thing I didn't want to finish eating. The two guards, one on either side of me, walk me through the building. I can feel all eyes on me. Everyone knows I've been summoned. I'm in trouble, going to be punished, or both.

I haven't seen the Inquisitor for almost a month. I can't decide if he has given up or if he has been busy with other prisoners, or maybe he really did get into trouble for going too far with me. Whatever the reason, I'm taken completely by surprise that I'm on his agenda today. I will miss weapons training. The fact that they even have me in weapons training feels so counterintuitive to me that I almost want to laugh each time I walk in there. Today, I'm not laughing.

They walk me right up to his desk. He ignores our presence for several minutes which leaves me feeling really uncomfortable, but I don't want to show it. This is obviously a new game. He casually sets the remote to my implant on his desk and tells the guards to leave. My eyes are glued to his tiny torture device. It is very clear to me that he is trying to get into my head, but he acts like he has made a dramatic turnaround and is now my friend.

"Thank you for joining me today. Elise." It's the first time he had used my name. "How are you feeling?"

I give him a confused look. His hand moves over the device and I quickly answer with the first thing that comes into my head, "Fine, sir, and you?"

"Lovely," he says pulling his hand away. "I would like to be your friend. I know we've had misunderstandings in the past, but know I was only doing my job."

He leans toward me and tilts his head to the side to look at me from under his brows. He reminds me of a bird and a shudder courses through me as his body language speaks to me saying that he cares about me and how I feel even though my head is screaming that it is a total lie.

"We're going to watch a movie together. Won't you have a seat?" His voice has changed too; now it's smooth and inviting, not bland like usual. The change sends more chills up my spine.

The couch he indicates looks normal, but I sit down gingerly just in case, right smack in the middle so that I have room to move. He sits so close, we're almost touching. It fills me with the urge to vomit all over his uniform or at least move away. I resist both. He pushes a button and clips begin to roll on the screen before me . . . clips from my time at school. They show days that I had laughed and was happy, days that I was with Malorie. My eyes are drawn to Jill because looking at Malorie makes me feel like there is a hard-boiled egg lodged in my throat. What is it about Jill that still makes me wonder if I can trust her? I can feel tears running down my cheeks but I ignore them and concentrate on Jill, still trying to analyze her motives. Then, I see something that changes my whole perspective. I'd always been suspicious of her. Heck, I'd even followed her once. Now with the view of the camera instead of my own eyes, I see her pass a note to an adult. What kid does that — in that sneaky way — in a crowded hallway? Someone who doesn't want to be seen, that's who.

The clip changes and shows Bren in class. He smiles at me and the videographer records my response. I pretend it means nothing. Out of the corner of my eye I see the Inquisitor open his mouth to speak, but his line buzzes and he turns to answer it instead.

"I asked not to be interrupted," he snarls.

"You are needed in quadrant seven, sir."

"I am running an interrogation."

"It's a code four, sir."

I watch him click a few keys on his tablet, his jaw tightly clenched. "Send someone to pick up 18A294E. I'm on my way."

Without another glance, he sweeps out of the room. I don't know if I have seconds or minutes but I don't think twice. I dive for the computer on his desk and start hacking. He has it password protected. Password . . . password. My eyes tear over his desk. Pictures, awards, and then over the walls . . . books. He loves books. My frantic gaze lands on an old hardcover more worn than the others . . . *1984* by George Orwell. I try several combinations before I hit on GOs1984.

I scan several files trying to get a feel of the setup. I need to create a back door for myself but I don't have time right now. I just need the lay of the land so that I will be ready when my next opportunity comes. They are self-contained here. All files have to be uploaded to the cloud. Forms are downloaded, filled out and shared. How archaic.

Footfalls sound near the door. I quickly erase my existence and shut the computer down. It hasn't finished closing out, but I'm out of time. I shoot around the desk and land back on the couch as the door opens.

"You should know my dear, that I have eyes everywhere."

I swing my head around. The Inquisitor stands there with the two guards and the technology specialist. I feel my whole body tense as they yank me to my feet. They drag me out the back door and down to the basement. "No . . . no . . . no . . ."

"I told you not to touch any unapproved electronics," he says in a voice that gives me chills.

Where had the camera been?

"See where she was," he hisses, snakelike to the technology specialist.

My guards keep on even though I struggle for all I'm worth. Into the showers we go and all the horrible memories I have of this room pounce upon me. They tie me to a metal chair, take off my shoes, run a wire around my ankles and dumped a bucket of water over my head. Metal — wire — water — holy hell — they are going to electrocute me. I struggle, cry, and scream. I have rarely been this scared. The Inquisitor comes in the door and laughs.

"You were a naughty girl, Elise," he says sounding pleased.

One of the many nameless guards brings in a battery large enough for a car and attaches the wires coming from my ankles. He shows me a remote and then hands it off to another black uniformed waste of skin. He flips a switch and a light begins to blink. I'm shaking. Then they leave. Seconds tick past. I'm panting. I move nothing but my eyes around the room, waiting. I move my head for a wider range and see no one. More seconds pass and I hear nothing but the rapid beat of my heart. I test the wires around my wrists. They are a little loose. I work at my bonds first a little, and then frantically, until finally my wrists and ankles bleed. I tip myself over in my chair and twist around until I'm free of the battery. I work and work until I'm free of the chair. I crawl to a corner, my chest heaving, but it feels like the room has no air. I gasp and attempt to control my shaking. They never flipped the switch. Was it all a cruel trick or is there more to come? My blood mars the white tile and tears run down my cheeks. My nose is running so I wipe it on my arm.

A movement by the door has me crab-walking backward as fast as I can.

"You are free to go, but next time you touch a keyboard without proper authorization, we turn it on," the Captain says calmly like this has all been a slight misunderstanding.

I rise unsteadily to my feet and approach him cautiously.

The doorway he is leaning in is the only way out. I press as close to the opposite frame as I can as I ease past and move toward the elevator. No one stops me. The door stands open. I look all around before I step in wondering what will happen next. Just as the doors are closing the Captain lunges, making me squeak, but all he does is throw in my shoes. The doors close and I slide to the floor in relief.

On the main level, I have to crawl out of the elevator. No one is around which I find odd but I'm thankful for it at the moment. I pull myself to my feet and with my back to the wall I limp back to the barracks. I almost cry when I get there, and think about going to bed, but decide I better hit the facilities first and see what I can do about my ankles and wrists. I throw up in the toilet before I can do anything else.

The girl with the rice is there like a wisp of smoke to hand me a towel.

"Are you my guardian angel or something?" I croak.

"Or something. How did you survive this long?"

"Very carefully."

"Clearly." She sighs heavily. "You are going to be a much bigger project than I planned on."

"You've said that before. Who are you?" I ask her again.

"I'm Reign," she sighs.

"Rain." I roll the name around in my mouth, but it feels off. "You make me think more of a big storm lurking on the horizon."

"No, you dope. R-E-I-G-N, like a queen."

Well, of course, I think sarcastically. "What do you mean by a 'bigger project than you planned on'?" I ask.

"I was sent by the Recalcitrants to help you," she whispers back.

"To help me? What does that mean?"

"I'm going to help you survive and then get out."

"So you have a plan, right?"

"No. You do," she says confidently.

"What? No."

"I know about you. You do have a plan. You may not know it yet, but you're noodling on something or you wouldn't have been mucking around in the Warden's computer."

"The Warden?"

"You don't even know who he is?" she asks with an eye roll.

"You mean the Inquisitor?"

"You call him that, but he's really the warden here and he's not a nice man."

"Really?" I say sarcastically. "Look, I thought the guy was in charge of interrogations. It's not like they wear name tags. It doesn't matter, it's how I think of him."

Reign rolls her eyes again and helps me over to a sink where she proceeds to apply some basic first aid to my ankles.

"What makes you think I was on his computer?" I ask innocently.

She gives me a don't-be-dumb look. "I know what goes on here. People tell me things and I'm observant. I saw them escort you out. I knew where you were going before you did. You've been gone for over two hours. The boy told me you were back. I had him watching. He's good at hiding."

"You know what time it is?" I ask amazed. I'm still guessing the time by meals, the position of the sun, and any guard's wrist communicator I can catch a glimpse of.

"I know where to look. Come on. We need to get you back to class before they come looking. For now, this is a safe place to talk if no one is here. I have more to share and I'll let you know where the cameras are later. When we are not in this room, you are not to speak to me unless I tell you it's okay."

"I understand."

"Good. Now come on."

"Do you know the boy's name?"

"I don't have to know his name. I don't have to know anyone's name. I just need to know who can be traded with."

She pushes me out of the latrines before I can ask any more questions. I limp to my class and Reign goes her own way. No one speaks to me and I make it my mission in life to fly under the radar and hide in the crowd. Getting singled out right now is really not on my to-do list.

Reign doesn't speak to me for two days and my huge quantity of questions grows exponentially. I begin to think I've imagined she ever spoke to me but fresh bandages and ointment appear on my bunk with the single grain of rice to let me know she's still around.

She finally snags me early in the morning before the guards have even come to wake us. The pressure of her sitting on my bed serves to scare me awake. She uses her fingers in the near dark to beckon me forward. Back into the bathroom we go, one of the few safe places to talk.

"The supply closet under the stairs is not bugged, but you

have to wait for activity in the hall so that the motion sensitive camera doesn't catch you. I tell time by looking at the guards' wrist devices, some forget to clear or cover them. There is also a device in the kitchen that shows the Coordinated Universal Time, but it's coded to display backward."

"What?" No wonder I couldn't make sense of the numbers there.

Reign rolls her eyes yet again. "When we get to the mess hall and you're in line for chow, look into the kitchen and on the back wall near the ceiling. Today I expect we will eat at about 7:00 a.m. The box on the back wall near the ceiling should read 00:00:41. Remember, it's backward so not really forty-one, it's fourteen and then minus seven for our time zone."

The solution to the weird box was so simple I was disgusted with myself for not catching on, but then I had been more worried about staying alive than I was about figuring out something that seemed inconsequential at the time. "Just to be sure I follow, seconds, minutes, hour and then the adjustment for our time zone."

"Yes."

"Thank you."

"They'll be here to wake us up in five minutes. I'll see you on the run."

I know better than to follow her right away so I go ahead and use the facilities. On my way back to my bunk I pass the boy who makes everyone smile. He looks so young and innocent while he sleeps. Kate is awake and is watching me in an appraising way. I send her a small smile but she just looks away. I sigh inside and continue down the row to gather the running shoes and sweatshirt I earned to use for these cold morning runs. I also pull out the fingerless gloves that were a gift from Reign.

I was told the first day, but I have relearned since that every privilege has to be earned. And when I say privilege, I mean basic necessities. I am still working on saving enough for a coat. No one warned me that first I would have to work off my bunk — each piece of bedding, my toothbrush, toothpaste, comb, soap, and clothes, so like everyone else I started out in debt. In addition, each day we have to work for our food. Even instruction has to be earned, but if you work hard enough you can earn extras like a paperback, government-approved book, or paper and pencils. It's harsh. The only way to stay close to even is to take extra shifts because regular assigned work shifts cover your food first.

Another week goes by so it must be November and I almost feel like I'm back in school — an even more highly militarized, controlling, authoritarian school, but a school nonetheless. They call it retraining or even reprogramming yet the feel of my old school is here in the things that are taught. It's the delivery that has changed.

I am still barred from any computer access. Concrete, tile, and metal are my whole world now, not wires and chips. Wires . . . my near electrocution flashes in my mind making me feel sick for a moment. In my heart, I know it is another of their games meant to break me, but I can play games. I can lock a piece of myself away. They still haven't gotten completely into my head, but I'm scared to death that eventually, they will. Reign is right; I have to do something before it's too late.

I am again sparing with Kate in fitness class. Could she help? She has more freedom than I do, but can I trust her? When she is out of my sight, what is she doing? We watch each other in the leery fashion that two cats do when they are new to each other. I will have to think carefully.

14

00100000 01100100 01101001 01110011 01100011

01101001 01110000 01101100 01101001 01101110

01100101 00101110

The lights burst on and I feel like I have barely closed my eyes, but then maybe I have. Sometimes they like to trick us. I'm not the only one taken by surprise; the sunny boy's hair is sticking out at odd angles. On him, it looks endearing. I get ready for our run and then try to sneak a peek at the guards' wrist devices. They are more elaborate than ours and are all usually locked and coded. Maybe next time — sometimes they are careless. I can't seem to stop watching and recording random bits of information in my mind. I will figure it all out. I am the one who will make the plan — except that I'm afraid my mind is imploding.

Running is hideous enough without being up for an extra early one. I'm still not much of a runner. I hate the way my chest gets tight and my throat burns, let alone the achy fire in my shins. Through practice and focus, I've learned how to avoid the stitch I used to get in my side, but the rest of it never seems to go away. If there is such a thing as runner's euphoria, I have yet to find it. I suspect the same is true for Kate and the boy since neither of them seems to be a good runner either. They lag behind regularly. Some folks run so smoothly that they give the illusion it takes no energy — that is not us. Today, I'm moving away from them as they lag behind. I know I'm fitter than I've ever been and yet the hate remains.

By my crude calculations, I figure we run about five miles each morning. I can make it the whole way now and I'm no longer the one at the back of the pack. It's still dark as we are finishing. Just as the buildings are coming into view, a blast rings out across the open space. We all dive onto our bellies and lay flat with our hands behind our heads like we've been taught. It doesn't pay to be last too many times. The first person to finish gets a voucher for extra food. Sometimes the last person is beaten; today they must have been shot. I wonder who it is.

I see movement and can't tear my eyes away from the small group approaching. Arms and legs dangle limply like a broken doll as two guards drag a small body past me. It's the boy from the end of my row. I try not to look at the hole in the side of his head, but I do anyway, unable to avoid the compulsion to watch. I clench my teeth together, praying I won't gag, but I can't keep my throat from closing up and my eyes from burning with the tears that I don't dare release. I had liked him. I liked his ready smile and his messy hair. I flash back to how his sleepy face looked just this morning. I didn't even know his name but he had been nice to me and I sensed a sweet gentle soul in him. He'd come in shortly after I was released to the general population and I often wondered how someone so young could end up here. Even orphans are kept at school. What could he possibly have done to anger the government enough to end up here?

I am sickened, yet not sickened enough — I am growing numb. I watch a guard pull Kate up from the mud where she fell to her knees, clutching her middle. This is why I can't let myself get close to anyone. It's too painful when they are gone, yet I hate what I'm becoming.

They have us come into the dining hall, where they serve us oatmeal, scrambled eggs and a piece of fruit. Today it's an apple, but I can hardly bring myself to eat. I remember giving my last apple to the boy. My eyes start to sting with tears again. I choke down as much as I can because I can tell by the way my body looks, I'm losing weight again. I know I need energy and I know they track everything — if I show that his death has weakened me, they will pounce on it and try harder to break me.

"Trays in. Morning rotation two!" A guard shouts into the nearly silent dining hall. *Nothing like a death in the morning to put a pall over the day*, I think savagely.

The female prisoner with the gray buzz cut, who I think functions as a handyman around here, slides in next to me as I dump my tray. "I'll miss him too," she whispers.

I just look at her, afraid to answer. Can I trust that she is here as a prisoner or is she a spy? I also wonder how she knows I care.

"Don't worry," she mumbles on the way out the door, "they won't notice what I can see in you. I'm a little empathic; I also know you will survive this."

I'm stunned, but I still don't know if I believe her. I know I need a friend, but I'm afraid to trust anyone. I'm still struggling to trust Kate and Reign. I sift through all I've seen and observed. I can't remember ever having seen this woman do harm to anyone. All I've ever seen her do is help so maybe she's okay. Maybe.

After weightlifting, I go to a session on pressure points in the human body. We learn to use them for fighting and healing. Then we study human physiology. It is no surprise to me that I'm good at this stuff. It's science. Not the kind I originally studied but still — science. It just seems so strange that they would teach me tools that I could use against them.

Reign snags me after class and pulls me into one of the supply closets she told me about. "I've got an idea," she blurts without preamble.

"Where have you been? I haven't seen you in over a week."

"I'm doing my job and the less you know about that the better. Right now I need you to do something."

"Other than miss lunch?" I flip back sarcastically. What can I say? I'm hungry after barely eating this morning.

Reign gives me an ugly scowl. "Don't be dumb. I know you're not! It's one of the few places they don't take attendance."

I sigh. "Fine, what do you want?"

"I need you to sign up for extra duty in the kitchen." Reign pauses to listen and check the crack at the bottom of the door for feet. "Let me know when you get KP. I found a girl who looks like you and you're going to trade places. She has a class in the computer lab."

"What?" I ask, appalled. "There is no way I'm going to try to get into the system again. I know they won't hesitate next time. They will just go ahead and kill me."

"I have a plan to get you into their system and I need for you to open a back door for the Recalcitrants."

"No way. They *will* kill me if they catch me."

"So what. This isn't living. It has to be you. I don't know how to do it."

"I'm not hacking in again. You know what they did to me last time. Are you nuts?"

"Do you want out of here or not?"

I give her one sharp nod even though my gut clenches up.

"Then suck it up and hack, sister, or consider this your permanent lifestyle."

I gulp hard. It will take every ounce of courage I have to pull this one off. My heart beats faster and my skin feels hot just thinking about it. I take some deep breaths and tell myself to relax. Reign pats me on the back, pockets something small from the shelves, opens the door and walks out like she belongs here.

I figure I better move quickly before I get into trouble for whatever she took.

I can feel a tremor in my body, but hopefully the guard who hands out jobs won't notice. Lots of inmates look nervous. Waiting in line to ask for a job helps me to compose myself. Right now I only have to do this one piece. Just this one thing . . . relax.

"Next." He sounds bored — good — he wouldn't look too close at me.

"I'd like to request KP for extra duty."

"Wristband." I hold out my arm. "Huh, lucky you. We have an opening tonight. You just saved some overworked scum extra duty," he sneers. "Report right after tonight's meal. You're on clean up."

I know it isn't luck. Reign has struck again. I hurry to lunch to see if there is anything left. Everything is being put away, but I can still snag an apple. *Another apple.* I help myself to water and spy Reign lurking in a dim corner, clearly waiting for me. I take a circuitous route as I munch. I go and stand near her and look out the window as if it's a coincidence I'm in the same location. The cafeteria is emptying quickly and afternoon jobs and classes are about to start.

"Did you get it?"

"Yes."

"Good. Meet me here at dinner. I'll have your new band. We'll switch the bands under the table and then for evening one rotation, go to the computer lab. You'll see that your schedule today includes a cleaning crew. It will give you a fresh layout of the building. Pin your hair back for work and then let it loose for the computer lab tonight. Don't look at any cameras. Let your wristband do the talking for you. If they ask, your name is Amy." Reign stops talking abruptly and runs into me — hard.

"Stay out of my way, grubber," she snarls.

I turn a blank stare in her direction and then flick my eyes to the guard who must have been watching us. He won't interfere unless there is bloodshed or we talk too long. If he thinks she hates me then he will be even less interested. I turn in my water cup and toss my core in the compost bucket. I check my readout and head for cleaning crew. How she knows my schedule before I do is a mystery.

She is right about one thing; my time on cleaning crew does give me a review of the whole building even though we are supervised by a guard the whole time we work. Our team of four goes room to room until we hit the computer lab and I get to remain outside and clean the hallway, but I get enough of a glimpse inside to know the lay of the land. Okay, so she is right about two things — this is also the closest I've gotten to the lab lately until today.

I finish out my afternoon shift half terrified and half expectantly as dinner draws nearer. When it finally arrives, my nerves have me so spooled up that I can barely think about eating. I run to the bathroom, get my hair wet and pull it all towards my face and then I walk to dinner. I get a tray and go sit where Reign had indicated earlier. I begin to worry that I'm not where she wants me to be. I take a bite but my stomach is in a knot. A guard comes and stands in the corner. Now how will we talk? After only an apple for lunch, I know that my body needs fuel so I choke down as much protein as I dare.

I don't see Kate anywhere. Part of me wonders what she's up to and part hopes she's okay. Finally, Reign comes in with a large group. She looks a little rough. She glances at the guard and then sits shoulder to shoulder with me anyway. She grabs my wrist and gives my band a quick painful yank, scraping off some skin. She forces the new one on before my hand can swell.

"See the tall chick with dark hair over there?"

I spot her and nod. "Follow her after dinner. She'll get you to the lab. Then you're on your own until the session ends. I'll find you after."

Reign glances around, takes a bite of food, and then grabs my arm again. As if by magic a pen is in her hand. She uses it to write on my arm while whispering, "That is the IP address where you need to send any information you can."

I nod once. The tall girl with the dark hair rises and so do I. I keep her in sight but don't follow too close nor do I look back at Reign. The girl I'm to follow turns in her tray and walks out. The moment she hits the doorway, I rush out behind her. She offers her wrist without looking at the guard and heads upstairs. I channel her and follow right behind doing exactly what she does. I work hard at not drawing attention to myself. I can feel sweat running down my back and beading on my forehead, but the guard at the lab lets me pass. I keep watching my target. There is an empty seat by her. I wonder if I dare take it. I sit slowly. She stares at her screen and then lays her arm purposefully on the desk next to her mouse. I look at her arm and back to her face. She does not look at me but rolls her arm and my gaze returns to it as a login and password appear, inked onto her skin. I quickly enter them and she wipes off her arm with her shirtsleeve. I'm in, so I don't look at her again.

I glance to the screens in the row ahead of me and using them as my guides, quickly open the proper programs. These are training exercises that I did when I was in sixth year. These people are not used to working in the cyber world. I will be able to hide what I am doing, but I'll have to work fast.

The room is silent except for the hum of the ventilation

system and the whir of about fifty computers housed in this room. This is my kind of white noise — subtle and smooth, calming and peaceful. Here we sit in a grid of eight across by six student inmates deep. There are four proctors in the room, one in each corner watching our every move. A camera in each front corner records the action in the room as well, so I keep my head down.

Action — bad word choice, there is a severe lack of action. And really, that's for the best.

Eyes move over screens and fingers flutter over keyboards. This class is taking a test. I laugh at the thought, being tested all over again, but I know how to beat this kind of test. They don't know who they are dealing with. Besides, I need to make them believe I am Reign's victim . . . today I am Amy. I hope passing with eighty percent, won't be too far out of character.

I shiver as cold air blows across my shoulders from the air ducts. The longer we sit the colder it gets. I know it is more than just sitting making me cold. They are conducting more than one kind of test here. I keep at the computer both testing and trying to break into their system while remaining unobserved. An older woman on the other side of the room raises her hand. A proctor goes over to her and there is some whispering I cannot make out. The proctor shakes his head. The woman wiggles in her seat but keeps working. An old man rises to walk over to a proctor but he doesn't get more than one step. The proctor has extended his baton and beat him to the ground with a single blow. In five swings the old man quits moving. I stop trying to hack for a beat and then go at it harder than ever. The minutes are ticking by and I have to build my shell and then I need to grant access to someone I don't even know, someone I have to trust blindly on the outside. A guard comes near and I switch screens back to the test. He glances at my work and moves on. Despite the cold sweat that is gathering at my lower back, I press my shoulders down and try to remain calm. I program in a virus that will send a ghost copy to the Recalcitrants of everything they send out of this place. Breathe.

They are hauling the old man out. My shell is not what I want, but it will have to do for now. Time is almost up. I hide everything I've done and hurry through some more testing for Amy. Not too good but good enough. I can feel tension in my neck and fear in my heart. The two men carrying the old man return and we are told to log out. My hands are shaking.

I walk down the stairs behind the group. I head to the back hall where most classes take place. As I pass the storage closet, I'm yanked inside. Too scared to utter a sound I turn to face my attacker with my arms up in defense.

Reign. I slowly lower my arms. Blood drips from her nose and she swipes at it like she's not aware of what she's doing.

"What happened to you?"

"Nothing. Did you get in?"

"Yes."

"Then it was worth it. Come on. Help me with her." Reign points to a lump in the back corner covered by a sheet.

"What did you do?"

"She's fine. She'll wake up in her bed. We're on laundry tonight. We'll dump her by her bed and make it look like she fell out of bed or something. The guards won't notice."

I realize I'm breathing fast and I can see black spots. It's not just my hands that are shaking now, it's my whole body. And Reign thought I had a plan. She's crazy. I'm no spy or secret agent. Reign swipes at her nose again, then pushes me to the floor, and forces my head between my knees. Now that the pressure has lessened, my body is overreacting.

"Pull yourself together!" she hisses, sounding mean.

I don't feel tough or brave. I'm not sure I even feel qualified. I am not that girl, but if I'm not, who am I? It is my job to get us out of here or at least try, right? Reign yanks off my band before I can protest, making the base of my hand red and sore. She hands me my old band and forces Amy's back onto her limp wrist.

"She'll be out for a while yet. Get to your class. If they ask why you're late, tell them you're not feeling well. Maybe they won't punish you for missing kitchen duty."

She pulls me to my feet and pushes some hair pins into my hand before she pushes me out the door. I pin my hair back from my face and run to a class on civilian management. They do stop me at the door. I am late but the guard waves me through with the "sick" cover. I'm pretty sure I look terrible. I spend the whole class waiting to be taken to the Inquisitor.

Class finally lets out and I stumble to laundry duty. Everyone else will be headed for bed. This is one of the jobs I hate most, not because it is hard but because it cuts into the little sleep we get. We are each assigned a cart to push to the dormitories. A mouse scurries over the guard's foot. He jumps and in the confusion Reign slips a note into my hand. I start pushing my cart and open the note inside it so that it is out of sight. I am to go just past the storage closet, tip my cart into someone and cause a huge commotion. I can do that.

I push my cart past the storage closet and take the corner too fast and on only two wheels. I let it career out of my grasp, causing the person behind me to crash into it. I wad up the note and stuff it in my pocket while the guard is leaping the carts in an attempt to avoid them.

"I'm so sorry!" I say. I make my voice as weak and submissive as I can.

The guard grabs the front of my shirt. "What are you doing?"

"It was an accident. I was trying to hurry. I didn't know they were so tippy."

"Ten demerits."

Damn. There went my coat for another week. I want to sigh, but I don't dare.

"Pick up the cart," he snarls.

"Yes, sir." I reach for the cart and wrestle it upright. I sigh inside as Reign passes me with her cart. We hurry on toward the dorm and pass from one guard to another for monitoring. Reign heads to the end farthest from the guard and positions her cart. The moment the guard's head is turned she shoves her cart into the aisle and dumps it. I quickly disperse my load and move to help Reign, who is just pushing Amy under her bunk with the toe of her boot. I pass out the rest of the load from where Reign left it on Amy's bunk.

I pray that we won't get caught. I can feel the nervous energy claw its way through my body as we work. It feels like everyone is watching us. Sweat is beading on my back and forehead. I pause to swipe at it. Reign gives me a dirty look.

I hear a small noise and my heart thumps crazily in my chest. I'm afraid it's Amy, but it's just her bunkmate who has climbed in above her. Reign kicks me to get my attention. The other bins have been moved to the center of the room to collect the dirty laundry. I quickly move ours into position. Then I wait while everyone puts their laundry in.

The panicky feeling won't leave me. I notice my hands are shaking and quickly grip the cart. The ones in front of me are moving. I don't think, I force my mind to blankness and follow along on the way to the laundry. Reign is stopped by the guard but a quick glance in her direction shows me that the guard is interested in her for something other than Amy. He is smiling at her and has boldly put a hand over hers.

My breath comes in quick bursts, not from exertion but nerves as I push the cart into the laundry. We park the carts and walk away. Tomorrow it will be washed by another team. Reign shows up and I breathe a sigh of relief. We walk back to the dorms without speaking. They have been darkened so we make our way cautiously with the dim red lights to show the way. No alarms are going off so it must not have been a bed check night.

As planned, we each go to our own bunk and get ready for bed. I listen to the breathing sounds. Most sound like they are close to sleep. I ease around the corner, sure to stay out of the red light's glow and move to Amy's bunk. Reign is already there, pulling her out from underneath. She takes Amy's shoulders and I take her knees. I'm amazed by how heavy someone can be when they aren't helping you. Her hips sag as we try to lift her onto her bunk. I'm really sweating now.

I'm worried she'll say something. I'm worried they'll notice something is wrong or that Reign will want me to hack again soon. I lay in my bunk, nervous energy boiling within me. My mind is churning and I struggle to slow my breathing. I expect at any moment, I'll be pulled from my bunk and interrogated. I don't know if I want to laugh or cry when dawn kisses the windows and the guard sounds the alarm to wake us.

I roll out of my bunk and into my workout gear. My nervousness has burned itself out, leaving me feeling dopey and out of it. My head hurts and I feel nauseous. I'm pretty sure that feeling is only going to get worse when we run.

My worry grows. I know that Reign is planning another way to get me into the lab. I'm so afraid of being caught that I'm sure I'm acting suspiciously, and I take as much extra work as they will give me to keep occupied and busy. I even have to make up a kitchen shift without pay since I skipped the last one. *Oh, joy.* But if I'm busy I can't think and if I can't think, I can't worry. A small sigh of relief washes over me when I hear the Inquisitor has left. There is no news about when he will return.

A week goes by and I finally have enough to get my coat. It takes every credit I have. I will be without toothpaste for a couple of days even though I stretch it as far as I can. They don't do much for teeth here. They don't take care of much of anything. They just run us until we die.

Die . . . no one has been shot in several days, not since the boy. Thinking of death makes me think of injury and illness which makes me think of Kate. Where is she, and what is she doing? I haven't seen her in . . . a couple of days. Is she in trouble, in isolation, or is she causing trouble?

00100000 01000001 01110011 00100000 01101001

01110011 00100000 01101111 01110101 01110010

I spend our morning run watching for Kate. I finally see her at the far back of the group looking awful but I can't get close enough to speak to her.

We are just starting to gather in front of the dining hall, but facing the gate, so someone new must be coming. I should have an opportunity to approach Kate when the alarm sounds and the guards are distracted. They move into position and the gates slowly swing inward. The new prisoner is led through the double gates between the guard towers. He stumbles and falls. It earns him a vicious kick from a guard. I blank my face, but inside I feel sorry for him. I've been in his shoes — helpless, hopeless, and afraid. They pull him roughly to his feet and it's all I can do not to let on that I know him . . . but it can't be him.

I have to be wrong. My mind is playing tricks on me. I have spent so much time pushing him out of my consciousness but he has stuck like Velcro, so that now I miss him so badly I'm creating him. I turn my head before I give myself away.

I swallow hard and sneak another look. He is dragged through the yard and into building one. I know where they are taking him. The first place everyone goes — the showers. I understand that it is to clean and disinfect us, but it also serves as humiliation. I feel for him.

The rest of us enter for breakfast. I just about convince myself that the new guy can't be Bren. Whoever he is, I'm glad that they don't put him in solitary. His crimes must not be very severe. I can tell even from a distance that he is scratched and bruised. He sits hunched and looks beaten, but then he turns and locks eyes with me. I feel a jolt travel through me and I suck in a breath. I am captured in his intense gaze and can neither move nor breathe. Electricity sparks between us with an almost visual arc. Reign kicks me sharply under the table but not before I see him tap out in Morse code, *We will get you out.*

I drop my eyes to the tabletop, my food left forgotten. I want to be alone — to feel — to think. I glance up when a guard contingent is sent to program his wristband. I wince as his bruised face is smashed onto the table and his arm wrenched behind him. I walk out at the earliest possible moment, desperate to fill my lungs with some clean, fresh air. Mostly I just can't stand to watch him be hurt.

Two guards are talking near the main doors to the grounds so I change direction and head back by the kitchen. I slide past the job desk where prisoners are already crowding in looking for work and hit the back hall where camera coverage is spotty and the lighting is poor. There's nothing back here so no one cares.

A soft footfall behind me jerks me around. This area is usually empty. Who besides me would dare? My belly pinches as fear grips me. I clamp down on a sob trying to choose which emotion to settle on. I can't decide if I should sigh in relief or despair. "What are you doing here, Bren? Are you crazy? I find it really hard to believe that you got caught, but I'd hate to think you did it on purpose."

He looks both ways and then moves in close so that I can see every bruise and scrape with clarity. "I came for you."

"Now you're in here and there's no way out. I've been searching, but they've put a new chip in me. It doesn't release a virus like the old one — now it induces pain and he says . . . he says it has a kill switch. So even if I break out . . . he'll just . . . I'd have to hack into the system controlling the chips first." I look into Bren's beautiful eyes — the ones I dream about every night, except now they are here and real and incredibly, vibrantly, fantastically green.

"We are getting out. There's a plan . . ." The waves of emotion I've been holding in crash over me. All the hurt, pain, and anguish take hold of my heart and squeeze it in a vice. I gasp for breath. I feel a sob rear its ugly head, but I can't let it go. My throat locks up instead. I won't hurt him. I won't let them do to him what they did to me. I know they will hurt him just to watch me suffer. Maybe it's all a trick and they brought him here just to torture me in a new way.

"Lise, what is it?" he asks interrupting my jumbled thoughts. The concern in his voice is almost more than I can stand.

My eyes sting with tears that I cannot shed—not now. I take two handfuls of his shirt and jerk him close.

"You should have stayed away," I gasp angrily, "and we shouldn't talk here."

"I'm just glad you're okay," he mumbles.

My eyes skitter around the back hall, watching for anyone to take an interest in us. "But I'm not okay," I whisper in a shattered, raggedy voice I hardly recognize as my own.

He pulls back and looks at me. My eyes are drawn to the fresh blood welling on his split lip. Talking must have reopened it.

"I'm sorry," I gasp, angry with myself as I reach out tentative fingers to touch it. I love those lips so much. It's the way they curve up at the outside edges, the way the bottom half is fuller than the top and the way his top lip comes up in two perfect peaks instead of just a smooth line. How could I hurt them?

He's talking, but I'm not listening. He gives me a gentle shake and my eyes snap back to his. "What did they do to you?"

I've kept so much in that when I finally open up, the words rush out like water over a broken dam. "They broke me, or maybe they didn't. Either way, I never told them about you. I talked about Malorie—they can't hurt her anymore. I talked about Jill too—I think she's dead or maybe she was a spy. I talked about school. They starved me, put me in solitary, beat me, drugged, cut and almost electrocuted me. They've messed around in my head and chopped off my hair. I'm not the same."

I press a hand to my mouth to stop the babble as I feel for the doorknob I know is behind me. My fingers hit metal, I turn the knob and slip inside pulling him in with me. I yank my shirt over my head. I have no idea what I weigh now, but it's a lot less than I once did. Old and new bruises cover my skin. Scars in shades of pink and white, depending on their age, move across me like a roadmap.

"Elise," he breathes. I hear pain, pity, and anger in his tone. He touches me with his warm hands. He is probably counting my ribs, but I don't care—not now. I unfasten my pants and show him my worst scar. It's puckered at my hip where they removed the old chip.

"I was awake when they did that They say I fought to get away so the sloppy job is my fault. I don't remember because of the drugs. I don't know which was worse—the drugs or the withdrawals. They left me in solitary until I was clean and cooperative. The funny part is—it was them that put all those chemicals in me in the first place, trying to get at the truth."

Bren's eyes slowly move up my ruined body to slam into mine. They actually hold tears. He starts to speak but I put my fingers over his lips. "Don't ever let them see you cry. To them, it's a sign of weakness. They will punish you so never let on that you like me or even know me. Do you understand? You can't let them know you care about anything. It's the first thing they take away."

Then I'm kissing him like I'll never get another opportunity. Electricity zings through me and my heart races. I feel warm and tingly in places that I forgot existed. My breath comes in short hungry bursts and I wish things were different . . . but they aren't. A sound leaves my throat—part moan and part sigh. I taste blood and I don't know if it's his or mine. I rest my forehead against his for a moment.

I start to push him away but my hand on his chest makes no impact. He slides his hands up my body, never taking his eyes off mine. He gently cradles my face in his palm and then he kisses me slowly and gently. It's the other end of the spectrum from where we'd just been. Maybe it's his way of telling me I'll be okay or maybe he wants to remind me who I was. The shattered girl that I am today is not the one he had known just a few months ago. I start shaking. He kisses along my jaw and down my neck.

"Lise," he breathes softly. "I would have come sooner but . . ." He doesn't finish, he moves closer, hugs me and then kisses me again. As his lips travel over mine, he runs his hands over me. He is the last person that handled me with care. Here, hands are made to deliver pain and abuse. I have nearly forgotten how good hands can feel if you aren't using them as weapons. How long has it been since I've felt anything good? I want to soak it all up so that I'll have something to hang onto. I slip out of my shoes, kick off my pants and pull his shirt over his head. He is pretty beat up too, but I'll win if we're having a competition for who is the poster child for the face of tragedy.

He looks like he's going to speak again so I quickly kiss him. I don't want to talk. I want to feel. Warm skin . . . a rapid heartbeat that isn't from running . . . soft puffs of breath . . . gentle sounds and the smile of softly curved lips. I open my eyes, I want to remember everything. I want to see it all. His eyes are still closed, his lashes long enough to brush his cheeks and make me jealous. His lips move over my skin, but he senses

me watching. He looks up at me and starts to speak again. No
. . . no talking, I think as I move in to kiss his lips yet again. I
kiss my way down his neck to his clavicle. I can name that bone
because they broke and repaired mine. I work my way out to
his shoulder and return to his neck.

"Lise," he breathes again so I bite him gently and put a hand
over his mouth. I have startled him. He picks me up and pushes
me into a shelf. It presses uncomfortably into my back but I
don't care. I want more and I know he does too. I can get lost
in this. I will get lost in this. I need this. He moves my bra strap
and finds another scar.

He pauses, waiting for me to answer his unspoken question. "They broke my clavicle one night when they didn't like
my answers to their questions. At least the questions stopped.
They took me to the infirmary and pinned it back together,
stitched me up and sent me on my way. They say that bone is
now stronger than the other one." I shrug but he looks so sad. I
don't want him to think about that stuff right now, so I slip my
arm from the strap. My attempt at distraction works.

I reach for the button on his pants and am just slipping it
from the buttonhole when the door bangs open. The Captain
fills the doorway. I still have nightmares about him from my
first days here. He's the one who broke the bone I'd just been
talking about. Did I jinx myself?

"What do we have here? A free show?" he sneers.

Bren spins around ready to fight but says nothing. At least
he knows not to talk back.

The Captain's eyes stay on me. "You moved in quick on the

new boy. I thought maybe you liked girls. I only see you with girls. I can't believe you were dumb enough to be seen. Guess you're not as smart as the Warden thinks you are."

I gulp, thankful that Bren still has his pants on. This doesn't look as bad. His fists are clenched and I know he's ready to fight so I put a hand on his arm. He doesn't know the rules yet. I have to protect him.

"It's nothing. He's just a boy I thought was cute. Let him go."

Bren cuts his eyes to me. He looks both hurt and angry.

"Just go," I add switching my gaze briefly to Bren as I move in front of him without moving my hand. I tap out, *Not safe*, against his arm out of the Captain's sight.

"No." Bren snarls through stiff lips.

The Captain smirks. "Maybe she wants a real man."

Bren's jaw clenches, but he shows no other sign of his anger.

"It's fine, he's only allowed to look," I say aloud as I send him another message, *Please. Trust me.*

"Yeah, but I can look at plenty. How about you do her and I'll watch," The Captain presses.

I'm afraid Bren is going to lose it as his muscles bunch under my hand.

Go, I've got this, I tap out, trying to save him, yet knowing he thinks it's the other way around. Bren shakes his head so I squeeze, digging what is left of my nails into his forearm and tap, *Go*.

Bren twists out of my grip, bends and angrily picks up his shirt, yanking it over his head as he stalks out. I can feel cracks fissure over my heart like before, in the woods, but I refuse to let it show. At least he knows better than to fight a guard, or worse, kill one.

I turn to the man from my nightmares and swallow. "What do you want?" My voice does not come out as strong and firm as I would like.

"I can't have what I really want right now so what are you willing to give so that I don't write this up?"

"What do you want?" I repeat. I have never bartered with him or any guard. I need a parameter to go by. I know now that sexual assault is not accepted and I can take a beating even though the very thought of it makes every bit of my smooth muscle squinch tight.

"Come over here and run your hands over me like you did to him and make sure I believe every second of it."

I take a breath and slowly move my reluctant feet. I have to pay for my sins — for any hope or joy that finds its way into my current reality. I can pretend I'm somewhere else or at least that I'm with someone else. I can do this, and I will do this, to save Bren from the beating he will get if I'm not believable. Then again, he might still get one if I'm not very careful. I can't have us on the watch list.

I touch his arm and almost jerk away.

"I'm not feelin' it yet," the Captain growls.

I try closing my eyes but he doesn't feel or smell the same. All the places in me that had been warm and shivery turn to ice. Can I fool him into thinking that a shudder of revulsion is something else? Maybe I can pull it off if I don't puke.

I step closer, my bare toes touching his boots and try again, still keeping my eyes closed. He moves a little and I feel the sting of a knife slide up my sternum.

I freeze and my eyes pop open. I look down at the fine red line building on the center of my chest. My bra slides down my arm and hits the floor and I begin to shake. He's going to do it. We're away from the cameras. It's my word against his. No one will believe me or care. Tears build at the back of my eyes and I feel like I've swallowed an entire hard-boiled egg.

"Show me like you mean it," he says again, his eyes never leaving my chest.

I can curl up and die or I can go down fighting. I begin to plot his death in my mind as I slide my hand from his arm toward his neck. I lock my eyes on his, move closer so that my left foot is between his boots and begin to cut off the blood flow to his brain like my instructors taught me. His eyes flicker like he's catching on and the door bangs open, just as his arm is coming up to defend himself.

Reign's tiny form fills the doorway. "Hey, Captain, you're not having fun without me, are you? I told you I was willing to barter. What are you doing with that skinny mutt? You're gonna hurt my feelings," Reign's seductive growl sets my teeth on edge, but she's in full vamp mode, right down to her stuck-out lower lip forming a pout.

The moment he turns his head I step away and scrabble after my clothes. He looks from me to Reign and back. "Maybe another time. I've got some paperwork to do and somehow I seem to be getting a headache," he ends giving me a significant look.

Reign closes the door. "That's too bad. I'd hate to let slip about prisoner 27C139A," she purrs calmly as she gives him a level look.

"Fine, no paperwork today, but we're square on that one." He brushes past her and is gone.

"What's wrong with you?" Reign snarls softly at me, the second he's out of sight. "I can't believe you burned this storage area. It was a stupid thing to do."

"I . . ."

"You know better. Are you hurt?" Her voice sounds worried, cutting the edge out of her abrupt words.

"Nothing that won't heal, except my pride." I pull on my pants and look at my ruined bra. I pull on my shirt and shoes and start to throw the bra away. Reign snatches it out of my hand. "What are you doing?" I snap, feeling hurt and confused.

"I trade in secrets among other things. He's not allowed to touch, but he has women prisoners touch him all the time. He takes it literally to mean he can't use his hands on you, anything else is fair game just like his knife on your chest. I've talked to his victims. He keeps asking them for more. Soon he'll be asking you for a blow job and you're not ready for that, so stay away from him."

"Why do you need that?" I ask, indicating my ruined bra.

"It's evidence. I can use it against him to get something I want. Now let's get you out of here."

"Why'd he leave it then?"

"Because he doesn't really care. What will they do to him? Slap his wrist? Give him a warning? Regardless, it might be worth something to him once he's cooled off."

Reign sends me on my way but takes the time to hide her new treasure in a ventilation shaft. I just hope it will do her more good than it does me right now.

I'm driven to talk to Bren. I feel like I have to make him understand before he gets himself hurt. It doesn't take long. I find him sitting outside the dormitory, looking into the distance. His elbows are on his knees and his hands cover his mouth. I can't decide if he's holding in vomit, rage, or tears. The way he looks fits perfectly with the nearly black clouds overhead. His eyes flit over to mine. They look haunted, angry, and tortured all at once. *He has to learn to hide his feelings better than this*, I think, worried. At least he's wearing a jacket.

"It's over," I whisper instead.

"What did you do?" he pleads, his voice sounding as rough as his eyes look.

"It's fine. Forget it. It's nothing."

His hand snaps out and snags my wrist. "It's not nothing."

I can feel the heat of his anger. He doesn't understand.

Reign walks up to us. "Let it go, lover boy. She saved your bacon. The Captain would have beaten the hell out of you or thrown you in solitary. She just had to be a little more degraded. It's no big deal for us, right E?"

My eyes turn to the ground and Bren drops my wrist. Degraded, yes, that's how I feel.

I hear the creak of boards and know that Bren is on his feet. "What's happened to you? This isn't who you are. Stay away from me — both of you," he growls softly, sounding more hurt than angry.

He starts to walk away, but Reign is faster. She stands in front of him and blocks his path.

"Bishop, she saved your ass. Be thankful and be supportive, damn it. It hurt her to do what she did, but she did it for you. She cares more about you than she does about a stranger looking over her goodies. She didn't sleep with him for heaven's sake. Hell, I've even shown him mine a time or two but then you've already seen them, so is it a double standard for you?"

We both gape at her.

"Well? It's okay for you to look at whoever you want, but she can't let him look? That is a double standard. How far would you go to keep your friend from getting a beating? She found her line. She bared her chest instead of feeling guilty about you getting bruised and bloody. Where's your line, Bishop?"

Reign and Bren? I wonder if my brain has audibly screeched to a halt. Well of course. She is tough, beautiful and mysterious. Of course he would be interested in her. I'm none of those things.

I start to walk away but now she is in front of me. "Stay focused. Stick to the plan and we all get out."

I try to push past her.

"Look at the bright side, sweetheart. All I did was break him in for you. I taught him everything he knows, and he knows a lot."

I freeze, my eyes popping wide. Is she kidding or serious? By the way Bren is looking everywhere but at us . . .

"Oh . . . my . . ."

"Did you think that when he got on the outside he was going to save himself for . . . wait for it . . . a sweet innocent school girl like you?" She throws her head back and laughs.

I feel like I've been slapped. My fist clenches and my arm cocks back to punch her in the face, but I stop. She isn't worth it. All she's ever done is cause me trouble and pain. I turn and walk away. To hell with dignity.

"Wait," Reign calls.

I pause — I don't know why — and turn. She tilts her head to the side of the building, her eyes begging me to come and look. I walk in the direction she indicated. I'm angry and hurt, but I won't make a scene. I hate spectators and we have already gotten a few curious glances.

"I'm sorry you had to find out like that, E, but it was my way of getting everything back to . . . never mind. Bren, look at this." Reign pulls down the front of my shirt before I can stop her, but I slap at her hand anyway. Bren takes a step closer and holds my shirt down so that he can see the blood that has beaded up and smeared in a mostly coagulated stripe down the center of my chest.

"I mean it, Bishop. She was trying to save you from a beating. She's had plenty so in her mind, what's one more? Besides, the Captain doesn't like boys, so it had to be her. You're the man with the latest intel from the outside, so focus on what matters here! We'll teach you the rules in here, but we've got to get her out of here because next time he'll do a lot worse," Reign says, sounding truly scared for once.

Bren goes still and serious and I feel another crack move across my heart. I guess I can still dream, but it looks like my reality with him is long over. I have ruined my chances with him. No, I'm just plain ruined. I'm not even smart enough to grab a coat. He releases my shirt and his eyes move to the trees as he thinks.

"I need to know more about these new chips and how to deactivate them. The Recalcitrants are moving in from the outside, but they are waiting for our signal. They know it's going to take time. We've got to bring down the communications and security so they can get in without all the prisoners being killed. We have so little intel about the inside. One prisoner who escaped a similar facility wasn't very cooperative. The one agent we got in here that came out the other side gave us what he could but it was only basics. Two others came out in body bags. There is one still here that is so deep undercover that not even I know who it is."

"Are they getting what I've sent?"

"Until you set up the backdoor for us we hadn't been able to hack the system. Now we can see files, but there is no one to ask questions about what we're seeing. Most of it is coded and we can't read it. Thank you."

I smile a small smile but Bren continues on, cutting his eyes to Reign, "You've been in the prison system the longest. I'm counting on you to help me understand how things work here."

"Did you miss me?" she simpers at him and I can't help but roll my eyes.

"Actually, I did." I feel my chest tighten another notch. "But no one we can trust has been *here* as long as Elise."

"There are plenty of prisoners who've been here longer than me," I say trying not to let my teeth chatter.

"No guards or prisoners we've planted have lasted as long as you."

I feel almost angry inside. Like I've had a choice in the matter! Maybe if they'd come to rescue me sooner — maybe if they had a plan, things wouldn't be like this.

"You're jealous," Bren exclaims. He actually sounds surprised. Reign steps away, but she doesn't go far. She stands watching the courtyard from the corner of the building.

I let my confused and mixed-up feelings show. I'm not sure that jealous is the word. I'm surprised about him and Reign, but she's right. I should never have expected him to wait for someone like me. I definitely feel hurt and maybe even used.

"You had a right to your own life outside. You barely knew me, so you sure didn't owe me a darn thing."

"Maybe I feel like I owe you something now," he whispers, moving closer.

"Why? Because I let the Captain cut me and get a look at my bare chest, so you wouldn't get a beating? You're welcome."

"Don't be so cold."

"Oh, I'm sorry," I croak sarcastically, "wasn't it you who was walking away a minute ago?"

"Yes, I apologize. I didn't understand."

"Don't." I'm afraid if he's nice to me, I'll cave. He is unwittingly doing more to break me in minutes, where they have not succeeded in months.

"Elise."

"Look, I should be dead . . . several times over. Maybe I'm part cat. God knows I've had way more than nine lives, but at the very least I should be completely crazy. And maybe I am, but they did one clear thing for me, they made me very angry. Now plotting revenge keeps me warm at night.”

“No. That’s not who you are.”

“You don’t know me anymore and trust me, you don’t want anything to do with who I’ve had to become.”

“Let me be the judge of that. Let me help you.”

“You don’t understand how screwed up my head is. For your own good, leave me alone.” Great, now I sounded like Reign, bossy, cryptic, and confusing.

“Elise, don’t for one minute think that my time on the outside was easy. I admit that I didn’t go through what you did and I’m still trying to assimilate it. I saw the reports. I read what they did to you. I didn’t want to believe it. I thought it was an exaggeration and you seemed so in control and okay when you read my Morse code in the dining hall. I thought the reports were all lies and then . . . then you showed me your scars and I knew it was all true. I didn’t come soon enough. I tried. I swear I tried. The person we had on the inside only knew that you were held below. They heard that you were being tortured and now we can’t find him. We don’t know if he’s here hiding or dead. We got Reign in here as fast as we could after we lost contact with him. We need her. She’s been in the system before. She knows how it works. I would have come in blind. The prisons run pretty much the same when it comes to the inside. She’s the expert. I just never should have let you get caught. I’m sorry.”

“I’m sorry you suffered on my behalf. I’m sorrier that you got yourself in here and may never get out, and I’m sorry that you're counting on me because, mister, your money is on the wrong horse. I'm going to get us all killed." My eyes burn and a sob catches in my throat. Why do people help me? I'm nothing but trouble.

I watch Bren cut his eyes to Reign and then he pulls me over by the tool shed and out of most people's line of sight. "I'm sorry. I didn't understand what you were trying to tell me in the storage room. I want you to know that my time with Reign feels like it was a lifetime ago. I care about her but I don't love her. I shouldn't have lost my temper. I was so happy to see you alive and . . ." He looks like he just doesn't know how to get the words out. He has that pained look in his eyes again that breaks my heart. "If I could have traded places with you, I would have done it in a heartbeat."

I don't know what to say, but I don't have to say anything. He saves me from that by pulling me into his warmth.

I pull back when it finally hits me. "Where did you get the coat? Newbies have to earn them?"

He looks at me blankly for a moment and then smiles. "They gave it back after they had me disinfected. I had some money on me. They let me trade the coat for the money that was not discovered when I first came in. I may not know everything about this place, but I've made it my job to study everything I could."

I smile at him. "I wish you were here when I first came in. I had to learn the hard way."

He reaches out and touches my face and then brushes back my super short hair. "I wish I would have been with you."

"Guys," Reign hisses. Bren breaks away and quickly walks

over to her. I take a little more time.

A new girl is being brought in. Two in one day is unusual. She is small and wiry-looking even from our vantage point, which makes it seem like she is only eleven or so. Please don't let that be true. Her hair is the color that usually comes out of a bottle or box but here it has to be real. My eyes are drawn to it like a magnetic force — it's the color of sunshine. It is a horrible time of year to come in. My heart squeezes. I don't even know her and I'm worried about her already.

hardly get to see Bren and maybe that is for the best. They have intensified my training, probably as a punishment for sneaking into the kitchen storage area with Bren, leaving me little time for anything else except to wonder how broken I really am. My nights are plagued by nightmares and my days are filled with avoiding the Captain. If my security breach has been noticed they are waiting for me to get careless. They would never let something like that go unpunished. I know my days are numbered.

Reign and Bren are often together giving me so many mixed feelings that I can't seem to separate them all out. I'm jealous, sure, but mostly I'm so scared all the time that I wonder if I'll sprout long ears and twitchy whiskers. I am the rabbit trapped in a too shallow hole with a pack of slavering wolves scratching at my burrow.

Reign thunks her tray down narrowly missing my fingers. I jump and she laughs. "Wallowing again?"

"Go away," I sigh in exhaustion.

"You have work to do."

"And you are going to get me killed."

"Maybe dead is better than being trapped here."

I give her a dirty look. It's all I have the energy for. When I turn my gaze back to the room, I see the new girl limp toward an empty table. My heart aches. I may not care much about myself anymore, but maybe I could save her. I should save Bren too. I guess I owe him that much.

"Okay," I sigh, "What do you want?"

"That's better. Meet me at the gardening shed after lights out."

"Fine," I huff. I'm not happy. Sure it's as safe a place as any to meet, but if they do a surprise bed check we're screwed.

Reign gives me her don't-be-dumb look making me think mind reading might be her super power. "No bed check tonight. It's not on the schedule."

I don't even bother to ask how she knows. I scan the mess hall again because it pays to be wary and alert. Kate is now sitting by the new girl. Better her than me. How she gets away with being nice to the new prisoners is beyond me. I would have been beaten and thrown back in solitary if I did those things. On the other hand, maybe that's where she is when I lose track of her. Maybe she doesn't care.

After dinner, I have double kitchen duty. I find it a great irony that the chef actually likes me. Clearly, he doesn't know that I'm hanging out with Reign, who is permanently banned from his domain. He won't serve her anymore either, but at least he doesn't deny her food. Perhaps he's not allowed. Today I'm washing dishes. Standing at the sink makes my back ache, but at least my nails are getting clean. I put myself in the zone and quietly hum what I can remember of an old song I used to like.

The normal kitchen clank and buzz stops suddenly. It can only mean one thing. I turn slowly and find three armed public safety officers. My heart beats faster as sweat beads up and chills chase down my spine.

"Prisoner 18A294E, you are wanted in the warden's office."

I take a breath and carefully set down the plate I'm holding. I start to wipe my hands but one of them grabs me by my arm. "Now!"

I can't control the shaking. I have to pee and my bowels are sending urgent messages to my brain. I'm falling apart. They drag me through the kitchen and to the stairs. I stumble and they shake me. Their anger shows in their reddened faces and white knuckles. Pain is coming. My breath rushes in fast bursts. I can't control it. I can't control anything.

The hall at the top of the stairs warps and bends. I haven't felt like this since they drugged me. The Inquisitor's door seems overly large; I imagine fangs bursting from the frame and shudder.

The office looks and smells like I remember. It takes my eyes a few moments to adjust after the brightness of the hall. Only the lamp on the desk is lit, throwing strange shadows around the room and giving his face a ghoulish appearance.

"Hello Elise," he drawls.

"Sir," I manage to force out past my overly tight throat.

"You may go," he says to my guards.

I watch them leave, but I don't move. I'm too scared.

"How are you feeling?" he asks like he knows.

"Um . . ."

"You have one of the newest chips installed. I wanted to try some new programming. I can tell by your response and elevated vitals that it is working perfectly. What would you say if I told you that we are working on some new technology and since you are such a wonderful subject, I thought we'd give you the chance to be first in line. Pain works on you, fear works on you. Next, I think we'll try the new built-in camera that records everything you see and has the special added bonus of us being able to send orders directly to you. I understand that it gives the recipient almost debilitating migraines but some things just can't be helped and this is for science and the good of us all."

My stomach rolls and I vomit on his expensive carpet. I take a certain satisfaction in it until I nearly fall in it when he hits the pain switch. He hits another button and screams into his communication device. "Get someone in here to clean up this mess and have her taken to the lab!"

"No!" I croak.

Two guards enter. I start backing up, but the Inquisitor is ready and zaps me with a jolt of pain so strong I curl reflexively into the fetal position.

This time, I will not be quiet. It takes four of them to get me down the hall as I kick, hit, scratch, and buck. If I'm going to be abused, I'm going to earn it. Now that the pain has stopped, reason is working its way back. I've got to get out of here!

My muscles strain. My left shoulder is screaming in agony as it is wrenched behind me in their attempt to subdue me.

"Son of a . . . Get a tranq for her," the guard to my left snarls.

I buck and my right leg is free. I quickly swing it in an arc connecting with the guard holding the other leg. The guards stumble. We are almost at the door to the hospital wing making a new wave of panic flood my system.

"Drop her here!" the lead guard yells. "Pin her and get a damn tranq in her."

I grab hold of the door frame in an attempt to peel myself away from them. I catch sight of the white shoes of a medic rushing toward us. Part of my brain notices that he is new to me as he tries to jab a needle into my arm. I feel more of a scratch than a pinch. The guards loosen their grip but I haven't felt anything yet.

I break loose and run into medical instead of away from it hoping for a place to hide or a way into the attic. Come on — give me something, anything. The pounding of the guard's feet is louder than my own heart. I'm tackled from behind. It sends me sprawling into an open doorway. I smash into a tray on my way down sending instruments flying. The doctor yelps in surprise. I look up and catch sight of a wisp of red hair under a scrub cap and a pair of blue-green eyes. With a crack, her foot comes down on a bit of the paraphernalia from the tray that has been scattered across the floor. Our eyes meet.

Kate.

Pandemonium breaks free as the lights go out. I claw and scratch my way to freedom.

"Where is she?" someone hollers.

"I've got her!" a triumphant voice calls.

"That's me, you idiot. Go cover the stairs."

A tone sounds and an announcement comes over the guard's communicator. "All hands to the yard! Code three."

"Leave her — she's got nowhere to go. We'll do a count later."

"Get down here now!" the communicator crackles again.

"What about Warden duty?"

"This takes precedence over that when there's a fight in the yard."

I don't want to waste a second of the confusion, I've got to get out of here. Someone steps on my fingers in their rush to restore order. A boot kicks the back of my head. My eyes water and I clench my teeth trying not to make a sound. I find the door frame and pull myself through.

I hug the wall, trailing my left hand along its surface as I rush toward freedom. Wait! The computer lab will be offline. I've got to hurry. I can hear the generators starting to click, trying to come on.

I make it to the door to the lab and ease inside, closing it behind me. I feel my way over to the cabinet where the laptops are locked up. Normally it would take a guard's wristband or another device to open it but with the power off . . . yes, I'm able to force the lock. I snatch one and its charger, wipe clean every surface I touch and then crawl onto a desk at the back of the room. I push the ceiling tile aside and pull myself up and into the attic. I'm so thankful that I helped with the electrical a while back. I quickly put the ceiling tile back in place and hide the laptop under some insulation.

I won't have to break into the lab anymore. Now if I can just avoid the surgery, otherwise I'm going to have to get really tricky about how I do things. I find the main beam running the length of this hall and work my way along it. I've got to get out of here before the power is restored.

I open a section of the ceiling and peek through. The emergency lighting has come on and this part of the building is busy. I'll have to try another location. Light coming through a vent catches my eye and I work my way toward it using the trusses as my guide like the electrician taught me. I smile a little when I find that it's loose enough to pull inward. I look outside. It's brighter than I expected, and I can hear shouting and running feet around the compound. I'm not far from the guard tower and it looks empty in the moonlight. I pull myself onto the roof and lean over to put the vent cover back into place. I wobble as I stand up, but then I walk along the peak of the roof away from the guard tower. Before I can think better of it, I turn and run toward the tower. I jump for all I'm worth as my feet hit the last of the roof and I fly into space, slamming into the guard tower roof, and knocking the air from my lungs. I slide down the slope but catch myself on the gutter and swing inside to lie panting for a moment on the floor.

I look around as I catch my breath and spy a communications device. I snag it and finding nothing else of value, lower myself down the outside of the tower on the darkest side. I cling to the shadows until I can join a group of prisoners milling around the yard.

The lights come back on just as I'm stepping into a group. My eyes quickly skim those gathered. I see Bren, Reign, Kate, the new girl, and a couple of other people I care about. I sigh in relief. They scan each of the prisoners ahead of us and send them to bed. I fully expect to be pulled aside so I edge over by Bren and touch his hand. He gives my hand a brief squeeze. I turn my head and pretend to cough as I pull out the communications device but keep it cupped in my hand. I pass it to Bren.

"I can't meet tonight," I whisper for his ears alone. "When they scan me, they are going to take me. I'm headed for surgery. They're implanting a new device in my head. It will record everything I see."

Bren's fingers clench painfully over mine. He starts to turn his head toward me. I shake mine once to let him know he needs to stop.

"I hid a laptop in the insulation in the attic. Top left corner above the computer lab. Save yourself. Good luck."

There are only two rows in front of us now. Bren gives my fingers one last squeeze and lets go. His body holds a slight tremor and I can hear his breath.

"Save yourself," I mumble softly once more just before I step up to be scanned.

Just as I expected, the scanner sounds an alarm as it passes over my wristband. Two guards take me while a third hits me with a jolt of pain so strong I nearly faint. I don't look at Bren. It takes everything not to.

The walk into the building seems to take forever. We move to the staircase and head up. I expect to go to the lab near the infirmary, but they are taking me back to the Warden's office. I don't know what to think.

His lights are on a little brighter now. His face looks tired and drained. When he speaks it sounds drained too. "With the power outage, all systems must be reset. Your gift is being postponed until another prototype can be sent. It seems yours was damaged in the power outage. I seem to have bigger problems than you on campus. I find that I must focus on a saboteur and an instigator. Go to bed. I'm done with you for tonight."

He waves a hand at me in a dismissing gesture. The guards take me back out and then stand with their backs to his office door. I look at them questioningly. One of them gives me the same shooing motion. I don't waste any more time and hot-foot it down the stairs and into the dorms.

The lights are out. I'm shaking with relief. I go into the latrine to take care of myself and to splash some water on my face. I'm alarmed to see a bit of insulation on my shirt. How did they miss that? I quickly take it off and shake it out. I take a moment to debate whether I should go get my jammies or go and see if Bren and Reign are meeting.

A soft footstep alerts me to someone else's presence. I whip my head around, but it's Bren. I sigh with my whole body. He may not be mine anymore but he is the only person in this place that I feel I can fully trust. I look into those amazing green eyes and know it's true. He is the one. I feel like I'm going to cry, but I know that if I give in, it will be even harder to stop.

I close my eyes for a moment and his arms come around me.

"They let you go." I can hear relief in his voice.

"Yes," I breathe. "For now."

"Come on. It's time to go to the shed. They have us all accounted for."

I leave my head resting on his shoulder for just a moment more. He runs his hand up and down my back. I want to close everything out and now I want to get out of here more than ever. I lift my head to signal to Bren that I'm ready and follow him out. The guard by the service hall is dozing. I don't question that; it was probably Reign's doing. Bren watches the camera. The second the red light goes out, he moves quickly down the hall and out the side door.

"Reign?" I ask.

Bren gives me a significant look. Yep, Reign.

He quickly leads me to the shed and we slip inside. Reign is not there yet but before I can worry, she is through the door.

"Aw, you look like you were worried about me," she says with a smirk.

"If you get caught we are all going to crash and burn," I growl back softly, feeling weary and tired of her games.

"What have you got?" Bren asks her. I'm sure he's trying to keep the peace.

"Something is up downstairs, but it's hard to find anyone who will talk. I have access to guards but not the tech guy in the basement. They keep him separate. The medical guy ordered some food and I happened to be available to deliver it. They let me take it down but I only got a glimpse. They definitely received some new equipment. Some of it was laid out and there were a number of boxes. We need to move faster. We need to get you back in the computer lab," she exclaims looking at me.

I look to Bren who nods and then look at her. "I stashed a laptop in the attic while the power was out. You cut the power, right?"

"Of course. A little bird told me that you were in big trouble this time." She smiles at me like the cat that ate the canary. "But good for you on the laptop. I take it you can work from there now? Did you take care of power? Can you hide your access? You can get internet?"

It was my turn to give her *my* best don't-be-dumb look.

"Good. You need to access medical and start wiping chips and not just yours. Do as many as you can so they have lots to recover. I hear that all prisoners are to be chipped by the end of the month and the new supplies confirm it. Maybe your chip will get lost in the confusion. You also need to infect their communications. Perhaps you can use a virus or a worm and see what you can do about disrupting security."

"Is that all?" I ask sarcastically. It's easy for her to make demands when she doesn't understand what I need to do. "You know that will take time."

"We'll sneak you out each night and you can work for a few hours and then sneak back in. It will take as long as it takes."

Bren's brow is wrinkled. I know he's worried even before he asks, "What about the other prisoners? Can they be saved? Can they be trusted? How is Elise going to get by on so little sleep?"

"Maybe she'll just need proper motivation. As for the others, trust no one. Our job is to save her — the rest are on their own, but we can at least leave the door open when we go."

I would like to save them all, especially Kate and the new girl, but I know I can't. I hang my head. I'm beat.

Bren reaches over and rubs a hand up and down my arm. "Let's call it a night. We can figure out how to get her into the attic tomorrow."

I'm so tired and emotionally drained that I stagger on the way to my bunk. I have muscles aching in places I didn't know I had muscles after my tussle with the guards. I even have a headache right behind my eye that I'm afraid will keep me awake, but my worn-down body has other ideas.

The lights come on signaling our morning run. I still hate running. It is worse in winter than it had been in summer. It's too cold to run without a jacket but you sweat with it on. It sucks. I wish we had some of the nice fibers that are made for this weather but none of us do. At least now I have Bren to watch. I never worry about him being near the end of the pack. Even Reign is a much better runner than I am. It seems like she can do anything and is beautiful too, but I've learned that her insides are not as lovely as the outside.

Just ahead is the new girl. I can hear bits of the conversation she is having with the woman who does most of the general maintenance of the building. I stumble when I hear she has just turned eleven. She is even younger than I feared. I pass them hoping to put her out of my mind, but I can't. She reminds me of the young boy who'd been too sweet for this place and paid with his life. I will try to do a few more little things to help her but I don't have much to spare, especially after I gave up all I could to help Bren get the minimum he needed for winter. Even Reign contributed to his winter gear but we can't chance getting caught when we have more important things at risk and giving her too much could expose us.

The girl, whose name I don't even know, is now lagging behind. I sigh and drop back to pull her along like people had once done for me. When the guards get too close, I dart ahead and then look back to see if someone else has picked up where I left off. Kate is helping her now, so I run on. I begin stretching when I reach the courtyard. I can see Bren and Reign so I inwardly sigh in relief and attempt to focus on my next task.

The last runners appear and start to stretch as well. The guards are not looking at anyone specifically so today will be a good day. No deaths mean a good day, in my mind anyway. The new girl is rubbing her arms but looks too beat to jump up and down. She has to earn a coat. A guard walks by and I hold my breath. She turns to speak to him. *No*, I scream in my mind. I start to edge her way, but Bren is closer.

"Everything here is earned!" the guard shouts, making both of us wince.

"Bu . . . but, coats cost lots and it's already winter," she whimpers softly, tears in her eyes and voice.

"Everything here is earned. You can buy things or kill him for his clothes," he snarls waving his hand at Bren, making my gut seize up.

"I . . . I can't," the girl whines. Kate looks like she wants to interfere but the maintenance woman has a hand on her arm.

"No?" The guard asks. "Well, it's done like this . . ." He pulls his baton and I lunge, falling into him and knocking him down onto the ice. I stay down praying he won't beat me with his baton, or worse, shoot me.

"Clumsy!" he screeches as he stands up. Redness has crept up his neck and floods his cheeks.

"I'm . . . I'm sorry!" I stammer.

He waves his baton at me and prepares to strike. From the corner of my eye, I can see Bren. He takes a step but hesitates. He wants to help me, but he is afraid he'll make it worse.

Reign knows the system better. She steps forward bravely and hauls me to my feet with one arm. "Come on, stupid, we're late for laundry duty."

I hear Kate's soft voice. "She doesn't know."

Reign pulls me quickly toward the laundry.

"It was your job to prepare her for her future here," the guard snarls back.

Reign tugs at my arm again and I quicken my pace, but jerk to a stop as a blast rings in my ears. I look back fearing for Bren. Reign jerks me forward, away from the chaos, but I still catch a glimpse of the girl who wanted a coat, the hole in her chest and the blood spreading over the cold, hard ground like a flower opening to the sun. A silent sob catches in my throat and I stumble. Someone else is not so lucky. I hear a muffled howl of anguish echo across the silent yard and catch a glimpse of Kate frozen, speechless, and stunned for a moment. Then I watch her collapse in on herself. Her shoulders curl in and she brings her hands up over her face, her head dropping.

Reign shakes my arm and whispers, "Don't look."

It's too late. The image will haunt me forever, but all I can think is, thank God it wasn't Bren.

I am too scared to work on the computer tonight but Reign insists it's a perfect night for it. Everyone is quiet and restless with the death of the young girl but none are grieving like Kate. I'm afraid for her. Reign insists that no one will be expecting a hack tonight and she reminds me that my days until surgery are shrinking fast.

"What if it's all a lie?" I whisper as I help her load another pile into the washer.

"It doesn't matter if the camera they said they'd install in your eye is a lie or not. Get your head in the game," she snarls back under her breath.

I say nothing more and return to work. I keep seeing the girl without a coat, a hole in her chest and a spreading pool of blood.

Our laundry time ends and I head to class. Today we are field stripping weapons. I've been doing it long enough that I can do it without thinking and that's a good thing because I can't get my thoughts to settle enough to focus on anything. Getting my head back in the game is a real joke. I want to curl up and cry, but I also don't want her death to mean nothing.

It's time for lunch. I know I need to eat, but it all tastes like sawdust. Reign is on the other side of the room pretending to ignore me. Bren sits with his back to a wall watching the room. He knows better than to acknowledge me in public. He also knows that if he shows me an ounce of sympathy I'll fall apart.

Kate seems to have the opposite sense and when I see the sorrow in her overly shiny eyes I about lose it.

"You should have sat somewhere else," I croak softly.

"I know where I'm needed."

"Kate," I grate, "You can't be nice to me. I'll lose it and I can't give you any sympathy or I'll really lose it."

"That is why you are special."

"I'm not."

"Elise, you are a survivor and you still have a big heart that you try to hide. Don't let them crush the part of you that cares. That is what they are trying to do. When you no longer care, then everything you do is just the job and you won't mind working for them. Don't let them win. I've been here a long time. I've watched so many prisoners turn into guards that I've lost count. For the most part, it's too dangerous to send them anywhere else. Some do go to jobs where they can be carefully monitored. Some are like me, kept here forever because their skills are needed."

"Why are you telling me this?"

"I'm not your enemy. I see greatness in you. You will be the one to end this travesty. You will be the one who figures how to get out and not only survive but bring the truth to the people. You have to bring it to them. I may not be your enemy, but the government *is* and not just to you but all of us who are not inside it. When did it become their job to decide who lives and who dies?"

"Kate, if they hear you . . ."

She leans even closer to me, her eyes overly bright. "You won't turn me in. When you go, take me with you. I have medical training. I'll be useful."

Curiosity grows stronger in me than my fear. "Why are you in here?"

"I was in love. I had an unauthorized baby. I knew what I was doing. My mistake was that I thought I could hide her." Kate stops talking and blinks hard several times. A tear slides past her lashes, but she doesn't seem to notice.

"Was that girl . . . ?"

"Yes." I'm amazed by how many feelings can fit into one small word.

"Do they know?"

"The Warden let me know that each time I was nice to someone he considered it a crime. Her death was my punishment. He will pay and so will the guard who shot her. He's paying already. He was my friend once. He's upstairs for therapy and I may have slipped him a little something in his food. It's unfortunate when one takes the wrong medicine. It can have lasting effects."

"They let you near him?"

"Of course not, but I can be . . . resourceful." The new look in her eye sends a chill through me.

I go from sorrow to fear like a switch has been flipped — maybe it's the gleam in Kate's eye. She's become reckless, dangerous and maybe more than a little unbalanced.

My wristband beeps, telling me it's a time for our next rotation. Kate rises as if in a trance and walks out, her tray forgotten.

I move what's left on mine over to hers and stack them. Then I get in line to turn them in. My thoughts churn as I wait.

At dinner, Bren sits by me. He begins tapping on my leg,

under the table. He tells me everything I need to know to get into the attic. I am amazed that he can communicate with me and quickly shovel in his food with the other hand. I am so focused on what he is trying to tell me that my own food is virtually forgotten.

Nod if you understand, he taps out.

I nod once like he asks. He gathers his tray and gets up and leaves without ever looking at me. I won't lie, I feel lost when he's gone.

It's my turn for custodial duties again. I'm thankful that I've earned enough credits to buy cleaning gloves. The chemicals they use are harsh and wreck my skin. Kitchen duty was bad enough and now my thumb is cracked and bleeding a little. My nails are peeling in layers too. At least I have nail clippers. They were one of the first things that I bought. I never appreciated all the little things that we were given at school to make our lives easier. I had taken so much for granted. I run my fingers through my hair to push it off my forehead. It must be getting close to four inches long by now. Parts of it are getting annoying, but I can't afford a trim and I have nothing I'm willing to give up in trade . . . yet.

I pick up my gloves in exchange for the credits I have and then head over to check in with the guard on duty by the supply closet. He unlocks the carts for us. There are four of us on cleaning duty. I don't pay any attention to the others; most prisoners are just nameless faces to me. I've learned to avoid attachment as must as possible; clearly, it doesn't always work for me.

I check the schedule attached to the cart. I'm shocked to

see that I have been assigned to the upper floor. I push my cart toward the service elevator and fully expect to be stopped by the guard there. He scans both my wrist device and the cart and then lets me into the elevator. I ride up feeling uncomfortable. This has got to be a trick. I am to start on the upper right side of this level. My first room appears to be an office. It is similar to the Warden's but smaller and finished in lighter colors. The feeling of oppression in the Warden's office is not present in this room. There are prints of the nearby mountains up on the walls and I find that I'm drawn to them. I move closer and just stare for a moment. They are so real, I can almost smell the mountain air and feel the cool moist breeze flutter over my skin.

I shake it off before I'm caught not working and check the routine attached to the cart; top down, dust, vacuum, polish furniture if any is present and then mop any hard surfaces. I pull the long handled duster from the cart and start the process of knocking down cobwebs and dust on the ceilings and upper walls. I dust the pictures slowly so that they can work their magic on me once more before I move on to the rest of the dusting. Just as I fight not to fall into the lovely mountain scenes, I fight to avoid the computer in the room.

The guard assigned to me and the other prisoner on this level leans on the open door frame and watches me work. Just when I'm feeling really uncomfortable he leaves. There have to be hidden cameras in this room. They have to be waiting for me to make a mistake. This has got to be a test or a trick. I pay careful attention to each shelf and picture frame as I dust but find nothing, and I know my not finding anything is not conclusive evidence. I finally get to the desk itself and itch to touch the computer, but I don't dare. Tempting as it is, I touch it with nothing but my assigned dusting wand. The guard looks in on me again, but I'm on-task so he disappears. I begin to vacuum and wonder if maybe the observation device is hidden in the cart or if they have finally given up on me. Do they believe they've fixed me? Nah, that can't be it.

I'm still dying to touch the computer, but I force myself to ignore it, knowing that I can use the laptop tonight and figure that if I get caught on this computer I won't be able to do the work I need to do.

I finish my chores, give the room one last check, and turn out the light. I push my cart to the next room, this time a classroom, and begin again. The next room is another classroom and then another office. This space is shared by eight people, including the Captain I fear so much. Each of the eight desks holds a computer and personal effects. Shelves split the desks so that there is a gap between each worker. A window at the end of this narrow room is made cozier by two overstuffed chairs for reading and a table with a lamp. I start to dust, but a flicker in my peripheral vision makes me turn. A monitor is coming to life and the subject on the monitor is me.

I feel as if I'm watching a natural disaster happen. I don't want to see it, but I can't look away. This is footage of me cleaning the first office. There were many cameras on me judging by the angles of the various shots flickering over the screen. A subtle movement of air lets me know I'm not alone. I clear my throat nervously, waiting for the pain that is sure to come.

I hold my body completely still as I slowly raise my eyes to see the Captain watching me.

"I am to let you know that your restraint has not gone unnoticed."

I just stand, unmoving. I can't decide if I should say something or not. Fear and outrage wrestle within me.

A leer cuts across his face as he strokes the handgun clipped to his side. I can't help it, I gulp. My reaction makes him laugh. I watch him go, but it takes two agonizingly slow minutes before I can stop the shaking and return to work.

Time passes, the fear eases, and anger fills the void. I finish my work and return my cart. While the guard checks it over and inventories my supplies, I slide a hand over and snag an almost empty roll of electrical tape and stuff it casually into my waistband. The second he gives me the all clear I walk straight to the latrine. I dawdle to be sure I'm one of the last in. I climb the shower divider and press open the window that Bren was supposed to loosen for me. It swings out easily. He must have found a way to lubricate the hinges. A guard stands just below the window. I freeze and watch. He swings his head slowly from left to right as if he is sweeping the grounds with his eyes. After twelve breaths, he strolls down the building and around the corner. I should now have five minutes to climb the building and disappear into the attic before the next one passes.

I ease my body out the window and stand on the ledge. I'm stronger than I've ever been but I wonder if I can do this. I rise up on tip-toe to reach the decorative edge, pull up and carefully move my feet to the top of the window. Now I can grasp the bottom of the second-floor window. I hear the scrape of boots. I work hard to steady my breathing. The next guard is early. I pray that if I hold incredibly still he will pass by without looking up. He stops right under me and looks both ways. Maybe I should just jump on him and find another way into the attic. I hold still evaluating my options.

Just as my arms are starting to shake, he moves off. *Please let me have the strength to pull up.* I manage to get an elbow on the edge. I try to push the window up, but it won't budge. *What happened? Now what?*

The window flies open and I nearly fall. A firm hand stops me. I flick my startled eyes to a darkened face.

"I've got you." I know that voice.

I'm pulled into the upstairs classroom and lab that the medical students use and collapse on the floor, shaking and breathing hard.

"You're welcome."

"Wh . . . What are you doing here?"

Kate's eyes and teeth flash in the dark, but I think it is more of a grimace than a smile. "I knew you were after something. You had that furtive look about you. I have hospital duty tonight, so I was in the right place at the right time and just happened to be looking out. I saw you climb out the window."

"You had time to actually look out a window?"

"They don't watch me like they do you. They need me. Before I was here I was a physicians' assistant. You know my crime. I made it worse when I spoke out against the government and the rest, as they say, is history. I have been a model prisoner up to now. I snuck away on a fake mission to the supply room, but don't worry, I wasn't followed."

I give her a skeptical look and go to check the hall for myself. When I look back I see that Kate has not moved from the swath of moonlight. "Told you so and yeah, I saw the look on your face. You need me. When you get out of here, take me with you. You'll need me."

"I want to trust you, but —"

"I know. They've made it hard to even trust yourself," Kate sighs. "Do what you need to do. I'll be missed in the infirmary soon. Be safe." She moves to hug me but stops just shy of doing so. I want to hug her too, but I'm not ready to fully trust her yet or maybe it's me I can't trust.

I watch her leave and figure out my next move. My planned point of entry into the attic was not from this room but I wonder . . . I look to the supply closet and figure that's as good an entry point as any. I try the knob but find it locked. I rummage in the nearby desk and locate the key. Important places are locked electronically, but no one here would be interested in stealing school or medical supplies.

Once inside, I climb the shelves like a ladder to get close to the ceiling. I push up the nearest panel and scan the area. It's dark but not so much so that I am completely blind. I can make it to the laptop from here and it saves me entering the halls on level two. This is safer. I haul myself in and close the panel behind me. It feels like it takes forever to get to the laptop, but I do eventually.

I run my hands over the surface and take comfort from its

presence. I can't believe that no one has reported it missing yet. I'm just thankful that I don't have another complication. Now that the laptop is in my hands I feel more focused. It may be uncomfortable up here, but at least I will be left alone. First I cover the built-in camera with a bit of electrical tape. Then I check and make sure that what I set up last time is still functioning. I look for any messages the rebels may have left me, but there is only one coded note saying that they are receiving a ghost copy of the nightly upload. I smile; it's working which means they are getting a copy of everything sent to the main government computer downtown. It's not state or even national, but district level is a start. I crack my knuckles and take a deep breath of the stale, tepid air. It's time to hack into our chips and see what other prisoner monitoring tech they have online.

I can feel the sweat beginning to run down my back in a combination of my earlier exertion and now nerves. My clothes are sticking to me. My hands are sweaty too, so I rub them up and down my thighs. My fingers slip on the keys and . . . I'm in.

I forget everything else as I stealth through their system. I find the programming that runs our chips and scan through the research notes on them. Each chip is assigned an alpha-numeric code and I only know my own. There has got to be more files. There! Data on each prisoner spools out before my eyes. I look at my own file first. Perhaps it is a mistake. I remind myself that what is in this file is only their version of the truth about me and it does not have to be my truth.

I have been pegged as a loner with passive-aggressive tendencies. I feel more comfortable with machines than I do with people, but I look to be trainable. I have survived this long and my skills mark me as being worth keeping. The programming that was tested on our trial location appears to have been a success but requires some minor tweaks before being released at other trials. Other trials! Oh — my — God. More kids will die!

I force myself to read on. It looks like they have not been terribly successful at correcting the glitches and some people are anxious to get *me* back on it. They want to know how I knew things and escaped their traps. Apparently, I could not tell them what I didn't even understand myself. Didn't they know I would never willingly hurt innocent people or help anyone else to do it?

I dig a little deeper and see that the Inquisitor has filled out a report stating that he believes that my psyche could be peeled apart and rebuilt to turn me into a killing machine. I could be conditioned to torture and kill. He is all kinds of wrong about that! My anger reminds me why I am here and refocuses me. It does not matter what he believes — it's what I believe that counts.

I start digging into the files on our chips. My goal is two-fold; first I need to find any information helpful to the rebels and send it on and second I need to figure out how to shut down the chips without hurting the people they've been planted in.

I find personnel files, building schematics, blueprints and wiring diagrams, all of which I send on. This will be more information than they've ever had. I hope it helps — Although I don't want to think about it, I know this may be all I am able to send before they figure out what I am doing. I'm irritated that I can find so little on the chips.

As I study the blueprints of the prison, a bunch of questions swirl through my mind. Where are the panels, subpanels, and main breaker? Most of the prison is made of concrete. Where does our water come from and where does waste go? We grow food here but not enough to sustain us. There are no animals kept here, so how do the supplies come in?

And then I know and almost feel dumb for not realizing it . . . but then I hadn't really had time to give it any thought. There have got to be tunnels here too. It seems odd to have them way out here . . . where do they go? I look again at the blueprints and find an anomaly on the lowest level. Someone will need to take a look — I don't think I'll ever be able to go down there again.

I move on to other things and find that all tools are inventoried, but what about kitchen equipment and eating utensils? Where could things be hidden? What areas are neglected? How can things be hidden in plain sight? I know that a butter knife can be used as a screwdriver and chisel. What in medical is inventoried and what is not? Could I adjust the inventory without it being noticed? My brain churns.

I switch to the inventory lists and study the tracking program. Inventory is entered by the shift leads of each guard section but reported by the guards. I keep following the thread to see what happens when numbers are off. There — notes on punishments of both prisoners and guards. I keep following the breadcrumbs of thought to see where they lead. Eventually, I'll have the whole picture of the system. I discover that supplies must be delivered on Tuesdays because of the bulge that happens in inventory regularly on that day. I also can see things dwindling throughout the week. I go ahead and send the inventory and some notes on how it's done. I worry about sending too much. Surely they have a staff to wade through all the data. I just need to focus on my part. They will have to decide what is important to the cause — that is not my job.

I look at the computer's clock. Dang, it's already after 2:00 a.m. My time is up. If they are going to do bed-checks tonight they will happen around 3:00 a.m. Depending on the shift change, which they still alter, I now know that it only varies within a fifteen-minute window on a rotating table. Each shift moves one hour forward every five days and then forty-two minutes back every two days. They think they are so smart. I need to be careful that I don't fall into the same trap.

Now that I've memorized the blueprints, I have four different routes I can take. I don't want to keep going in and out the same way and beat a path. I have always believed that there are cameras everywhere; now I see that isn't the case.

Cameras focus on the main areas, the stairs, and elevators at all times. They must believe we are too scared or too dumb to try anything else. They do not consider how desperate we could become. I also see that the cameras cycle in all other areas. They don't have them on in all areas all the time. I think I'll try leaving through the infirmary tonight. The cameras in that location are off so I only have live people to worry about in that section.

I confirm that all the file transfers I've started are complete and then I shut down the computer for the night and hide it under the insulation. I can't have it overheating itself or anything else. I'm going to have to find a way to get power to it soon. The battery is nearly used up. Maybe I could work with the electrician again and steal an outlet jack to wire in. I know how to do that now — I will always be thankful to him for inadvertently teaching me.

I listen carefully at my access point. I count to sixty just to be sure and then carefully lift the lid. I do it slowly and only just enough to peek. It would be cosmically stupid to get caught now. I neither see nor hear any movement so I move it back further to take a better look. I'm right by a camera, but the indicator light is off like it should be.

This section of the infirmary is curtained off. It's meant for the terminally ill and contagious patients, but no one is here now. I slither out and hang by one hand as I move the ceiling tile back into place. I rest one edge on my fingers, drop onto the hospital bed and land with a soft thud. I jump silently to the floor and then straighten the bedding. I look at the ceiling tile and think it looks undisturbed.

I listen again. Soft footsteps let me know someone is coming. Once they've receded, I move close to the curtain for a look. The coast is clear so I head to the outer wall in search of a window.

The first one I find is a fixed one. The sweat from the attic that had dried begins again and my stomach squeezes. The next window is also fixed, adding to my anxiety. The third one is operable. I sigh and slide it open and look around. Two guards stand talking near the guard tower. If I'm careful the corner edge of the building that sticks out will hide my descent.

I struggle to find a foothold. Just when I think I'm balanced, my foot slips and I hit my chin on the window ledge, clacking my teeth together with an audible crack. My eyes water, but I manage not to cry out. I find another place to put my foot and work the window closed. Inch by agonizing inch I work my way back down, trying not to look at the ground. I force myself to concentrate. Sadly, I will have to go all the way to the ground and then climb up to the shower room window.

When I feel my feet touch the ground I want to cry for a whole other reason, but I crouch low and run to the shower room window before I can be caught. I want to cry for a third time when I see the window is open for me, and I jump and snag the edge. I'm shaking by the time I get an elbow on the ledge, but I pull myself onto my belly and then on in. I teeter on the edge of the nearest stall as I pull the window closed. I slide down and lean against it for a moment, panting.

Reign has left night clothes for me, hidden behind a sink drain pipe like Bren told me she would. I take a quick shower, dress in the night clothes, and roll up my day clothes. Tomorrow is Bren's turn for laundry duty. He'll see that they go unnoticed in the laundry room.

I walk past the end of his bed prepared to drop them off. His hand snakes out and gently grabs my wrist.

I wait, expecting him to say something. He doesn't. He pulls me close and hugs me fiercely to his chest. I can feel his heart rate slowing. His breath makes my hair flutter. I relax and let my arms settle into a comfortable position around him. I feel my own breath and heart rate slowing. We are alone in a crowd of sleeping humanity. I want to sleep and I want Bren to hold me while I do it. I believe that if he does, the nightmares won't come. I wonder if I can trust myself to wake up before the guards arrive for our morning run.

Just as I'm about to suggest it, he releases me but keeps my hand. He takes me to my own bed, kisses my forehead and walks away. I pull myself onto my bunk and hug my pillow, pretending it's Bren.

18

The alarm for us to get up comes much too early, but I realize that I can't remember having had any nightmares. I dress quickly and I run my fingers through my slowly growing hair, pin back the annoying bits and sigh. My old school life would be a dream existence now.

Our five-mile early morning exercise regime is its usual awfulness. I don't get the pain in my side anymore, but I still hate the run. The only thing it is good for is a chance to communicate with Reign and Bren. I find her in the crowd and work my way over to her position. I don't look at her, I just run next to her until the guard on the ATV is out of sight.

"I need an outlet."

Reign doesn't look at me either. "What do you mean?"

"I need an outlet from the electrician, wire cutters, a knife, a chunk of wire about a third of a meter long, and a screwdriver that fits the screws in the outlet."

Reign slides me a glance. "It's gonna take time."

"You have until tonight. I'm running out of battery."

Reign curses under her breath and picks up the pace. I watch her move through the ranks until I sense someone next to me.

Bren quirks up one corner of his mouth in our version of a smile before he asks, "What'd you say to her?"

"I told her what I need for tonight." I risk a glance at him and then change the subject. "I get why you volunteered for this. I don't understand her motivation."

"She's a criminal. This is better than her alternative. If she does this, we'll clear her name."

"What do you mean?"

"She's wanted by both sides for various crimes."

"But you trust her."

"I know her story. She didn't have a choice and the government made what she did sound worse than it was. Her crimes, in the eyes of the Recalcitrants, are small and petty by comparison."

"Someday you will tell me."

"You make it out of here, Sunshine, and I'll tell you everything you want to know."

I start to smile a real smile, but Bren bumps into me to remind me where I am and who we are before I make that fatal mistake. I hope I remember how to smile when I finally get out of here.

We come up to the main yard where everyone is gathered before breakfast like usual. Some are stretching and others are talking softly, but all are waiting. The line of three guards standing in front of the door is a good deterrent. We are moved into two lines, which is not common.

Each of us is wanded by one of two guards before we are allowed into the mess hall for breakfast. They do these random checks periodically, but this one feels more sinister somehow. I half expect to be pulled aside, but they let me pass and then it's all I can think about as I wait my turn to get my share of break-fast. I can only assume that some missing items have been noted.

This morning when I look at my oatmeal I actually have feelings of contempt toward it. What I would give for a fried egg sandwich or an omelet. I can still remember the feel of it in my mouth . . . fluffy, salty, the bite of onion, the mustiness of mushroom, and best of all, the savory taste of bacon and melted cheddar cheese. I have got to get out of here.

After breakfast, I go in search of a job. There is nothing available in electrical, but I can get a janitorial shift. I take it hoping for a break. When I get to the closet to check out my supplies I pay careful attention to how it is done and everything in the room. I watch to see how items are recorded and wait to see if chemicals are measured or weighed. I don't want to get caught staring, so the moment the guard's attention is on one of the janitorial carts I study the shelves. I can see all the supplies I need, they almost seem to sparkle tauntingly behind the wire mesh grid held in place by framing and locks, so close but out of reach.

I do a quick inventory of the rest of the items in the cabinet and then of my cart. It's my turn to be prepped for work. The guard is lazily checking off my items. He starts to mark his tablet.

"Wait," I say as an idea pops into my head.

He looks at me in surprise.

"Last time I cleaned the warden's office there was a light out."

"That's maintenance's problem," he snaps.

"But if he knows you know about it and didn't do something . . ."

"All right, all right."

He sighs and unlocks the cabinet and reaches for a standard bulb.

"No. It's one of the specialty ones he has over his pictures and plaques to highlight them."

He turns startled eyes on me. I try to look as small, nonlethal, and trustworthy as I can. From behind my lowered lashes, I watch him shake his head and reach again. While he is twisted away reaching for the highest shelf, I grab a small coil of 220 wire and shove it into the back of my pants, covering it with my shirt.

He thrusts the bulb into my hands. "Now get to work. You're running behind."

I nod my head and then push my cart out of the storage room. As I work my way down the hall, I scour my brain for a place to hide my prize. Images flash in my mind; an empty classroom on the second level, classroom supplies including tape, and an old wooden teacher's desk to tape the wire under. I will enter the attic through that same room tonight. The best part is they are too cheap to monitor anything up here in the hall or other important areas since most prisoners aren't allowed.

It feels like forever before I can finally get to the room I targeted. The moment the guard leaves to check on the other janitor I snatch up the needed supplies and tape my wire into place. The squeak of his boots alerts me to his return. I quickly grab my dust mop and take some swipes at the floor. I finish my job, crack a window open and double check my tape job before I leave.

I get to clean a new area today that gives me a window into the lives of the guards. I discover that most of them sleep in one of four rooms; each has ten twin sized beds with five on each wall. I check my sheet. All linens are to be changed today. It is my job to strip the beds. It's a good thing that I don't have to make them because I never showed any aptitude for hospitality so a perfectly executed hospitality corner will never happen on my shift. I dust the lamp over each bed and the small tables between them. Clearly, this is just a place to crash between shifts because no personal items are in sight. I quickly finish the vacuuming and move on to the rooms belonging to the shift leads. These rooms each contain two twin beds, two desks, and two closets. I recognize some of the guards in the photographs over the desks. It does give me a little insight into who has families and who is married to their job. When I reach the farthest desk, I see a picture of the group who took me down . . . and an unconscious me. It hurts to see myself trussed up like a turkey and tossed like yesterday's trash in the back of the military transporter behind them. My stomach churns and I tear my eyes away and finish the room. Did they put it here for me to find?

The Captain's room is quite a bit larger than those of the shift leads, but then I know he is here full time. The room is strangely sterile. No pictures and only a few books are present.

The books he does have are telling — all are military history and warfare. I'm drawn to the window. It does not look over the camp but toward the trees. Perhaps he dreams of life outside these walls too.

The rest of the morning crawls past. I fight the urge to curl up in a corner to nap. At lunch time, I take my tray and look for Reign. She catches my eye and then looks away with a slight shake of her head so I move over to sit by Bren. I press my leg from the knee down into his, hoping that no one will notice. I don't want any attention on us, but I need to feel him, to know that everything is as okay as it can be. We have almost survived another day.

Lunch ends much too quickly, but I know that Bren will pass on the information that I tapped on his leg with Morse code. I pray that Reign has better luck this afternoon with the outlet but I prepare myself to deal with it on my own — that and a screwdriver as well as something to strip the wire.

I'm deep in thought when Kate bumps into me passing off a scalpel as she does it. "Good luck," she breathes before pressing on down the hallway. I palm the tool until I can get somewhere to hide it better. This must be what Reign has arranged in place of a screwdriver, the wire stripper, or maybe she sent it to me for defense. It won't work as well as a wire cutter but then it's really not the best choice for a screwdriver either.

At dinner, I sit across from Bren. He holds one of my feet between his. I slide forward far enough on the bench to hook my free foot around his ankle. It is not enough, but it will do for now. Reign walks past and gives me a look. Then she flicks her eyes to the windows and back. I take it I'm to meet her outside.

As soon as my tray is cleared I walk out and look for a probable meeting spot.

"Hey!" I turn towards the voice. "I've seen you skulking out here before. It kinda makes me think you're up to something."

"No, sir," I answer softly. "I only wanted some fresh air."

"Let me see your wristband."

I hold out my arm obediently. Inside I'm shaking, afraid that I'll have to find a new way to meet Reign. I look toward the ground but scan the area with my peripheral vision.

"You have five minutes before work detail begins."

I feel like I've been let off easy, but I only nod once and then move away from him as I continue to scan the area. The garden shed seems most likely and sure enough, my eye catches a flash of movement. I glance around and then take a circuitous route to the shed while trying to walk with purpose. Reign snatches my elbow the moment I'm close enough.

"I got it but you owe me big. Do you know what I had to trade for this?" she asks, shoving the outlet into my hand.

I just look at her and wonder, *Do I want to know?* Probably not. "I appreciate your sacrifice but you're not the only one who —"

"I don't care what you think. Just get us out of here."

I can hear a tremor in her voice, hidden under a layer of sarcasm and hate. For a moment I'm afraid of her, of what she will do. She is not like me. She will get even with the people who hurt her and I know that I do not want to be one of those, but I can't help myself, I have to know.

What happened to you? How'd you get here?" I ask her

again, feeling sure I won't get an answer this time either.

The anger stays, but I see something else too. Reign gets a faraway look in her eyes and I can see her as she once was. I can see her as a scared little girl, beaten and abused. Forced to do things she was not ready to do.

Her voice starts out in a whisper I can barely hear. "When I was ten, I was pulled out of school. My parents had been in an accident and I was put on a plane and flown to this coast. I would now be the ward of my mother's second cousin. I was supposed to go back to school, but he kept me home. He had me cook and clean for him. When I first came, the weather was bad and I understood not being allowed outside, but come spring I longed for fresh air. I remember standing by an open window just so I could breathe it in."

Reign's eyes have gone closed and her shoulders have curved inward as if she is trying to physically protect herself from the memory. "When I was twelve, he started coming into my room at night." This time, she shudders lost in those memories.

I watch her swallow and then her eyes slowly open to take in the world around her. I know she is struggling to hold herself together.

She takes another breath and continues her story. "By the time I was thirteen, I was pregnant. He kept hoping I would lose it. He continued to keep me locked up, which wasn't too hard considering the rather remote location. I had not met even one neighbor in my time there and hadn't a clue which way to run. My baby was born at only thirty weeks. Back then I didn't know that was too soon. I labored for thirty hours before delivering a little boy and finally fell into an exhausted sleep holding him close. When I woke up, he was gone. My captor had smothered him."

I watch the emotions travel over Reign's face. The sadness is washed away by hatred as she turns her eyes back to me. "I fed the sorry son of a bitch rat poison for five days and then I cut him when he tried to come back to my bed. I left and never looked back. The Recalcitrants found me first and sheltered me. They had a counselor among them who helped me, but the best help came when they taught me to fight. I learned quickly. By sixteen I was going on raids, but by seventeen I was captured and put in a place like this. They didn't chip us at that facility."

Reign stares at the distant pines for a few breaths and then continues like I'm not even there. "I had kitchen duty one day and took advantage of it. I was chopping celery when the deliveries arrived. I stabbed our fat, slovenly cook and ran right past the startled delivery guy. I took his truck, drove for a while and then ditched it on an old service road. I eventually rejoined the resistance but it was help you or be locked up. They think I'm dangerous."

No kidding, I want to say aloud, but I'm afraid — afraid of what she's become and of what she will do.

"Time's up. Go before we're caught." Reign practically runs away from me. I watch her as she goes. Her pain recedes with her but what she said will always be with me.

I go to my evening class, feeling like I'm there in body only. Phantom images of Reign float in my head. I'm broken and can't even help myself so what can I possibly do for her? I walk to my next job in a daze. This time, it's Bren who stops me to pass off a stubby screwdriver. A few steps later, Kate passes off wire nuts, and I hadn't even thought to ask for those. The items burn a hole in my pocket until bedtime. I'm so afraid I'll get caught, I shake.

I nearly slip and fall on the otherwise uneventful climb to the attic. The bag I put my tools in remains secured to my waist. The guards didn't find it when they tossed everyone's footlockers today, but then I'm smart enough not to keep it there.

My first task is to wire in my outlet. I find a junction box, carefully open it and remove the wire nuts. I prep the loose pieces of wire and the outlet. Ten minutes later, I'm ready. My heart leaps when I plug in the computer and see the icon showing it's charging.

I study the system to see if any of my trespasses have been noted. Finding no evidence of that, I follow more threads. I send each file on to the rebels after I look at it. I still do not hear from them. My eyes burn but I keep at it until I'm nodding off. I shut everything down and hide it as best I can, just in case.

I only have to stop once on the way down to wait for a guard to pass. Bren meets me long enough to take my dirty clothes and then he's gone, silent as a shadow.

My neighbor has to drag me out of bed in the morning. All I want to do is sleep but I have more important things to do. Thinking about disabling the chips is the only thing that keeps me going. I nearly nod off in my citizenship and government class. I find it a huge irony that they teach that subject until a quote from school pops into my head, "History is written by the winners." Maybe what they are teaching here is not the truth, but what they want us to believe.

Now I have a new reason to stay awake and pay attention. I want to separate truth from lies. I evaluate each sentence I hear or see in print. I compare what I remember to what is being presented now. What is the same? What is different? And all the while I wonder, what is their agenda?

I manage to get through the day, putting part of my attention on my surroundings and the rest of it on the job I must do. At bedtime, I brush my teeth with the rest of the prisoners and wait impatiently for lights out. I stare at the ceiling, afraid to close my eyes, but after what feels like forever, the room goes dark.

Tonight, when I finally get to the laptop, I get hung up on the Inquisitor's notes on all his prisoner experiments instead of doing my job. This man is the greatest evil I've ever known. He must be put down for the greater good, but I don't know if I have what it takes to do it. The message line opens and char-acters appear. I stare at them as the seconds tick by. I doze off and jerk awake as my chin hits my chest.

Are you okay? The cursor is blinking in the hidden chat box I established.

How do I answer that? I don't even know what okay is any-more. I come back with the best answer I can think of, *I will be.*

The cursor flashes but no more characters appear. I send the Inquisitor's notes and leave, still unable to hack into the chips far enough to answer my questions. I feel like I am as far from disabling them as I was when I first got here.

Reign meets me in the bathroom tonight to get a recap of what I have accomplished. I can tell that she is frustrated with the slowness of my progress. Part of me admires how well she is holding her tongue, considering. I'm sure being here brings back horrible memories for her. I think I am asleep before my head hits the pillow.

19

01010010 01100101 01100011 01100001 01101100

01100011 01101001 01110100 01110010 01100001

01101110 01110100

Today is even rougher. I'm crashing. All I want to do is sleep. I find that it is easier to stay awake when I'm on my feet. It's even better when I'm in the cool crisp air of morning and evening. The snow is long gone but the bite of winter still hangs on in the darkness. I'm thankful that the dryness of the area doesn't leave the brickwork slippery as I climb.

Having gotten away with it before, I'm feeling more confident as I make my way to the attic. When I slip, I give myself a mental slap and remind myself not to get cocky. I sigh with relief when I'm tucked into the relative safety of the attic. Sitting in the warmth with the darkness wrapped around me, I yawn so hard my eyes water. It happens over and over so that I can barely see the screen. I'm not reading as carefully, but I'm sure to send it all on. I pray that I'm helping, and I hope that I can trust the Recalcitrants. Everyone lies, everyone has their own agenda — can I even trust myself?

I slip the last few feet down the building but it's Bren who meets me in the latrine tonight. He pulls me in for a hug and we slide to the floor together.

"You're cold," he whispers into my hair.

"I'm tired."

"You can do this. I believe in you."

"I'm glad someone does. I've got to crack it soon. I'm so tired, I'm running on fumes."

"Did you learn anything new?" he asks softly.

"Mainly that the Inquisitor, Warden, I mean, is every bit as sadistic, ruthless, and cruel as I felt he was. Apparently, I'm not the only one he's . . . shared his gifts with."

"I don't know what to say," Bren whispers, his voice catching. "'I'm so very sorry,' just doesn't even come close."

"He needs to be put down, but even after all he's done to me, I don't know if I can do it. Maybe if I caught him torturing someone else I would be moved to act." Now I know I have changed if I think I can really hurt someone, and I don't very much like who I am anymore.

"Don't worry about that right now. Until you kill the chips, there is nothing we can do about him that won't come back on you or the others unfortunate enough to be chipped."

"Nothing? I can come up with something. What's more important than ridding the world of his evil?"

"We need the chips disabled, Lise. Then we need to get our escape plan and supplies finalized. After that, we can worry about him."

Bren says the words with all the calm authority of a leader. I need to learn to be more like that and less like me. His arm is still around my shoulders. I lean over until my head is on his chest and take comfort in his steady heartbeat. I slide my arm around his waist knowing it's only a moment in time, but I feel safe. When did I last feel like this? I snuggle in a little closer and remember the last time I was with him. I pull up each image of when he held me. No matter what his past with Reign, this moment is mine.

I pull my head up and take a deep breath by his neck. He smells different than I remember. The underlying scent is the same, but the soap used here to wash our clothes and bodies is harsh and cheap with a medicinal quality.

I want so badly to kiss him but I don't know what he'll think. Maybe it's remembering those good moments when he first found me, or is it just Bren's draw? I have always found him so appealing. Before I can change my mind, I touch my lips to his neck. His skin feels warm against my mouth. His body stiffens for a brief moment and then he relaxes, tilts my chin up and kisses me.

"I believe in you," he whispers against my lips. I can feel him smile before he gets serious about kissing me. I want to stay right here, but my body is beginning to feel desperate for sleep. "You're exhausted," he says gently.

"I'm sorry," I reply.

"Don't be. We all need you. It's my job to take care of you and I'm not doing a good job of that. Let's get you to bed."

I feel myself blush even though I know he means for me to

sleep. I watch him pause and observe the dorm. The way he glances around the corner makes me think of all the spies I used to read about back in the library at school. I almost giggle. Bren takes my hand and leads me to my bunk where he tucks me in like a child, complete with a kiss on my forehead. As I close my gritty eyes I swear I hear him mumble, "Sweet dreams." Even if it's my imagination, I hold the wish close to my heart.

Sweet dreams are not a gift I receive. Nightmares plague me and when I'm awake, numbers, symbols, codes, and fragments of random data swim in my head. I feel pressure building. It shows in the kink in my neck, my short temper, and the pain in my head. I have lost the ability to self-soothe. I am unable to calm down. Not letting it show is fragmenting me from the inside out.

The lack of sleep is catching up with me. I find myself taking catnaps during sit-down lessons and at lunchtime instead of eating. As much as I want to get out of here and as much as I know others are counting on me, I have to drag myself back to the attic. I will have to insist on a break before I give myself away.

My eyes widen and I'm fully awake. I have found a disturbing piece of information . . . Portland was only the first. Seattle, San Jose, Los Angeles, Salt Lake City, and Phoenix are up next. I see a thread to a demo and follow it. I watch in horror as red blooms over the screen, exploding at each city and spreading east. My breath is coming fast — I have to remind myself it is just a demo — young people slaughtered like cattle, all to quiet the resistance and get them to surrender.

Does the government believe they're retraining me? Who can I really trust or does it even matter? What if I die? So what?

I don't want to live like this. I don't want to live in a world where no choice is my only choice. Was it better to be blissfully oblivious like I used to be or was I ever really that way? I knew things were wrong when I was at school. Back then I could do nothing about it. What can I do now? All I know for sure is that I will not be anyone's puppet.

I try going at the chips in a new way. If they are installed by medical then maybe they can be found in that data stream. It is one of the few places I have not looked. I can almost feel the seconds ticking by.

Yes, there, surgical procedures on each chip. I see a list of who has them installed so far, and follow the links to patient notes. I capture each file and send it on. Independent thinkers, difficult prisoners, and those with specific skill sets are all singled out and chipped.

By virtue of escaping the trials, I have made it onto the list. In my file are notes on what they did to me and how I responded. Pain, fear, and adrenaline explode in my body. A ragged sound more animal than human escapes my too tight throat.

I take a moment to just breathe, slow my racing heart, and relax. "I am in the attic. I am helping people. I am okay." A calming mantra, I repeat the three phrases two more times.

I become aware of a strange icon in the lower right corner of my screen. When I switch from the medical notes to another tab, it disappears. Switching back to the medical notes, it reappears, so I decide to take the plunge and click on it. A summary appears showing all the work I did on the live game and its virtual twin. There are also notes about the multi-player game release. I still can't believe they're actually going to release it for the public, at least until I read the details.

There will be subliminal messages embedded in *The Curse of the Underworlders*. These messages will reprogram the citizens who are on the verge of rising against the government. They are targeting certain personalities. These people will receive a mental push that will topple them over the edge. They will be so enthralled by the game that they will lose interest in life, forget to eat, and will eventually die. Numbness replaces my anxiety. This is why they want me back. This is what the Inquisitor is conditioning me for. If I no longer care about anything, I will be able to hurt people. This is what he meant when he referred to me as his tool.

What they have already done is bad enough. Without me to fine tune the game, they'll collect data from all players. They will then use that data to inform the game and make it even more deadly. The scenarios will continuously be reconfigured. I gulp, I can't help it.

I send everything on then shut down the laptop — my head spinning, and my heart squeezing in my chest. My cheeks are wet with tears I didn't even realize I was shedding. I feel utter despair.

I can barely get my act together to make it back to the latrine window. Reign meets me inside but I'm so shaken that I can hardly talk.

"What?" she asks, looking worried. "Is it the chips? Can't you break them? Are they on to you? Were you caught? What?"

Reign reaches out and shakes my shoulder. I take a

breath and let it out slowly. "What they did to us, my year group — they're going to do it in other places. It wasn't that I didn't know, but now it was all too real, staring back at me from that laptop."

Reign's face shows determination. "Did you send that piece of information?"

"Yes," I sigh. "But that's not all." I take another breath, trying to control the tightness in my chest. I can feel Reign's impatience, but she holds her tongue. "They are going to release the virtual game I worked on. They're planning to turn people into mindless zombies by planting subliminal messages in it. People will forget to eat and will eventually die. It's my fault. I did this." My voice hitches on a sob. Tears stream down my face. I just can't hold it in anymore.

Reign sits next to me and awkwardly pats my shoulder. An almost hysterical giggle bubbles up when I realize I'm probably the only friend she has who's an actual girl, making her social skills even worse than mine.

"Don't lose it now. We're not out of here yet." Her voice sounds disgusted, frustrated, and worried all at once.

I suck in a damp, shuddery breath. "I'm okay," I say even though it is *so* not true.

I wish for comfort, oblivion, something — I will find none of those things in Reign. I walk listlessly to the sink and splash water on my face, then pull on the nightwear that she left and drop off my dirty clothes where they will be collected in the morning.

I should go to my own bunk but I can't. I trudge over to

Bren's. I gently reach out to touch his shoulder but of course, he's awake.

"What's wrong?" he asks in a nearly silent whisper.

I shake my head and sit next to his hip. He starts to sit up, but I push him back. I stretch out on the very edge of his bunk with my back to him. I just need to know he's there. He pulls his blanket from under me and then shares it with me. He curls around me like he did long ago to keep me warm. I have missed this. I have missed him. We agree that it's dangerous but I will risk being caught. I need this.

Bren wakes me before the guards do. I'm able to slide out of his bunk and creep back to my side without anyone obviously noticing. I just reach my bunk when the morning alarm sounds. I change direction and head for the bathroom to beat the crowd.

I would go about my day with a smile on my face, but I'm too scared that I'll be called into the Warden's office at any moment. I make it a point to avoid everyone, allowing me think-time to figure out my next move on the laptop tonight. There's a shift in the air, and I feel something. What is it? Turning slightly, I try to take in more of the room. No one is paying any attention to me, except — wait — Kate is staring at me. She breaks eye contact first. What was that look on her face? Fear — worry — anger?

I put her out of my mind and focus. The rest of the day passes faster than I would have imagined and soon I'm back in the attic with a new approach in mind. I look at our chips again from the medical side. For some reason seeing Kate has made my mind think of medical — instead of programming. I try to figure out what makes them tick biologically. I take a deep breath of the musty attic air and I feel hopeful for the first time. The chips are energized by our bodies. If I change the chemistry . . . What would it take to change the chemistry in a buffered system? No, I'm better off short-circuiting them and setting up false signals. To set that up I need to understand the current signals and patterns. I start by studying my own chip. I know what I've been doing when I've been under extra stress or sleeping. When I first look, all I see is a big mess. I force myself to relax and the code begins to unravel. My perspective changes from two dimensional to three dimensional and the lines of code separate into distinct patterns and threads.

I will start by replicating my own patterns and have them repeat at random intervals within limits. I don't want it to appear that I'm sleeping at three in the afternoon. I plug in a special code so that sleep always happens in the same timeframe, give or take seventeen minutes. I swear I can almost feel my newest chip inside my neck — evil, sentient. A cobra waiting to strike.

Now I have a way to make it look live when it is shut down. I set up a file for each person chipped. Questions swirl in my head as I work. Each chip includes a GPS tracker that activates an alarm when we leave the grounds. It also shows where in the compound we are but only latitudinally and longitudinally — it doesn't include our elevation — their mistake. All they would know about me right now is that I am in the correct section of the building but not which floor I'm on or above for that matter. A smile spreads over my face.

I still need to figure out how to shut them down. Populating the phony data is taking longer than I wanted it to. My brain keeps noodling around how I can deactivate the kill switches. Should I disrupt the chemistry, fry, or short circuit them? I don't want to simply turn them off so that someone can come along and turn them back on. Whatever I do, it will need to be permanent but done in such a way that I don't activate the kill switches. I don't want anyone else to suffer like Malorie did.

My mind begins to wander. Once I take care of the chips, then what? How are we going to get out of here? Bren was the last one in. He must have a plan in place to get us out. It was just the chips that were a snag, right? He just hasn't had a chance to share the escape plan with me. My mind tumbles back to the chips. Where is the signal coming from? The places that send and receive the data are not the same. I know that much.

I continue to mumble to myself as I search and click. Suddenly there it is. I begin a hack into the signal. I want to get in unobserved and I want to share it with . . . or do I? I want the Recalcitrants learning from this, but I don't want them to start thinking they can do the same thing. One human controlling another is wrong. Each needs to be the captain of his own destiny.

I feel myself slipping into the world of 0s and 1s, data and bytes. The code flows over and around me, absorbing me. A sound startles me. If a guard is up here, I'm as good as dead. I hit keys as fast as I can to hide my work as I flip the monitor around to blind whoever is up here. I squinch my eyes closed and feel my way as quietly as I can through a truss, where I freeze and listen.

My breath is coming fast and my heart is trying to pound its way out of my chest. I'm afraid it is so loud that the guard will hear. I feel my body shaking as I wait for the pain that will surely come. I hope to make a break for it when the laptop is reached.

"Lise?"

I know that voice.

"Lise, it's okay. It's me," Bren's voice whispers into the near silence.

I sigh audibly. A moment later his hand fumbles over my leg and then settles on my knee.

"You're okay," he mumbles softly and I know that it's true, but only because he's here.

"Bren," I respond softly. "I lost track of time and was wrapped up in corrupting the chips and I wanted to send the information on but then I thought I shouldn't. I don't want even the Recalcitrants to have too much power. No one should control another and—"

My babbling is cut off by his lips.

"Relax," he says softly against them. "It's almost four in the morning. I was worried."

"You were?"

"I don't want anything to happen to you."

"Because I'm your ticket out?" I ask, hating myself for asking it but wanting desperately to know.

I can hear Bren sigh. It makes me wish I could see his face better. His voice is soft and soothing as he speaks, "I do want to get out of here, but I don't just care about that. I care about you. You matter."

I feel his arms come around me and a sense of peace flows

through me. This is where I belong. I've got to get him out of here. He deserves a better life. He is the one who has to be saved. I decide to kiss him some more, figuring I've earned a little happiness.

"I should get you to bed." I can hear both worry and regret in his voice.

"I'll survive. Tell me how the rest of the plans are coming. No one tells me anything."

I feel Bren smile. "It was decided that none of us should know everything. That way if we are caught we cannot tell them what we don't know."

"Is Kate one of us now? Has she been accepted into our group? I saw her watching me and the look on her face—"

"She is. Reign tried to recruit her not knowing she was already the agent inside. It turns out Kate was always one of us. She has gotten information to the Recalcitrants many times."

"What? Really?"

"She is the one who confirmed you were here."

"She never let on—you never let on."

"Kate told me that she helps to patch up a lot of the brutality that happens here. She has also had to deal with a number of bodies. Helping the resistance was a way to help her control the rage. She may be a genius. She figured out how to get us intel by hiding it in the dead bodies. Another member of the Recalcitrant team collects the bodies from this facility and removes the intel hidden inside."

I can feel Bren's voice rumble through his chest as he speaks; combined with his heartbeat, it is a soothing sound.

"Amazing. I can't believe they haven't caught on."

This time, Bren isn't smiling. "It wasn't hard, Lise. To them, a dead prisoner is nothing but garbage. Our people gave them a proper burial after trying to identify them."

The thought that our own government cares so little about us makes my eyes burn with angry tears. I change the subject to get the horrible images out of my mind. "Tell me about what's in place for our departure. I'm getting close here. I need to know what's next."

"Once you have cleared us to move forward, it's time for Kate to go to work on her side. Reign and I have been studying the blueprints you captured. We will take out the power and then we run."

"You make it sound easy."

"You keep thinking that," Bren replies softly, then changes the subject. "It's not comfortable up here. How do you stand it?"

"I stay focused on my job. What I'm doing is much more important than my comfort."

"And that, my dear, is why I care just as much about you as I do about getting my insulation-coated, cramped-up backside out of here."

I giggle and throw my arm over my mouth so I don't laugh out loud.

"What is Kate's part?" I ask to get my mind off Bren.

"She has access to all kinds of wonderful pharmaceuticals. I believe she is looking to incapacitate the guards. She'll need help, though. You've had kitchen duty before so it will probably be you."

"Oh boy." My voice drips with sarcasm.

"Come on, Geek Girl, close up shop. You've got to be up in an hour to run."

"I can't wait," I say in the same sarcastic tone.

Bren waits while I close out the computer. I find that even though I'm super tired, all I can do is smile. "I'm glad you're here."

"Me too."

"Gee, and you could be sleeping."

"Trust me, when you're up here, I never sleep. I need to know you're okay."

"Thanks, Bren."

He pulls me to my feet and then gently pushes me against a truss. My breath catches as he leans into me again and touches his lips to mine. "This should have been our hello and welcome kiss. This should have been what it was like to see each other again. Not that moment in the hall, in the storage area, and what came after — this."

Suddenly I'm wide awake and tingling all over. His body pressed against mine makes my whole torso feel both light and tight like something is about to explode. One of our hands tangles in the other's hair and then I'm using both hands to pull him closer. I spread my feet a little wider and start to wrap a leg around him too when my other foot starts to roll off the beam. Bren catches me and we laugh softly.

"One day we will be in a place worthy of you. Clearly, this is not it. We should go."

I nod and smile, as I squeeze his fingers. He goes through the hole in the ceiling first and then replaces the tile for me. He sends me down the building while he keeps watch and then true to his word, tucks me into bed. I'm happy about the moment we stole, but I know it isn't enough.

00100000 01010000 01110010 01101111 01101010
01100101 01100011 01110100 00101100 00100000

Morning is so harsh and painful that I wonder if I would have been better off not to sleep at all. I drag myself through our morning run in a daze. The only thing that keeps me going is learning bits of the plan from Bren at one point and later the rest from Reign. They will take jobs in the garden so that they have access to tools. I feel sorry for them because I know they are going to be in for some hard labor, removing the dead plants and turning the soil with shovels in preparation for spring planting. Their plan is to take out the generator and damage the power supply while they're out there. I am to start signing up for regular shifts in the kitchen so that I am in place when the time is right. Kate is working on obtaining some kind of synthetic drug that she won't tell me about.

Before we even go to breakfast, we sign up for jobs. We have a better chance of getting what we want but we run the risk of missing out on food to do it. I'm lucky to snag the last bruised, spotted banana before I have to be at this morning's assigned class.

By lunchtime, I feel like death and figure I look like it too. Kate slides in next to me and I barely acknowledge her existence. I am so worn out that I seriously consider napping through lunch instead of eating.

"You are taking the rest of the day off to rest," Kate says as she moves her hand over my tray.

"What?" I ask, feeling perplexed. "You know I can't do that. They would never let me." I take a bite of mashed potatoes and then a bite of precut chicken. I wonder fleetingly if I'll remember how to use a table knife if I ever see one again.

"You have run yourself down to nothing. It's time to recharge." I watch Kate pull apart a bite of chicken with her spoon and fork as I process what she said. I shift my gaze to her face and stare at her for a full minute. In my mind I see her hand moving over my tray, realization dawns, and then my stomach begins to roll.

"I gave you something to make you throw up," Kate says, confirming my fears. "I will take you to the infirmary, where I will give you an IV of much-needed electrolytes, vitamins, and fluids, and then I'll let you sleep. You're no good to us in this shape. Besides, you've been looking worse and worse over the last couple of days. They will be fooled completely."

"But I have work to do." I feel a little guilty, but mostly I'm afraid of Reign.

"Trust me, honey, it will keep and the rest of us need to be ready as well."

"Okay," I start to answer, but I'm seized by an overwhelming, uncontrollable urge to empty my stomach. I half raise but don't even get turned before what little made it to my belly hits the table and bench. Nearby prisoners dive out of the way and a couple gag. I start to sweat and want nothing more than to lie on the floor. I wonder if Kate is trying to kill me instead of help.

Kate calmly takes me by the arm, pulls me up and walks me out the door.

"Where do you think you're going?" the guard at the stairs asks.

"I'm taking her to the infirmary. Just look at her."

I try again to lie on the floor, which seems to be all I can think about at the moment. Radio chatter comes over the guard's com about a cleanup in the dining hall. I burp and dry heave. I pant and then swallow hard trying to control myself. The guard who stopped us must believe our story because he calls for someone to take us up.

A guard shows up almost immediately. He asks Kate what's wrong with me and then takes my other arm and leads us to the elevator where they let me sit on the floor. My stomach gives another heave and the guard jumps back and puts in a call to have someone meet us with a barf bag and to send someone else to clean up the elevator.

I'd be smiling at the inconvenience, but I know a prisoner is going to have to clean up after me and that makes me feel bad. Kate leads me to an empty bed, hooks up the promised IV, and swears she'll watch over me while I sleep. The last thing I see is her earnest blue-green eyes as my own drift closed, even though a part of me is afraid to give in.

From utter, cottony darkness to scared spitless, I jerk awake wondering where I am and whether or not I'm safe. Pale blue LED lights glow softly overhead. Storm cloud gray curtains run from the wall above my head to past the end of the bed. The bed across the aisle that aligns with my feet is empty while the curtains block the rest of my view. An IV drip nearly out of clear fluid runs into my arm. I quickly search for any pricks, incisions or other marks to see what they have done to me now. Finding none, a sense of relief gently trickles through me.

I'm just getting my breathing under control when a sound alerts me and then my curtain flutters. A slender hand with clean, neatly trimmed nails clutches it.

Boots are headed my way. I start to pull my IV.

"Nurse!" A deep voice barks.

"Yes, sir," Kate's voice replies calmly. The clean nails should have told me who it was. Only medical people can stay that neat around here.

"Where's the doctor?" I know that deep voice too.

"He isn't feeling well, sir."

"Who's in there?" My stomach pinches.

"Currently, we have . . ." Kate pauses as if she is thinking. "We have 18A276B, 24C382T, 19A679Z . . ." I hear her take another breath.

"Forget it. Did they get rechipped?"

"Not all, sir. Like I said, the doctor is sick and —"

"Can't you just do it?" The Captain gruffly interrupts.

"No, sir," Kate replies, sounding innocent. "I'm not allowed."

"I hear 18A294E is up here. Be sure she gets her special procedure done before she leaves."

"I'll inform the doctor and confirm that her new equipment is in stock."

I hear the boots march away and realize I can feel adrenaline surging through my body. The hand still hovering over my IV line is shaking.

I hear a door close before Kate finally moves. She is pale and has dark circles under her eyes. The turned down corners of her mouth lift when she sees me and the life comes back into her like clouds moving away from the sun. She immediately puts a finger to her lips.

I feel like she can read my mind when she starts whispering. "Bren and Reign are fine. Another prisoner was killed in the testing of the new chips. This time, they cause a tiny explosion which ruptures blood vessels causing aneurysms." Kate puts a hand on my arm when she sees the tears begin to well in my eyes.

"It's no one you know. He's someone from the other dorm. It just pushes up our time frame. Both Reign and Bren are ready for their parts and I have acquired what I need to get started. The test I ran on you worked great so I tried it out on the 'good' doctor so that he would be otherwise occupied while you were here," she ends sounding more than a little acidic. We both know he is anything but good and an awful lot like some of Hitler's doctors from history were said to be.

"Wait. You tested it on me?"

"I was confident that it would work and I brought you right here just in case, so what's the big deal?"

"Really?" I couldn't decide if I should be hurt or impressed.

"I wouldn't hurt you. There was only a small risk. Please understand. You needed rest and it was the perfect opportunity to test my concoction."

I sigh but another thought takes hold in my fuzzy brain urging me to swing my eyes from side to side, taking in the curtains. Kate shakes her head. "There is no one within five beds of you and I'm the only one on duty at the moment. It's about three in the morning. You were out for almost fifteen hours. Are you ready to work?"

"Yes," I whisper back. "But if I'm fine, what about the doctor?"

"I'll keep redosing him at random intervals. Now stop worrying about my motives and go do what you need to do. The cameras are off like they usually are up here in the middle of the night, and the bathroom is down the hall," Kate says while pointing. "You have until roughly four-thirty until surveillance is back online in the hospital section. See if you can make it to work before then and I'll see you at breakfast like usual."

This time, I don't stop myself from giving her a hug. When I do, I hear her sniff and mumble, "Thanks, friend."

"No, Kate. Thank you. I was fried. I couldn't have gone another day without rest."

Her smile gives me hope. She pulls my IV and slaps a bandage on it before shooing me down the hall.

When I get back to the cubicle I find Kate cleaning the room and fresh clothes waiting on the foot of the bed. She catches me looking at the ceiling and smiles.

"You can get where you need to go from here. I'll make it look like this space was never occupied. If the captain of the guard asks, I will say that the doctor still isn't well and I was not authorized to keep you. As for the data, well, it must have been misfiled or misentered somehow. Whoops. It's really hard to keep track of everything all by myself," Kate winks at me as she finishes her message.

I dress quickly, hop up on the bed, and push a ceiling tile out of the way as Kate moves over to glance both ways in the hall, and then turns back to see if I need help. We share a quick smile before I heave myself through the opening, and I give her a saucy wave before sliding the ceiling tile back into place. Taking a moment to look around, I head for the laptop. I have a lot of work to do.

My heart races when I discover a number of files have changed. They are on to me or at least realize that someone has been in the system. I go over everything and feel like there is no way they can track it here and to me specifically. I dig a little more and find that nearly all the prisoner records appear to be corrupted, but — *you can't hide what you're doing here, Warden.* I've already sent on most of the data, notes and JPEGs to the Recalcitrants. I know they have the real files somewhere, but I wonder if it matters — I don't need them anymore. I just need to find the data on the chips and finish my work. Now that my mind is clear it should go faster.

I'm relieved when it does. I know who performed the ugly destruction of the current system. It had to be the IT guy I helped weeks ago. I close my eyes and think about him. Could he have played me? Was he doing it now?

I take a back door in to look around to see if I can find any trace of him. I reskim his record, but I've made adjustments to mine, so he could have done the same. I note several recent changes to his file, so I give up on that and look for any other computers online. If they are smart enough to cover their tracks I'll find nothing, but I hope . . . yes, there it is. There is only one on and it's in the Inquisitor's office. I crawl in that direction.

Angry voices waft toward me. I can't make out what they are arguing about yet. I crawl closer and remove a chunk of insulation. They instantly become louder and clearer.

"I'm telling you it had to be her!" That voice I would know anywhere — it belongs to the Inquisitor.

"As much as I'd like to think so, I just don't see how. A better question would be, how much information has been leaked? You don't even have a full record of what has been accessed." This voice is calmer and thoughtful.

"I didn't have that kid killed for nothing. I wanted information and if I have to torture my way through every prisoner here I will!" the Inquisitor rages. "Someone knows who breached our system. Someone has at least seen another acting suspiciously!"

"Bartholomew, think about what you are saying. If too many die there will be questions," the calmer, deeper voice replies.

"So what? If they find out we've had an information breach, heads will roll and mine is NOT going to be one of them."

"Since you're so sure it's her, just make her your scapegoat," a third voice suggests reluctantly.

There is a moment of silence in which I can hear keys clicking on a keyboard and then a long beep.

"Sir, there is a severe storm warning in effect." That third voice is familiar. It has to be the guy I worked with when the Inquisitor sent me to repair the classroom computers.

"Oh good," the Inquisitor huffs moodily. "Just what I need."

"Now Bartholomew, perhaps —"

"Shut up, Irving. Tell me what you've got on the girl, Dale."

"I've got nothing, sir. Her file is no more altered than anyone else's. She has been doing her assigned duties and has not caused any trouble."

"You can do better than that! Who does she talk to? Who does she spend time with? Eat with, sleep with?" I can feel the venom in the Inquisitor's voice.

"I'm telling you, sir. There is no good intel on her. She is patternless, friendless and has no apparent boyfriend. Despite the rules, you know what they try and we catch most of them but not her. She is not tied to anything that is missing or any misbehavior. She is either incredibly smart or she isn't who you thought she was. If it's her, I've never seen someone hide so well in plain sight."

I can hear the Inquisitor snarl and begin to pace. I wish I could see what is going on but the holes in the ceiling tiles are too small. I begin lifting more pieces of insulation hoping for a break.

"I know it's her!" the Inquisitor snaps.

"If it is, I can't prove it," Dale, the IT guy, answers back. His fear shows with the catch and slight quake in his voice.

"We don't have to prove it. We just need to flush her out. We need to scare her into giving herself away."

"Are you sure nothing was leaked, Dale?" Irving asks.

"From this end? No. But there is chatter out there. The Recalcitrants are on the move. They have started releasing propaganda. They know things they shouldn't know," Dale responds.

A loud smack makes me jerk, but it is not me who has been struck. "This is your fault. What good are you? You were supposed to be smarter than her."

"I'm not the one who set up the security. You asked me to test her. I did. She is capable but not as smart as you think." Now Dale sounds hurt and angry.

"How do you explain the missing laptop?"

They know! I think so loudly, I'm half afraid I've spoken aloud.

"Maybe it's a simple miscount," Irving tries to sooth.

"A simple miscount?" Inquisitor Bartholomew rages. "No, there is one unaccounted for. There is nothing simple about it. It's her, I'm telling you."

"It's been missing for days. It probably got broken and tossed out. Who would want to get in trouble? Have some prisoners check the trash."

"If she has it, when would she have had time to use it? If she has it, where is it?" Dale asks. "We've done a thorough search with zero sign of it. Every outlet has been accounted for. All laptop cameras are picking up appropriate footage. I also bribed three more prisoners to keep watch — just like you asked."

"How long can the battery last?" Irving asks.

"Eight hours tops," Dale responds.

"Then it's dead by now. The thief will need power, so train all cameras to the outlets."

I sigh. Well, at least I know where they'll be watching for the time being.

"Where is she now?" I hear more key clicking and hold my breath.

"She must be in the dorms. Her tracker shows her right under us."

Or over, I think with a smile.

"It's late. Let's call it a night and discuss this more over breakfast." Irving suggests.

"Fine. Continue your recruiting as time allows, Dale. Approach her and try to make friends. If she's lonely, maybe she'll spill the beans to you."

I hear a chair push back and know I need to hurry. I have to beat double-agent Dale back to the dorms.

"Not you, Dale," the Inquisitor says in an oily voice. "You have a hacker to isolate before you can go to bed."

"Yes, Warden," Dale responds in a weary voice.

I decide there is nothing to be gained by staying so I double check the laptop to be sure it is secure and then cover my tracks from where I entered all the way to my exit point. I scramble down the outside of the building at a reckless speed and slither through the bathroom window, knowing I'm running late.

Three shadows separate themselves from the darkness. I

drop low, ready to roll away and make a break for it.

"It's us."

It takes half a beat for the words to register. Reign, Bren, and Kate are all waiting for me.

"We need to talk," Reign says in a harsh whisper.

Oh boy.

"There's a storm coming," Kate blurts.

"It's the perfect cover," Bren adds.

"We're not ready," I argue.

"We're out of time!" Reign snarls impatiently.

"I need more," I reply, trying to sound reasonable.

"Then you're going up there and work until you're done."

Bren slides Reign a frustrated look. I guess I'm not the only one who finds her bossiness irritating.

"They'll notice," I say.

"We have it covered," Reign interrupts.

"But —" I try.

"Listen, we have a plan. You work and stay focused. We'll take your bracelet and pass it around so it looks like you're where you're supposed to be," Reign insists.

"We have a number of people ready to fight," Kate adds.

"You have about forty-eight hours until the storm hits and we make our move," Reign says firmly.

Fear clenches my gut and squeezes my chest. I can't help it. I look to Bren.

"I can't," I say as firmly as I can muster. "There are things I simply cannot do with just the laptop. I need access to the servers."

"Then we will find a way to get you that access." Bren's voice is soft and low, soothing.

Before I can protest further, Reign has a firm grip on my wrist and yanks both my ID bracelet and strips of skin away from my hand.

"Holy hell!" I yelp in response.

Blood wells in a couple of places but before I can get upset, Kate grabs my arm next and applies a cool cloth she had ready. The smell of medicine stings my nostrils and the thought that I've been hijacked stings my pride. While Kate fixes up my hand I tell them everything I can remember about the Inquisitor's plans.

I am fully expecting Reign to back down, but she pushes harder. "This is why we have to move. You have got to finish those chips or you aren't going to make it out of here. Our window is closing. Quit fooling around and do it already!"

I want to say something back, but I seem to upset her more when I confront her. "Fine but I have to be seen too or they will notice."

Reign's face brightens like she's pleased and then her scowl is back in place. "Fine, but you have a deadline. You figure it out. Come on Kate. We've got work to do."

"Wait," I say and then quickly tell them about Dale and his spies.

Reign looks unimpressed. "I'll take him out and then the folks reporting to him will lose interest."

"They will notice," I warn again.

"Then I'll make it look like an accident."

I want to say more, but Bren lays a hand on my arm, so I

shut my mouth.

I watch Kate and Reign go, but Bren remains.

"What?" I whisper, knowing he has something to say or he would have left as well.

"You can do this," he repeats softly as he tucks a bit of hair behind my ear.

I move in to give him a quick hug. I can feel the rumble of his voice through his chest when he speaks. "Here is what we are going to do."

"Always the leader," I say, feeling frustrated. I wonder why I can't even have a moment to myself.

"I'm not your leader. Elise, I'm your friend, your teammate . . . no, I'm your partner in this."

I close my eyes and hang my head so that my forehead rests on his chest. "My friend, my partner," I repeat listlessly.

Bren moves his hands to my face and gently encourages me to look into his eyes. "I want to be more than friends. You know that. But first, we have to get out of here."

"I guess," I whisper, knowing he's right, but I don't like it.

Bren moves his face closer and touches his lips quickly to mine. I feel both hopeful and broken-hearted. All too soon he moves back.

"You can do this. If anyone can figure out how to shut down the implants, it's you."

"It isn't done here. The data is held off-site."

"But they have access here, right?"

"Yes."

"Then trick the system. Communicate false files and we'll

remove the chips later."

I nod, knowing that scenario will only help those who make it to the Recalcitrants.

"When we got the weather report, I went ahead and damaged the generators. They are not scheduled for another test until next week, so we have to make our move before then."

"Okay."

"I'll take down their power grid when the storm hits. We can do this. Be brave just a little longer."

I nod again. What more is there to say? Bren hugs me tightly and releases me before giving me a gentle push toward the dorms. At least he recognizes that I have a good head on my shoulders and that I am capable of making thoughtful decisions. He also knows I take direction much better from him than I do from Reign. It isn't necessarily what they say but how they say it that matters. He asks and she tells. I don't do bossy and I hate bullies. Reign can be both.

I sneak into Bren's bunk again and sleep without dreams. By some magic all his own, he is again able to wake me just before the alarm wakes everyone else. He pretends that he doesn't know me until we are halfway done with our morning run. He moves next to me to whisper, "Change of plans. Reign decided you're right. If the Warden calls you to his office, we can't fake that, as much as I wish we could. So you will get your bracelet back and will only have time to work at night."

"I can handle it."

Bren is quiet long enough for me to look his way. His lips are in a firm straight line and his eyebrows are drawn in and down.

I scan the runners — no one is listening, so what's he thinking?

"I will disable their weapons," he continues, sounding like he's lost in thought.

"How," I interrupt.

He just gives me a look, telling me with his eyes it is *need to know*, and I don't.

"We need you to take more kitchen duty and we'll get you into the attic tonight. This is just about your last chance. Disable the chips, however, you can, even if it leaves a trail or they can see it. Kate heard they're bringing in another doctor, day after tomorrow — time is up."

As if on cue, big, fat drops begin to fall from the brooding clouds. First, they're far apart, but soon they are falling thick and heavy, quickly soaking us.

At breakfast, Kate slips a wristband on me that is loose enough to go over my hand. "They'll notice," I mumble just loud enough for her to hear.

"They are too busy with other things right now." Kate's eyes slide to the latest guard to be overcome by her mystery disease. A guard hurries in our direction and Kate quickly hands me today's vial. "Kitchen duty—four drops per guard's tray."

My palms instantly slick with sweat and my heart races. The guard is still on a path right to me. My alarm grows, but then I realize that he is after Kate for her medical expertise. She leaves her tray behind, knowing that I will take care of it. I'm terrified for her; if they figure out that she is the orchestrator of their illness, they'll kill her. Rain continues to fall, confirming that I am out of time.

I condense our leftover food and garbage onto one tray, stack them, and get in line to turn them in. I watch the guards from the corner of my eye. They are all talking more than usual and appear nervous with their shifting eyes and constant fidgeting. I catch part of a conversation as I head out the door to the main hall.

". . . my second shift in a row, with so many sick."

I overhear another guard talking as I wait in line for an extra job. "I hear the doctor is still sick and now about a dozen of the guards are down — must be one nasty flu."

"The questioning will continue regardless."

"They won't question us will they?" The younger guard asks, sounding as nervous as he looks.

I don't hear the reply. The line has moved on and I don't want them to notice my eavesdropping. I have to clear my throat twice before I can ask for kitchen duty. The guard looks me over and studies the roster. I'm afraid I won't get my request. His communicator beeps, distracting him. He quickly scans my prisoner band and waves me on. I have to keep myself from running to the kitchen.

Lunch prep is already underway when I reach the door. Once I'm there I rack my brain to figure out how in the world I'm going to be able to get to the guards' food. The chef begins assigning jobs. I'm tasked with chopping vegetables. I look longingly at the food the chef is preparing for the guards. How can I get the poison into it without being seen? Wait . . . I can be seen. I need to not be noticed. I need a distraction. My eyes skitter over the kitchen as I consider and throw out scenarios. The chef is in an area where there are no rubber mats on the floor. I snag a bottle of oil, uncap it and dump it as I walk behind him. Now I wait.

I collect my twenty-five pounds of carrots while keeping my eye on him. He gets oil on the heel of his shoe, but nothing happens. I grind my teeth. I'm running out of time. I need an alternate plan. *Chop. Chop. Chop.* I'm desperate, I've got nothing better. I walk up behind him, my knife low at my side, point down. I turn it to cut him, but he slips, falling with a huge clatter before I can touch him. I drop my knife on the counter and step closer to the guards' trays.

Everyone is coming to his aid. The guard slips and falls also. This couldn't have gone better if I'd planned it. I drop poison onto as many trays as I can, but I'm too amped up to carefully count the drops. I'm shoved out of the way by the assistant chef, or sous chef, I've learned he's called, and dump most of the vial on the fifth tray by mistake. The guard radios for medical and clean up. The sous chef yanks on my pant leg.

"Get those delivered!"

"Yes, sir,"

The chef is throwing a fit — screaming that his elbow is hurt and directions for lunch prep all jumbled together making him sound crazed. The guard and sous chef try to calm him. The other two prisoners on duty with me are backed into corners, trying to look small. I grab the delivery cart and load the first four trays. Then I try to figure out how to better disperse the poison. I quickly scoop the contaminated eggs onto tray six, divide it in half and put part back on tray five. Before I can divide it again the sous chef is yelling at me.

"What are you doing? The food is getting cold. Go. Go!"

The sous chef then fusses as Kate and a prisoner aide hurry

in. Kate and I make brief eye contact. I push the cart past where I left the oil bottle, put it with the other condiments on the cart, and wheel it toward the door.

As I pass the shelf where the oils are kept, I pick up the guilty bottle from the cart, wipe it clean with the cart's towel, and put it back on the shelf. I say a little prayer, hoping that no one noticed and that everyone is distracted. Camera coverage is spotty here at best, but then that's a secret that I shouldn't know.

Another prisoner meets me at the service elevator and relieves me of the cart. By the time I get back to the kitchen they are walking the head chef out. The cleaning crew is just starting on the floor so I return to the carrots. My heart beats double-time for most of the shift.

I keep my head down, praying that I will escape the Inquisitor's scrutiny today as he wades through the prison population. Only half of those who go to him for an interview come back and the ones who return look shaken, scared, and gray as the sky. I swear I can smell doom.

After dinner, I see the prisoners who had disappeared during the day are lined up and marched out through the back gate and into the woods by four armed guards. The first six prisoners each carry a shovel. Nerves clench my belly and fear dances down my spine. Going into the woods at night with shovels is not a good sign.

Tonight, I return to breaking our cyber chains and replacing our signals with fakes. Doing it well enough to hide it is taking time I fear I don't have, but if I'm caught before it's done, then what was the point?

In the morning, while we're on our run, only the shovels and guards have come back, leaving the prison population shaken. I hear whispers among the guards as I pass a couple in the hall, "They know someone was in the system, they just don't know who . . . yet."

The dining hall is unusually quiet. Kate snags me at breakfast, passing me another vial. She softly whispers to me that she and Reign have taken out a few unfortunate prisoners during the night so that it will not look like it's only the guards going down with the mystery flu. A couple of drops on a few specific toothbrushes are all it took to make them sick. I pray that it goes unnoticed that nearly all of them are friends of the guards or people Reign suspects of being Dale's recruits.

I get in line at the job desk behind Bren and Reign who again take work outside so that they can access the generator and the incoming power line. I worry about both of them too. I catch sight of their hands and noticed that they have blisters, cuts, and scrapes from all the shoveling. Their nails are dirty and broken from picking rocks out of the ground by hand. No wonder Reign wants me to hurry; she must hate this kind of work. I ask for more kitchen duty. They are so short staffed that it's easy to get.

Today, my dosing goes much more smoothly. I am tasked with pouring orange juice for the second shift, so it's easy to drop a small glop into the carafe and then distribute it among the glasses. I suppress the urge to wave goodbye as the cart rolls past and focus on the tureen of soup being prepped for the first shift's lunch that is underway. When the sous chef walks away, I walk past and empty the rest of the vial.

I head to my morning class. I can't tell if I'm aware of things starting to go wrong or if it's all my imagination. By lunchtime, the rumors begin and I know I'm not dreaming. It starts with whispers; the doctor is sick and now the guards are catching it. I threw up in the dining hall, they wonder if it started with me. Was I patient zero? Several people send me furtive glances. A shift will be shorthanded. A rumor begins that backup staff may be sent from the nearest town, but they don't know the cause of the illness so they are reluctant to expose anyone else. I smile inside.

I listen shamelessly to all the gossip. I go to my next class where a prisoner is hauled out of her seat and escorted roughly out of the room. The instructor barely blinks. The guard at the back is called out before class ends. Neither comes back.

I can feel the panic starting to rise. The system is crumbling. Two more guards have taken ill and many are mumbling. Guards are now being questioned about the security breach and more prisoners disappear. Everyone eyes each other suspiciously. Dale the IT guy has vanished and I don't know if he is among the sick or has been hidden away. The wind has picked up and rain continues to fall in earnest. Thick sheets of it cascade down obscuring everything outside under skies so dark it appears to be nearly night.

Tonight I go to the laptop for the final time. This is my last chance to do what I can remotely before we try to get me down to the servers. Bren will head to the weapons room to damage what he can while the prison sleeps on, oblivious.

Kate and I will continue to poison the guards, me from the kitchen and her from the infirmary. I figure we can get whatever Kate concocted into nearly every guard's tray before their meals are delivered. At breakfast, Reign surprises me when she passes me a vial and tells me it's for the guards' water. It looks like today I will be on janitorial duty. I will add the chemical to their bottled water when I replace it as part of my janitorial tasks.

I check in and get my cart. The vial is burning a hole in my pocket, so to speak, except that I have slipped it inside a tear in my waistband. They will only notice if they pat me down and I don't think there are enough healthy guards to waste the effort. Kate set the rumor loose that it is a new strain of virus which has them looking in another direction.

I try to appear calm, but I know my façade is cracking. I can feel it. The guard looks me over carefully, slowly, menacingly. He points to his eyes, to me, and then back to his eyes, telling me without words that I am being watched.

I know better than to say anything.

"Cart four," he growls.

I pull it out and go over my checklist as I wait for him to clear me to go to work.

A hand comes down on my cart. My eyes jerk up towards the guard's.

"I recognize you even beaten up, skinny and with your hair hacked off."

And I recognize him.

"The Captain had me brought on special. My talent was

being wasted watching civilians. I'm here to watch you now. I don't know how you got the jump on us in the woods, but I plan to find out."

"Other . . ." I wanted to say *others have tried*, but I stop myself.

"Think what you want. I've got all the time in the world."

But you don't, I yell back in my mind.

He steps closer, almost touching me, his breath hot on my neck. "I'm watching."

I recoil slightly and he flips me around pushing my back into the cart. He starts to pat me down.

"You're not allowed to touch," I squeak.

"I am if I'm suspicious. New rule, 'all prisoners are subject to search at any time.' And I'm feeling suspicious."

My heart begins to beat wildly. This is no ordinary search — he is trying to humiliate and intimidate me by feeling every part of my bra and the full length of my legs.

"How about a cavity search?" he asks as he trails his fingers up my sides.

I bite my tongue and stand very still, the vial burning at my back. He holds my gaze. I refuse to look away. I can feel the seconds ticking by.

"You need help, Mike?"

That's right. I had promised myself that I would remember the guys who captured me, but that was a lifetime ago. Mike shifts his gaze to the Captain. I hope he hasn't read anything in my eyes.

"No, sir."

I try not to sigh.

"She clean?" the Captain asks.

"Yes, sir."

"Then let her get to work. Somebody needs to clean our bathroom with the flu going around and it is not going be us, right, Mikey?"

A slow smile slithers over Mike's face, making fear congeal in my gut. He reaches past me, brushing my chest once more for good measure before he snatches the cleaning gloves off my cart.

"Have fun," Mike sneers.

I push my cart out of the room, gritting my teeth. The Captain's face holds the same kind of sly smile. He puts a hand on my arm at the door.

"You could buy those gloves back if you want."

I stare at him and say nothing.

"The rules have changed since last we met in this room. Remember that."

I gulp and he laughs. I practically run to the service elevator. The guard there releases me to go up. I know I'm on camera but I lose it for a moment anyway and lean against the back wall to take a moment to recover. I take a deep breath as the doors open and push my cart to the first assignment on my list. Where had Mike come from? He hadn't come in the front gate with the usual fanfare. As far as I know, no guards have come at night. This has got to be another entrance not shown on the blueprints.

The guards' quarters are not as nice as the Inquisitor's office but much nicer than anything the prisoners have access to. I am taken aback by the oddity of how much it looks like the staffroom at school that I happened to see once in a while as I walked by and an instructor happened to be entering or exiting. Two men are playing cards and a third is reading. None of them acknowledge my existence. As I clean their kitchenette I get a feel for the room. I wipe down the outside of the cabinets and then methodically go through them as I've been instructed. The fourth cupboard I open surprises me. It contains a chute. I pause to consider where it goes.

"You don't need to clean that one. Just dump the dirty towels in," one of the card players barks at me.

I quickly shut it and move to the next cupboard but my mind whirls. The chute is not in the plans. I find it careless of them to let me see it. I finish wiping down the cupboards and then I confirm the camera location and move my cart into position. I drop down behind it and quickly pull out the vial. I take the water jug off the bottom and set it by the dispenser. I remove the old one, dumping my vial into the reservoir at the same time. I put the new bottle on and breathe a sigh of relief. I move on to dust the blinds and empty the trash, where I quickly stash the vial.

I must have gone invisible again because the guards don't pay any more attention to me. I gather my things and move to my next project, their bathroom/locker room. When I get there, I find that they really are filthy pigs. The bits of previously consumed food clinging to the toilets about gag me. I carefully go over my cart and find a lone, forgotten glove and some chemicals that I could only hurt myself with. I can't make a bomb with what's here and they won't even work on the toilets without a lot of scrubbing. I pour the bowl cleaner in the toilets and let it do its job while I head over to scrub the sinks. I hurry so that I don't get caught with a glove on; I'd hate to have it taken away. I want to finish the toilets one-handed before they do, but I'm on to mopping the floor before anyone comes to check on me and the glove has long since been returned to its hiding place.

I feel relief when I can move on to the vacuuming and dusting of their living quarters. I glance out the window and see that the storm is getting worse and even though it's pushing lunch time, it looks like night. Through the window I see a dozen more prisoners marched out the back gate with one guard. I have never seen such nervous people in all my life, but then I am one of them — the scared, the helpless. My sense of urgency builds. I don't want to be helpless anymore.

By the time I return the cart, several more guards and a couple of prisoners have fallen ill. It's strange not to have guards posted at the dorm. They now only cover primary positions like the gates and the offices upstairs.

At dinner Kate lets me know that they're not even monitoring the infirmary anymore. With so many of them there, I suppose they find it unnecessary.

I sneak away to the attic feeling almost relieved. For good or for bad — this is it. I slip back into the system and make one more tweak. Our chips are offline and my dummy program is running. Before I move on to my next task, I do a quick search to see if Dale is online, but there are several computers running. I give up on that to program in a virus and leave it to do its work. I check the laptop's clock and see it's time for me to meet up with the team.

I remove the vent cover; the wind catches it and it flies right out of my hand. I realize it is too dangerous to scale the outside of the building with the wind and rain. I'll have to do what I can from the inside.

I could make use of the laundry chute in the guard's quarters. The halls are darkly quiet but nearly all cameras are on with the shortage of live guards to monitor things so the halls won't be safe. I will have to travel the attic to the guards' quarters.

Wind whistles through the opening I left at the vent. I feel a sense of urgency as I try to navigate the attic trusses. One slip and I'll be through the ceiling but I am now behind schedule. Stress tightens the muscles in my neck and shoulders making them ache and my palms are slick with sweat. I don't know if I'm more scared or relieved when I get to the guard's section of the building.

I listen carefully at the break room before I remove a ceiling tile. The room is dark. I come down on to the kitchenette counter. The light under the door goes out and I can hear the emergency generators trying to kick on. I slide to the floor and find the sink. I start counting cupboards until I find the door covering the chute.

Not everyone could fit through here. I take a breath. This is risky. I could get hurt in the fall. I ease myself in and try to pull the door closed behind me as I brace myself by pushing my legs against the sides. I hear the distinctive pop of the sheet metal as I force it out of position. The cupboard won't quite close, but I suppose it doesn't matter at this point. I start my decent just as I hear the breakroom door hit the wall. I'm afraid to move. I don't want to make a sound. My legs threaten to cramp so I try to focus on my breathing.

The cupboard door starts to move. It may be above my head but if they shine a light in here, I'm doomed. I catch a breath and hold it, torn between letting go and dropping fast, giving myself away, or waiting.

I hear the squawk and crackle of an old-fashioned radio.

"All hands meet at the dorms for bed check."

Some dirty clothes are dropped on my head, then the cupboard door snaps shut and the footsteps recede. I blow out the breath I was holding and move awkwardly down, cringing each time the chute pops or creaks. When my feet run out of chute, I take another quick breath and free fall into the pile of dirty, smelly laundry.

I scramble out, snag some clean nightwear and climb the shelf to slither out a window. I run the length of the darkened building. Flashlights sway at intervals as the guards try to keep track of the exterior. I pick my moment and scale the outside of the dorm to slip in through the latrine window.

I practically fall into Bren's arms. "You're late. I was worried. Are you ready?"

"No. They're doing a surprise bed check. Go. Go!"

I strip out of my damp clothes and pull on the nightwear. I roll up my day clothes and stuff them behind a toilet hoping they will go unnoticed.

I hear a voice mumbling commands so I flush and walk to a sink. I turn on the faucet and a flashlight beam smacks me in the face.

"What are you doing?" the guard queries abruptly.

I don't answer; I just turn off the faucet, face the light beam and shade my eyes with a dripping hand.

"Back to bed," he snarls.

I shake off my hands and wipe the rest of the moisture on my pajama pants while I follow him into the dorm. I watch what I can in the dancing beams of light as I walk to my bunk. They aren't scanning us — so their equipment is not receiving. It's working. They are doing a manual count. I barely get onto my bunk before they're leaving. Bren is there a heartbeat later, pulling me down.

"Quick, we need to get you to the basement. Follow me."

Without the red lights to guide us, I would have had to touch each bunk, but Bren navigates just fine in the dark. I grab on to the waistband of his pants and let him lead me out.

"Wait. My shoes."

Without a word, Bren swings through our latrine to grab them. When we reach the dorm's outer door I see Reign squatting by the lone guard who is prone on the floor.

"What did you do?" I gasp.

"Relax, Princess. He's sleeping. I doped him with a gift from Kate." Reign looks at me with a smirk and adds, "Now get going."

The outer door is locked, but Bren is prepared. I throw on my shoes while he fiddles with the door. At some point, he has lifted a manual override key and uses it to unlock the door. Everything is happening both too fast and too slow.

"Go on," Bren says. "I'll be right behind you."

I say nothing. I wish for so many things that my thoughts

jumble. I take a steadying breath and put my hand to the latch. The wind rips the door right out of my hand with enough force to be painful. It's the perfect kind of diversion — natural, not man-made. The time is perfect to make our move. I run for the main building. The wind howls and someone screams. Some people are terrified of storms. I am not one of those. I almost feel sorry for the prisoners Reign is releasing as a further diversion.

With a tremendous crash that sends a vibration through the ground and then up through my legs, a piece of the gardening shed hits an arm's width from me. I can't stop or even slow. I leap over it and go through the doors. Of course, they couldn't connect the ground floor like the upper level. While the power is down, I must make it to the servers. I have programs to set in motion for when the battery backup comes online. I have to be fast. I have a limited amount of time to get it done and get through the gate before I'm trapped inside forever.

22

stop inside the entry to the main building. Although I know chaos is gaining a foothold, I'm surprised there is no guard here like there is in the daytime. It feels eerie. I have just a moment to register the feeling before Bren skids in behind me.

"Come on," he says, taking my hand. He hurries past the stairs and behind the kitchen to the service counter where jobs are assigned and supplies are given out.

"The elevator will be down," I remind him.

"We're not going to the elevator."

Bren slides a hip onto the counter and swings his legs over. He drops down on the other side. I lean my elbows on the counter and peer over trying to figure out what he's doing in the beam of the light from the flashlight he'd snatched from somewhere. I watch him pull up his sleeve to reveal a five-digit code, which he dials into a trap door I'd never noticed.

"You never told me about this so that if I was questioned I couldn't give it away. If the system was hacked it couldn't be me because I couldn't get to the servers. You just better pray the system down there has enough juice to do what I need."

Bren snorts before he answers. "If you were them, what system would you get power to first? What system would you be sure was on the emergency battery backup? The one you will need to use to call out for help and upload all your important data from, right?"

"Point taken."

"Lise, you can trust me."

"I have to trust you. There is no other option that makes any sense."

He gives me a quick smile. "Ready?"

"I hope so," I reply, feeling nervous again.

Bren pulls two semi-automatics from his waistband, hands me one, and aligns the flashlight's beam with the barrel of his. "Open the hatch, keeping the cover between you and the hole, just in case."

I check the safety and shove the SIG into the back of my pants. I've cleaned these and fieldstripped them, but they've never once let me fire one.

I do as he asks. The beam is suddenly overly bright to my eyes as he shines it into the hole and I cower behind the cover. When he's satisfied, I watch him slide down the ladder without even using the rungs.

He waits at the bottom for me, but I can tell he's watching

carefully by the way he swings the flashlight in all directions. I take a deep breath to steady my nerves and follow him.

"Where to, beautiful?" he asks when I hit bottom.

"I don't know. I thought you did."

"Nope, but you know where it isn't from your time down here, so lead on."

I shrug and move away from the cells and showers and into the other section. Bren opens each door cautiously, ready for anything. I wish I was brave and tough. I worry about actually shooting a live someone with a heartbeat. They can't be all bad, right? They're just doing their job, but it's them or me. Who would have thought that I, of all people, would suffer from too much empathy? I've known pain and I don't want anyone else to feel it—not like I did—not ever.

I stop and listen, but all I can hear is Bren so I put a hand on his arm to stop his movements too. It's the hum of machine—my kind of machine—it calls to me. I point to the door that hides the sound. Bren has me put my back to the wall on the hinge side; he drops down on the other side and turns the handle. Beams of light burst from the room followed by the discharge of weapons that nearly deafen me. I curl into a ball with my back to the wall, my hands over my ears and wait for the cacophony of sound and hail of bullets to end.

It takes only a moment to give myself a mental slap. I need to help. I open my eyes. Bren is crouched down on the other side of the doorway firing in. No one is rushing out. I roll into position the next time Bren fires and sneak a peek into the room from the floor. One guard is down and unmoving; the other is cowering behind the desk and firing blindly through the open door at desktop height. I crawl forward. Bren's eyes go wide as he shakes his head at me. When I don't stop, he latches onto my ankle. I scowl over my shoulder at him. A bullet whizzes above my head and I gently kick him loose. He changes tactics and fires again to give me cover.

Their exchange continues as I crawl toward the desk. I scuttle around the edge and glance around the corner. Dale, the IT guy, is huddled under the desk the guard is firing over. I lunge and take the shooter to the ground, his semi-automatic flying from his hand. I punch him in the throat before he can recover. Dale holds shaking hands in front of him.

"That's no guard," Bren says, leaning over my shoulder to haul him out.

I smirk. "That's Dale. He works for the Warden as his personal computer guy."

"Get off me," he wheezes to Bren who is pushing his back uncomfortably into the desk.

"I could just shoot you," Bren offers.

"You won't. I've passworded the system. You can't get in without me."

Bren cuts his eyes to me. I roll to my feet and shrug.

"What makes you think I need a password?" I ask casually.

"Why else would you be down here except to get into the system?"

I glance at the only lit monitor. It is indeed password protected, but is it encrypted?

Since I haven't responded, Dale tries again, "It was you who took the laptop; it had to be. I respect that you were clever enough to take it but you ran out of battery a couple of days ago. No one saw you at an outlet so now you need to hack from here."

"Have you been down here the last couple of days, Dale?"

"Yeah, why?" I'm not going to clue him in, but it did explain why Reign couldn't get to him.

The backup radio at the guard's hip squawks, "All hands to the yard—dorms are compromised."

Dale moves and Bren puts his full attention back on him. "No, no, Nerd," Bren hisses.

Dale throws his hands back up in the air.

Bren speaks without looking at me, "Get to it."

I look at the keyboard for a moment. What do I know about this guy? What would he use for a password? What does he value? He has an overinflated value of himself. He wants to be important.

I touch the screen. "Invalid password," appears in the pop-up window. I smile. "Touch the screen please," I ask of Dale.

"No," Dale whines, sounding petulant.

Bren moves his SIG closer.

"No," Dale repeats. Bren moves and fires a shot into the unconscious guard, eliminating his ability to ever tell anyone about us and letting Dale know he's serious.

"Okay, okay," Dale whimpers as he leans forward to touch the screen with his right index finger. "Invalid password," appears again.

I close my eyes and visualize. "Use the middle finger of your left hand."

Dale reaches toward the screen but with the wrong finger. Bren shoots him in the foot making him yowl in pain.

"Do what she says or I'll aim higher — maybe just go right for the heart like your buddy on the floor over there and then we can use your hand to open it ourselves."

Dale gulps. Tears are running down his face and the foot he's holding in the air is dripping blood. He reaches for the monitor again with a shaking hand. This time, access is granted.

"Come on, genius," Bren snarls at Dale. Then he speaks to me, "I'm on to my next task."

I'm already at work so I just nod. He will be releasing the prisoners down here to create a bigger diversion. Dale whimpers and cries. Bren sets one guard's standard issue SIG on the desk by me, keeps the other and the extra clips for himself, and drags Dale out the door. I hear it lock and refocus on my job — to disable all the cameras and then bring down communications. I begin to scramble the chips and destroy the files on all the ones that don't include kill switches; those will have to be dealt with later. We don't have time for surgery. I begin running the false chip signatures that I had created earlier and send the Recalcitrants the files of the folks with kill switches in the hope they can find all of the escaped prisoners and remove their hardware.

The weather reports have dictated our window of opportunity and the worst of the storm is about to hit so I return to breaking everything and wiping as much as I can. From here I can access everything. I quickly send out the message to the Recalcitrants letting them know the prison has had a mutiny and then I add a worm while I'm at it. It will eventually eat everything that is left of this network. It will also be replicated onto any device that tries to access this system. They will now have a nearly impossible mess to recover from. They will have to admit their failure and reformat from higher up the food chain. When they establish that link — the Recalcitrants will know where the hub's servers are located with the tags I've added.

The emergency battery lighting comes on — I check the computer and confirm it is the expected protocol that happens when the generator fails to come online. I also see that replacements are scheduled to arrive at dawn. It's time to meet the others.

My mind wanders to Bren damaging all available weapons while I was in the attic earlier and I hope the ones that are left won't be the death of us. I shake the thought away and refocus on my task, setting the central computer to direct all the systems linked to the prison to flicker and eventually go to static. I wipe all prints off the keyboard and all the other surfaces we may have touched.

Grabbing the extra SIG, I listen carefully at the door before I take a look. The halls are eerie with only the emergency lighting working. Thanks to Bren they are working on the battery system which should only last for about 90 more minutes. I have to say a part of me admires their triple deep safety plan but I admire Bren more for being able to beat it.

I step into the hall. It's silent so everyone must be out. I walk back to the access point before I lose the lights and listen with my whole body before I climb up the ladder to the main level, regretting that I didn't have time to find the underground entrance that I know has to be here.

I don't see Bren. I'm already nervous and the added pressure puts my body into overdrive. I slip through the hole and crouch for a moment to listen. I hear footsteps pelting toward me and look for a place to hide. I want to get away from the hatch and there is no room under the counter so I move into the hall. The door to the kitchen is locked. I about have a heart attack on the spot as I lunge toward the storage room.

"Relax Lise, it's me."

I breathe out a sigh. I can't think when I've been happier to see anyone. "Have a little trouble with the guards?"

"Just a little," Bren answers with a smile. I realize I love that smile. "Let's go."

I freeze. "I can't."

"What? Why?"

"Before I go, I have to do one thing. I have to see the Inquisitor. I have to do something about him."

"What you need to do, Lise, is leave. He will be punished by the government. It isn't your job."

"I can't trust them to do it."

"I remember what you said about him once, but killing someone is not who you are."

"Maybe it is who I am now."

"It's not. Let it go."

"You go on. I'm seeing him."

Bren closes his eyes. His face goes expressionless and then he says softly — just one word, "Okay."

We walk toward the unguarded stairs. I glance out the main

doors as we pass and I can see a horde of prisoners, some trying to crawl over and some trying to break down the gate. A few have engaged the guards who remain untouched or less affected by Kate's flu. People are going to get hurt and I can't stand to watch so I run up the stairs.

Bren follows me on down the hall to the only door with light coming under it. We each put our back to the wall and he slowly turns the knob.

A guard is ready for us, but Bren is faster and has him disarmed before his weapon is fully drawn.

I pick it up from where it clattered to the floor and move on to the inner office. Bren and the guard struggle, but I know who will win. I open the door to find the Inquisitor packing papers, books, and his laptop into a box. For some reason, all his awards and diplomas come into sharp focus; Bartholomew Augustin Rehnquist.

He freezes and looks up, the papers almost glowing behind him.

"You!"

"Things aren't going like you planned are they," I say coldly.

"I knew you were behind this."

"I think you may be overestimating my skills."

"And yet, here you are with a gun pointed at me."

"True, because it's what one has to do with a rabid dog beyond help."

"This will not end here. You can kill me, but you won't win. Go ahead because you're too late to stop what you really want to stop. I got out of you what there was to get. The trial goes live in Seattle next week."

I hesitate. Bren's right, despite what he has done, this is not who I am. If I do this, I'm just like him. Perhaps I could hold him hostage and force them to shut it down?

"After all I did to you? You've got nothing to say?"

I can feel myself begin to shake. He still has a hold on me. I change my mind again. What I have done is nothing compared to what this monster has done.

He must almost see my thoughts whirling around because he smiles like he knows a secret. "I knew with enough time, I'd get through. With the right persuasion, I'd learn your deepest secrets. You feel guilty for creating the game. The weight of every student death rests on your shoulders. You know *you* are to blame."

Sweat and heat gather at my back. I'm burning from the inside out and I'm afraid he knows it. I've never felt such hate and loathing for him and what he's made me. I am the monster.

"Here we are and now I finally understand, you truly are wired differently." His gaze shifts. "*And* I also see who helped you in the woods. I understand who always helps you. I know who was always at your side, if not in reality, then in spirit. I know who runs you. We are blessed to be in the presence of royalty. I should have recognized you sooner. You went to school together — I did not realize you had met. You were his student and you still are. He's the prince of the Recalcitrants and you, my dear, are a pawn."

I find myself grinding my teeth. I didn't mean to give anything away but clearly, I have.

"Oh no, not my pawn . . . you are his pawn," the Inquisitor continues.

Pressure is building in my chest. I have to make him stop talking. I raise the old SIG Sauer another notch and flick the safety. My hands are shaking, but I must do this. Surely I won't miss at this range. It's like the game — I've done this in the game. I can do this in reality.

"Go ahead," the Inquisitor repeats. Then he lunges for my remote. He presses the button but I'm still standing here — no pain. My finger loosens slightly on the trigger. He pushes the button again, a look of confusion on his face, and then cocks his arm back to throw it at me. My finger twitches in response, my shot is high skimming along the side of his head, but he drops to the floor, the sound still ringing in my ears.

Bren darts past me so fast he is nothing but a flash of movement. In one fluid motion, he has the desk lamp in his hand and smashes the Warden, my inquisitor, across the temple. Bren waits for a beat to see if he will move and then throws down the lamp. The LED flickers and goes out. Bren walks purposely toward me and puts a hand gently over the SIG, lowering it. Then he carefully takes it from my numb hand.

Bren grabs my elbow and pulls because I can't take my eyes off of Bartholomew Rehnquist's blood dripping onto his expensive carpet. As Bren gives my arm another tug all I can seem to think is how mad he's gonna be when he realizes he bled all over it. A giggle pushes its way up and out. Bren throws me a worried glance. It's probably because the giggle came out sounding a little hysterical.

"Are you okay," he asks, sounding as concerned as he looks.

I decide that now is a good time for the truth. "No."

He gives my shoulder a squeeze and kisses my forehead. "The first one's the hardest. Process later. We've really gotta go, Lise."

I take a deep breath and nod. We burst out of the Warden's office and hit the darkened hall at full speed. A guard staggers toward us, flashlight quivering.

"Stop!" he barks in a weak voice, but we don't. Bren launches himself and plants both feet in his chest. I am right behind him with a kick to the guard's head. This one will stay down, but there will be more.

We fly down the stairs. It's only a few feet to the outside door from the bottom. The Captain steps from the shadows and fires. I swear time slows and I can hear the bullet moving through the air. Bren pushes me and I slam into the wall as the bullet tears across my arm with searing pain. I fall more than I run down the rest of the stairs while I watch in awe as Bren tackles the Captain to the ground. I get my feet under me and run, skidding to a halt next to the combatants. I have to do something! Bren's hand is bleeding. I watch it slip off the SIG the Captain is trying to aim at him. I kick the Captain's hand for all I'm worth. The weapon flies free and I run after it. I pick it up, turn and . . .

He has Bren on his back and is choking him. I move forward, press the safety to confirm it's off and then shove the SIG to the side of the Captain's head. He freezes, my finger twitches, and warm blood sprays over me. I smell powder and iron. I can taste it. The Captain falls to the side and Bren pushes him off. He's saying something, but my ears are ringing.

"Are you okay?" I shout.

My vision is blotchy and then shrinks to a dot. I'm falling. No, it's more like sliding.

01100100 01101111 01110111 01101110 00100000

01101100 01101001 01101011 01100101 00100000

01110100 01101000 01100101 00100000

feel rain splatter on my face. The air I breathe is fresh and clean. Bren is holding me. We are moving toward the gate. It looms over us, dark and terrifying. Everything comes back in a flash. I struggle and Bren drops me just in time. My stomach heaves as I fall to my hands and knees. What little was in there all comes up. I crawl through the now open gate expecting to be shot down or for my chip to reactivate and explode, but nothing happens.

I stagger to my feet. Bren grabs my arm and we break into a run. We run away from the torture, the pain, the smell of blood, and the vision of the Captain, whose death is on my hands. I stumble as I run trying to wipe his blood off my skin.

"Come on, come on!" Bren yells.

Then I hear another voice, "You made it."

I am slammed from the side and almost fall over from Kate's exuberance.

"We haven't made it yet," Reign says darkly.

I can make out prisoners fleeing in all direction and I can hear distant shouts and scattered gunfire.

The farther we run, the quieter the gun reports and shouting become. Soon all I can hear is rain, distant thunder, pounding feet, and the inhale and exhale of my breath. I keep my eyes trained on Bren's back and clear my mind. I will have time to think, later.

We pause, hands on knees, sucking air in great gasps. The four of us step apart and listen, each facing in a different direction. Bren gives the signal and we move out. We skirt the town that supports the local farmers, ranchers, and prison. According to Bren, there is an auxiliary unit posted here but from this distance, all appears quiet. Either they have not been alerted or they are being stealthy. My gut tells me that it is not their style so they just don't know . . . yet.

Bren starts walking again and we follow like baby ducks. Even Reign is quiet. We are all too tired to run. I don't know about the others but my feet hurt and I have shin splints along with my injured arm. I hope I don't need stitches. The bleeding seems to have slowed but I can't really tell. I can't remember when I last ate and I need to get my mind off my misery and onto something else, anything else — just not the Captain . . . and blood . . . and death.

My thoughts are interrupted by a siren. We look back and see the town coming to life.

"Come on!" Bren yells again and I make my body move faster. I notice I'm not the only one who can barely manage a jog; Kate is lagging behind even me. Soon we are walking again. All activity seems to be moving away from us, back toward the prison.

I begin to fantasize about a bed and maybe some painkillers. I stumble, jarring myself enough to create a new ache but also enough to wake myself back up. It only lasts for a few minutes. I am soaked to the skin, cold and shivery, but I am alive and for the moment, free. I notice Bren slowing. He almost seems confused which is odd. He shares a look with Reign. She moves into the lead. I start to ask what's going on when I'm interrupted by a sudden movement. Figures that had been well-camouflaged burst from the ground. They quickly subdue Reign. I turn to run.

"*Stop!*"

I don't.

"Stop or we'll shoot them."

This time, I listen, slow my steps and turn around. I place my hands on my head. Kate has a man on either side of her, holding her firmly between them. Bren is on his knees with a gun to his head.

"No," I say hoarsely. I clear my throat and try again. "It's me you want. Let them go."

"Identify yourself."

"Elise Andrek."

My words are met with dead silence. I blink rain out of my eyes and wait.

"Confirm identification."

I start to open my mouth to respond, but a man steps

forward and holds a device up to my face.

"State your name again," he says harshly.

"Elise Andrek," I say slowly, watching his piece of technology in fascination. I raise my eyes slowly from the tech to his face, which is covered in paint. I can also see bits of grass and debris stuck to his uniform in intricate camouflage.

"It's her," he says turning to his superior.

"Let's go," the officer answers.

The soldier takes my arm and walks me forward toward a hole in the ground where a grass covered trap door has been propped open. One by one my friends are lined up behind me.

The opening is no bigger than a city manhole cover. Rungs lead into blackness. Another soldier goes first, activating night vision goggles as he descends. I am pushed gently from behind. What the heck, they haven't killed me yet. I go down rung by rung, feeling my way but not seeing. I land hard at the bottom of the ladder, expecting another step where there isn't one. The cool dampness makes me shiver harder, my teeth chatter. My captors push me on.

We make many turns and in no time at all, I am hopelessly lost. I'm pushed through a series of curtains that I cannot see but merely feel. Just as the sky lightens before dawn, my surroundings lose the inky blackness I was becoming used to. One more curtain and we enter a box lit by some kind of red lighting. Once we are all inside, a door swishes shut behind us and the left-hand wall slides open to reveal a larger room filled with monitors, computer stations and operators wearing headsets.

"Welcome, Elise."

I turn at the sound of my name. A small scarred woman with a regal bearing and iron gray hair stands stiffly to the side. There is something both familiar and frightening about her.

"Who are you?"

"We are Recalcitrant. The government named us, but we take it to heart."

Bren has said nothing, so I'm not sure what to think. I glance at him, but he is staring straight ahead giving me no clues. Shouldn't he be telling them who he is? Shouldn't he be asking for help or . . . He's waiting for me. He's giving me the chance to show them I'm a leader.

"May we have some dry gear before we move on?" I ask, trying to be brave, strong, and worthy of their help.

The woman laughs. "Move on? Hardly. From here you move forward. Consider yourself recruited by the resistance."

"I think that has already happened. I've been sending you information."

"And we appreciate it, but our work is not done. Follow me, please."

"You know who I am, who are you?"

"You may call me Patton."

"Patton? Is that your name?" Surely she isn't named after the historic general?

"It is my call sign and all you need to know me by."

I give her a hard look. The stiffness I had noticed earlier remains and she has a limp. The handgun strapped to her left thigh surprises me. Most people are right-handed. Then I notice the curled fingers of her right hand.

"You were in a serious accident," I say bluntly.

A small smile curves up the undamaged side of her mouth. "My accident was being the guest of Bartholomew Rehnquist in his early days. Looking at you, I would say he has become more skilled, though I'm sure you're no less damaged."

"I'm sorry for your pain," I say hoarsely, looking her right in the eye.

"And I yours. We survive and we move on. Those of us who are brave enough, work to stop the damage." She pauses to open a door. "Here we are."

She has led us to a small room where we are faced with an odd arch encircled in plastic. A technician sits behind a control panel nearby. I turn and look at her for clarification.

"Step in. You each need to be scanned."

"I'll go," Bren says as he brushes past me. He boldly steps into the machine and holds his arms above his head, his feet spread apart. It whirs and beeps in response as beams of light swing around him. Patton steps closer to a screen on the wall and I follow. Images of Bren's systems begin to generate in the multiple screen segments.

"What all is it showing us?" I ask, filled with curiosity.

"We are looking for unseen hardware mainly, but it also shows his bones, nerves, circulation, etcetera."

"I have some hardware."

"Then we need to deal with it before you can go on. We are shielded here, but if they are able to start tracking you again, you will be found in no time once you are outside our walls."

"Won't they go to where I last had a signal?"

"I'm sure they will, but they won't find anything worthwhile."

"Huh," I reply, thinking they may be overconfident. I switch gears to the thing I can control. "So you got the data I sent?"

"We did."

"Then you know what piece of tech they installed in me. Do you have a doctor on staff who can handle a procedure like this?"

"Just a field medic."

"You know my chip is wired into my spine more or less, right?" I paused to point. "At the base of my skull. Are they skilled enough to . . . ?"

"You brought your own medic, right? She can do it because after all she's way more than a simple medic and she personally assisted in many installations. More importantly, you saved her life. She'll be motivated."

I gulp and glance at Kate who looks unusually pale.

"Next," the technician states and Reign steps forward. By the looks of Kate, it may be a race to see who throws up first, her or me.

Kate goes next and when it's my turn Kate asks for lots of pictures of the chip's capsule and its location. Her forehead is beaded with sweat and Bren looks worried. He and Reign are reluctantly escorted out by the technician. Patton leads the two of us to a room with a strange chair in it. On closer inspection it is quite miraculous and looks like it can be moved to accommodate the human body lying or sitting, facing it or away from it. Patton has her field medic adjust it so that I can sit with my face resting in a padded circle.

"My medic will stay and assist," she tells us.

I look at Kate. Her arms are crossed in front of her and her face looks pinched. This could kill me or paralyze me, yet she looks more afraid than I feel. Maybe I've done all I really need to do to stop the game. Maybe my last task is to help Kate to have the confidence to become the doctor she should have been. I can trust Kate or I can stay here indefinitely. I take a deep breath. "It will be okay, Kate. I trust you."

Kate bites her lip and nods so I move over and sit in the chair. Her touch speaks the words she's afraid to say aloud. Her gentle hands wrap my hair up and out of her way with a long strip of gauze. Then she swabs my neck with a solution that makes my eyes water. I feel the prick of a needle and try to relax. I can feel pressure but not pain. I try to ignore the sounds of surgery and the tugging sensations, which I sense more than actually feel.

She pauses periodically and looks at the pictures of my device that they have up on screens all around the room for her. When her forceps scrape something that sounds like bone, I have to force myself not to gag. I feel huge relief when I hear something hit the metal pan on the tray next to me with a twang. Patton, who had been standing off to the side, eagerly takes it and gives it to her medic with quickly mumbled instructions. I'm sure they are going to study it. I would have liked a look myself. I hear the medic leave. Kate's attention stays on me as she begins to put my flesh back together. When she's done she covers it with a bandage and then takes a look at my arm before she cleans and bandages it too.

"All done," she says raggedly as she wipes sweat from her forehead.

I wiggle my fingers and toes and then gingerly climb out of the chair. Kate tosses her gloves on the tray and removes the scrubs they had given her. Her eyes look red and there are dark circles under them, but I can see relief in them too.

"Thank —" Before I can finish the rest of the sentence she is hugging me.

"I was so scared I'd hurt you." I can feel the truth of her words in the hug. When she pulls back, I can see it in her eyes as well. I feel okay. She has earned my trust.

"I believe in you, Kate."

She makes a funny sound, part laugh and part sob. Patton smiles at us. It's a friendly smile but it makes me feel awkward. "Come. I'll take you to the others," Patton says sounding pleased.

I look over a small room where open shelving lines all available wall space. A table with six chairs holds center stage. Four piles of dark clothes and boots rest on its top. Reign sits in one of the chairs with her knees pulled to her chest. She has touched nothing and actually looks worried, or maybe scared.

"Get changed. Food will be here in a moment. We are leaving in twenty minutes," Patton says.

I start to thank her and realize she is gone. I look back to the table where Reign and Kate are each going through a pile and realize Bren is missing.

"Where's Bren?" I ask Reign.

"He was upset that they wouldn't let him stay with you. Someone came for him and he left willingly. Nobody told me anything," she answers bitterly.

I strip quickly, careful of my wounds and then redress in the provided clothes. They are nothing much, but a big improvement over our previous attire.

The smell of hot food hits me before I can see it and my mouth waters. We are each given a small plate of plain roasted chicken, mashed potatoes, peas and a glass of water. Bren's clothes still sit on the table, making me worry.

I try to eat slowly, but it has been awhile and I'm incredibly hungry. Bren shows up looking serious as I'm shoveling in the last bite. I watch him carefully, but he isn't making eye contact and the wrinkle between his brows tells me he's not ready to talk.

He quickly changes, his food arriving before he is finished. He forgoes lacing his boots for sustenance. I don't even try to speak to him because I know our time is about up, but I very much want him to say something. Patton is back before he is done eating. I feel frustrated. I want to know what's going on.

"Come," Patton says briskly. "We don't want to waste the darkness."

We are led down a level and then along a hallway that feels like it goes on forever. I notice cameras along the route. At the end is a guard station. I know Patton is important by the way the two men down here snap to attention when they see her.

"Is he ready?" she asks them.

"Yes, ma'am," the shorter one answers.

"Through that door," she says to us. "Good luck."

Through the door is an underground supply depot. I smile. I recognize the stamps on the crates and boxes. Whatever is in here has been stolen from the government. Bren was right.

Whatever is going on, it is way bigger than me. It's time for me to be part of the solution. I step forward as a surprisingly young man approaches.

"I'm Ridley. You are to be crated and shipped downstream."

"Did you say crated?" I ask, feeling appalled. To be honest I'm not sure if it is more a fear of small spaces or of this pirate I'm trusting my life to that has me nervous all over again.

"It's okay," Bren says softly next to my ear. "This is our way to the main camp."

I clench my teeth and nod once.

"Visit the facilities. You'll get no more water until you arrive. You will not be let out and there will be no potty break. I suggest you sleep. It's gonna take about three and a half hours to get you to your transfer point."

We each take a turn in the depot's bathroom and then he leads us on board where crates are stacked on deck. He shows us to an enormous one that has been propped open. "This is it, your happy home for the next few hours. Try to relax."

I sigh inside before I climb over the edge. I crouch down in my corner and wait while the others join me. I settle in and try to relax like Ridley suggested. I figure that with our backs to a corner and our feet stretched toward the center, they would touch in the middle. It is too low to stand but we will be able to crouch or sit without difficulty.

Leather straps have been mounted to the inside of the crate for us to hold on to for balance and support. We have also been provided with a small hand ax for emergency escape purposes and a special container for anyone who can't hold their bladder.

We have nothing else but the clothes on our backs, our wits, and one another. A random thought floats through my head from my gaming days. If this were a game we'd be set. We have Kate our healer, Bren our fighter, and Reign our thief character. What did that make me? What is my value here? This is survival 101; there is no tech required. The thought depresses me and makes me feel useless.

The lid goes down and is nailed into place. Bren nudges my foot. I know it's him by the direction and feel. He wants to know if I'm okay. I'm not. I've resorted to my imagination to fill the void. If I let myself think, I know I'll break down. If I let myself think, I'll see the Captain's death all over again. If I let myself think, I'll be back with the Inquisitor. Is he dead like the Captain?

I draw in a ragged breath. I will be okay. I say it over and over to myself. The engine roars to life. I gulp as I feel the barge move and shift. I remind myself to relax. Finally, the predictable motion and steady beat of the barge's engine lull me.

I don't know if hours or minutes have passed. I hear something, but I might be half dreaming. I wake myself up and listen carefully. It's a shout, but it's so far away and muffled that I can't make it out. I take a slow deep breath and concentrate. The engine stops.

"Prepare to be boarded." Now the voice is clear and it makes my gut clench. Prepare to fight is more like it. I can hear my crate-mates moving. A bump and shift let me know another craft has come alongside.

I don't know what I'm expecting — a bribe, maybe? Our

captain is neither argumentative nor solicitous. In fact, he sounds bored. The voices come closer and are much clearer.

"What's in this one?" the new voice asks.

The tarp is ripped off. I can almost see, as early dawn hits the slats with weak greenish daylight. I glance from Bren to Kate and then to Reign. I can tell that each of them is listening and looks ready for anything. They look more determined than scared and that lifts my own flagging spirits. Bren is reaching very slowly and carefully toward the ax.

"It says parts."

Bren unties the ax. I'm holding my breath. I let it out really slowly so they don't hear.

"Yes," replies our captain.

"What kind of parts?"

"I don't look in 'em. I just move 'em."

"Aren't you curious?"

"I'm not paid to be curious," Captain Ridley responds.

"Guess that's why you're orange, right?"

"We all have a job to do. We can't all be public safety. Who would get you supplies, keep your streets clean, and wash your uniforms?" Now Ridley's voice holds a little bite.

"Open it."

"Sure, no problem."

My stomach pinches and my heart races.

"As soon as you produce the appropriate documents, I will open any crate covered by your paperwork," Ridley continues.

I sigh when I hear his words.

"You don't sound like the usual grubbers from maintenance

and transportation," the public safety officer sneers.

"Our assignment has to do with our aptitude, not our intelligence." Part of me wants our captain to go on and part of me wants him to shut up before every crate is opened and we're exposed.

I hear footsteps moving away. The movement of the barge combined with my nerves makes me feel ill. I silently roll onto all fours and suck in some deep breaths. At least the air is cool.

The public safety officer begins talking again, but his voice sounds very different, almost wheedling. "Sir, I have stopped a shipment . . . yes, it's suspicious. It is not on my roster . . . it's the Mayweather; IMO is 4780381 . . . Yes, sir. Yes, sir, but I know how important to you it is that we . . . I would like to look in the crates anyway, but the captain is requesting documents . . . But, sir, don't you think . . . Yes, sir, I understand."

There is a moment of silence and then the rude tone returns to the officer's voice. "Give me your vessel documents and bill of lading."

"Rory, get the man a copy of what he wants."

"Yes, sir," the second mate replies quickly.

All grows silent except for the lap of water and the creaking of the barge.

I can't stand it anymore. I need . . . what? To know everything's going to be okay? Forgiveness and acceptance for all the grief I've caused? Is this it? After everything am I going to die now? What if they send me back to prison? My heart hurts. Can we feel our hearts breaking? As the thoughts chase around in my head, one thought remains constant. I don't care so much what other people think, but I do care what Bren thinks and I wonder why he doesn't hate me — if we're caught they will be punished because of me.

I glance over at the person I care about most. He has a wrinkle between his brows again. It's his worried look. Clearly, it isn't just me who expects the worst.

I hear feet scurry toward us. "Your paperwork, sir."

I hold my breath.

"All looks to be in order. You may go."

I hear more footsteps and the bump of the hulls. Then the engines come to life and we are moving again. I count slowly to one hundred. Nothing has changed so I crawl over to Bren. I feel weepy and I don't want to give into it. I can't give into it. He puts his arm around me and I listen to his heartbeat.

After several minutes of quiet, I figure it's safe enough to whisper. "Where were you after they removed my chip?"

Bren sighs. "I was angry that they wouldn't let me at least watch. A lieutenant of Patton's came for me and he took me to where I could observe. Then while Kate was stitching you up he took me to their communications room so that I could send a message to Melodia. Some things changed while we were unable to communicate. We can't go directly to her. We have to be reprocessed. I guess it's for the best but I don't like it. We're short on time and we've been through enough already. You've been through enough already, but it is out of my control. I can't change anything and I hate it."

"Sometimes it's all up hill. I guess."

Bren squeezes my shoulders. I loop my arms around him

and lose track of time. Soon I'm drifting in and out of sleep. As long as I hear Bren's steady heartbeat, I'm calm.

A soft thump on the crate wakes me. Captain Ridley speaks softly, "I want to wish you luck. You'll be unloaded soon and the dock is monitored so don't make a sound."

I start to thank him, but I hear him move away from the crate and then from a distance, I hear him bellowing instructions to his small crew. Activity builds on board and I strain to listen. Bren is also alert and I suspect that he has been the whole time. The barge changes direction and the engine sounds change, soon followed by the motion. Listening to the voices, I glean that the cargo is about to be off-loaded. In no time, there is a loud thump against our crate. We are lifted and swing for a few moments. Bren holds the ax, blade down against the bottom of the crate, ready in case we fall. My mind tumbles around wondering if it is better to fall into the water and risk drowning or to fall onto the land where we'll surely break bones.

I feel whatever is holding us release. Before panic has a chance to take hold we land with a thud strong enough to make my teeth rattle. A small engine roars to life and we're moving once more but with a different motion; this time, it's vehicular.

Reign pretends to sleep but I can see Kate's eyes flash through the gloom. Narrow strips of sunlight try to cut lines through the crate making us look like old-time prisoners in striped uniforms. I close my eyes and try to channel Reign.

The driver takes a fast turn, rocking us to the side and I open my eyes. I have no idea how much time has passed or even what direction we are going other than generally south, but I know by the sun's position that it has to be early afternoon. A shadow passes over us and stays so long that it seems like it must be clouding up.

The truck comes to a halt and the engine is cut. No one speaks, but I can hear the scuffle of many booted feet. There is a light thud and the truck gives a lurch to the side. Bren grips the ax when what I assume is a pry bar is applied to the side. With a crash, the side of the crate pops open and Kate nearly falls out. I throw a hand in front of my eyes to block the piercing light.

"Out! Hands on your head. Knees in the dirt." The voice is male, deep and gruff.

Kate slides out first. The light is still so bright that my eyes are watering, rendering her nothing but a silhouette. Reign goes next and I follow behind her before we make them angry. I can see enough to know that these people are not wearing black so I'm willing to do as they ask. Bren follows me out after I hear the thunk of the ax being left in the crate. I kneel next to Kate and put my hands on my head.

My eyes are adjusting. I'm happy to note that we're back in Douglas fir country. Dampness is wicking into the fabric of my cargo pants at the knees. I take a deep lungful of the clean, crisp, fresh air.

I notice that a tall lean man has taken an interest in me. I meet his gaze. "You don't act like a hardened criminal." I recognize his voice as the one who ordered us out of the crate.

"I'm not," I reply, trying to keep my voice calm.

"We'll see about that." The speaker has control in his voice with a hint of fear.

What I can see of his face looks grim. He is dressed much like Bren was when he found us underground. I glance to the others. They are all armed, all wear boots and most have their faces obscured by a scarf or hat. Some wear dark glasses, all wear long sleeves and a few even have the kind of gloves the construction personnel wear.

I swing my gaze back to the speaker, who I take to be the leader or at least the spokesperson for the group, "What do you want?"

By the way his eyes crinkle, he must be smiling. "I want you to tell me everything."

I look to each of my friends and try to communicate with my eyes that it is time for one of them to speak.

"Don't worry. You each will get a chance to spill all of your darkest secrets." He turns to his followers. "Separate them and take their statements."

They are armed, I'm not, and since no one else is putting up a fuss, I let them haul me to my feet and escort me down the graveled road. Soon it is so narrow that the trees touch over our heads, obscuring the storm-gray sky. I smile to myself; no helicopters, drones, or satellites could see through this. I begin to see a number of low buildings and yurts with plenty of needles and greenery strewn across the roofs.

Kate and Bren are taken off toward the left; Reign and I are led on and then to the right. I quickly lose sight of them through the underbrush. Of course, they would leave me with Reign. We walk on and on moving ever farther apart. I look back over my shoulder and find that Reign is now also gone. I'm on my own with two guards. They lead me into a squat building of cinder-block. My first impression is that I'm in a multipurpose room of some sort. There is a cot, a kitchenette, and some cupboards. I'm pushed into an old folding chair placed by a rickety table. I feel like I'm in someone's home — no, wrong word — domicile? Someone lives in this meticulously neat yet tired room.

The female captor pulls off the scarf wrapped around her face and tosses it onto the scarred tabletop followed by her cap. I feel surprised and don't try to hide it. She is older than I would have suspected, maybe close to mid-fifty. I'm immediately curious about her. She just doesn't fit my mental profile of a rebel. Her long hair is captured in a stylishly messy bun, a streak of gray giving it character. Her eyes are bright and inquisitive. She sits in the folding chair opposite me. When she speaks her voice is educated and cultured.

"Tell us about your work on the game."

I see no reason not to answer so I do. The Inquisitor already got this out of me anyway. While I am talking she takes a few notes on a pad of paper that her assistant has retrieved from a drawer. How very old-school of her. He also sets up a camera to record our interview and then he stands guard and watches me.

"Tell us about your trial."

Again a fair question, so I answer honestly but briefly. What is it about her? I find myself wanting to talk to her. I want to trust these people who are against the government I've grown to hate. If I'm wrong and it's all a trick I'm not sure what I can do about it. I'm so tired.

"Tell us about your escape."

"Which one," I ask, a small smile touching my lips. "Through the underground, right?"

"How did you know which I was referring to?"

"You seem practical and organized. I feel like you would want information chronologically."

"Yes." A simple one-word answer and I am not surprised. She wants information from me and doesn't want to give too much away. I tell her about Malorie and Bren. My voice grows thick at times with the painful memories, but I keep talking. I am not sharing anything that the Inquisitor didn't already get out of me except for Bren. This is the first time I have talked about him. The time for protecting him is over. He is answering his own set of questions with another Recalcitrant. My thoughts swirl — Patton had my chip removed — she turned us over to Ridley who gave us to these people. I could trust them, couldn't I, or did it even matter at this point?

"Tell us about your capture." I have to close my eyes to face this one.

"Tell us about prison." I shudder. I can't help it. This is difficult to talk about, but people have to know about the atrocities that happen there. They cannot be allowed to go on. I cry as I tell my story. I show them the scars and wipe my nose on my sleeve. As much as I want to curl into a ball and pretend that it never happened I know I can't. If this is the only thing I can ever do to change the world then I must. I have way too many marks in my negative column to make up for.

When I stutter to a halt she presses once more, "Tell me what happened after you walked out the gate."

I go on a little more, talking about running and the sounds I heard. I talk about the sleeping town and then alarms, where I stop again.

"Go on," she says after a long pause.

"I do not choose to volunteer any information about what happened next."

"Why?"

"If anyone had assisted me at this point in the story, then they deserve to be protected. If I am questioned again I will do the same for you. I have given you plenty to validate and you have the four of us. Let us go on to do what we feel we must or don't. Share the atrocities of the prison system or don't. At this moment there is nothing further I can do so I choose not to say anything else at this time."

"We will consider your words," she says formally.

I watch her rise. They silently gather their equipment and leave, locking the door behind them. I remain in my chair, listening and observing the room. I hear nothing but the whispering of the trees. I don't see any obvious cameras so I get up and start searching the room. I meticulously go through each inch of it. A few minutes in, someone comes to stand outside my door. Whoever it is, they don't interfere with me, so I ignore them and continue my search. I am happy to find no sign of cameras but then there is no other technology either. I have running water and my own bathroom. Unless I want to throw soap in my guard's eyes, smother them with a pillow or strangle them with a blanket, I've got nothing. Not so much as a nail file or pen has been left behind.

I feel incredibly weary, so with nothing else to do, I make use of the cot and fall asleep almost instantly.

24

01100011 01101000 01101001 01101100 01100100

01110010 01100101 01101110 00100000 01101111

01100110 00100000 01110100 01101000 01100101

Food and water are delivered every six hours as near as I can tell, with no means of keeping time except for what I can see out the window. When I am asleep, they simply leave it on the table. I have had five deliveries now. I've been separated from my friends and left alone long enough that I have gone back to incessant worrying. I can't change anything. I can't fix anything. I can't even take care of myself. I feel like I'm held together by my skin — skin that burns in response to my overactive system. I pace the room. The guard still stands outside my door. I don't know why they bother. Where would I go by myself? Without supplies, I can't make it back to the hub from here and I've got to stop the scenario from going live in Seattle in five days. I need a plan.

It's like prison, yet different. I lock out my window, but all I can see is trees and rain. Guilt lies heavily on me, a backpack full of bricks pulling on my shoulders. I know everything is my fault. I should have been smarter. I should have realized what I was doing sooner. I'm scared. I want to curl up in a ball and cry. My throat is growing tight and pressure is building. My breath comes faster, fogging the glass and I begin to shake.

A knock at my door startles me. I swipe at my eyes, take a breath and go to open it. Bren takes one look at me, steps inside, and hugs me close while pushing the door shut with his foot.

"I thought I wasn't allowed to see you," I say, my voice cracking.

"We've been cleared. We can head to the city now," he replies calmly.

"Oh boy?" It comes out on a sob.

"You've been busy beating yourself up again. Come sit," he says as he drags me to the bed. He sits at the foot of the cot and pulls one leg up to face me.

I sit with my legs crisscrossed so that my knee is touching his. I swipe at my watery eyes again. "I'm sorry. I'm better when I'm doing something. I can't stand all this time to think."

"I know. That's why I'm here. I thought that if I came to tell you we were cleared, we could also talk about some other things that have . . . well, been weighing on my heart."

"Oh?"

Bren reaches out and picks up my hand. His skin is warm and calloused. I can't seem to take my eyes off our entwined fingers.

"Remember when I first came to the prison and you and I . . . had a misunderstanding?"

I look up from our fingers to his face. "We don't have to talk about that."

"I think we do. I want to you know about Reign."

I turn my lips in and bite them. I don't think I want to know, but Bren doesn't give me a choice. "We rarely had time to talk in prison. We were nearly always watched and monitored. It was never safe. I was in a dark place. The government leaked that you were dead after twisting anything you ever did to dark and ugly. 'Terrorist' was one of the kinder terms they used."

Bren takes a breath. "I was devastated when I thought they'd killed you. I had been looking for you for three months and blaming myself for your capture and then Reign came along. It started and ended in a short time. We were both drinking and sharing our personal miseries when things went too far. It was a mistake. I ended it and the next day . . . a report was released from a man on the inside."

"The guard who came in as a spy — What did he say?"

"His report was about a girl with an iron will; someone who wasn't allowed to use computers anymore. There was a rumor that she was the girl who built the game. The Recalcitrants released the news that you had done it without knowing the purpose. You were reprofiled and that intel was released to the public. Many started talking about how you had always been smarter than you let on, that you could beat the system. You became a symbol of hope and then even people outside the Recalcitrants began to believe. People started saying that you could outthink a computer and I was afraid. If I was hearing it, what was the government hearing? I knew I had to find you, to rescue you, but then they had rechipped you and it was too dangerous to take you out. All I could think about was what the government tells us, 'that everyone must follow the rules and there is not room for disagreement and that everyone has a role to play to make the system work'."

"I'm being used by both sides aren't I?"

"In a way you are."

"I don't want to be part of anyone's game."

"I know, Lise. They made you what you are. You did not create the monster. They did this."

"I want to shut the game down permanently and then I want to be left alone. I want to put this behind me."

"Where will you go? What will you do? How will you live? You need a plan that goes out farther than a week."

"I don't know — right now I can't look that far ahead. I can't see past the game."

"Work with me. Together we can bring down both the live trials and stop the release of the online experience."

"I have to fix this."

"Please, let me help you."

Another knock rattles my door. Kate pops in with a first aid kit, sandwiches, and a big smile.

"You look gloomy. Cheer up! I've got food."

When I don't reply, she tries again. "Well then, grumpy, let me check your neck and arm."

"Why are you so happy, Kate?"

"They need me here. I can do some real good. I can pay my debts." She removes my bandages as she talks, inspects everything and redresses my wounds.

"I'll miss you," I whisper, my voice catching.

"I'll miss you too — until I see you again."

"How can you be so positive, Kate?"

"Many bad things have happened to you that you never deserved. I figure the universe owes you some good. This here, these people — they are *my* good."

I can feel my eyes tearing up.

"I will see you again," Kate insists.

I hug her close and try to pull myself together. "I'm happy for you, Kate. You deserve to have a real life among people who value you."

"I believe in you." Kate whispers. How can they all be so positive and forgiving when it comes to me? One more squeeze and she pushes me away to wipe her own eyes. She pats my shoulder and continues, "You're all set."

She holds out her hand to Bren who pushes past it to hug her instead.

"Good luck and take care of her," Kate says.

"Good luck to you, too. I will," Bren answers.

Kate leaves, shutting the door softly behind her and a bit of her sunshine leaves with her.

Bren picks up my hand again. "If you ever want to ask me anything about Reign, you can."

I nod, feeling drained.

"I need to tell you something else," Bren says softly.

"Why do I have the feeling I'm not going to like it?" I grumble.

Bren's mouth moves into a straight line. He closes his eyes

and I hear him sigh. "Reign is coming with us."

A bunch of emotions race through me. "She doesn't have anywhere else to go and they won't let her stay here," I guess.

"I'm sorry," he says, confirming my assumption.

Now it's my turn to sigh. "She's an enormous, bossy, pain in my ass, but she can be useful . . . sometimes."

Bren chuckles and hands me a sandwich. "Into every life, a little Reign must fall."

"You're so punny," I respond and then we sit down to eat in companionable silence. When we're done we continue to sit together and watch the woods from the doorway and try to soak up the sense of peace that floats in the gentle breeze teasing the boughs.

Bren is so quiet that I turn to look at him. His eyes are closed and his breathing is steady. He may have fallen easily into slumber but as tired as I am, my mind won't let go. I know I must go back to the city to get into the government computer and shut down the game. Just as important, I have to let out the truth. Bren is right. I started this and I have to finish it. I can see Malorie's face and I feel my throat grow tight. I squeeze the sob for all I'm worth because I don't want anyone to know. The tears can't be stopped, they pour uncontrollably down my cheeks. They leave hot trails behind and I swipe at them angrily. Breath leaves my body in a harsh huff and comes back in with a shudder.

I attempt to kill the fear and loss with logic by thinking beyond myself. What happens when you overthrow the government? What will rise up in its place? Will you leave the world a better place?

It is not for me to decide who should govern everyone. I just know that what is in place is not working and has to be changed. I know that I am not the person to run things. There are people smarter than me for that so I choose the devil I do not know over an intolerable present. It's time to suck it up and sneak back into the place I'd hoped I'd never see again.

I wake Bren and lead him to the bed. I want to hold him and rest because I don't know what the future holds anymore.

In my dreams I'm back in the trial, trying to save everyone, but no one will listen. My view pans out and my other self becomes no more than a rat in a maze. The view pans out again and I am running the program where my other self is a character on the screen.

I wake to full darkness and footsteps followed by a knock. I roll out of bed trying not to wake Bren and walk in my sock feet over to open the door to the woman who questioned me.

"Time to go." Her voice is gentle, almost hopeful, yet concerned.

Bren comes to stand behind me. "We're ready."

We follow our guide back to the main area where a few ancient trucks are parked.

We are directed to load up in the back of one. Reign joins us. I'm still trying to both figure her out and decide how I feel about her. I'm not sure what use she will be at this point, but I worry about what she'll do on her own.

The truck bounces back down the deserted roads toward the river, but it is not our final destination. I couldn't see where we were loaded to go to camp, but it definitely was not this stretch of train track where I see the river sparkling with moonlight dancing on its surface.

The engine is cut and the truck comes to a stop. Our armed companions exit the cab. The woman who questioned me waves us down. Part of me would like to know her name, but I understand why she doesn't share it.

She encourages us to move close. Our driver stands with his back to us and his assault rifle ready. We move to form a small circle with the woman. "The train will slow here as it enters the tunnel. You will climb into the empty boxcar. If it is stopped and searched you are on your own. Otherwise, its final stop is a place you know." She puts a finger on Bren's chest over his heart. He nods so he must know what she means.

"The train will be here in about five minutes. Good luck and thank you for the information you all provided us with." She reaches out and clasps each of our shoulders.

"Come on," she says to the driver.

I watch them get back into the truck and drive away. I almost wish they were going with us. Bren takes my hand and leads me to some shrubbery near the mouth of the tunnel, Reign follows. I can't read the look on her face.

Our wait isn't long. I feel the vibration in the ground before I can see the train. It is so much louder than I expected, but then I have never been this close before. The female Recalcitrant is right; the train does visibly slow — nearly to a stop.

Just as I'm wondering which car to select, Reign points, "There."

Almost as obvious as a "pick me" sign, the next to the last car is emblazoned with the graffiti "defy authority" and the side door is slid open.

Reign jogs forward and jumps gracefully on board. I hesitate, but the train is speeding up.

Reign looks out the doorway and waves us forward. Bren makes it just ahead of me. I fall to my hands and knees and just stay there for a beat getting a feel for the moving platform.

"You all right?" Bren asks.

I really don't know what to say. I'm bombarded by feelings and emotions I can't put names to. The enormity of my task is overwhelming.

Bren puts a hand on my shoulder. "Lise?"

"I'll be okay," I gasp, and roll onto my back. The cold air rushing in the door is refreshing but chilling. I have mixed feelings when Reign pushes it closed. Bren leaves me be for a short time, but I can feel him watching.

I know I need to pull myself together. I must pretend that I'm fine for Bren. He and Reign are sitting side by side with their backs against the front wall of the car. I pull myself to my feet and stumble a little as I try to get my sea legs.

I sit on Bren's other side. "I'll take first watch," I say trying to sound brave, confident, and in control.

Bren gives me a questioning look.

"Great," Reign says and promptly curls up on her side with her back pressed against Bren's thigh for warmth. He raises his eyebrows at me in the darkness — I can feel it more than see the response.

"It's okay," I say, trying to convince him. "I'm okay. I need to think."

He reaches over and squeezes my leg in support and understanding, rests his head against the wall and closes his eyes.

I'm jealous for a moment. He has one job — to look out for me; I have to save the world. Then I think about how unfair I'm being.

The rhythmic sounds of the train lull me. I begin to seriously consider how I can stop the live action game from rolling out. How can I prevent the distribution of the game and how can I destroy it? They will have been building traps for the fake trials for months. It's more than just computer code. How do I get the word out? Are there any government officials or public safety personnel that can be trusted? They can't all be bad, can they? But then who would believe someone like me? I've got to make someone believe. I need help. I can't do this on my own.

Reign whimpers in her sleep, making me realize, we are all broken — just how much varies across the board. I feel sorry for her and for every life that has been damaged by the very people who say they are here to protect us. I wake her when I judge a third of the time has gone by, but I don't share any of my thoughts — she would not appreciate them.

I close my eyes not planning to sleep. Next thing I know, Bren is shaking my shoulder. He gives me only a moment to wake up and gather my thoughts before we are leaping from the train. I hit the ground hard, skinning my hands and knees in the gravel, but the sting has me fully awake.

Bren runs and we follow in and out of parked boxcars on

the multiple tracks. We slow to a walk as we leave the yard and try to blend in with the suburbanites.

As we walk, I notice our surroundings less and Reign more. Her posture has stiffened. Each time I glance her way she looks more and more nervous. It's the little things that give her away — the twitch of her eye and the flutter of her hands. She won't look at me. She stares at Bren's back but I feel like she doesn't really see him.

I pull in a deep breath of the city outskirts — concrete, fuel, and an array of plants and humanity fill my nostrils. With the smell comes a flood of memories — of Malorie, of our bus trip to our trial — of my early life here before I was sent away to school.

I'm surprised when Bren enters a building just as the sun bursts above the horizon.

Now damp mustiness fills my nose and the murky dim and disuse speak to me in ways I don't understand. Neither Reign nor I utter a sound. Bren walks confidently toward the back. His line of sight is focused midway down the hall. He turns right at a branch and walks down the side hall. A short distance down, a worn metal door hunkers like a fugitive. I know he's going to stop in front of it.

Dusty cobwebs rest in the upper corners. Bits of litter and piles of detritus decorate the floor, but the door opens on silent well-oiled hinges. Alarm bells ring in my head. I start to reach for him to stop him, but he eludes my grasp, steps on in and looks directly at the camera I notice in the upper left corner. Fear bursts through me, but then I see the indicator light on the camera blink twice. It must mean something to Bren because he shuts the door behind us and leads us down the stairs.

My heart races when I see a trap like one used in my trial. I dive for Bren's knees and bring him to the ground before he reaches it. Reign scrambles into a corner and takes a defensive pose.

I hear applause.

"Nicely done, E," a new voice says softly.

Bren sighs. I look up to see a flock of underground people who look oddly familiar.

"You know, E, the government isn't the only entity who can build a trap and we turn that stuff off when friends are present."

"I . . . I know you," I say, scrambling to my feet.

"Yeah and you owe me a scarf too. Now let's get out of here before we have the unwanted kind of company."

Bren is on his feet and dusting himself off. His body language tells me he's not concerned and then he is wrapped in an enthusiastic hug by the man who calls me "E." I decide to walk next to him.

"You have me at a disadvantage, sir. You know my name, but I don't know yours."

Bren answers instead. "This here is Uncle Malcolm. He watches over Melodia."

The man snorts. "I do try, but she doesn't make it easy."

I give him a better look. He could be the vendor from the market. At the time I hadn't given him a good look, but now I do. He had sported a full beard at the market, but now it's stylish stubble. His dark hair is cut short now where I have the feeling it was longer at the market. He is a little taller than Bren but the walk . . . yes, there it is, the way they hold themselves and their gait is identical, their looks are not so much so. Like Bren, he is more wiry than bulky, however, that is where the resemblance ends.

"You don't look like a bodyguard," I venture.

Malcolm turns his face to me and smiles, though he keeps walking. I like the way his dark eyes crinkle up and now I notice the gray in his sideburns and beard that make him look wise. The style of his short hair finally registers — he hasn't quite let go of . . . "You used to be public safety."

"I'm retired, don't worry."

We continue to walk on and my mind churns. "Wait. You quit. But how? They don't allow anyone to just quit."

"They do when they think you're dead."

Wow, this man had to have given up a lot to be here. He had to believe strongly in his convictions to give up everything to support them. A wave of unworthiness washes over me again.

I look from face to face. Of the other three with Malcolm, none has said a word to me and none are introduced. That probably makes it better for them if I am recaptured by the government. I can't give anyone away if I can do nothing but roughly describe them. I try to smile at them, but they won't make eye contact. Normally, I would feel snubbed, yet this is different. Something is scratching at my attention. I glance at Reign. She won't meet my gaze either. As I watch her, I realize that she is acting furtive and almost angry. It makes me somewhat concerned since she is not her usual confident self.

I decided to bite the bullet and ask. "Are you okay?"

"I'm fine," she snarls back at me in a harsh whisper. She pushes past so I reach for her but Bren puts up an arm to block my attempt.

"Let it go. Give her some space," he suggests.

I nod in acknowledgment more than agreement. Why not? I have enough problems of my own.

After many twists and turns in the underground space, I am hopelessly lost. No matter what the government does to me, they will never be able to get this location out of me. We pass through a door with three cameras focused on it and down yet another hall. The door up ahead is guarded by live people behind what I suspect is a bulletproof shield of clear material.

The other side reminds me of the market though the atmosphere is different. This one is smaller and looks like it could be broken down and moved at a moment's notice. I soak it all in and breathe deeply. Sounds wash over me. They're happy. A lull snags my attention; it's as if the whole market is holding its breath.

Melodia approaches and wraps me in her arms giving me a sense of peace that lightens my heart. I feel happy. I feel at home. The market breathes and then a shiver skitters up my spine. I open my eyes and see Reign, whose eyes tell me she hates me and that I should watch my back, making me feel conflicted and confused. Can't she feel the good vibes in here?

We are led to a well-guarded room lit by many lanterns; their distinctive hissy roar makes me uncomfortable. The largest round table I have ever seen hunkers down in the middle of the room and looks like it has been set for about sixteen people.

Pillar candles burn in a starburst shaped pattern across the center of the deep green cloth.

I move up next to Bren. "What's going on?"

"It looks like brunch and a planning session. They operate in a council fashion here. People request to be on the council and then are voted in. It's all volunteer and anyone who wishes to help is welcome as long as they pass the scan."

"The scan?"

"Our system for making sure that no one is a spy."

"Do I even want to know?"

"Nope."

I glance at Bren. His answer was uncharacteristically abrupt, but he's not looking at me, he's watching Reign. Her eyes slide between us. Then she crosses her arms and turns so that we are out of her line of sight.

01100001 01101110 01101001 01101101 01100001

01101100 01110011 00100000 01111001 01101111

01110101 00100000

Malcolm calls everyone to the table. I am separated from Bren and that makes me uncomfortable. I am however next to Melodia which is a plus. She doesn't seem to be the one in charge. A man closer to Malcolm's age appears to have that honor and by the look of him, he was once a member of government. He speaks and I quickly tune out, taking more interest in the delicious food before me than a boring planning meeting.

I'm startled out of my own private food induced heaven when the sound of my own voice touches my ears. Part of my interview with the Recalcitrants is on the big screen. I'm talking about the game. My cheeks grow warm.

"What do we need to do to stop this atrocity?" the ex-government man asks. Crushing silence fills the room. "Elise?"

I clear my throat. "It's bigger than our hub." Why hadn't I paid attention to what was being said? "They have plans to take it live in other hubs, starting with Seattle in a couple of days. I believe that if I can get into our hub's main computer, I can —"

"You're a child. We have programmers. Send one of them," A female council member interrupts.

Arguing breaks out around and across the table. I sink back into my chair, feeling Reign's glare scorching me over the tabletop.

Melodia touches my arm. "Are you ready?"

"What?"

"Are you prepared to reprogram the live game?" Melodia clarifies.

"I don't have a choice. It has to be done from a main terminal and I have to see the screens. I can't walk anyone else through it — there are too many variables and nuances."

"Then it is you who shall go." She gives my arm one more pat and then reaches for a small silver bell that I had assumed was to call a waiter or something. All voices cease immediately.

"My friends, I appreciate your deep dedication to this matter. Each of you has come to a decision based on the information you were provided, combined with all your past experiences. I am here to tell you that nothing in your past has prepared you for this moment in time, or for this girl. Not one of our programmers can do what she can."

"But she basically created the game. She is Oppenheimer!" the female council member argues.

"She did so without understanding what she was doing

because she was not given the whole picture," Melodia returns.

"All the more reason not to let her go," the councilwoman retorts.

"She deserves the chance to fix this. She was tricked. That will not happen again."

I wait for someone to argue with that. Several seconds pass and then miraculously I begin to see nods around the table. Soon voices are raised again, this time, they are saying "Aye."

I try to stay alert, but my full belly soon has me nodding in my chair. Melodia herself walks me to another room where bunk beds line the walls.

"Get some rest, dear. You are not needed for this part."

"Thank you," I whisper.

The door closes but opens again almost immediately. Reign practically slams it behind her. She opens her mouth, closes it, and then paces the room.

"What's your problem, Reign?" I ask, unable to leave her alone any longer.

"You are."

"Me? What did I do?"

"You're the 'it' girl," she snarls.

"What?" Now I'm completely perplexed.

"They want to be you or know you. They listen to you. You're so sickeningly nice, loyal — you have integrity."

"I don't understand."

"I hate you. Couldn't you do one selfish thing — ever?" she whines.

"I am selfish and I've done terrible things," I reply softly, beginning to understand.

She growls. "Shut up — I don't want to hear it. The self-doubt, the unworthiness — you're so . . . humble. I do something bad and I get punished, you get . . . celebrated."

"I'm sorry you're hurting."

"Don't. Don't you do that. Don't be nice, not to me. I can't even have Bren because of you."

"Bren?" I wonder how this became about him.

"The one thing that was good in my life and you took it away. You didn't even have to be there — your freaking memory was enough."

"I thought you agreed to end . . . wait, you lied — you lied to him to protect yourself."

"Yes."

"If you knew who I was, why did you help me?" I ask in bewilderment.

"I was curious. I needed the money, and I wanted freedom — especially freedom."

"I'd say your goals have been met. Why are you still here?"

"Bren told you the truth. I've got nowhere else to go. I've got nobody else, but I do have a mission. I can help stop what's happening and yet I can't stand to watch you with him. So then what am I to do? As much as I despise you, I hate them more."

"I'm sorry. What can I do?"

"Of course you're sorry." She throws herself onto a bunk with her back to me. Soon she is asleep — it takes me much longer.

01100001 01110010 01100101 00101110 00100000

01011001 01101111 01110101 00100000 01110111

01101001 01101100 01101100 00100000

As soon as I'm awake, I look for Reign. When I don't find her, I feel a sense of relief and then I feel ashamed for having it. Next, I go looking for Bren, but I don't see him in the lounge or dining hall. I don't really see anyone around and my belly growls, so I go on into the kitchen.

No one is here either. There is some kind of schedule up on the wall, making me believe that they share the workload. The area is older yet clean and neat. I begin to rummage through the cupboards, looking for something to eat, but there are so many choices after what I've been used to, that I feel overwhelmed. When was I last allowed to make a choice about much of anything? I open the refrigerator and I am confronted with more choices. I sigh.

I finally end up with a banana and some kind of oat-based

cereal with milk. I eat it standing by the sink. Instructions for washing dishes, waste disposal, composting, and recycling are also posted. I follow them as best I can. As I finish, one of Malcolm's crew, who led us in, appears.

"Elise?"

"Yes?"

"I'm Erik. I was asked not to introduce myself yesterday for safety reasons."

"I understand. It's nice to meet you, Erik."

"You too. I'm to take you to Melodia."

"Where is everyone?"

"They are receiving their instructions or going through practice exercises. You were to be left to sleep as long as you needed."

"Um, thanks, I guess. Will you tell me what's going on?"

"No."

"No? I don't understand."

"That is not my job."

Part of me wants to yell at him but I can see that he feels bad about keeping me in the dark so I let it go and follow him back past the lounge and into a small room that is set up to do makeup and costuming. I am fascinated by the array of clear plastic, labeled drawers that cover nearly every inch of wall space. I am somewhat reminded of the room where I was first made over. There is a stylist's chair, tool cart, and wash sink but this room is much more. I skip over the ordinary and pull out a drawer containing prosthetic noses.

I hear the door open and assume it's Erik leaving but instead, Melodia stands in the doorway. She smiles at me and then pushes me gently into the stylist's chair.

"What are you doing?" I ask, curious but unafraid. After all, what could this tiny woman do to me that has not already been done?

"I am going to change your appearance," she answers simply.

"Aren't you too important to do stuff like that?"

"None of us is too important to do any job that needs doing," she replies as her eyes crinkle.

She gives my short mop a good once over and then trims the sides and evens up the raw edges. I watch her in the mirror, fascinated as she pulls chunks of hair up between her arthritic fingers before giving them a snip. Her weathered face holds a look of deep concentration. I am much more interested in watching her than I am in seeing the outcome of what she's doing.

She lays the scissors aside and stirs a bowl that was set off to the side. She begins to paint my hair. I find the smell intriguing. It almost smells good, fresh, and not like bleach or ammonia like I expected. She uses a dryer on me for several minutes before washing out the paste.

I return to the chair by the mirror. She puts more goo in her hands and rubs it over my head before drying me once more.

"Now I'm going to apply some semi-permanent face paint. They will have to look hard to know it is you under all this."

"Okay," I reply hesitantly.

Soft brushes tickle my skin as cool dampness flows over the surface of my face. Melodia does not let me look at the end result. She hustles me into a corner behind a screen and hands me clothes.

The blue of technology both terrifies and thrills me. The fabric is nice, but the fit is a little off. I pluck at the front and wonder if I would have been able to fill it out before I lost so much weight.

"How's it going?" Bren inquires from the other side of the screen.

I step out and his eyes go wide. "You look . . ."

Having not seen myself I don't know what to think.

I must have a fantastic look on my face because Bren is quick to correct his words.

"I mean you look so different. I'm impressed."

"Melodia does good work."

"Yeah, she does, but that's not what I mean. It's you. You are very versatile. You looked good before and now you look good in a different way. That is impressive."

I must still look skeptical because he adds, "You look great, unlike some people who, when they color their hair or whatever, look odd."

I laugh. I can't help it. "You're doing fine. You don't have to try so hard."

"Okay," he smiles back. "Maybe I wanted to build you up before I go over what happens next."

"Uh-oh."

"It's not horrible, just a little uncomfortable. You are going to get a type of contact lenses and a listening device."

I can feel my face change. Hadn't Kate just rid me of all the trackers and implants?

"Come on, Lise. Don't give me that look. These are temporary and removable. A very small team needs to go in. It's important that we have backup and tech support. The things we can learn —"

"Stop. No. Just no. I am never giving that kind of power to someone again."

"But, Lise."

"No, Bren. I was tricked into it last time and now I will fix it, but I will not give volatile information like that to anyone. I will break the system or die trying and I will not share."

"Okay, no tech for you. I will still have an earpiece so that I can receive intel. It's time to meet with the rest of the team."

Bren opens the door for Malcolm. Reign is behind him looking focused. She is silent and does not meet my gaze. Malcolm starts speaking and I put my full attention on him.

"Our people will do what they can for us from here. The volunteer decoy teams are ready and will begin leaving. We are to roll out at intervals and all are taking different routes into the city. Our tech team will divert some cameras, some will be put on a loop and others will go to static. We are going to the staging area and to get there, we will be taking the new tunnel."

"What tunnel?" I ask, feeling perplexed.

"While you were . . . gone, we finished construction of the tunnel going under the river. Trust us to get you in. You know what to do once you get there."

"I do."

Malcolm instructs me to redress in underground style clothes and to pack up the blue technology outfit for later. I step behind the screen and do as he asks. I can hear the murmur of their voices but not what they're saying. When I step out, Bren hands me a backpack for my clothes and they proceed to test their tech. Malcolm tries one more time to get me to at least wear an earpiece, but I refuse. He and Bren share a look, but he relents. I'm probably being childish, but I'm done with giving away the inner workings of my mind and will not let the Recalcitrants become like the government.

Malcolm leads the way on yet another underground tour that leaves me directionless. An hour into our journey I can tell that we are definitely descending. The way is lit and appears to be watertight. We pass through a series of rubber-gasketed metal doors. Fear and anxiety make pressure build in my body. I begin to shake as I imagine being trapped down here and the water rising — I can't get it out of my mind. My skin grows hot, my breath comes fast, and my hands begin to shake. The edges of my vision darken.

Bren reaches out and squeezes my sweaty hand. Just as I'm ready to ask if I can sit for a moment, I notice a rise in the floor and automatically pick up my pace to a near jog instead. Malcolm slides me a glance and picks up his pace as well. Only the upward twitch of his lip lets me know that he's on to me too.

I suck in some deep breaths and will myself to relax. Malcolm leads us up a ladder, through a hatch, and down a passageway. Things begin to look familiar and my anxiety rebounds. I recognize this underground thoroughfare. I begin to hyperventilate when I see a discolored spot on the floor. I glance to the left — this is where Griffin died and over there is where I hid watching. Tears blur my vision.

"It's not safe here," I whisper.

"It is now. We've cleared it," Malcolm reassures me.

"There are cameras. They can see us."

"We have control of these cameras. A lot has changed here, E. Trust me."

I follow Malcolm and will my mind to go blank. He pauses before a metal door that has been forced open. I glance up ahead and see a squad of Recalcitrants faced away from us, blocking the way.

I follow the others inside where two more armed Recalcitrants wait. One nods at Malcolm and we move on. Soon it's clear that we are in the lowest level of a building. We have made it downtown.

Malcolm leads us up five flights of stairs. My thighs are starting to burn so I'm thankful when he exits the stairs. Another team of Recalcitrants waits on the darkened landing. One holds up a hand for us to wait, speaks quietly into his com, and then leads us into the deserted hall. He has us wait out of sight until the elevator is open and he's cleared it for us. We all go in and he pushes the button for the 19th floor. Two more team members are waiting for us when the doors open. We head down the hall and enter an office suite that has been taken over by the Recalcitrants.

All kinds of surveillance equipment, from audio to visual and heat sensing to signal recording, stand in front of every window. Most have operators nearby. I spot Erik who takes off a headset and walks toward us.

"Glad you made it safe and sound, sir," he says to Malcolm

as he practically comes to attention.

"Thank you. Is everything ready?"

"Yes, sir. This way please."

We follow Erik into an internal conference room. A tall woman enters through another door and sits at the head of the table. Erik leaves through the door we entered and shuts it behind him.

"Malcolm."

"Helen, this is Elise, Bren, and Reign."

"Elise. So you're the little lady who unwittingly released the monster." I feel my cheeks grow hot. "It is nice to meet all of you. Welcome to the forward command center."

Helen points to her right. "Behind this wall and out the windows, you can see the building in which the servers you need to access reside. You will be given an opportunity to observe it before you enter the building tomorrow morning."

She touches some buttons on a remote which cause the lights to dim and a screen to power on. "This is the main entrance where you, and several others made to look like you, will enter as if you are a worker. You will then proceed to the second floor where each of you will enter a cubicle. You will remain there until you receive a message that it is time to go to the conference room. Once there, you will pick up the equipment that we have ready for you. Synchronous to this, an attack will be taking place in Seattle to divert the live game up there. With the government's eyes on Seattle, it is the perfect time to make our move here."

I watch closely as she runs through several screen shots of

the building's interior and maps of the second-floor cubicles, conference rooms, offices, stairs, elevators, and so on.

"The government, as far as we know, is unaware that we have infiltrated this building. We had a different plan in place you see, but we are willing to give you one chance. Our plan is now plan B which we will execute even if you are still in the building. Do you understand?"

The room grows silent, making my gulp extra loud. "So you're saying that if we aren't careful, we won't make it out alive?"

"Pretty much."

"You're serious," I exclaim, feeling nauseous.

"We all have to make sacrifices for the greater good."

I can tell that she is deadly serious which makes me begin to pant as pain builds in my chest and I forget how to breathe. In prison, I was ready to die — now I am afraid. I've had my taste of freedom and I like it. I want to tell her to go with her plan.

When she begins speaking again, I feel like she can either read my mind or my body language is screaming at her. "We all agree that the servers must be accessed directly not remotely." She waits for my nod then continues, "If you really can break into them, you can stop this insanity and you will save lives. You know the system — we don't, so you can do it faster, smoother, and with a higher percentage chance of not being caught. It would take us too long to hack in. We've been trying to get in from the outside for six months. We put our best hacker inside; he didn't make it out. Our new plan was to blow up the servers, but it will damage the building and hurt innocent people inside and it would only shut them down until they could get set back up. The charges have already been set. What do you want to do?"

"Go in." I wonder if I ever really had a choice.

Helen smiles at me. "Good. You will go through the front door — that will be least expected." She continues to lay out the plan to get us in and me to the basement where I can begin to unravel all the evil I have done. She ends with our exit strategy.

I don't know how long we are in our meeting in the window-less room, but the sun has moved a long ways. Food has been laid out and is waiting for us when we walk out. We quickly fill plates and then go over to the windows to watch the workers leave the building. I concentrate on how they look, how they carry themselves, and attempt to discern if they are speaking to anyone. For the most part, I see relaxed shoulders, smiles, and mouths moving in conversation. It's clear to me — they don't know what hides in the bowels of their building, I'm sure of it.

My mind drifts and I become less aware of what is in front of me and more aware of what is in the distance. I sense . . . something. I keep looking out the windows as I make my way down to the corner where I stop. I stand looking through the glass at the bridge I crossed with Malorie and Bren. It feels like it was a lifetime ago. Emotions well and surge in me. "For you, Mal — I'm going to fix this. If I don't make it, I hope you're waiting for me. I need my friend — I've always needed you."

I tear my gaze away and force myself to sit near Bren on one of the couches where I try to rest and relax, but I can't seem to do either. I glance over at Reign, asleep on a loveseat with her legs curled up so she'll fit. She is peaceful and innocent in sleep, but

I know she can be deadly. I wonder if I will ever understand her. Beautiful on the outside and prickly on the inside, I don't even know if I can call her friend. Bren reaches out and touches my hand. He twines his fingers with mine and for now, it is enough.

01001001 01001001

27

01110000 01100001 01111001 00100000 01100110
01101111 01110010 00100000 01110100 01101000
01100101 00100000

The sun touches the glass and Helen comes to wake me, but she is too late, I've been mostly conscious all night. She has me repeat back the plan to be sure I've got it and then she releases me to breakfast which I cannot eat. The minute someone comes to help me get ready, I gratefully leave it.

I quickly shower and dress in technology blue, complete with a new ID badge. The young man assigned to me touches up Melodia's work on my face and restyles my hair. He adds a pair of glasses with no hidden tech, he is sure to show me, and then I'm free to return to breakfast.

Reign comes out of another room dressed in the white of engineering, her hair artfully rearranged and makeup on her face. She looks like a model and I feel like dirt. Bren steps out and I forget her for the moment. I had forgotten how handsome he can look in slacks, a button-up shirt and dress shoes.

I go over the plan in my head as I wait for the "all clear" to move on. Work begins at 7:00 a.m., but all citizens are still on curfew so no one, except public safety and maintenance, will be on the streets until at least 6:00 a.m. Workers will flood into the building at about 6:50 a.m. We are to enter with that crowd, pass through security with our fake IDs and wait with the group at the elevators. From there we go to the second floor and walk to our assigned cubicles. At 7:33 a.m., I am to go to conference room D and close the door. The others will appear at random intervals. A Recalcitrant posing as a public safety officer will be waiting. They will unlock a cabinet and leave. We are to take weapons and a special keycard that will override their system which has a laser identifier.

That is all the further I get when we are cued to go. I follow Malcolm into the hall and back to the elevator guarded by our people. We all go down to the second floor and then take the stairs. I realize that I am unclear as to how many groups are posing as us at this point, but three will be moving in like us, from this location.

I may not know what to make of Reign, but I've already come to consider Bren's Uncle Malcolm a friend. I watch him with his freshly trimmed visage, and I worry. He is impersonating a public safety officer, so if he is caught it is an especially serious offense. If he is caught with me it will mean his death.

We exit the building, farthest from our target, seconds apart and at random intervals. As we wait our turn, I get a good look at the other groups. My three doppelgangers look enough like me to even fool people I know well. One group goes right, and the rest of us head left to circle the building. One group crosses the street at the same corner as us, but they make the walk signal and we wait for the next one. The other group heads up the street to cross at the end of the block where I can see the group who turned right is just crossing.

All four groups are regathering at the cue to enter the target building's main entrance. I focus on trying to blend — to look like everyone else. Some workers are chattering around me, innocent and unaware. They sound like they are baffled by the curfew and heightened security. Others are talking about weekend plans. I feel both jealous and disgusted by their simple life and simple view of their circumstances. To be fair, if I was standing here with Malorie, our discussion would have probably sounded similar.

We finally enter the building's lobby and security is thicker than even I imagined. I purposely breathe slowly through my nose. Ten scanners run in a row across the width of the entry. It might have been a grand entry before it was cluttered with this junk. There is no way to make these look pretty and they slow down the flow, filling this side of the scanners with people. Another, much smaller, group waits at the bank of elevators.

My skin is flushed with heat. I can feel dampness around the edges of my hair, under my arms, and at my back. I pass through the scanner without it beeping and move to the elevator. I see that Malcolm has taken up a position as if he is working. Reign has made it through, but I've lost sight of Bren. I force myself to remain calm. The elevator doors open and Reign and I step in. Suddenly this feels like my trial all over again. Just as the doors are closing a hand slips in, making them bounce back and then Bren steps inside. I breathe a sigh of relief.

The doors open at level two and we are presented with a maze of cubicles. I go over the map in my mind. Go right, down three rows, walk in and go to the far side, turn left and go up two cubicles. There are pictures here and a girl in a few of them who looks a little like me.

I unclip my ID badge and run it past the scanner, mounted on the computer screen. Nothing happens. I take a breath and do it again. Nothing. I clench my jaw. A couple of people walk past my desk. No one says anything. I swipe the card again. A third person walks by, she stops and walks back. I do a double take and quickly cover my reaction with a blank look.

"You having trouble?" Jill asks.

My eyes flit to her ID badge and immediately back to her face. "No ma'am," I say softly, purposely deepening my voice a little.

She gives me a hard look but then moves away. I feel like I'm imploding. Jill Johnson, not the name she used at school but definitely her. She was spying on me at school and she is watching for me now, but she is looking for the old me. Surely they have given her updated pictures. What if she did recognize me and is turning me in this minute? I should have taken the communication device. I feel sick thinking about it. She wears the crossover uniform marking her as technology but also as a liaison with public safety. It is not common, but on this floor, it would remind workers that they are being watched — always. As if the camera and recording of the sites you visit and time spent on your computer are not enough.

I swipe my card once more and it takes. I quickly log a bathroom break and run for it before I heave in my cubicle. I see Jill standing off to the side, studying me, but she doesn't follow me into the facilities. I'm thankful as I look at myself in the mirror that I don't really look like the person I remember. I'm pale but otherwise I look a whole lot better than I feel. I'm just so very different inside and out. I splash some cold water on my face and let it run over my wrists. I blot my face with a paper towel and check my makeup to be sure it is still in place. I walk back to my cubicle and pretend to work. Jill walks by but doesn't pay any special attention. In school, she thought she knew me but she never did.

I check the time clock on my screen. It feels like time is crawling by. I work on the items that I am supposed to accomplish, but it is so simple, I am quickly bored. I decide to cause a little trouble and open a back door where I can work without being observed. The normal activity will be recorded, but what I do here will not. Jill walks back past and I quickly switch screens to the work I have been assigned. I wonder how Reign is doing in her department. I know Bren will be fine.

Once Jill has gone past, I look for news on the prison. I find nothing, literally nothing, as if it has been completely removed from the system. I look for Bartholomew Rehnquist. He has not disappeared. He has been hospitalized and is awaiting a court hearing. I also find a small obituary entry on the Captain. Part of me is sickened and part of me realizes he can't hurt anyone anymore. In an odd twist, my Inquisitor is being blamed for his death and the prison revolt. A few have been recaptured and placed in other facilities, but close to eighty prisoners are still at large.

I note the time once more — funny how it flies by when you find something to do. I close out everything but the basic program I am to be running and then sign into the meeting taking place in conference room C. I catch sight of Reign just ahead of me and walk into conference room D where Malcolm is speaking to another person dressed as public safety. Bren enters behind me.

No words are exchanged now that we all are in the room. The guard uses a special keycard to unlock the cabinet and hands each of us a special stunning weapon that holds multiple charges but is nearly silent. The downside is that you have to be close to your intended target. He hands each of us a different ID badge and takes our old ones. He touches Malcolm on the arm and then he leaves. It has all taken only moments.

One at a time we leave the room and head for the stairs that will take us to the basement. Two burly public safety officers, looking like special ops, rush past me. I keep walking but my breath is coming fast.

Just before I enter the stairs I see them escorting one of my doppelgangers to the elevators with Jill behind them. I quickly push through the door and lightly sprint down the stairs before I'm seen. Malcolm sees my panic and uses his keycard to open the door to the subbasement stairwell.

"What's wrong?" he asks, the moment we are out of camera range.

"They just arrested one of my look-a-likes. We have to hurry."

Malcolm begins speaking into his com and Bren takes my arm and hurries me on. At the next panel, he swipes his card and the door swishes open. We move on and now it is my turn to enter the main computer bay but my card isn't working. I know we haven't mixed up the cards since each has a photo on it.

"Try again," Reign says, sounding nervous as she comes up behind me. "We're running out of time."

No kidding, I think, and swipe, again nothing happens when I do, so I crack open the panel. Clearly, something was miscoded. Bren arrives and we study it while Reign watches our backs.

"I got this," Bren says as he yanks two wires loose and shorts them. The door slides open and I rush in with Reign behind me. I look back at Bren.

"Go on," he says calmly. I've got to cover this up and I'll watch for Malcolm. He should be here by now."

I nod and move on. This part of the task is mine. I walk to a terminal. I examine my card carefully. There are scratches in the strip. I swallow hard and remind myself to remain calm. I take a breath to settle my nerves. I peel the thin plastic layer off the front of my ID badge and smooth it over the strip. If they look at my badge now, I'll surely be caught. One more breath and I give it a swipe. Nothing happens for a beat and then the little light switches to green. Reign hands me her card so that I can enter the twenty-three digit access code that has been typed into the back like a regular ID number in case it was confiscated. It takes. Relief sweeps through me.

I breathe calmly for the first time today. I am in the digital world where I feel at home. It's time to work. I concentrate and forget about Reign for several minutes until I feel her twitching behind me. Her agitation shows in her wild eyes and drawn weapon that she swings from one access point to another.

I try to keep working, but it's no use. I give Reign a look and notice she is practically sweating. "What?" I snap at her.

She's wearing her wary look again. "Just hurry," she rasps, her agitation clear.

It feels like role reversal. For once I know what I'm doing and she does not, so I return to hacking and try to ignore her. After several minutes I suggest that she go check on Bren and Malcolm. I sigh when she stomps away. I'm in, and with the peace I can concentrate on corrupting the online game. Now as it is played it will corrupt and destroy itself. I remove the subliminal messages and begin to remove all signs of my trespass. I see Reign stalking back toward me so I switch gears and begin seeing what I can do to disrupt the live action game. I can't kill it altogether from here but knowing how they programmed our chips, I know I can disrupt the kill signal permanently for all students currently implanted with the device. They will have to reprogram that feature individually. I just hope I've gotten our side enough time.

I start breaking down the student GPS trackers when my terminal goes into safety mode, the lighting changes to red and alarms begin to sound. I wipe the board with my sleeve. The terminals around me are all shutting down. Reign grabs my arm and yanks me down a row of circuitry panels. I couldn't save them all. I needed more time.

"My com is down," she yelps. "I don't know what's going on."

"It's a normal safety procedure. The Recalcitrants will expect it. They will hack through and you'll be back up soon."

"But if they don't hear from us they'll blow the system down here!"

"Calm down. We have a few —"

A distant boom interrupts me. A few beats pass and then the only door to this room blows. Reign's eyes go huge and then we're running down the row. I wonder where Bren and Malcolm are but at the moment our job is to get to a safe place. Uniformed public safety officers with flashlights, their weapons drawn, swarm the door. Reign pulls me toward a ventilation shaft. She pops the cover off and we slither inside. She snaps it back into place with a soft *snick*.

"Where are they?" one of them barks.

My heart is thudding so hard in my chest that it hurts. Reign yanks insistently on my sleeve so I follow her deeper into the ventilation system. She whispers into her com quietly enough that even I can't hear all the words, so it must be back up already.

"We have about ten minutes to get out of here. Did you get it done?"

"I think so."

"You think so?" Reign sounds angry and scared.

"It's done. I did all I could."

A flashlight beam cuts into the space silencing us but doesn't touch us.

"Not here." I think I hear one of the men say.

"Come on," Reign breathes.

We crawl quickly through the shaft. When Reign stops I bump into her. I watch a small screen light up. It looks like a mini GPS unit complete with building schematics. She studies it briefly and then leads me on and then right at the next intersection. Soon we're at another vent cover where she listens carefully and then removes it and slides out.

"Clear."

I follow her and replace the cover. She pulls out her device again and speaks into her com.

"She says it's done. We're in a storage room in the northeast corner. There is a service elevator to our right." She pauses and listens. "Yes, we're headed there on your 'Go'."

Reign's head is bent forward and her body is still, but her eyes are watchful. "Time to move, Princess," she says shifting her gaze to me.

I grit my teeth so that I don't punch her. I follow her out, saying nothing. If she has resorted to calling me "Princess" again, then I have already irritated her somehow. We walk down the hall until she holds up a hand. We wait until she has gotten some sort of signal and then we move on to the service elevator. We force open the doors and swing over to metal rungs set into the side. It is going to be a long climb.

When we get to the first floor, some sort of evacuation is already in process. Reign is mumbling again, sharing intel with our side. It looks like they are using face recognition devices before anyone can leave. I see Reign nod. Apparently, we are on to plan C, the back door fire escape.

I feel like a fish, fighting my way against the current, but no one seems to take any real notice of us. The crowd thins as we get closer to our goal. Reign stops and turns to me. She begins speaking and I can tell that she is angry, but although she looks at me, she is talking into her com to them.

"Where are you?" I hear her say over the general din. I watch her peek around the corner in front of us.

"Not good enough! We're at the fire exit and they have it covered," she growls and then grows silent for several minutes as she listens. She has stopped looking at me, but now her eyes zip back. Whatever she has heard, it isn't good. I wish I could hear or at least understand the look on her face.

I hear a sound behind me and start to turn. Reign kicks in the door next to me and shoves me inside. I feel confused. Wasn't that Bren I saw? I struggle for a moment, but she takes me down and my head hits the floor as my weapon pops free. I'm stunned. I don't know what's happening. Four doors — *or is it two doors?* — open at once and figures move in both. Then Bren is at my side.

"Are you okay?" he asks.

I nod and wince. I reach up to feel a goose egg rising on the back of my head. "Reign went —"

I'm cut off by several shots being fired and then the thud of running feet. I swing my head around looking for a place to hide, but stop and hold my head in my hands hoping that will control the throbbing.

"Stay," Bren yelps, jumping to his feet.

I watch him go out the door we had all entered and then

I focus on listening to the sounds outside the doors with my eyes closed. I crawl over to the door that Reign exited. I hear nothing so I crack it open. I see four bodies in the hall, none are moving. No, wait, the smaller one is. I realize that the alarm has been cut and then a sound, small and delicate touches my ears.

I crawl toward the sound. Reign's head and shoulders are propped up against a wall. I have to crawl over a guard to get to her. Not long ago, in my other life, it would have freaked me out but now I'm more worried about her.

Reign looks so tiny. Blood blooms from three holes in her chest. Her weapon and the one she must have taken from me lay to either side of her. By their positions, I'd say she'd been double wielding them. I know she cleared the exit but for what? Wouldn't the Recalcitrants have come? I crawl closer and press my hands over two of her three wounds.

"Why?' I beg. "Why did you do it?" Reign blinks and looks up at me.

"As much as part of me . . . hates you . . ." Reign struggles to pull in a shallow breath. The gurgling sound of it lodges a sob in my throat and I push more firmly on her wounds. "I . . . I love you. You're the only . . . only real friend . . . I . . . I've ever . . . h-h-had."

"Reign?"

The look in her eye changes.

"Reign . . . ?"

Bren skids to a stop next to me. "I told you to . . . never mind. She's gone, Lise. We've got to go. Malcolm has them convinced we're in the crowd at the entrance."

"No." I cry as I pull Reign to my chest. I've lost too many people.

"Elise, she did this for you. Don't waste it. We need to go."

"We're bringing her."

"We can't. We need to get you out and she'll slow us down. We need what you know to finish shutting down the games."

I kiss her forehead and lay her down. Bren takes one look at my bloodied shirt and huffs out a sigh. He bolts into an office and is back in seconds with a jacket. It's too large but it will do.

Once my shirt is concealed and Bren has checked his weapon and grabbed her com, we move to the fire exit.

"What about her weapons?" I ask.

Bren wipes them down and puts them back in her hands. "We need to leave them to help make the story convincing that she acted alone."

Bren takes my hand. "Are we go?" he asks our invisible helper and then he's pulling me through the door. Just as we clear the door I hear the first boom and feel a vibration travel up my legs. Malcolm is waiting at the end of the alley. He's now wearing the colors of medical branch.

"You're okay," I sigh and I can feel more tears burning at the back of my eyes.

"Not yet," he answers gruffly and then he's pulling me down the street with his arm around my shoulders as three more explosions shake the sidewalk.

We walk three blocks, sirens screaming in the distance and I can hear helicopters in the air. Screens activate up and down the street and then I freeze — It's my voice I hear amplified over the PA system. Bits of the recordings the Recalcitrants edited are playing. I am distracted but Bren urges me on and soon we duck into an alley, turn our jackets inside out and move on. I glance at Malcolm who is now in hospitality green.

In a few more blocks we enter a doorway. It turns out to be a pub. We head for a booth at the back passing it by and enter the back hall. Malcolm leads us through a door marked *Employees Only*. He walks up to a shelving unit that swings open at his touch. A tight circular staircase waits inside. My brief glimpse of daylight is over.

01110011 01101001 01101110 01110011 00100000

01101111 01100110 00100000 01111001 01101111

01110101 01110010

At the bottom of the stairs is a metal door. Malcolm places his hand on a small panel next to it. I don't see anything happening but then suddenly I can hear a mechanism moving. The portal swings open to a hall and after two more similar contraptions, we enter a room. Lights come on as soon as we enter. It looks like we have access to technology along one wall. Bunks are set into another, the third contains a kitchenette, and the fourth is covered in shelves of supplies broken by a door. I open it and find a small bathroom.

We wait for five long hours for the extraction team to get to us. They bring new disguises and then we are off again, dressed as a group of underground people. They return us to the secure location where I last saw Melodia. I burst into tears when I see her and she wraps me in a hug. Maybe it's just me or maybe it's the warmth and sadness I can sense radiating from her.

"I'm sorry that you lost another friend, sweet girl. You are not alone. Our losses have been heavy and many of our friends are gone too. I promise you will survive."

Her words turn my tears into sobs. She holds me, saying nothing further, but I can feel her love and commitment as almost a year of pain flows out of me.

They keep us for ten days. I pay attention to very little. I am invited to meetings that I don't attend. I do as I am asked; no more, no less. Finally, a decision is made — I am to be moved to a satellite facility for the safety of people here. I have been wondering who I am. The clothes I wear are not mine but then nothing is. I have absolutely nothing to call my own and now I have no way of earning anything more. I am here by the grace of these people; they own me and the services I can provide. They tell me that my message is still being played at random intervals and that over half of the Seattle hub's children were saved. They expect to save even more in San Jose and Phoenix. I guess it's a start.

Bren finds me in the common room. I like it best because the lighting here feels like real sunshine. I stare at the scenic photography on the walls and pretend I'm outside. He tells me it's time to prepare for our next journey. We will travel alone this time. One day Melodia and Malcolm will join us, but for now, they are needed here. This time, we will not be going at night. We are going to hide among the masses. I follow Bren through the tunnels until a patch of sunshine takes me by surprise.

Daylight filters down through the grate. It's the first real light I've seen in days. I slowly climb the ladder, cautious of the slimy, slippery rungs. Bren is still fiddling with a device so I make sure my footing is secure and then . . . I push up on the grate. It makes a horrible grinding sound. I wait, scared to death of being caught. Finally, I move cautiously into the daylight. It seems so wrong somehow — the bit of sun that breaks through the clouds making everything extra bright and shiny. Leaves shouldn't be this green, I think resentfully. It feels like the rest of the world is celebrating the loss of my classmates, Malorie, and Reign. It makes me angry.

Topsiders, I know their name now, are afraid of the tunnels. No one goes down there unless it is their job to do so, but I know the tunnels are not the scariest thing out there. I don't understand the topsiders, living their lives like a bunch of sheep waiting for the slaughter. They give and give and never expect anything in return until one day they are no longer necessary.

Bren crawls out behind me and replaces the grate. He touches my elbow and we begin to walk.

"Have you ever noticed how the bright green of new spring leaves practically glows? Those crazy fluorescent green leaves come back every year, always marching on and not knowing or caring about my life or whether I live or die, they just know that they must go on," I say to Bren.

His look tells me that I must go on too, but he squeezes my hand to lessen the sting. We walk much as we did the first time we left the city. We go to the same deli on our way out of town, but this time, the woodsman, Josiah, joins us. He grins at me across the table. Bren gets up and we leave like normal customers and pile into his Jeep.

"Good to see you again, Miss E.," he says enthusiastically once the doors are shut. "I knew you'd make it."

We go back to his place and I wonder if I'll get more of his biscuits and gravy; sadly it is not to be. Another truck is waiting for us. The lady who interviewed me at the wooded camp hops out with the same gentleman who drove us to the train.

"Hey!" she says with a big smile as she hugs us both. "We are honored to have you come to work with us. We have left false leads as to your whereabouts all over the place. The California and Nevada hubs have just fallen. Idaho and Montana are next. They won't be able to send students to trials anymore. "

"That's good," I say, feeling rather numb.

"None of this would have been possible without you," she grins.

"I guess."

"The game went live and it's a dud. That's thanks to you too."

I sigh. I don't know what's wrong with me. It just feels like what I did is not enough.

"She just needs a little time," Bren says to smooth things over for me.

I say very little on the ride to camp. When we get there I'm stunned by the number of refugees. It was practically empty last time I was here.

My appearance is first met by silence and then the floodgates open. People want to hug me, touch me, and thank me. How can they do that when it is my fault that they are here? I feel utterly overwhelmed. Bren puts a protective arm around me and backs them off with softly spoken, kind words and a big smile.

Days turn into weeks and I get used to the people here, the stares, and the odd treatment. I have become a sort of strange celebrity. I try to remain gracious but their attention is painful for an introvert like me. At first, we have separate cabins but I keep sneaking over to Bren's. The Recalcitrants soon discover that leaving me with him means that the screaming I do at night from nightmares is limited.

I try to do what I can with the tech they have here, but I am bored in my work and left to wonder what my real purpose is now. It has got to be more than keeping the computers going for the Recalcitrants, but what if it's not. Maybe this is all I deserve after the massive damage I've done . . . even if it was unintentional. There are things I cannot fix — it's not for me to do, yet I have a hard time letting it go.

"I feel like I should do something," I say to Bren one sunny afternoon as we meet for our daily lunch.

"You are."

"It's not enough."

"You did your part."

"I feel like I should do more." I watch some children playing under the trees. They are quieter than you would expect. I wonder what the answer is, for me and for them, and then I remember that we are all broken — just to varying degrees. More importantly, the only person you can ever really fix is you. One must remember their mistakes enough to not repeat them, instead, let them go. "Maybe I'm starting to believe you."

Bren kisses my forehead and goes back to work. I miss him

the moment he leaves. I secretly count the minutes until we will meet again at dinner time. After dinner, we do our community chores and then return to our cabin to do our own. I understand that I finally have the simple life that I asked for, although it is not quite what I had in mind.

At bedtime, I snuggle close to Bren. He is my anchor. I try not to be too needy though he doesn't seem to mind. I sigh and drift to sleep, knowing that he has my back tonight, like always.

"Wake up sleepy head. I want to show you something." Bren's voice is soft, low, and teasing.

I don't want to go anywhere, so I snuggle closer to his warmth. At first, I snuck into his room, but now I don't care what anyone thinks and since he doesn't seem to either, it's now the norm. I can't sleep without him. Perhaps I will never be able to let myself relax enough to sleep on my own. I'm too damaged to be normal anymore.

Bren disentangles himself from me and gets up. I won't lie, I pout. I had been sleeping peacefully and for me, that is a real feat.

"Really, come on. It will be worth it," he says, smiling.

"I doubt it," I grouse as I roll out of bed. I dress quickly in the chilly air. Bren keeps smiling and waving me forward like he has the best secret ever that he's dying to tell me. I pull on my boots, hurry through my morning routine and follow him out into the darkness.

He leads me a short ways from our cabin and pulls out a blanket that he sets on the ground and flips over a log. He pulls me down onto it and holds me close. I close my eyes but he has other ideas.

"No sleeping. You are here to watch the sky."

"Ugh, I'd rather sleep. I think I've earned it."

"You are such a grouch in the morning. This will be worth it. Trust me."

The sky is a frosty blue-gray, still dark enough that most things are in silhouette, but low on the horizon and creeping up into the clouds is the most magnificent fuchsia-orange color I've ever seen. It makes everything begin to glow as the sun creeps higher.

"You stare at it like you've never seen a sunrise before." I can hear the smile in Bren's voice.

"I think this one may be the best." He just smiles at my response and turns his gaze back to the wonder of nature. I feel like it needs more explanation. "Maybe it's because I feel safe for the moment, but everything just seems . . . brighter, fuller, bigger . . ." I end on a sigh.

"You don't have to explain it. Just enjoy the moment and let everything else go."

He pulls me closer and kisses the top of my head. I hope I can do that, at least until I close my eyes and the nightmares come again.

"I'm here with you. They won't come."

I smile because he knows what I'm thinking. Maybe with him here, there really is a chance they won't and just maybe I have a real shot at being free.

"And besides," he says after a dramatic pause, "I've arranged for pie — Marionberry, right?"

"You remember that?"

"It was an impressive list you gave me. I'm sorry it took me so long to deliver."

"You were a little busy."

"I will never be too busy for you, sweetheart."

"So, know-it-all, what do I do with the rest of my life?"

"You live, Lise. You live."

"**The past** is history
The future a mystery
But today is a gift . . .
that's why they call it **the present**."

-**Bil Keane**, *American Cartoonist*
(October 5, 1922 — November 8, 2011)

About the Author

Lauren Lynne graduated from both Oregon State and Portland State universities with degrees in education. She is the author of the young adult fantasy, action-adventure series, *The Secret Watchers*. Lauren focused her *Secret Watchers* series toward teen reluctant readers, but has drawn in enthusiasts of all ages. She's passionate about sharing her love of reading and writing with everyone.

The Pacific Northwest, with its vivid and varied panoramas, is where Lauren makes her home. When she's not writing, she can be found spending time with her family, working with students, reading, gardening, or hiking around Mt. Hood, the Columbia River Gorge, or the Oregon Coast.

The Recalcitrant Project is her first dystopian young adult novel. To learn more about Lauren and her current and past work, visit LaurenLynneAuthor.com.

R\Users\ADMIN>command/find /TRU

FINDING TRU . . .
TASK COMPLETE.

R\Users\ADMIN>command/execute /TRU

LOADING SYSTEM ITEMS . . .
TRU SYSTEM READY.
ADMIN CONFIRMATION REQUIRED.

Confirm Execution   . . .   [Y] or [N] ?

R\Users\ADMIN>command/ |

01010100 01101000 01100101 00100000 01010010
01100101 01100011 01100001 01101100 01100011
01101001 01110100 01110010 01100001 01101110
01110100 00100000 01010101 01110000 01110010
01101001 01110011 01101001 01101110 01100111

SOON...|

For this and other exciting titles, visit:

www.WyvernsPeak.com

www.twitter.com/WyvernsPeak
www.facebook.com/WyvernsPeak

Sign up for our newsletter, get free stuff, and be the first to know when new books from your favorite Wyvern's Peak authors are released.

Follow Lauren Lynne on Twitter
@LLynneAuthor

Like Lauren on Facebook
www.facebook.com/LaurenLynneAuthor

Visit her website at
www.LaurenLynneAuthor.com